# Holiday EverAfter

BY

LARA
(LOS ANGELES ROMANCE AUTHORS)

Holiday Ever After

Copyright © 2016 Los Angeles Romance Authors

Edited by: Mackenzie Walton
Cover: Nora Flite, Depositphotos
Interior Design: Ophelia Bell
Acknowledgment - Copyright 2016 Maggie Marr
Foreword - Copyright 2016 Beverly Diehl
My Vegas Bad Boy - Copyright 2016 Nora Flite
The Year of the Rooster - Copyright 2016 Mia Hopkins
Christmas Daze - Copyright 2016 Marla Murphy
The Twelfth Month - Copyright 2016 Kathy O'Rourke
No Room at the Inn - Copyright 2016 Beverly Diehl
Hopeful at the Holidays - Copyright 2016 Cami Brite
A Lares Christmas - Copyright 2016 Claire Davon
Bed of Sweet Surrender - Copyright 2016 Kadee McDonald
Ghosted: Christmas Present - Copyright 2016 Roxann Breazile
The Santa Shack Up - Copyright 2016 Susannah Erwin
My Oktoberfest Escapade - Copyright 2016 Jewel Quinlan
Home for Christmas, Act 2 - Copyright 2016 Teri McGill
Sorcha in Snowflakes - Copyright 2016 Kate Bigel
The Christmas Encounter - Copyright 2016 Tema M. Merback
Glow - Copyright 2016 Pamela DuMond

ISBN-13: 978-0-9977314-3-9
ISBN-10: 0-9977314-3-5

# TABLE OF CONTENTS

The contributors are generously donating all proceeds from this anthology to Los Angeles Romance Authors (LARA).

# ACKNOWLEDGMENTS

An anthology, is by nature, a group effort. A collaboration, of sorts, of talented and creative people who come together to present stories for you, the Reader. There are many volunteers who made this LARA anthology possible. First thank you to all of our contributors. Thank you to the anthology director, Beverly Diehl, whose vision brought this anthology to life. Thank you to Ophelia Bell for her patience and dedication. Thank you to Nora Flite for her contribution of not only a story but also a great looking cover. Thank you Claire Davon, this year's LARA Secretary for her help with the anthology. Thank you to Rick Ochocki for coordinating the blind submission effort. Thank you to Maria Powers for blind judging submissions. Thank you to our editor Mackenzie Walton who did a great job. Thank you to Mia Hopkins for help with the blurb and back cover text. Thank you to all the members of LARA who have belief, dedication, heart, and talent beyond measure. Finally, thank you, Reader, for spending time with these stories, it is my deepest wish that you enjoy our anthology filled with holiday stories.

- Maggie Marr, LARA President 2015-2016

# FOREWORD

The fall and winter holidays are a great time for yummy food and yummier romance.

In the spirit of giving, the Los Angeles Romance Authors (LARA) Chapter of Romance Writers of America® presents this sweet and steamy anthology of holiday short stories from USA Today bestselling writers, talented debut authors, and not-yet-but-soon household names.

We can't guarantee a Happily Ever After in your personal life, but *Holiday Ever After* offers plenty to keep you warm on a chilly fall or winter evening, from your own Mr. Scrooge, to a bad boy stripper, to a Navy SEAL, to the sexy exchange student next door. Historical, paranormal, contemporary—we've mixed all genres together like the tastiest sweet-and-spicy fruitcake (or alternate holiday treat of your choice).

If you enjoy these stories, please leave us a review, and recommend this collection to your friends. Authors *live* for review and encouragement, especially the newbies I am so pleased to include here.

*\*sends the reader a virtual Christmas cookie\**

~ Beverly Diehl
LARA's Anthology Coordinator
2015-2017

# My Vegas Bad Boy

## By Nora Flite

I t was Christmas Eve and there was a candy-cane striped dick gyrating inches from my face.

That's right.

Christmas Eve, in Vegas, at a *male strip club*. Oh just wait, it gets even better! You see, I was in the middle of a bachelorette party for my best friend, surrounded by Greek God muscle-bound men gyrating in my direction, and I—genius that I am—had forgotten to pack any sexy underwear.

That meant I was wearing ugly as sin panties you could barely feel right *calling* panties, underwear fit for getting covered in sticky sweat at the gym. Torn up, gray things that were too big and definitely weren't what I wanted anyone seeing me in.

*Not that it matters,* I told myself. *One: strippers don't go home with horny screaming bachelorette girls.*

*And two...*

*I haven't been out on a date in over a year, anyway.*

That wasn't about to change just because this was Vegas.

"Hell yeah!" a woman screamed next to me, making me wince. Glancing sideways, I realized it was the bride to be herself. Shelly and I had been friends since college. She was the sort that gave you advice but never practiced what she preached.

She was also gorgeous...and wearing a crown that proclaimed her Queen of Marriage Land. That meant every half-naked guy was carefully migrating over to her chair, enjoying the rain of money her friends and I were tossing around.

I cheered as loud as any of them, trying to force myself to feel the excitement I was sure I should be feeling. My best friend was getting *married!* We were in fucking Vegas on Christmas Eve in the biggest male strip club I'd ever seen! The combination should have been so over the top I'd be forced to have a good time.

And I wasn't. Not one bit.

I was sure this was the worst Christmas ever.

Shelly met my eyes. I put on a giant smile, not wanting her to catch me being moody. I mean, I wasn't even upset, I was just—what's the word? Drained? Uncertain? I'd thought that a night of debauchery in Vegas would take my mind off of *things.*

It wasn't working.

All the candy-cane dicks in the world couldn't change that.

Reaching for my drink—because alcohol can solve any problem—I absently slid my attention back to the stage. My fingers never found my glass. They didn't even get close. Each tiny fiber in my body had locked up, my brain struggling to handle the explosion of shock that ricocheted through me.

I'd gotten used to the men jiggling their nuts and rocking their hips. Yeah, they were sexy, but they were also kind of silly. After an hour of sitting in the club, I'd figured I was numb to the provocative entertainment.

Then I saw him. Or rather, I saw that he'd seen *me*.

If you could have taken the slow drum beat and gritty bass line of an R&B song and given it life, the guy on stage would have been it. He was perfectly solid, from his shapely calves and flexing thighs to the long long *long* way up to the horizon line of his jaw.

He was dressed in a pair of tight red briefs, black suspenders stretching across his flat stomach and over his defined chest. His shiny skin—was that oil?—was covered in vibrant tattoos.

Once, when my father was very ill and we all expected him to pass on, I'd gotten the courage to get a tiny heart with his name needled into my shoulder. It had hurt like a *bitch*, as if I was being stung by a thousand bees the size of poodles. Also? My father recovered from his close call, so I had a memorial to a living man on my skin.

The point is that I *know* how much tattoos hurt. And this guy—this piece of ovary-throbbing man flesh—was coated in them like they were suntan lotion. Imagining the fierceness you'd need to get through so much pain had me sitting straight up in my chair.

When he smirked at me, my heart stuttered. Like I said, he was watching me. In the flashing stage lights his narrowed eyes looked orange. The closer he got, the more I realized they had to be brown, maybe caramel.

He swayed closer, moving with the beat of the music. His hand slid down his carved abs, inching with determination toward the obvious shape of his massive prick. I stared at him—at it—and at him again. My mouth felt like I'd been licking cotton balls all night.

*Oh hell, don't think about licking anything right now. Especially not balls.*

My knees twinged in pain; I'd been crushing them with my fingertips. This mystery man was almost on me. I'd forgotten where I was, what was going on around me, all because he was like some truck on fire careening my way and I was too damn stupid to jump aside.

"Excuse me?"

I jumped and spun, knocking my empty glass off the stage-rail so that it shattered onto the floor. The waitress who'd spoken to me jumped back, and around me, I heard shouts of surprise from my friends. *Right, my friends. The bachelorette party.* Fucking fuck, had I gotten that distracted by this chunk of mancandy?

Shoving my chair back, I scooped up a crumpled napkin and bent down to pick up the bigger chunks of glass. "I'm sorry!" I shouted over the music. "I'm such a klutz, I'll clean this up!"

The waitress flapped her hands, grabbing my wrists. "No, no! Leave it alone before you get cut up!" Her laugh was easy, calming me some—but not entirely. "People do it all the time. I'll sweep it up and get you something new."

Shelly yelled something my way. I spotted her waving at me. Our friends were watching me, their smiles gigantic and strained. My cheeks were on fire, but I waved back at them, shrugging like it was all a stupid accident. Like anyone could have done what I had because the waitress had said as much.

But I knew better. I'd knocked my glass over out of nervous reaction.

Right in front of me was the cause.

He was kneeling down, but it wasn't a subdued pose. The stage made him tower over me, his torso a row of dips and dives I could have lost myself in for hours. When he leaned in, his grin cutting ear to ear, his voice was soft as velvet. I felt it between my thighs.

"You know," he said, "Girls don't usually break stuff because of me until I get them home."

"Break stuff?" I asked with a blink.

"You know. Like the bed frame."

Shit. I really needed that new drink. "That wasn't because of you," I said flatly. "I'm just...tired. And the glass was slippery." I was a terrible liar. His laugh told me he knew that, too.

His face swung closer to mine. "I'm Toxic. What's your name?"

*Toxic?* I almost laughed, it was such a fake name, but fine. Two could play at this game. With a quick look at the strippers in their peppermint red and white thongs, I put my lips near Toxic's temple.

I wanted to whisper. You had to get close to whisper.

When I spoke, I accidentally brushed my mouth on his skin. "Candy."

"Candy?" he asked, pulling away. There was a flash of something dark in his eyes. I didn't know if he was upset that I'd just kissed his temple or because I was giving him a name faker than his. "You don't seem sweet enough to be a Candy."

Leaning back in my chair, I adjusted the top of my emerald green dress; Toxic watched my every tiny movement. "Sure I am. Sweet, happy Candy. That's me."

"Well," he said, sliding his legs over the edge of the stage. "I've been watching you since you came through the door, and you definitely don't seem happy."

His knees moved to either side of my shoulders. Not only was I eye-level with the bulge in his tight tight *tight* briefs, but I was trapped. "Um," I said—it came out too quiet. I tried again. "It's my best friend's bachelorette party, of course I'm happy."

"Uh huh," he chuckled. Ever so softly, he traced his fingers down the side of my throat. In spite of myself, I lavished in the buttery sensation he created in my belly. "You're not fooling anyone, *Candy*. Something is bothering you."

I didn't like being interrogated. I shot another nervous look at Shelly, but she couldn't even see me behind the wall of man-ass in her face. "So what if I'm not having a great time? You get paid either way."

"Ouch." Toxic slid his hands farther, until one of them was wrapped in my hair. He was strong, his grip pure steel as he forced our foreheads together. His breath burned along my skin. "Baby doll, if you're not having the best night of your life, then I'm failing. And I fucking *hate* to fail. Get me?"

I was breathing from the top of my throat. "I—kind of. Okay. Maybe I'm not having a great time, but it's got nothing to do with you."

"Doesn't matter." He sat up, reaching over my head. The waitress had returned, clearly not wanting to get in between us. Toxic took the glass from her, handing it to me. On impulse, I wrapped it in my hand, but he held on. "I'm not letting you out of my sight until you start smiling. It's a matter of pride."

He was already helping, because I felt my grin start to grow. "Stripper honor is more intense than I imagined."

Laughing, he cupped the back of my head with his free hand. The feel of his nails on my scalp made my whole head tingle. "You don't know the half of it. Drink."

So I did. I let Toxic control the flow of alcohol, his touch firm but sure. Whatever the waitress had given me—I think I'd been drinking Screw Drivers—burned down my pipes. Before I was out of breath, but only just before, Toxic released me so I could suck in a desperate gulp of air.

"Fuck," I coughed, my eyes watering.

"There," he said softly. "That's the first hint of a real smile."

Flushing at his observation, I wiped at my mouth. I could still feel his fingers in my hair even though he'd stopped holding me. "I can't get too crazy. Tonight is for Shelly."

Toxic followed where I pointed. The other male dancers had surrounded her in a circle, showing off the various ways they could pluck dollar bills from her mouth.

He said, "I'm pretty sure she's fine."

"Still, I can't get drunk in case she needs me."

"You don't need to get wasted to have fun." His knee rubbed along my upper arm. "Not with me."

Fucking hell, I believed him. I was insane and lonely and *hating* that I was feeling bitter toward Shelly. I could never tell her about any of it. I could only try to bury the whole mess of emotions.

And Toxic was offering me a pretty convincing method of doing so.

He stepped off the stage, reaching out for me. I hesitated for a split second before grabbing his hand, letting him help me to my feet. Some people noticed us going toward the rear of the club, where the curtained off rooms were. No one stopped me.

The only person who *could* have stopped me was… well, me.

But I didn't want to.

"Here," Toxic said, guiding me into the tiny booth. It was darker here, the music softened by the walls and heavy cloth. A giant burgundy-colored couch fit against the corner, the only piece of furniture—the only anything—in the room. "Sit down."

Licking my lower lip, I asked, "What are you going to do?"

His eyes held a shadow. "Make you smile."

I was glad for the couch; my knees had gone weak and useless. I nearly fell onto the cushions. Toxic arched over me, not giving me a second of air that was free from him. I hadn't noticed it until now, but he had a strong coffee and almond scent. It made me hungry; I blamed my drool on that and *not* on how he started rocking his hips deliciously.

He dove at me, his hands gripping the couch above my head. One thrust, two, he moved with patient precision as he brought his body toward mine, never quite touching. I'd always thought lap dances would be silly. I never imagined enjoying one. Not until this.

After such a long stretch of celibacy, of not wanting—though I swear I'd tried—to get close to another man, I was feeling the familiar twitches of excitement. Toxic was everything I'd never searched for. I didn't go after guys with tattoos; definitely not men who took their clothes off for money.

But here I was, lying beneath a man who was a pure galaxy of ink. And it was fucking amazing. He toyed with a suspender, drawing my eye down his body. I looked where he told me to, I followed along and fell under his spell.

Toxic was a showman, but this was more than a performance. He turned, winking at me and showing off his ass. I started to giggle, blushing at his actions. Then he was on top of me, removing all humor and replacing it with a low-boil of heat in my belly.

One knee came up on the couch, pushing his mostly hidden erection into my line of sight. I bit my tongue, forcing a squeak down. I had a strong desire not to let him see he was getting to me; his piercing stare said it was a waste of time trying to hide it.

Nuzzling my throat, he traced a fingertip down to my navel. "I can smell how much you want me," he whispered.

Tensing, I made a useless noise. "I—it's not like you don't want me, too," I finally blurted.

His eyebrows went up. "Oh, I do." Making sure I was watching, he palmed his hard-on and growled, "I want you bad, sugar. I want to fuck you until you can't open your eyes."

I would have sat there like a lump, but he took my hands, placing them on his stomach. The hard shape of his abdominals became harder when he breathed in. I shifted on the couch, feeling my own sticky inner thighs.

Toxic swayed hypnotically, his nose brushing mine. I was crafted from nothing but a pure, wickedly hot need to see this man naked—to fuck him hard and fast, and damn anyone else who thought that was wrong.

His lips were a smirk that was going to kiss me. Would it be silky, would he be cruel? Did a man like him kiss the way he danced—with rhythm?

I wanted to know.

The moment was shattered by a flap of the curtain and a single strangled moan. "Josia!" Shelly sobbed, stumbling into our private room.

"Shelly?" I gasped, baffled by her appearance. I didn't have time to ask questions, she was falling sideways.

In a great panic, I shoved Toxic off me and hurried to catch her. She half-sat, half-knelt on the floor, her eyes barely focusing on me. "Josia, there you are—listen, please listen. I love you, so listen."

I said, "She's had too much alcohol. I need to get her to her hotel room."

"I'll get some help." He started for the curtain.

Shelly clawed at my dress, speaking too loudly. "You're such a good friend, okay? Okay? I'm so so *so sorry* about Nolan. I am! Listen, I am!"

I froze there, cradling her close and wishing I could shut her up. Uneasily, I glanced at Toxic. "It's fine, Shelly. I told you before, it's fine."

"But you used to *love him!*" Sniffling, she hugged me violently. "But I love you! So don't hate me for marrying him!"

Ah. Fuck. This wasn't what I needed right now. Outside, I heard voices—people calling for Shelly. "In here!" I shouted back. Toxic, who'd stopped where he was to stare down at me and my drunk friend, looked me dead in the eye. I wanted to say, *Now you know why I was having such a bad time tonight.* I didn't. I stayed silent.

A pack of women burst through the curtain, knocking Toxic aside. "Here she is!" One of them—Tina—said. "Josia, is she okay?"

"Yeah," I said, helping Shelly to her feet. "She just needs water and sleep."

Together, two of the girls helped Shelly from the room. Tina sighed, and I saw the dumb Queen of Marriage Land crown in her hand. "We'll get her set up."

"I should help," I said quickly.

"No, no. It's fine. We can handle it." Her smile was genuinely apologetic. I had the terrible idea that all of them knew what Shelly had said to me. Maybe I was stupid to think it was a big secret.

After all...Nolan and I had dated for five years.

When the curtain fell back, Toxic and I were alone. Absently, I adjusted my dress. My heart was thumping, but no longer from excitement. This was good ol' faithful anxiety.

"Come with me," he said, grabbing my wrist.

Startled, I pulled back. "What? Where are you taking me?"

Toxic forced me out of the booth, giving me no room for argument. "You stopped smiling," he whispered, just loud enough so I could hear him over the music. "I promised to fix that. Remember?"

Unable to speak around my thick tongue, I let him guide me. I didn't make a peep even as we headed through a dark hallway, not even when we popped out into a parking structure and I realized we were in public—and that he still had on nothing but red briefs, suspenders, and a pair of fucking boots.

"You should get some clothes on," I blurted out, looking side to side. Did anyone see us?

"I figured you liked this outfit, though." Grinning, he stopped beside a black convertible, the top was down. To my amazement, he yanked out a key from his shoe. The locks popped, he opened the door for me.

If I wasn't insane before, I clearly was now, because I climbed inside.

Toxic had a plan. He drove us out of the underground lot without hesitation, showing me how skilled he was as he navigated the packed streets. It was the middle of the night on Christmas Eve—were *all* of these people avoiding things like I was?

When he broke out onto an open stretch of road, I stopped thinking about anyone else. Toxic made the tires squeal down the asphalt, daring any cops to chase after us.

Astoundingly, we were left alone. He went faster, like he sensed we were immune to arrest. The wind was chilly, reminding me painfully of the snow I wasn't going to see this holiday season. I had a soft spot for my hometown in Connecticut, a pit that ached to be filled with snowmen and my breath in the night air.

*But I'm here,* I reminded myself. *In the desert. In Vegas.* I'd have to make do.

With nothing on the long strip in front of us, Toxic challenged the engine of the convertible to its limits. I was screaming—cheering—and I hadn't realized it until my lungs began to burn. My hair whipped into my eyes.

I should have been terrified...

And I wasn't.

Toxic was confident, I saw it in the way he was focused on the road. His knuckles were bloodless from how he strangled the steering wheel. The sensation of my stomach dropping out made me remember I wasn't invincible.

With my heart expanding, I yelled, "We don't need to go so fast!"

He shot me a side eye. Pressing a button, he closed the roof, saving my face from the brittle wind. My ears thumped, still ringing from the white noise. He stopped the car so suddenly that I strained against the seat belt.

Panting, I twisted, finding him staring straight at me. Toxic's lips were split in a breathless smirk; I had the sense that he wanted to bite me, to taste me. "Were you scared?" he asked.

"A little," I said. "Why did you do that?"

Smoothing a hand over his thick hair, he didn't break his stare. "To make you forget."

My nostrils flared with how obvious the answer was. It had worked—I'd stopped thinking about Shelly and the wedding. I'd been caught up in the moment, torn between fear and adrenaline as this stranger careened us down a dark road.

The Vegas Strip was far behind us; I saw it shining in the distance. Carefully, I studied the man who sat beside me as if he was a coiled spring. Toxic was no longer relaxed, but I didn't know why. I understood so little about him.

I did have one thought, though. "You weren't supposed to make me forget," I said slowly. "You were supposed to make me smile."

His mouth tightened. Rich shadows slid over him, but they couldn't hide his mostly naked body. I could see how his chest flared, and I definitely saw the way he sized me up. He'd done that a lot tonight.

"You want me to make you smile?" he asked.

My fingers came down, unclicking my seat belt. I started to say, "Yes." I never managed it. Toxic exploded at me, all muscle and wicked lips that had held back from taking me earlier. I'd known he'd ached for me when he'd danced. His hard-on had been...quite the sight.

I still wasn't ready for how hot his mouth was.

And his fucking *tongue*.

He kissed me like I was the oxygen he needed to live. Strong, solid hands cupped my cheeks, his weight pushing me against the window. It was cold, a scant relief with how this man was doing his best to melt me.

If he thought I'd just lie there while he had his way, he had no clue who I was. Quickly, I wrapped my fingers in his suspenders, using them to hold him close. I *felt* his reaction, his lungs expanding, his tiny inhale.

Toxic reached down, finding the zipper on my dress and cutting it down my spine. The fabric fell away, exposing my breasts to the air. That was when he finally ended our kiss, leaning away as he gasped. "You're fucking gorgeous, baby doll," he said severely.

If making me smile was a bet, I'd lost it a million times over.

When he went to lift up the hem, I grabbed his wrist. "Wait," I said.

His chuckle tickled through my soul. "I'm not sure I can."

Chewing the side of my lip, I gathered myself. "I'm wearing really, really ugly panties."

Toxic paused, his eyebrows knotting together. "Okay?"

"So, you know. Just a warning."

Pointedly, he took my hands and placed them on his chest. Then he reached down, tugging my dress off my hips, revealing the gray, torn, and definitely not-cute granny panties. I was ready for him to laugh at me. Instead, he stared into my pupils while he slowly—ever so patiently—pulled my underwear away.

"These," he said, tossing them out the window of the car, "don't matter. I'm not going to see them ever again, and neither are you."

There was no *way* that should have turned me on, but holy fuck, I was soaking the inside of my thighs. Scissoring my legs, I shivered. "You owe me a new pair."

"Deal." Gripping my knees, he flipped my legs over my head. As if he was tasting the most exquisite, delicate dessert ever, he licked my pussy from bottom to top. His face shined with my juices. "Reach into there," he said, tapping the glove compartment beside my head.

I was dizzy with lust, it took me a minute to understand. Popping the compartment open, I saw the silver pack of condoms. I didn't even have to dig for them.

Whatever part of me found that a little player-esque was buried too deep beneath the hot throbbing need for Toxic to fuck me. I hadn't wanted sex so bad in far too long.

But I wanted it now.

*Look at the upside,* I thought, handing him a foil packet. *You're using protection.* I didn't need to add "Got knocked up on Christmas Eve" to my current list of reckless decisions.

Toxic licked his thumb, reaching down to stroke my clit. I whimpered, wriggling while he watched. "Get in the backseat," he growled. The hot grit in his throat made me jump up eagerly, stumbling over onto the other cushions.

There was enough room for me to lie down fully in the backseat. He sat on my thighs, his weight comfortable. At this angle I saw what I'd witnessed earlier in the club—his cock was straining against the material of his briefs.

I had a sudden terrible worry that he might make a joke, something about me being a Ho Ho Ho, or stuffing himself in my chimney because it was Christmas.

My ex had made *awful* jokes.

But Toxic just slid his briefs aside, his shaft bouncing heavily into the air with the weight of his arousal. The tip was shiny with precome; my clit twitched, my insides tensing. He was as big and thick as I could have imagined.

And…if we weren't about to hook-up, I *would* have gone back to my hotel room and imagined.

Deftly, he rolled the condom down his cock. I was shaking with anticipation. He jerked himself, smirking down at me. "You like this, huh?"

Nodding furiously, I said, "Yes. Fuck me, stop teasing me."

"You don't want to wait?" He choked the base of his dick, and I swear, it swelled further. "You look like you want to wait."

"Shut up," I said, wrapping my heels around his back and forcing him closer to me—damn, his grin just kept spreading. "And fuck me."

"Only because you asked so nicely, baby doll." Burying his mouth on mine, he sank the tip of his fat cock-head into me. I grit my jaw, hissing as he stretched me with every single inch of his length.

The ridge of his cock scraped over the roof of my pussy. I was sweating already, my toes cramping as I urged him on. I wanted—I needed—to have this man inside of me. I wanted to tingle with orgasm, to forget every bad part of my last year. My last…five years?

When did I begin the count? Before the breakup, afterwards?

Toxic groaned, thrusting in to his full depth and erasing my ability to think about anything but how he was stuffing me. My insides rippled, milking over him as he started to shift backwards. His strokes were short, quick—he had less patience than I expected for someone who was used to dragging out a performance.

"Did you want me to fuck you before I gave you that lap dance?" he asked into my ear. His teeth nipped, lifting goose bumps. "Or was it after?"

A red fog coated my brain. My tongue was too soft, too sensitive; speaking was turning me on as much as his hips grinding over mine were. "The start," I moaned. "When you looked first at me."

His cock flexed inside my tight walls, his speed growing. Reaching under me, he dug his palms into my ass. Toxic drove me hard into the seat, fucking me to a rhythm that was quickly breaking down. He needed release as badly as I did.

"I can't hold off," he growled, his chest sandwiching against my hard nipples. "Come for me, do it. Squeeze your pretty little pussy and *come!*"

He didn't have to tell me twice; I'd been on the edge for some time, his filthy mouth was the nail in my coffin. Sobbing, I vibrated from head to toe, pressure exploding through my cells. My lower belly clenched, liquid heat slipping down my skin as I came violently.

Toxic was close behind, his muscles locking me into place. He held me steady, his last thrusts loud—obscenely wet. His cock thickened, pushing the condom—and me—to the brink. Through the latex I felt him come, his length pulsing without an end on the horizon.

We both gasped for air, our bodies trembling together with the aftershocks. I felt fucking amazing, spent and relaxed and better than I had in ages. The tension that had been in my body had been removed by the expert skills of this unfairly sexy stranger.

*Stranger. That's right.* Gingerly, I pushed him off of me, grimacing as his cock slid free. *Toxic is a stranger, that isn't even his real name.* In spite of that, he'd treated me better—made me feel better—than anyone had in far too long.

That should have been too wonderful to be marred by anything. But I'm not lucky enough to be so simple. I've always had a taint of paranoia; a need to understand. As I watched him dispose of the condom, I sat up on the seat. There was a tiny indent from the buckle in my lower back; I ignored it. "Toxic?"

He looked out the window, as if he'd sensed my serious mood and wanted nothing to do with it. "Yeah?"

"Why did you put so much effort into cheering me up?" I wished he'd look at me.

Then he did, and I wanted him to stop.

There were slivers of tragedy mixed into those caramel irises. It morphed the color, turned his warm gaze into something sad and painful. We'd met just over an hour ago, but I felt like I knew him.

Or at least I knew this part of him.

The hurt.

"Three years ago," he said suddenly. "That was when my fiancée broke up with me. I don't blame her, not really. I was a mess—still am." He chuckled. His smile didn't reach his eyes, his voice gritty and low. "She knew I'd become a dancer after we split, but she didn't know I worked at that strip club. Not until she showed up for her bachelorette party."

My ribs became too small; there was no room for my lungs. "That's awful," I whispered. "I'm so sorry."

"Don't be." Reaching over, he slid his arm around my shoulders. I was crushed against him, acting like the one thing keeping him tethered to the present. "I saw how excited she was. How happy. I'd never seen her smile so much." His eyes went back to that moment, wistful. "It hurt so fucking bad, even if I was glad for her. That pain…it's unforgettable."

He kissed the top of my head and said, "I recognized it tonight when I saw you."

Breathing through my nose, I clenched his arms around my middle and squeezed. "You couldn't have known what was wrong."

"Not exactly," he agreed. "Not until that girl burst in and ruined our private dance. She made it pretty obvious."

Shame rolled up my neck, warming me. "Shelly deserves to be happy. I didn't want to feel so awful about it. It's just…there was a time when Nolan was being terrible to me. She was the one that made me see we were wrong together. It's hard to swallow that they're getting married, after everything, I guess."

I expected Toxic to give me more advice. His fingers rubbed along my shoulder, then through my hair with absent comfort. We behaved like long lost lovers, not an idiotic, reckless woman and a wild—but sexy, yes, very sexy—stripper.

Finally, he broke the silence. "My name is Darius, not Toxic."

Snuggling against his bare chest, I traced one of his tattoos. It was a long yellow snake, its fangs deep in an apple sitting on his bicep. "I have a confession, too. My name's Josia, not Candy."

His laugh came out like a snort. "I'm shocked, just shocked! It's almost like your friends weren't all shouting that at you earlier."

Grinning, I shrugged helplessly. "Keep my dark secret safe, that's all I ask."

He rumbled with laughter. I joined him, letting him rock me in the backseat, his heat swarming my brain until nothing in the world existed but him. I'd never meant for this situation to go so far, but...I didn't mind.

I kind of loved it.

Sleep took over, softening the last of the alcohol so that when I finally awoke, I was free of a hangover. I didn't even have a headache. I was, however, extremely confused to see Toxic—Darius, I reminded myself—sitting in the front seat of the car.

The pink sunrise glistened over his smooth skin. The edge of his nose was strong, his eyelashes thick and swooping. It would have been picturesque, except for the fact that he was swearing under his breath, twisting his key over and over in the ignition.

"Shit," he mumbled.

Rocking forward, I hung over the driver's side seat. "What is it? What's wrong?"

He flicked his eyes back at me, his smile going crooked. "Morning, sunshine."

"What's wrong with the car?" I insisted.

Rubbing the side of his neck, he said, "I left the battery running while we were getting busy last night. It's dead. We're going to have to walk back."

Letting my jaw drop, I sat up and tested the key for myself. It clicked, but nothing more. "You're serious." Instinctively I reached for my pockets, remembering that I didn't have my phone on me. I'd forgotten my purse in the club; it had become unimportant while I was under Darius's spell.

We were fucked.

For a long while I sat there. Something bubbled in me, the pressure rising. I didn't know what it was until I started to giggle. I couldn't stop, I was in tears. It was too funny, too stupid! Wiping my eyes, I gave him a long kiss that left us both breathless. "I guess we better get walking."

"Look on the upside," he said, helping me out of the car. "It's Christmas. People are obligated to help each other out on this day, aren't they?"

As we marched down that stretch of road—him half naked, me underwear-less in my dress and carrying my heels in my hands, both of us holding out our thumbs to catch a ride—I realized something.

This wasn't the worst Christmas ever.

Maybe Vegas didn't have snow, something we were both grateful for in our current state, but it had allowed me to finally, after such a long time, let go of my bitter feelings that had burrowed deep into my bones.

Toxic laughed, gesturing at every car that slowed for us but never fully stopped. I found myself copying him, the sound echoing into the sunrise-orange sky. This ridiculously over-the-top stripper in his Santa-themed underwear that barely hid his ass or anything else…

He'd done what he'd promised he would.

He'd made me smile.

What better Christmas gift could I have ever asked for?

## About the Author

Nora Flite is a USA Today Bestselling author of some of the dirtiest bad boy romances. She always pushes the limits in her romances, whether it's between a hitman and his target, or a rockstar and his newest band member. Also? She adores men with tattoos. Just a fact.

Website: www.noraflite.com

# The Year of the Rooster

## By Mia Hopkins

*Yŏu yuán qiān lǐ lái xiāng huì.*
Fate brings people together no matter how far apart they may be.
—Chinese saying

\* \* \*

It's winter break and campus is deserted. Iris Cheng and I pass each other in the hallway like two ghosts who haunt the same dorm. For one week, we exchange a daily hey and a smile. Then we retreat into our separate rooms and shut the doors.

Like almost everyone else on this floor, Iris is an international student from China. I'm here because I'm the only resident advisor who's studied Chinese—well, one semester of Mandarin, anyway. This doesn't even matter, really. The international students either all speak English or avoid me completely.

On Monday of the second week, I get up early, work out at the gym, take a quick shower, and get dressed. Before I lose my nerve, I knock on Iris's door. When she opens it, she's wearing a sweatshirt, yoga pants, and expensive-looking Nikes. We're both structural engineering majors. She's one of the few women in my department, and I'd be lying if I said I never checked her out during lectures. She's kind of tall for a girl, with a squarish chin and deep-set eyes. She's pulled her hair back into a ponytail. Her ears stick out a little.

I'd be lying if I said I didn't think she was hot.

"Abel?" She's smiling, but her voice is wary. "Is something wrong?"

I try to sound casual. "No, everything's fine. Just wondering if you wanted to go down to the dining hall. With me. For breakfast. I mean, if you haven't eaten already."

She pauses. I'm not awkward around girls, but there's something about Iris that unnerves me. I'm kind of relieved when she finally says, "Sure. I was about to leave. Let's go down together." Her English is clear and precise. She has a slight Australian accent.

Over cold cereal and coffee, we chat in the nearly empty dining hall about classes we've taken and our favorite local student haunts. We live twelve steps away from each other, and still I'm surprised by how limited our shared experiences are. This is the fallout of attending a big university, I guess—proximity means nothing. We're basically strangers.

To my surprise, we begin having breakfast together every morning. I don't flatter myself—winter break on campus can feel like solitary confinement, and any kind of human interaction is good. But with each passing day, Iris's smile comes more easily. She asks me more questions about my life. Pretty quickly, formality fades between us until—just like that—we're friends.

On Christmas Day, I call each of my family members one by one. They're all off on their own adventures. My mom is taking her first vacation back to Mexico in more than ten years, my sister is on a semester abroad in Costa Rica, and my brother Lucky just bought a house with his new fiancée—I doubt he'd want me dropping by for tamales.

I'm happy they all have something good going for them, but I'm nostalgic for the Christmases we used to spend together. We were poor as hell for a long time, but we always celebrated. To save money, my sister used to draw a Christmas tree on a piece of newsprint and tack it to the wall. We'd put our presents under it—small stuff. Socks. A couple of candy bars. A box of crayons. I think about these things as I ride my bike to church and light some candles for my family.

In the afternoon, Iris and I go for a hike along the creek. Nothing is in bloom. It's quiet and cold. Clouds are rolling in.

"Do you miss your family?" I ask her, because I sure as hell miss mine.

"No. Not really."

That's a surprise. I search her calm face. "Why not?"

She shrugs. "You grew up with your family. I didn't."

I know from our breakfast chats that her father owns factories and her mother is a doctor. From her designer-label clothes and her thousand-dollar bike, I guess Iris's family has money to burn.

"I lived in Chengdu until I was nine," she continues. "Then I was sent to boarding school in Sydney and high school in Canada. Now, I'm here in Davis. I see my mother and father once, sometimes twice a year."

Wind fills the trees. I zip up my hoodie, and Iris digs her hands into the pockets of her down jacket. "Do you ever feel nostalgic?" I ask.

She stops for a second, blinking. "Wait a second." She takes out her phone and checks the translation for *nostalgic.* "No," she says, putting her phone back in her pocket. "Sometimes I miss my home-stay family in Vancouver. Sometimes I miss my Australian classmates. But nostalgic? No." She shrugs and we keep walking. "I'm not really a sad person." I listen to the soles of our shoes on the dirt trail. Iris says, "I like to live in the present. Like this, here, with you. This is good."

Maybe because I'm sad. Maybe because it starts to drizzle and Iris doesn't seem bothered at all. Maybe because she knows herself and—God help me—her cheeks turn bright pink when she's cold. Whatever the reason, after two weeks of getting to know her, this is the exact moment I start to fall for Iris Cheng.

"Hey. Come here," I say.

She steps close to me and I put my arm around her. She smells soapy and sweet, like rose petals. Without another word, we walk like that back to the dorm. When we arrive, she gives me a quick hug.

"See you tomorrow at breakfast?" I ask.

"Yes. Tomorrow. Breakfast." With a smile, she goes into her room and shuts the door.

\* \* \*

All my friends have secret crushes on Abel Garcia. With his wavy dark hair and muscles, he looks a little like Jon Snow from *Game of Thrones*. For a long time, I didn't get his appeal at all. But in the last few days, I've slowly started to understand.

My roommate is back in Guangzhou for winter break. Almost everyone is back home in China. The wealthier students are on shopping trips in New York or London. I'm not jealous; I like the quiet. I read ahead in my classes and catch up on my Korean dramas. For as long as I can remember, I've always been somewhat of a loner.

So it surprises me I've been enjoying Abel's company. Of course, I noticed him in some of my classes, but we've never really talked. He asks a lot of questions during discussions. He's friendly and smart; the professors adore him, even the gruff ones.

After Christmas, we've been a bit shy with each other. Having his arm around me on the walk home should have felt wrong—I'm not a big dater and I'm not interested in boyfriends, especially not now. But being close to him felt better than it should have.

We haven't touched each other at all since then.

Not that I'd mind if we did.

At breakfast on New Year's Eve, Abel asks me if I have plans for the night. One of his friends is having a party at Emerson and he wants me to go with him. I don't like drunken parties, and I tell him so.

"Are you always this blunt?" He's smiling, so I know he's not offended. Sometimes American irony is hard for me to pick up.

I look up *blunt*. There's a translation app on my phone. "Yes," I say.

"All right, no party." He lifts an eyebrow. "How about movies? Do you like movies?"

"As long as they're action movies. With explosions. Not too much talking."

"Perfect. How do you feel about Chinese food?"

I laugh. "My favorite."

Abel looks a hundred times hotter when he smiles. "Okay. Movie night in my room. Nine o'clock. Wear your rattiest pajamas. Bring your pillow."

That evening, I look up the word *rattiest*. Is he serious? I spend two hours in the women's restroom shaving, waxing, plucking and exfoliating. I even paint my nails. I put on some nice underwear, stuff I haven't worn since I broke up with my boyfriend in Vancouver last year. Over that, I wear my rattiest pajamas, as instructed. But I put on some lipgloss and mascara, too.

This is Abel Garcia, after all.

At nine fifteen, I'm at his door.

"You're late. Traffic?" He looks down the deserted hallway.

"Lots." I thump his shoulder with my stuffed panda as I walk inside.

As a senior and our floor's resident advisor, he gets a room all to himself. He's pushed the beds together to make a double, and he only has one desk, so the room feels spacious. He's neat; there's no clutter or dust. The only decoration is a silk Mexican flag tacked to the wall, red and green with its determined eagle clutching a snake. A framed photograph of his family sits on his desk. In the picture he stands next to his handsome-cowboy older brother, a pretty sister, and a beaming, young-looking mother.

Abel and I sit cross-legged on his bed and have dinner out of paper cartons. He calls this "Chinese takeout" but in reality, it's American-style Chinese food. It's pretty good, but we don't eat any of these dishes back home.

"How do you celebrate New Year's Eve in China?" he asks through a mouthful of noodles.

"Nothing special. But we celebrate the Lunar New Year in January or February. It's called the Spring Festival."

He listens carefully as I tell him what I remember from my childhood: family reunions, lanterns, fireworks, dumplings and new clothes. Children receive money in red envelopes called *hong bao*.

"This was the Year of the Monkey," I say, "so the *hong bao* had monkey designs on them."

"What about this year? The one coming up?"

I can't remember the word in English. I pull out my phone, tap in the characters, and press translate. "It's the year of the cock," I say.

Abel laughs so hard, he almost spits out his soda.

"What?" I'm annoyed but genuinely puzzled. I haven't screwed up my English in a long time.

"I'm not laughing at you, I'm laughing at the translation." His laughter fades, but he's still smiling. "Do an image search for the word *cock*."

I do it. The first ten pictures show exactly what I mean. But the eleventh picture surprises me. My face turns hot, and I know I'm blushing.

I look at him. "Really?"

"Really," he says.

I turn off my phone. "English is weird."

"It is." He reaches up and tucks a strand of hair behind my ear. I blush harder when his fingers brush my cheek. "Say *rooster* next time and you won't run into any trouble."

When we finish our meal, he cleans up. He rigs his battered laptop on the nightstand and turns down the lights. As I try to get comfortable on his bed—Abel's bed, I remind myself with a giddy smile—I'm impressed by his choice. He's found a streaming version of *The Avengers* with Mandarin subtitles.

"I settled on a movie with subtitles because I don't want you to miss anything," he says, and presses play.

"I understand English," I say, faking offense.

"You don't have to keep pretending you understand English, Iris." Before I can use it to hit him again, Abel grabs my panda and shoves it under his head. His arm comes around me automatically and I don't remember anything feeling better—except for the last time he put his arm around me on Christmas Day.

"Are you comfortable?" he asks, snuggling close.

"Yes."

I drift off almost immediately. When I wake up, I'm curled up against Abel's side, my head on his chest. He's sound asleep, warm and solid beneath me. I blink in the darkness. The movie is finished and his screensaver is up. I glance at the clock. It's a quarter past eleven.

As I lift my head, Abel stirs. He puts a big hand on the back of my neck and slowly pulls me close again.

"Wait." His voice is deep and soft. Gently, he slides the elastic from my ponytail. He runs his hands through my hair, and his fingertips brush my scalp. I shiver. I rest my head once again on his hard chest.

We're quiet for a long time. I listen to his breathing and lie very still. Unwanted feelings rise up inside me, bringing along some hard truths. I pretend to like being lonely. But I don't like it. Not at all.

"Tell me something about you that I don't know," Abel says. His touch feels amazing. "A secret."

I swallow hard. I have few secrets, none of them particularly exciting. "Okay," I say softly. "My major."

"Your major?"

"Yeah." I close my eyes. "Eight years ago, there was a very big earthquake in my hometown. I was living in Australia. I watched everything on the news. I couldn't go home. I couldn't reach my parents. For two days, I thought they were dead."

Abel's hand stops moving. He doesn't say anything, so I keep talking.

"They were lucky. They survived. But 70,000 people died in that earthquake." I take a deep breath as I remember the nightmares flickering on the TV screen in my boarding school's dormitory. I was the only student from Chengdu. "The worst thing I saw were the children. Their schools were not built properly. The buildings collapsed on top of them. With China's one-child policy, many parents lost their only son or daughter."

I move closer to Abel. His heat envelops me as he holds me tighter. "I promised myself when I grew up, I would build the safest schools. Schools that would survive the most powerful earthquakes. So I came here, to California, to study structural engineering and seismic design."

He's quiet for a long time. Silently, I worry that my confession is too heavy, too serious for him. Guys don't want seriousness before a hookup. I lie still, fighting off regret.

Beneath my hand, his abs flex—they're so hard. He sits up in the darkness and puts his finger under my chin. "I want to kiss you, Iris. Is that okay?"

My lips tingle. Actually, my whole body tingles.
"Okay."

* * *

I n the faint light from my laptop, Iris's face is relaxed. Her lips are parted slightly, and her dark eyes are fixed on my mouth. Her calm expression throws me off balance, and my heart is trying to punch its way out of my rib cage. I angle my head to kiss her. When my chest rests against hers, I finally feel the truth— she's breathing hard.

She's as excited about what's going to happen as I am.

"You're so beautiful," I whisper.

I take my time. I stroke her cheekbones and her chin. I'm gripped by a deranged desire to make this moment last as long as possible. I graze my thumb along her bottom lip, back and forth. Her warm breath hitches and washes over the back of my hand. I keep stroking her. I cup the back of her neck, nestling my hand between her skin and her warm, silken hair.

"Abel," she whispers, "kiss me."

So I do—but not where she expects. Softly, I kiss her forehead. I kiss both her cheeks, then her chin. She closes her eyes and grasps my shoulders. I kiss her throat and she jerks against me, her body arching against mine.

I start to press soft open-mouthed kisses to her neck when she pushes me back, eyes wild.

I'm surprised. "What's wrong?"

"Stop messing with me," she whispers.

She grabs my face and smashes her lips against mine. Heat explodes between us like a solar flare. She combs her fingers through my hair and grips it, pulling me closer. We're both breathing hard, drawing deep, frantic breaths. When Iris opens her mouth slightly, I take the opportunity. Our tongues brush against each other, and every nerve in my body ignites. My brain goes dark, sucked into a black hole of pleasure.

We make out for what feels like hours. We're so enthusiastic I nearly knock the laptop off the nightstand. Iris giggles at me as I shut it and put it aside. I turn on the lamp to get a better look at her. Her cheeks are flushed bright red, her hair is a mess, her T-shirt is sideways, and her smile—God—her smile is radiant.

She holds out her arms. "Come here."

I collapse into her, kissing her neck as she strokes my back. I let her drag my T-shirt over my head and watch as she takes off hers. I lay on my back and she climbs on top of me, running her hands over my chest. Her bra is purple with tiny white polka dots. It's playful and sexy at the same time, just like her.

She sits up. "Okay?" she asks. Her pupils are dilated.

"Okay," I say.

"You want to…?"

"Okay," I say again, like a dork.

I watch as she stands up and strips off her pajama pants. Her panties match her bra and suddenly I realize

I'm not the only one in the room with ulterior motives tonight. She grabs her stuffed panda by my head, puts it on my desk, and drapes my T-shirt over it.

"He shouldn't see this."

Her goofy smile crushes my heart. I lunge at her. She squeals as I carry her back to bed and cover her with kisses. Her bra disappears, followed by her panties. Soon my clothes are gone, too. And now we're lying together, tangled up, skin-to-skin, and I'm so deep under this girl's spell, I think I might be dreaming.

She lets me touch her, kiss her, taste her. She watches me as I work my way down her body, savoring her. When she opens her legs, I lose myself in her, observing the way she responds to each caress. Soon I discover her sweet spot. I stay on it, grinding her down with a slow, steady rhythm until her thighs flex and she's trembling.

"Abel," she whimpers.

She comes against my tongue but I keep licking her, drawing out her orgasm. Her face tightens up and goose bumps cover her body. As I watch her, I feel bulletproof. I've never made a girl climax so fast.

When she's finished, she kisses me once more and wraps her cool, delicate fingers around me. I'm so turned on, it hurts. We look down together.

"Big rooster," she whispers, breathless.

We're laughing as she strokes me. Awkwardly, I reach into my nightstand, grab a condom, and roll it on. I'm so close that there's no art to my game at this point. She guides me and I hold myself still, right at the edge.

"Ready?" I ask.

She nods.

Iris grasps my forearms as I slide deep. Her eyes are glassy. She is so naked, so vulnerable, so insanely sexy beneath me, I have to shut my eyes to keep from shooting off too fast. My other senses scramble to take over—I smell the rose petal essence of her hair, I taste the earthy sweetness of her pussy, and I feel...everything. Sex has never been this incredible.

She pulls me down into another kiss. An over-whelming need to thrust grips me. Her muscles tighten around my shaft and I groan, shaking from the effort of holding back.

"I'm not going to last long," I whisper against her lips. "I'm sorry."

"Don't be sorry." She kisses me once more. "Don't worry about that at all."

I hold my breath and lift myself higher. I begin to ride her. Pressure builds inside me. When I open my eyes, I see that hers are closed. She is panting softly. Her entire body is flushed and glistening with sweat.

"Iris," I gasp. "Look at me."

When she opens her eyes, I come so hard my head snaps back. Pleasure races through my veins, burning away all of my loneliness. Iris holds me tight. I might be moaning. I might be yelling. I have no idea. It doesn't matter—we're the only two people on this floor. We can be as loud as we want. We can run naked down the hallway banging pots and pans if we want to.

When I come to, I realize I've collapsed on her. She's stroking my back. "Are you okay?" she asks.

I manage a grunt. Slowly, I get out of bed. I clean up with some tissues, turn off the lamp and lie back down next to her. My muscles have turned to liquid. I'm exhausted, barely lucid.

"It's almost one o'clock." She strokes my damp chest and kisses my neck. "We missed the countdown."

Yawning, I pull the blankets over us, wrap my arms around her and squeeze. I kiss her sweet lips in the darkness, and nothing has ever tasted so good.

"Happy New Year, Iris."

"It is," she whispers.

## About the Author

Mia Hopkins writes lush romances starring fun, sexy characters who love to get down and dirty. She lives in the heart of Los Angeles with her roguish husband and two waggish dogs. For more information, please connect with her on Twitter @miahopkinsxoxo.

# Christmas Daze

BY MARLA MURPHY

## CHAPTER ONE

L ady Grace smoothed her plain green dress and announced, "Lace be damned." Tromping into the woods, she raised her fist to God. "Why did you make life easier for boys?" She plopped down on a stump and mumbled, "You have to be male."

A gust of wind shook the overhead branch, dumping snow on her head.

"I'm not in the mood for a snowball fight, thank you." Grace brushed the snow from her head and looked toward Heaven. "I propose a truce."

The sun came out for the first time in days, sending light spiking through the wind-blown branches and creating a crooked hopscotch pattern in the snow. Enticed by childhood memories, she whooped aloud and made a game of jumping from one dazzling sunbeam to the next.

Taking no notice of the cold until she tripped over a root and fell face first to the ground, Grace spit out, "Bollocks," along with a mouth full of snow. "Sorry." Then, "Hey, I thought we had a truce."

With legs sprawled, she shivered as a gust of wind whooshed under her skirt, catching it on a thorny bush. Displaying her bloomers to every woodland creature who cared to look, she struggled to free herself.

A deep chuckle invaded her revelry. "Well said. Bollocks, indeed. You look to be in a bit of a tangle."

With snow dripping from her rosy nose and clinging to curls nearly the color of the snow itself, she let out a yelp and tried to roll over. "You there. Close your eyes."

"Hold still. You're making it worse, and if I close my eyes I won't be able to see what needs to be done here."

She could only imagine how much of her undergarments were visible. Collapsing back into the drift, she managed to keep her head out of the snow. "Just get me free."

He pulled to untwist the skirt., "Tell me your name, miss, and where you work."

*Oh, no. In this dress he thinks I'm a servant.* Grace felt him gently tugging and grit her teeth. "The skirt is ruined. Just tear it."

"Stop squirming. Tell me, do you work for the Hamptons?" He released the last of the thorny branches, and Grace tried to stand and wiggle away. As her foot slipped on an icy spot, he grabbed her up by her waist before she could land back in the briars. His breath tickled the back of her neck as he whispered, "Or perhaps you're the bar maid at the tavern down the road?"

"Unhand me. Or you'll be meeting my brothers on the dueling field." A shiver passed through her, but it wasn't caused by the cold breeze. When curiosity triumphed over embarrassment, she gathered her courage and turned. Momentarily stunned by the face of the man with a gentle touch and rude questions, she became lost in the warmth of his dark brown eyes. They were almost as black as his wind-blown hair. *Oh, dear God. Handsome and cheerful?* His next question and lop-sided grin brought her back to her senses.

"How will you compensate me for my assistance, miss?"

*He's laughing at me.* "You're daft. I asked for no aid."

"Still, you received my help. I claim a forfeit for my trouble." Tapping his finger on his lips, he blew a lock of hair from his eye, and said, "I suppose a kiss will suffice."

Grace stepped back from the rogue, gifted him with her dimples, and shoved him over the stump into the snow. Giddy, she ran away laughing, wishing she could have stayed for a kiss, and regretting she wasn't his barmaid.

## CHAPTER TWO

B ridge rode up to the portico at the Hamptons' estate, still musing about the maid with the flax-colored hair. She shouldn't be hard to find again. She was a pretty girl with shapely legs and a behind begging to be caressed. He had gotten a quick look at her bloomers, until his mother's voice in his head scolded him for not looking away.

The ancient doorman allowed Bridge no farther than the massive entryway. Despite the fact he knew Bridge was family, and a merry gathering could be heard in the parlor, the haughty old stickler would see if the Hamptons were *at home.*

Bridge didn't have long to wait. General Hampton stomped toward him, inspecting his brother-in-law from top to bottom. Grabbing Bridge's outstretched hand, he growled, "Bridgeton, I see you are finally here. The other guests arrived days ago."

Alice rushed toward her brother, arms open. "Bridge, you look half frozen. Have you been out rolling in the snow again?" She gave him her impish grin and moved her arms up and down at her sides as if making snow angels in the air.

He chuckled, lifted her off her feet and swung her around. "There's my sweet Ally. I'm afraid your angels will be a bit wider than the last ones we made."

The general growled. "Be gentle with my wife."

Alice smacked her brother's shoulder. "Behave. You know I'm increasing."

"How many does this make? Twelve? Fourteen?" He loved to hear her laugh.

"This is the second, and well you know it. Jeremy has talked of nothing else, since he heard you were coming."

"How is my nephew?"

The general's chuckle softened his chiseled face. "He has been driving us crazy asking when you would arrive."

Alice teased, "I assume you've been hiding from Father until you have a fiancée on your arm. A few young ladies are here waiting to meet my titled single brother. But first you need to get dry and warm. I'll send the general's valet to you."

A hot bath eased his muscles, abused from the hard ride from London. After he sent a fussy valet away, Bridge entertained himself with his hands between his legs, thinking again of the playful maiden. He could carry her off to Gretna Green, and spend the rest of his life bedding the prettiest girl he'd ever met, if he didn't have obligations as an earl. Damned nuisance, grooming to become duke. He could have used a brother to take away the pressure of siring an heir. His bath cooled, as did his mood. *I'm destined to spend a virtuous life with a proper lady. Too bad Ally can't inherit the title.*

Now warmer and better dressed, Bridge laughed about his encounter with the free-spirited girl that landed him in a snowdrift. It had been fun teasing her. Later he'd slip down to the tavern and pay her a visit, but for now it was time to deal with Father's ultimatum. He'd find a suitable girl, charm her, put a ring on her finger, and get her with child.

Bridge braced himself as he waited for the doorman to precede him into the salon. "Lord Bridgeton." Stopping in the doorway, Bridge made a reconnaissance of the room, noting faces and exits. Taking his sister's extended arm, together they entered the frilly, giggly fray.

## CHAPTER THREE

Lady Grace inhaled roasting goose and pungent mincemeat at the kitchen door. Knocking snow from her boots, she made her way to the ovens. Alice had given up reminding her to use the front entrance.

Sweet Aunt Alice. Some women would not have welcomed their husband's wild niece into their home. Grace had been sent to the general in London, hoping his wife could influence her. Alice tried, but Grace's first forays into society had been disastrous. The general soon whisked them off to his country estate for a house party, giving Grace an opportunity to practice on a handpicked list of guests most likely to overlook her social blunders.

Backing closer to the ovens, Grace closed her eyes. The space between her legs pulsed pleasurably as she relived her encounter with the handsome man. His angular features had made him look menacing, until that crooked grin. It was his mouth cocked to one side as he demanded a kiss, that had her pushing him into the snow. *Forfeit a kiss, indeed.*

When the cook admonished, "You stay in those wet clothes, you'll be spending Christmas in bed," Grace heeded the warning and ran off to her room. She was chilled, and as she entered her bedchamber she found a warm bath awaiting. Nancy looked up from adding sweet-smelling oils to the water. The young girl had been promoted from the cook's helper when Grace arrived, and learning to be a lady's maid had come easily to her. Grace not only valued Nancy for her creative fingers with unruly blonde curls, but for her good nature and ability to keep a confidence.

The soak revived Grace's body to match her happy mood. She tried not to fidget as Nancy worked her magic, wrapping soft braids around her head and ignoring the few curls that escaped to bounce around her face. She had spied her new silvery-blue dress draped across her bed, and was anxious to wear it. As Nancy finished lacing the dress, Lady Alice tapped on the door and entered.

"Grace, you are lovely. I concede, the ribbon suits you better than the lace. It's a rare gift you have of looking at a fabric sample and imagining the finished dress."

"Thank you for having the trim changed, Aunt Alice."

"Shall I accompany you to the parlor? My brother has arrived. All the guests are present and waiting for dinner to be announced."

Inhaling deeply, as they walked the hallway, Grace commented on the holiday aromas. Clove-spiked oranges nestled next to the dusty blue berries on the juniper boughs laced up the stair railing. As they made their way down the stairs, Grace whispered, "You know I'd rather be curled up with a good book than have to tolerate these people one more evening. It's not too late. I can slip off to the library and no one will miss me."

"Please make an effort, Grace."

"Nobody likes me. The men stare at my bodice, the women chatter, and they all make my head hurt. Anne and Mary are the silliest and I still can't tell them apart. And their cousin makes me ill. How can someone as beautiful as Lady Charlotte act so ugly?"

"I know the twins are flighty, but they're young. I've seated you away from them, and I'll keep an eye on Lady Charlotte."

"Thank you. Those clingy geese honk over every eligible man in the room."

"My brother will add to that number. I think you'll like the earl."

"Oh! That's right. He's titled. Wonderful. The geese will flock to him, leaving me to gander where I will."

Standing in the drawing room doorway, Alice laughed aloud at Grace's clever comment, drawing attention to the two before Alice guided Grace toward her brother. "Bridge, may I present Lady Grace, the general's niece? Lady Grace, this is my brother, Lord Bridgeton."

## Chapter Four

B ridge fought the urge to cast up the mulled wine he had stupidly imbibed on an empty stomach. General Hampton's niece? With the words tumbling through his head, he barely remembered to bow. "Lady Grace."

He couldn't look away. Taking short breaths, he waited for her reaction. He was met with a blush, a clumsy curtsy, but no hysterics. Looking as if it would take too much effort to move her facial muscles, she didn't blink, until her eyes came alive with mischief. "Good evening, my lord. You seem familiar to me. Have we met?"

Before she could say more, the twins grabbed each of his arms and started plying him with questions, each simpering a bit louder than the other to gain his attention. He continued to ignore the silly fifteen-year-olds, along with Lady Charlotte, who was tapping her foot and glaring at Lady Grace. Bridge had been flirting outrageously with the older—and most striking woman in the room—until he saw Grace standing in the doorway. From then on his eyes never strayed from Grace's face, even as her blush deepened.

Lady Charlotte stepped up. "Lady Grace, you must visit my room before you retire, dear. My maid can mix a cream to dampen your complexion."

It was said loud enough to gather the attention of several in the room. Watching Grace's hands become fists—the white of her knuckles in sharp contrast to her reddening upper torso—Bridge stepped in. "I warrant Lady Grace's blush only enhances her beauty."

As dinner was announced, Alice extracted a tittering twin from each of Bridge's arms, and assigned partners for the procession to the dining room.

Across the table and two chairs away, Bridge studied Lady Grace. *God, she's magnificent.* Hell. For a moment he had considered marrying her when he thought her a serving girl. Finding she was of a suitable station to be a peer's wife, he could now think of nothing else.

*I know she's smart. Will keep us both entertained. Courageous. We could travel the world together. Who would have thought a chance meeting with a pretty girl in the woods could be the answer to my problem? I need to think, and if Lady Charlotte doesn't stop babbling, I'm going to reach across this table and throttle her.* As annoying as she was, he couldn't fault the chatty woman for trying to find a husband.

*My God!* His sour stomach lurched as he grew pale. His eyes moved down the table to the golden girl tossing him her dimples. *A husband? Am I dense? Was it a chance meeting? Did you wait for me with your dress hiked to your waist?* He closed his eyes. He was so taken with his snow maiden that he would forgive her. He could think of nothing else.

## Chapter Five

Grace had trembled on wobbly legs when her handsome stranger had been introduced as Alice's brother. Now he sat near the head of the table, looking deep in thought. Charlotte sat across from him, looking perturbed by his inattention.

Her eyes wandered back toward the head of the table. Earlier he had come to her defense when Charlotte embarrassed her, but now something was causing him distress. She flinched at his intense scrutiny. *What happened to the amusing man from the forest?*

After dinner, Alice invited the men to forgo their brandy and join the ladies for the lighting of the yule log. Grace rushed ahead to the parlor and commandeered a hiding place behind a heavy velvet curtain. Feeling safely shielded in the window well behind the fourteen foot tall Christmas tree even Queen Victoria would envy, she chanced a peek. The older men stood around the hearth, embellishing stories of their youth. The ladies sat nearby, keeping an eye on the wassail bowl and the children trying to sneak a cup. Young people maneuvered each other into position under the mistletoe. So far Charlotte had not been able to catch Bridge, causing her to sigh and tap her foot. Aunt Alice, tired of her pouting, insisted Charlotte accompany the twins at the piano.

Bridge hadn't budged from where he leaned against the wall. Grace watched him study the room, suspecting he was looking for her. She inhaled the fresh scent of the evergreen and absently stroked the rich drapery, moving it to take another peek through the branches of the massive tree.

Glancing at a shiny ornament, her smile faded. Staring back at her reflection from the silver ball was Bridge, who had crept up to her side. He sported a sly grin, looking like a cat holding a squirming rodent.

Her insides commiserated with the poor mouse as she whispered, "Bollocks."

"Indeed. Did you overhear your brothers, or did you learn that word from a beau, my sweet?"

"I beg your pardon, my lord. If you were to know me better, you would learn I am no one's sweet anything."

"So I've deduced. Your perfidy is remarkable, but I'll acquiesce to your request."

"You talk nonsense."

"You begged me to know you better, and I accept the challenge."

"You intentionally twist my words. Go away, you devil."

"You don't intend to pay your due?"

"I owe you nothing, you foolish man."

"I freed you from a thistle. You repaid by knocking me into the snow."

"A trifle action, my lord. You'll have brutal punishment awaiting when I tell my brothers of your crude questions."

"I believed you a tavern maid, grateful to be rescued. Nevertheless, it was not well done of me."

She threw back her head and quietly laughed in his face. "So, me lord, can I bring ya a tankard of ale while ya stand there a gawking at me?"

"There's the saucy wench I thought you to be. How long did you have to lay in wait for me? You must have been quite cold by the time I came along."

"Wait for you? Are you a simpleton? What kind of noddycock travels off the road anyway?"

"Perhaps one who stops to admire the half-frozen creek and hears a woman giggling in the forest. Perhaps a gentleman too curious for his own good. And too gallant to avoid a conniving maid looking to better herself."

"Your conceit is laughable."

"Don't you dare walk away. You will explain yourself. Why were you without your maid, alone in the woods?"

"You can't be related to Lady Alice. There's not a kind bone in your body."

"So you *have* been studying me. Come here, and I'll acquaint you with my bones."

"Cretin."

He cocked his brow. "Shrew."

"You are impertinent and you bore me. Go away." Shaking, she stepped away from her safe niche to find her uncle approaching.

"I wondered if Bridgeton had lost his mind conversing with the tree. What's this about impertinence, Grace? Do I need to have him flogged?"

Grace grimaced, trying to imagine how much the general overheard. "No, thank you, Uncle. I can handle this fribble."

Bridge smirked. "And if Lady Grace can't manage, her brothers can call me out."

"What nonsense is this, Bridgeton? Grace has no siblings. She's an only child."

Excusing herself, Grace escaped, her face glowing as red as the holly berries adorning the mantle.

# CHAPTER SIX

Nancy opened the draperies much too early, but the aroma of honeyed hot chocolate at her bedside enticed Grace to open her eyes. The sun was out for the second day, making everything brighter as it bounced around her pale yellow bedchamber.

Nancy, holding up her riding skirt, called out, "Good morning, milady! Lovely day for a ride."

Somedays Grace wanted to muzzle the cheery maid, but not today. Not only had Nancy pilfered the last of the orange cream cakes, but the blessed girl had come up with the perfect solution to clear her head. "I'll wear my breeches."

"You told Lady Alice I got rid of them."

"If she sees me, I'll tell her I retrieved them from the rag bag."

Quickly dressing, Grace headed out her room towards the servants' stairway. It was the spicy scent of bay rum that alerted her to his presence before Bridge pulled her into the linen closet and held her by her waist.

His breath tickled. "Good morning, my lady. Nice breeches."

"Strange accommodations, my lord. Your sister couldn't find you a better bedchamber?" *God. Will he kiss me? A forfeit? Who am I kidding? Just kiss me before a maid finds us.*

"Ah, my funny little rabbit, you ran away last night before answering my question."

Her breathing became labored in anticipation for what was to come. *If you don't do it soon, I may die right here, a maid never to be kissed.*

"Answer my question, Grace. Is it a husband you want? Were you trying to trick me? Were you waiting for me in the snow?"

"Oh! Let go, you ignorant oaf." She ran down the hall, still an unkissed maiden.

It didn't take her long to reach the stable. As Circe was being saddled, Grace asked the stable master to point out the earl's horse. The last thing she wanted was to run into him riding this morning. Or ever again.

Maybe.

# Chapter Seven

Bridge nodded to the early risers leaving the dining room. Left alone with a footman, a grumbling stomach and a sideboard Alice had seen stocked with his favorites, the food was of no interest. He closed his eyes and held emptiness in his chest.

*What's wrong with me?* As soon as he asked her, he regretted it. *Answer my question, Grace. Is it a husband you want? Were you trying to trick me? Were you waiting for me in the snow?* Her once quickening breath when he had pulled her into the closet shriveled to cold hardness. While his mind taunted that she must be a brilliant actress, it was his heart that held the answer.

He had watched her run away, knowing there was no need to revisit the accusation. He had conducted himself shamefully. His mother, Alice, hell, even his father would have been outraged. "One question, and I'll release you. Are you with child?"

The silence was maddening, as no breath escaped from either body.

"It's not your concern."

Gritting his teeth, he asked, "Just how many men have you lain with?"

She'd had enough. Pushing against his chest, she tossed her head. "I don't keep count of trivial matters."

"You little fool. You need to give the babe a name."

"I'm a virgin, you pig-headed toad." Pushing away, she ran down the servants' steps and out the kitchen door. She had not been waiting to trap him.

*What was wrong with me? I'm a horses' arse. I don't deserve her favor.*

A few bites into the breakfast he barely touched, he spied Grace riding away from the stables like she was evading an army of demons. He jumped from his chair, headed to the stable, saddled up, and rode off to follow her.

He caught sight of her again as she entered the woods. He tied Adonis to a branch and crept down to the creek. He found her sitting at the river's edge, leaning against a tree singing a song about holly berries. Watching her hand stroke the smooth rock, polished from years of spring floods, left his cock dancing in his breeches.

She looked upward as white snowflakes freckled her nose. She stopped singing, and called out, "What a delightful surprise!"

His heart seized with pleasure, until he realized she wasn't talking to him.

Her throaty voice flowed across the patterns of the light- and shadow-dappled landscape. "Must you always have the last word? Dropping a snowball on my head?

Not very gentlemanly of you." She raised her hands to catch the flakes. "But thank you for this peace offering. Now. Please do something about Lady Alice's brother. Maybe send the fool on an errand until the house party is over?"

"Where would you like—?"

Surprised, Grace cried out, tossed her head, and ignored him.

"If I'm sent away, perhaps you'll come with me?"

"You've said enough today. Must you sneak up on me, too?"

"Were you just asking one of your brothers to come to your rescue?"

"You are insufferable. Come, Circe, our morning has once again been tarnished."

As she turned to face him, a brilliant light shone on her face. Transfixed, Bridge was rooted to the snowy ground as if he too were one of the giant firs arising from the mist. But for the dejected look he had put in her eyes, she was an angel illuminated from above. Never had he seen such perfection, and once again he regretted every stupid thing he'd said to make her sad.

He struggled to say something. "Circe? Your mare is a witch who turns men into pigs?"

"She is. Not much of a trick."

Before Grace could utter another word, Bridge took her hand. "You had the right of it. I am a cretin. A jackass. I behaved abominably. I don't deserve your forgiveness, but please allow me to apologize. I'm the worst kind of fool, Grace." As he brushed his lips across her hand, he felt her relax.

"Yes. You behaved badly, but how can I stay angry with you after such pretty words? We all make mistakes, but we don't all have the courage to admit so." Glancing at the sky, her shy smile held a touch of amusement. "I admire a brave man."

Pulling her lightly against him, he felt her soften as he inhaled her warm breath, tasting of oranges and chocolate. "You have my gratitude. You're a fine lady to allow me a second chance." He placed the softest of kisses on her lips, and murmured against them. "Thank you. Sweet Grace. You are delightful. I could kiss—"

Giggles and chatter intruded on their paradise. "Lady Charlotte, wait for us. Are you sure he came this way?"

Bridge stopped, rested his chin on her head, and whispered, "Bollocks. I'll draw them away from the woods. Meet me in the library in an hour." His crooked smile broadened, crinkling his face up to his eyebrows. "I haven't finished this fine apology."

Before Grace could answer, he was astride Adonis, and with a wink, he was gone.

## CHAPTER EIGHT

The kiss had been heavenly. Before leading Circe the long way home, she stood for a time, attempting to catch her breath and swaying with her arms wrapped around herself. Looking up at God, she grinned. "What?"

Grace was early to the library, and was surprised to find Bridge setting up tin soldiers on the library floor, only to have Jeremy knock them over with his chubby fist and laugh so hard he rolled over on his side with a case of hiccups. When Bridge stopped tickling him, he began setting the soldiers into formation, looking up when the child called out, "Look, Auntie *Gace*."

Bridge kept his smile on her, until Jeremy threw a soldier at his face

Grace knelt beside the child. "Jeremy, I doubt a good soldier would hit his commander. But if it were to happen, I'm sure he would apologize at once."

As Jeremy whispered something to Uncle Bridge, she watched as the two packed away the soldiers in a beautifully wooden box. Jeremy clutched it to his chest when the nanny arrived to retrieve her charge. He saluted Bridge, bowed to Grace, and the two left.

When Jeremy and his soldiers marched out, Grace gifted Bridge with her best dimples. "You have a way with him. He's lucky to have you in his life." *You'll make a good father.*

"He's wonderfully curious, isn't he?"

A shriek and a clatter emanated from the hallway, followed by the sound of a slap and a wail. Rushing out of the library, they were the first to come upon a chaotic scene. Charlotte was examining the flounce on her skirt, raising it a bit higher when she spied Bridge. The nanny was retrieving the scattered soldiers, and Jeremy stood crying and holding his cheek.

Bridge gently pulled his little hand from the child's face and handed him his handkerchief. The General stormed out of his study. "What in the blazes is going on here? Jeremy, cease…" He stopped mid-sentence when Bridge turned Jeremy towards his father. In a low voice, the older man asked, "What happened to your face, son?"

Jeremy stood tall and said, "That fat *uggy* one hit me. *Thew* my men."

Charlotte shrugged. "Blame the nanny. The urchin was running through the hall. Look how he ruined my dress."

Little Jeremy was not finished pointing. "You're the bad old witch in my book."

The general glared. "Apologize."

Charlotte stared at the child. "Fine. I forgive you for saying I'm big."

"Are you dense? Lady Charlotte, apologize for hitting my son. At once."

Bridge reminded her, "And he didn't call you big. I believe he said fat."

Grace added under her breath, "And ugly." Bridge grinned.

Charlotte batted her eyelashes at Bridge. "Now don't be silly, my Lord. Everyone looks big to a baby."

Jeremy shouted in an attempt to be heard, "I am not a baby. I am *fee* and a *haff*."

Alice arranged for Jeremy to have tea alone with his father. When told of the treat, Jeremy's sniffles waned and his sweet baby smile returned.

Bridge held his hand out to the nanny. "I'll repair the hinge and bring it to the nursery."

\* \* \*

Later, dressed for dinner in a low-cut silk gown and emerald earbobs to match, Grace sat contemplating the kiss among the snowflakes. It had been commanding, yet his firm lips had been gentle.

Nancy chattered as she caught Grace's errant curls and tucked them, along with sprays of orange blossoms, into the intricate braid. "So. Cook said Lady Charlotte is having dinner in her room. You'll be seated across from the earl. Now he can just look across the table."

Grace beamed as she headed to the doorway. "Nonsense. He doesn't watch me and will not be looking at me."

"Just remember to show them dimples. I have two pence on the betrothal." Nancy's cackle rang out all the way through the open door.

Grace turned back in the doorway, and teased, "Wagering with the footmen? Nancy, I'm shocked."

Moving into the hallway, the gentle aroma of the orange blossoms danced around her head and mingled with the warm scent of cinnamon. She looked up to discover sticks of the spice tied to a bouquet of mistletoe. She was certain the pomander had not been there this morning.

At the sound of Bridge chuckling, she looked around to see him leaning against the door to his room. Laughing, she picked up her skirt, but he was at her side before she could run.

"Ah ha, my pretty."

"You don't play fair, my lord."

"I rarely do. And look, I've caught a little rabbit in my snare." As he brought his hands to her shoulders, he whispered, "And only had to tarry here most of the hour to catch her." He leaned forward. "Let's see if it was worth the wait."

Grace leaned in and murmured, "Do you intend to talk to my lips, or kiss them, my lord?"

Bridge nibbled and teased as he breathed, "Open for me, you little minx, and I'll show you."

Grace grew faint in his arms, reveling in a kiss that was more than she ever dreamt the touch of lips could command. Until the general cleared his throat.

Bridge grinned, pointing above him, and, to keep his sister and the general from seeing the bulge in his breeches, turned Grace toward the stairway. Descending a few steps, they glanced back to see the general with a smile on his face as he and Alice were locked in a tight embrace under the mistletoe.

## CHAPTER NINE

Bridge delivered Grace as far as the door to the salon before he excused himself to readjust his clothing. Anne and Mary motioned her to join them. They talked hair ribbon colors until Grace was ready to strangle them. Mary, or maybe it was Anne, leaned across the chaise.

"Did you hear about Charlotte? She's not sick. I think she's up to something."

Grace continued to ignore them, glad they were interrupted by a voice that sent waves of pleasure through her as it found a nesting place between her legs. *Such wonderful new feelings.*

"If you'll excuse us, ladies, I'm escorting Lady Grace to dinner."

She rolled her eyes as they walked away. "Must you move like a panther coming up behind me? It's most unnerving."

"I like making you nervous. I like the way every thought crosses your face. You need to work on that. I knew you were going to push me into the snow a moment before you did it. I let you escape, you know."

"No. I didn't know. And it's not pretty of you to tell me so."

"I'll leave the pretty to you, but I'd be lucky if you sat at my gaming table."

"Must I put up with your teasing all evening, my lord?"

"Most likely. You are easy to play with, and I'm fascinated by your rosy cheeks."

"Quiet. My uncle is watching."

"Will he have one of your brothers call me out?" Bridge was still laughing as he seated Grace, whispering so only she could hear, "I'll gladly play with you anytime, in the game of your choosing. You only have to ask, pumpkin."

# CHAPTER TEN

The third day of sun put everyone in the mood to explore the countryside. Sitting in a sleigh across from Grace, Bridge admired her rosy glow and the delight in her eyes. He marveled at the thrill he experienced when near her, and the torture he went through last night as he imagined her curled beside him after a rousing night of lovemaking. This afternoon he would formally ask her uncle for permission to court her.

Grace would make the perfect wife. Passionate, smart, funny and wild, a good woman. From the moment she pushed him into the snowdrift, he had been intrigued. He'd wed her, nestle himself between her legs, and they'd have a lifetime of happiness together.

The sleighs returned to the manse after two hours. Laughing as they knocked the snow off their boots, Bridge grabbed Grace, pretending she was slipping on some nonexistent ice on the portico. Nuzzling her hair, he said, "Save all your waltzes for me."

"Your sister says no more than two dances with one gentleman is proper."

His eyebrows danced up and down, as he grinned. "Unless we are betrothed."

Giving him a playful thump on his chest, she said, "So you could have more than two dances? Seems a shallow reason to leg-shackle me, my lord. I mean, a lifetime with one man?"

"I don't know. Such a playful clever girl could keep me laughing for a couple lifetimes."

"Are you ever serious?"

"Not often, my sweet. Meet me in the orangery in an hour, you little minx."

She nodded. His eyes followed as she scampered off.

Alice joined him. "She's a remarkable young woman."

"She is. I've grown quite fond of her, Ally."

"Don't break her heart, Bridge."

With a reassuring smile, he kissed his sister's cheek and left to search for the general.

## CHAPTER ELEVEN

N ancy worked quickly to brush out Grace's wind-tangled tresses and lace her into her white velvet gown. Lady Alice entered carrying an elegant flat box. "Beautiful job, Nancy."

"Thank you, milady. I attached the flower like you asked."

Trying to rush to the conservatory to meet Bridge before dinner, Grace jumped up to give her aunt a kiss on the cheek. "The gardenia in my hair was your idea, Aunt Alice?"

"Yes, dear. Sit down. The general and I want you to have something."

Grace's heart pounded faster, but not in anticipation of the gift. She was late.

"Look at you, Grace, fidgeting like a schoolgirl waiting for her custard."

Holding out her hands—because if she didn't move she was going to tackle her aunt and gag her—Grace said, "I beg your pardon, Aunt Alice, but I can hardly wait. Let me see."

Grace pulled on the bow, opened the lid…, and was rendered speechless.

"The general had one of his mother's neckpieces reset. The earbobs are there in the center. Shall we try them on?"

"Oh. Lady Alice. They're exquisite."

"Yes, well, they are now. She had a good eye for jewels, but her taste was a trifle gaudy."

"It's a wonderful gift. This is why you encouraged the velvet be cut so low?"

"Yes. I regretted pushing you, but that is the neck-line these rubies deserve."

"They are magnificent. Thank you, Aunt Alice. Look how the light catches the color. I can hardly wait to be swirled around the room under the ballroom candles."

"They aren't half as beautiful as you, my dear. Now come, I've checked the dining room, but I want your opinion on the ballroom flowers."

There was no excuse that wouldn't sound ungracious after accepting such a lavish gift. Keeping her smile in place, she followed her aunt, but her mind and heart was in the orangery.

## CHAPTER TWELVE

W here was she? The general had given permission to court her. The orange blossoms teased him to a wicked frenzy, and he knew the scent would forever remind him of Grace nestled in his arms.

Giggly voices warned him the twins were nearby. *Not now!* He stepped behind the wall fountain. He believed he hadn't been followed, so he wasn't concerned when Lady Charlotte glided in and glanced at the bench he had recently vacated. He strained to hear her over the damned dribbling fountain.

"Well, I feel sorry for the earl. Her maid says she's sick every morning. I'd tell the poor man, if I thought we'd not be overheard. He must think me a pest when I follow him. Maybe he'll ask for a waltz tonight, and I'll be able to warn him."

Bridge leaned against the wall. By the time the three left, his breathing had become difficult, squeezing his heart until he felt nothing but emptiness. Only his brain worked, mocking and screaming. Minutes later he stepped out of the glass house, leaving behind the cloying stink of orange blossoms.

# CHAPTER THIRTEEN

She was horribly late. Grace almost tripped on the hem of her dress as she rushed to the greenhouse, praying he was still there. Giddy, she rounded the corner in the hallway and bounced off Bridge's tight chest. He took a step away from her.

Laughing, she put her arms around his waist. "Apologies. Your sister kept me busy."

Stumbling when he removed her arms from his body, she reached to steady herself and looked into his dead eyes. It took a moment for the light in hers to fade as he walked away.

People remarked on his absence at dinner. Grace didn't eat much, but that wasn't the reason she now stood in the ballroom feeling hollow, wobbling with nothing inside to keep her upright. Cold as the ice sculpture on the table beside her, she fought to keep a pleasant face, as her insides continued to melt into a great emptiness, drip by horrible drip. *What happened? He hasn't looked at me once.*

Taking Grace's fist, her aunt loosened her fingers, allowing the once pristine velvet to return to its natural fold. "I'm sure crushing your dress won't help."

Grace grimaced, but didn't take her eyes off the couple swirling around the ballroom. He'd already danced with the twins, and three others. This was his second waltz with Charlotte, who looked demure as Bridge held her close to his chest, whispering into her hair. *If the weasel-brained idiot can't see what a conniving woman he has in his arms, he can go to Hades.*

A sob caught in her throat as she watched the man she loved dance Charlotte onto the snowy terrace. *God, help me. I love him.*

Within seconds Lady Alice caught her husband's attention and nodded toward the French doors. It was just in time for him to see Bridge and Lady Charlotte sneaking away. Soon the general had escorted them both back to the ballroom. Charlotte looked unhappy. Bridge was cool, but Grace's eyes were on his mouth. *Those lips will never touch mine again.*

The general put his hand on Grace's arm. "Are you daydreaming, dear? The gentleman asked for a dance."

## Chapter Fourteen

Bridge held Grace away from his body. His smile was more of a grimace. It was the only part of his body not deadened with rage as he watched the deceitful woman in his arms. "Is this your normal way of finding a dance partner? Sending your uncle to drag me inside just as I was about to become betrothed? No. Don't. You'll not abandon me on the ballroom floor."

"I'm feeling ill. Let me go, Bridge. I beg you."

"I thought that happens in the morning."

Looking to the ceiling, she whispered, "Where's the man I was to meet in the orangery?"

"Stop it, Grace. I'll not be your suckerfish. You'll begin to show soon. Will you stay on here, living on my sister's charity? What? You have nothing to say?" How could you betray me?

"I wonder which of us is the bigger fool."

The music ended. His hand continued to claim her wrist. "Why trick me, Grace? Why not be honest—come to me for help? Oh no, you will not faint." Shaking his head, he sighed and escorted Grace to an alcove. They could speak privately while in view of others. "What kind of spell have you cast? God help me." They sat side-by-side for several minutes, staring at the dancers. "You played with my heart. And betrayed me."

Moments of tension-filled silence went by. Grace sat frozen. Bridge's voice turned toneless. "You will sever all ties with your lover, and return these rubies and other gifts. I'll purchase a cottage for you and the babe. Contact my solicitor when you are in need of funds. This is goodbye, my sweet treacherous love. I wish you and the child a long, good life. I leave in the morning. You'll not see me again."

As couples danced nearby, Grace gazed at his face as if memorizing it. "You should stay for the excitement, my lord. History will be made once again. It's to be a holy birth, for I am a maiden. Untouched, but for our stolen kisses. There is no baby, and I would never accept a cottage. Or your charity. You poor arrogant fool. Goodbye, Lord Bridgeton."

Bridge nodded, escorted her to his sister's side, and bowed. Slipping out of the ballroom, he made it to the general's study. With a generous sifter of fine brandy, he paced. The urge to scream or argue or trade punches consumed him. *No baby? Had Charlotte lied then?*

The second drink had him questioning his sanity. *The general should call me out. I nearly proposed to Charlotte hours after I asked his permission to court Grace.*

After the third drink, flashes of light drove sharp pain behind his eyes and out the back of his head. Though the spirits had him rattled, he remembered something was wrong. Something important. *Grace.* He slipped into the kitchen, where the cook took pity and made the coffee strong enough to return him to his senses.

## Chapter Fifteen

Bridge roamed the manor like a caged tiger, having barely survived the worst night of his life. *Is she ill? Ignoring me? Pretending I've already left?* There had been finality in Grace's sorrowful eyes. *I've lost her.* His heart couldn't take it.

Trembling, he opened the note Anne slipped him, and read Grace's words. *Thank God.* The sweet forgiving woman was giving him another chance.

He loved her, and tonight he would tell her.

# CHAPTER SIXTEEN

Lady Charlotte had spent hours practicing Grace's handwriting. She sat in the darkened room waiting for Bridge to enter, confident Anne had delivered the message. Smiling smugly, she pulled at her bodice and released the breasts that were increasing in size every week.

The light from the hall illuminated Bridge as he opened the door. Anne would be close behind, ready to scream when she discovered them together. Leaving the door open to the hallway light, he entered. "Grace, why are you sitting in the dark?"

Charlotte's heavy perfume assaulted him, as he was shoved onto the chaise, his face smothered by her breasts. He pushed her to the floor and stood. Comprehension was immediate, even as he yelled, "What the hell?" He wasn't surprised the figure standing in the doorway holding two lamps had seen enough. The damage was done. Bridge now had a fiancé, just not the one he loved.

Charlotte had no help getting up from the carpet. She looked shocked to find the old footman coming through the doorway and making his way in to light the room. He was making a point of not staring at her breasts. She whipped around as the general and Lady Alice stepped out from behind a drapery, each holding a glass of wine.

The general's voice was louder than usual as he faced the stone-faced earl. "Good evening, Bridgeton. You're looking a bit pale."

Lady Alice was relaxed. "Calm yourself, Bridge. We discovered Charlotte's plan. We're here to witness the deception. Charlotte, repair your bodice and have a seat."

The general's face was dark with rage. "Save your questions, Bridgeton. As this concerns my niece, ask Lady Grace to join us. I believe some apologies are in order."

## CHAPTER SEVENTEEN

G race paced her bedchamber, confused, mortified, and outraged by Bridge's words. It was time to leave. She had spent the day writing carefully worded notes to Alice and her uncle. She would send for her trunks later, she'd ask the boy at the inn to return Circe when the mail coach arrived, and not to worry about her. She packed a few items in her valise when Nancy wasn't around to see her, and kept an eye out for Alice as she stopped in often to check on her. Evening came, and she had a dinner tray sent up, saying she was retiring early.

Dressed in her trousers, she carried her valise down the back stairs and made her way to the kitchen where she lit a lantern and slipped out through the kitchen door.

Knowing the servants were having their Christmas party at the cook's cottage, she would have to saddle Circe herself. In the near dark and with frozen fingers, it took longer than expected. Tying her valise to her saddle, she climbed on the mounting block, and let out a yell as someone pulled her to the ground.

"Hello, rabbit. Where are you off to?" His deep voice resonated through her, further shaking her already chilled body.

"It's Lady Grace. Please go away."

"How far do you think you'll get in this weather?"

"As far as the inn. Circe will be returned tomorrow."

"You've packed light."

"I'll send for my trunks when I'm settled."

"And where will that be?"

"As you said, it's not your concern." Her voice was low and sad.

Bridge winced. "That was not well done of me. I was an idiot for believing Charlotte. I should have trusted you, Grace."

"Lady Grace, and thank you for the apology. I could use a hand up, please."

"Not on your life. I've caught you again, and this time I'm not letting go. I was wrong. I'm here to beg your forgiveness one more time."

Her voice was lifeless. "Think no more on it. I'm leaving."

"Hey. Where's the feisty girl I met in the woods?"

"She grew up. She had the joy knocked out of her, but has recovered enough to move on. I've made my decision to live alone, and please myself. I'll wear trousers when I want, and eat marzipan before breakfast. I'm using my inheritance to buy a cottage near the sea. I've left letters."

"It's freezing out here, and if you won't come back inside where I can better grovel at your feet, I'll be forced to take extreme action."

When she shook her head, he grabbed her hands, knelt in the cold hay and looked up at the rafters. "I need some help to convince the lady to stay. Can you give me a hand here and change her mind?"

"Don't mock me, Bridge. And it's not my mind. It's my heart that's broken."

Standing up, he whispered, "Then let's ask your old friend to mend it."

"And don't mock him either." A sudden gust of wind buffeted them, blowing out the flames in the lanterns. The thunder shook the stable so intensely, Grace jumped into his arms.

Shaking, she remained cradled against his chest, feeling cherished as he held her like the most precious of creatures. As he nuzzled her hair, he asked her forgiveness, promised to love and trust her forever, and gave her the best kiss of her life. She returned the favor. Enveloped in a blanket of warmth, they remained cuddled together, relishing the sense of peace they had discovered in each other. They walked hand in hand to the parlor, to announce what everyone else already knew.

Fifty years later, they would still be telling the story to seventeen grandchildren, Bridge swearing it wasn't thunder that shook the stable, but booming laughter descending from above.

# ABOUT THE AUTHOR

Marla Murphy, contemporary and historical romance writer, is a former hippie war protester, street vendor, advertising creative director, boutique owner, and national award-winning painter. She dives into each venture with joyful determination, and has a tendency to misbehave. Murphy lives with her original husband in Los Angeles.

Website: marlamurphy.com

# The Twelfth Month

## By Kathy O'Rourke

### December 2ND

### Casey

Normally at 8:45 a.m. on a Tuesday morning everyone would be gathered in the lunchroom trying to get an extra mug of wake-up coffee, but not today. Today, the lunchroom is closed with an "under decoration" sign posted on the door. You see, Annie, the company's resident party planner, has enlisted a group of Christmas warriors to put up the last of the holiday decorations, and they need the room.

Unfortunately, my cubicle lies directly across from all the commotion. Pointing at the box she's placed on the floor right outside my work area, I whine, "Annie, come on, don't hang anything right there, please."

She rolls her eyes at me. "Casey, stop being such a Scrooge. "

"I'm not a Scrooge, I just think you're going over-board."

How much more crap do they need? There's already a fully decorated Christmas tree in the corner by the boss's door and the winning results of the annual wreath-making contest hanging proudly on each partic-ipant's individual cubicles. Plus, Marty has a Hanukkah menorah, plastic dreidels, and chocolate gelt sitting on a small desk right outside his office, and not to be left out, Dwayne has strung the lunchroom with strings of black-, red- and green-colored lights and placed an altar containing the seven symbols of Kwanzaa right next to the microwave.

Seems like enough to me.

Molly, my only true friend at work, squeezes her way past Tim and Gary, who—under Annie's direction—are trying to hang a snowman mobile from the ceiling tiles right in front of my cubicle.

"Morning, sunshine," she says in a hoarse voice. I can't help but notice that her eyes are bloodshot and her hair looks like she just got up and ran a comb through it.

I whisper, "You sound and look like shit."

"Went out last night with some friends," she says as she opens a little white bag she's carrying and hands me a glazed donut. "What a big mistake, didn't get home until after three."

Mocking concern, I say, "Aww, poor baby, today's gonna suck, huh."

With a half laugh, half grunt, she tries to rip the donut out of my hand. "Give that back, you unsympathetic, ungrateful bitch."

I'm fast; swinging my chair around, I toss the donut in my top drawer. It's now so far out of her reach she'd have to climb over me to get it. Triumphantly, I announce, "Not gonna happen, it's mine now."

Tim, who flirts with everyone, male and female, spies the bag of food. Putting a hand on either side of my cubicle's entrance he gives Molly a come hither smile. "Pretty girl, do you have an extra donut in that bag for me?"

Giggling and falling for his charm, Molly opens the bag. "Of course, take whichever one you want."

I roll my eyes and mumble, "Pushover."

"So, are you ladies coming to the holiday party next week?" Tim asks between bites of his chocolate-covered goodie.

My skin starts to heat up and it feels like bugs are crawling up my back. I'm not stupid; the only reason he included me in his question is because I'm sitting here. He's not interested in me; he has the hots for Molly. But who can blame him? She's got the body of a cover girl and an outgoing personality to match. Me, not so much. I'm plain. The kind of woman who is invisible to men. Plain Casey Reilly, that's me.

Batting her eyelashes, Molly answers, "Of course, I wouldn't miss it. I even bought something new to wear."

"Good, we're gonna have fun." Tim chuckles and wiggles his eyebrows.

Giggling like a damn schoolgirl, she answers, "I can't wait." Turning to me, Molly asks, "Casey, you coming this year?"

"Nope," I snap.

"But…" Molly starts.

I interrupt, "No buts. I never attend these things."

Tim adds, "Why?"

"I have my reasons." Turning around to face my desk, I switch my computer on, hoping they'll get the hint that I'm done talking about this.

My aversion to all things holiday is already in full force. I was a no show at my Aunt Alice's house for her yearly Advent dinner, and yesterday I mailed off my RSVP with the "not attending" box checked to the formal Christmas charity ball my cousin is throwing.

Molly gets my not-so-subtle hint and blows some air out in a silent whistle. "Okay then, I guess it's time to start the day." Turning sideways, she slips past Tim and heads off to her own little box located three down and one to the right.

Tim leaves next, but not before adding, "You know, you might actually have fun. You should think about coming."

"Not gonna happen," I say over my shoulder as I get ready for a day full of helping the senior citizens of Paradise Village, San Diego, California. I've worked here since earning my bachelor's degree in gerontology. I love helping our residents stay healthy and happy.

I overheard Molly talking about going shopping for presents after work and want no part of it, so at 4:59 p.m., I sneak out the back door. My plan is to get away fast and clean.

My phone chimes just as I reach my car.

*Text from Molly: Someday you need to tell me why you hate the holidays (sad face)*

*Me: Someday I will... See you tomorrow (tongue sticking out emoji)*

How can I explain that bad things happen to me during the holidays? My grandmother—my storytelling, cookie-making nanna—died baking gingerbread men when I was eleven. She was taking a tray out of the oven when she grimaced and grabbed her chest. She was dead before the paramedics even made it to the house. I was there and watched her take her last breath.

Then Ben, my favorite cousin, the water balloon king, was blown to smithereens by an IED in Iraq three days before Christmas a few years later.

But worse of all, my parents were in a car accident along with my younger brother on Christmas Eve three years ago. Hit by a semi-truck that skidded on black ice, my parents died instantly, but my precious little brother, Flynn, lingered on life support until finally succumbing four days later.

So yeah, I hate December and everything associated with it.

Needing dog food and a few other things, I stop at the Albertsons right down the block from work. Located right in the middle of the village, the parking lot is full of golf carts, the chosen mode of transportation for many of our seniors. The lot is crowded and I end up parking way in the back next to a Jeep with a surfboard strapped to the top.

Grabbing a shopping cart, I head straight for the pet aisle, where I wrestle a 26-pound bag of Iams Senior Formula dog food into my basket. Naturally, I pick up some treats for my best friend too. Next, I pick up a loaf of whole wheat bread and a package of sliced provolone cheese, then stop at the deli counter. Damn, it's crazy busy. I contemplate buying packaged cold cuts, but the deli's are so much better, so I take a number and step back to wait my turn.

* * *

## MARSH

Grandma's request for thinly sliced ham—Boars Head black forest ham to be specific—has me waiting in this long damn deli line. You think being in the service I'd be used to long waits, but this is frustrating as hell. These senior citizens are too damn picky. Ms. Q-Tip Hair has rejected the size of the slices being cut three times now and the clerk is trying her hardest not to get angry.

Per the number on my ticket, forty-four, I have at least a fifteen-minute wait since they just called number thirty-five.

Bored, I start to people watch. Standing amid the elderly customers is an attractive, brown-haired young woman. I swear she has the most amazing smile I've ever seen. Yes, she's smiling, not at me, but at the people waiting around her. Then she does the sweetest thing; she taps the shoulder of a frail elderly woman who looks unkempt and disheveled, whispers something in her ear, and then proceeds to fix the woman's misbuttoned blouse, straightens her sweater and brushes her hair out of her eyes.

The clerk yells, "Thirty-seven!"

I need a closer look. Since I only have a handheld basket, I have no problem maneuvering over to where she's standing and pretend to look at the packaged sandwiches in a case by her left side.

I scope her out. She's pretty in a down-to-earth kinda way, freckles across the bridge of her nose and hair that looks free of all those fancy gels and things. The PVSD insignia on the pocket tells me she works here on campus. And even though her clothes are loose, I can tell she has curves in all the right places.

She's pretty, kind, and spotting the large bag of kibble in her cart, an animal lover, too. I've seen enough. I'm going in. After a deep breath, I point at the dog food in her cart. "You recommend that brand?"

She gives me one of her smiles; I like that it's just for me. A twinkle appears in her light blue eyes when I smile back at her.

"Yeah, my old guy loves the stuff and I swear the formula helps keep him in good shape." She looks down at the basket and adds, "It has anti-oxidants, Omega 6 and 9, too."

I chuckle. "You sound like a walking TV commercial."

She gives me a sly smirk. "Nope, I'm just reading it to you."

I laugh, lick my finger and give her an imaginary chalk mark. "Touché."

She blushes and asks, "So, what kind of dog do you have?"

Before I can answer the clerk yells out, "Thirty-eight."

Out of habit, I check my ticket. "I'm number forty-four, what are you?"

She groans, "Forty-six."

"We could be here a while."

Letting out a big sigh, she adds, "No kidding." Then she gets back to business. "So, what kind of dog do you have?"

Embarrassed, I confess the truth. "Sweet thing, I don't have a dog. I just wanted a reason to talk to you."

Her face turns a lovely shade of pink and she lowers her eyes. "Really?"

"Yeah. I watched you take care of her"—I nod at the now buttoned-up lady— "and I just knew I had to meet you."

She surprises me with, "Well, let me introduce myself then. My name is Casey Reilly and I really do have a dog. His name is Champagne, but everyone calls him Champ."

"Marshall Holden, Marsh for short." I offer her my hand and she gives me a good solid handshake.

Her hand is soft and has a bit of a chill to it. "Nice to meet you, Marsh." She gets a puzzled look on her face and asks, "What are you doing shopping at Paradise Village?" Before I can answer, she starts to laugh and jokingly adds, "I know you're not a senior citizen."

I chuckle and shake my head. "You're right, I'm not a senior. My grandmother lives here and she sent me to pick up some things for her. And you?"

Pointing at the patch on her pocket, she tells me, "I work here and live two blocks from here, so this store is convenient for me."

"That makes sense," I respond a little too quickly.

Nerves get the best of me and I stop talking. Oh shit, what now?

\* \* \*

## CASEY

This guy is cute. His eyes are dark, and what's with the extra-long eyelashes, damn! He's muscular but not overdone like a weight lifter. His high-and-tight haircut, the set of dog tags around his neck, along with the skeletal frog tattoo on his lower arm, firms up my conclusion: he's a Navy SEAL. Dressed in jeans and a tight white T-shirt, he is one hot man.

"Are you active duty?"

"Yeah, just got stateside two weeks ago."

I snicker and ask snidely, "And you came to see your grandmother?"

He answers a bit defensively, "Yeah, why?"

"I've heard stories. SEALs are known to party pretty heavy when they get home...you know women, booze, sex." I roll my eyes at him. "They don't visit their grand-mothers."

He gives me a look of surprise. "How'd you know I'm a SEAL?"

I point at the tat on his arm. "I live in San Diego, remember? I know what that means. But rest assured, I'm no Frog Hog. I have friends who act like groupies but not me."

With puppy dog eyes, he points at his heart. "You cut me to the quick, Sweet thing. You don't like SEALs?"

"God, that's not what I meant. I like SEALs, Marsh, I just don't chase after them," I tell him in an attempt to clean up my faux pas.

"Well, smarty pants, I *am* a SEAL, have been for five years. And the stories are all true. I did party for about a week and then all I wanted was a good home-cooked meal and a clean, soft bed to crash in."

"I get it."

The clerk behind the counter calls out, "Forty."

Like little robots, we both double-check our tickets. This seems so ridiculous to me, I smirk and in a deadpan voice ask him, "I'm still forty-six—are you still forty-four?"

He gets my joke, throws his head back and lets out a hearty snort. "Good one, Casey, good one."

A second clerk appears behind the counter. "Forty-one."

"Well, it looks like you're coming up fast."

He points to my purse. "Give me your phone."

"Why?"

"I want to see you again and I'm going to put my name and number in your contacts."

This can't be happening. Meeting a cute Navy SEAL who wants to see me again? My hands shake, but I hand him my phone. He winks.

When he's done, he hands it back. "Now call me so I can put you in my contacts."

"Okay." I quickly hit dial and his phone rings.

Then he winks at me again. "Got it."

The first clerk yells, "Forty-three," at the same time the other calls out, "Forty-four."

He raises his hand so they can see him and moves up to the counter, all the while keeping his eyes on me. He looks like he wants to eat me for dinner. My whole body tingles. It's been a long damn time since someone even noticed me yet alone desired my company.

When he finally turns around to talk to the clerk, I see that he is just as fine from the back as he is from the front. His ass looks down right bitable in his jeans. Lord have mercy, he's wet panties material for sure. Plus, he's nice, real nice.

When it's my time at the counter, I get a pound of rare roast beef, thinly sliced, of course. Rolling my cart to the checkout line, I spot Marsh in the "ten items or less" line with his wallet open. He sees me and waves while mouthing the words, *I'll wait over there*, pointing over by the big sliding glass doors.

"You didn't have to wait for me," I tell him when I'm finally done with the cashier.

"Oh yes I did," he answers in almost a shocked manner. "I need to help you put that huge bag of food in your car and make sure you know I meant what I said."

Showing my brat side, I ask, "And what was that?"

In mock anger, he responds, "Now listen here, Sweet thing, I definitely want to see you again. You got a problem with that?"

I give him what I hope is a sexy look. "Not at all. I'd like that."

As serendipity has it, the Jeep parked right next to my car belongs to him. How is that even possible? He whistles the tune to *The Twilight Zone* as we both laugh at the strange course of events. As he's loading the dog food in my trunk, he says, "How about meeting me for coffee tomorrow?"

I can't help myself—I have the urgent need to touch him. I put my hand on his arm, right on top of his sexy tattoo. His skin is warm to the touch and I feel a tingle all the way to my panties.

"Sorry, I have to work all day, but I could meet you after. Say, for an early dinner or something?"

He surprises me by grabbing my hand and pulling it to his lips. "Sweet thing, I'd love that."

Turning my hand over, he places a kiss in the middle of my palm, sending an electrical zap right through me. But more than that, it's the connection between us that gets to me. I don't want him to go.

After a moment of just looking into my eyes, he stutters, "I-I gotta run, but I'll text you later with a when and where."

All I can say is okay as I watch him climb into his Jeep. As he drives away, I lift the palm that he just kissed to my lips. "Oh my God, what just happened?"

\* \* \*

## DECEMBER 3ᴿᴰ

When my phone chimes at six a.m., I giggle because I know it's him.

*Marsh: Gotta report in. Sorry. Dinner when I'm back?*
*Me: Of course (sad face)*

My mood sours instantly. I wanted this date. Actually, I needed it.

\* \* \*

## DECEMBER 4TH

My phone dings, it's another text, and for some reason my hands shake as I read it.

*Marsh: 4 days in and out. See you when I'm back. Stay sweet.*

*Me: Stay safe*

Does that mean four days total or eight days? Damn, I'm not sure. Then fright takes over—after all, it *is* December.

* * *

## DECEMBER 9TH

I'm an anxious, fucked up mess. My nights are filled with restless dreams, and my days full of questions. How can I react this way over someone I just met? Is he okay? Am I losing my mind?

Each day I've gotten worse tempered. Granted, my fellow workers are used to my foul moods, but now I'm even snapping at my beloved seniors.

I keep my phone with me at all times, even taking it to the restroom. I want to know the minute he texts. Today is day five. If he meant four days total, he should be home today.

At midnight, I give up and fall into another night of dark dreams.

* * *

## December 11th

I call in sick, ruining my perfect attendance record. Lack of sleep has me unfit to even type today. I have to stop doing this to myself.

Molly is coming over after work. I asked her to. I meet her at the door dressed in old sweatpants and a wrinkled SOA T-shirt. "Hi, Mol."

She looks me over as she steps inside. "You look like death warmed over." Then taking a whiff, she adds, "And it stinks in here, like wet dog."

Champ, hearing the word dog, starts to thump his tail on the hard wood floor.

"He's been inside all day with me."

Opening the sliding glass door to my backyard, Molly turns her attention to my dog. "Champ, come on, buddy, go outside for a while, please."

Excited, he wags his tail as he scoots out to play.

"Leave it open, please; let's air the place out a bit," I tell her.

Not feeling the need for small talk, I start right in. "Molly, I'm a mess. I've met someone and it's driving me crazy."

With her eyes popped wide open, she answers, "You met someone, really?"

I tell her all about Marsh, our chance meeting, and his text messages.

Molly, ever the romantic, claps her hands together and answers, "Oh Casey, sounds like kismet to me."

"I just wish I'd hear from him. I know he's on a mission, but I need to know if he felt it too. If he felt the instant connection." Adding a pathetic little laugh, I add, "Or was it all in my head?"

Molly pats my hand. "He's in a situation he can't control, honey. Give him an extra week and then if you don't hear anything, text him."

Smart. I can do that. "Okay. I will." Enough about me—I ask, "How was the office party? Did you have fun?"

Red-faced, she whispers, "Yeah, and I went home with Tim."

"Tim? Girl, tell me you're lying."

Shaking her head, no, she says, "I really did. You know I've been crushing on him for a long time." Smacking me on the arm, and then fanning herself, she spills the beans. "He's so damn good in bed, Casey. I must have had four big O's that first night."

"Really?" My mind goes to Marsh and imagining what he would be like as a lover.

Molly adds, "Can I tell you a secret?"

"Of course."

She leans in close to me. "He's kinky—he likes to be in control. You know, like a Dom."

"BDSM? And you liked it?"

"Loved it." She walks over and slides my outside door shut before speaking again. Then she lays it on me. "He spanked me and made me get on my knees."

I snort, "Wow."

"Yeah, and it felt so good," she says in a very satisfied way.

"Hmmm, did you call him Sir?"

She giggles and nods yes, then gets serious, "You can't tell anyone or tease him at work, Casey. I would just die."

"I won't. I promise. So, are you two, like, a couple now?"

Beaming, she shakes her head. "He says he wants to be. I need a little time to decide. But we're gonna see where it goes."

I reach out and hug her. "I'm happy for you both."

Yeah, I'm happy for them, but I'm jealous as hell all at the same time.

I get no text today.

* * *

## DECEMBER 14TH

At 5:45 a.m. my phone rings. A strange feeling comes over me when I spot that the call is coming from an unknown number. I scramble to turn my bedside lamp on.

"Hello?"

A deep male voice asks, "Is this Casey Reilly?"

Somehow I know this is about Marsh. Goose bumps appear on my arms and my heart starts to beat so fast I hear it in my ears. "Yes, this is Casey Reilly."

"I'm Ryan, one of Marsh's team members. He wanted me to—"

I cut him off. "Oh God, please tell me he's okay, please."

"Yeah. He's in the hospital in Germany and will be stateside in a few days."

"Hospital?"

"Yeah. He got hurt, but the docs have patched him up. He just has to wait for them to release him and then he'll catch the first plane home."

"Hurt?"

"Sorry, I can't tell you anymore, but Marsh insisted I call and tell you he's gonna be late getting back."

"Thank you, Ryan. I have to admit I've been worried about him."

"This your first time waiting on him?"

"Am I that obvious?"

He snickers into the phone. "Yeah, you are." Then he adds. sounding serious, "I'm not gonna lie to you, it's never easy. but you'll learn to deal with it."

"I sure hope so. Thanks for calling me, Ryan. It means a lot."

"You're welcome. Take care of my boy."

\* \* \*

## DECEMBER 16TH

It's been two days since Ryan called. I know I'm being impatient, but every minute seems like an hour and every day a year. Am I building this up too much in my head? Is this even real?

\* \* \*

## December 17th

9:32 p.m. My phone rings. Oh my God, it's him. I turn the TV to mute and answer in a breathy voice, "Oh my God, Marsh."

His voice sounds tired as he speaks. "Hi, Casey."

I hold back the tears that threaten to give way. "It's so good to hear your voice. Are you okay?"

I hear him sigh and blow air into the phone. "Yeah, I'm fine. Honey, I'm on my way, I should be there tomorrow afternoon."

He sounds far away. "Oh, thank God." I hesitate, then add, "Ryan told me you were hurt."

"Damn, the bastard wasn't supposed to tell you that. I'm beat up, but I'll survive."

I admit, "I was worried."

"I know you were, Sweet thing."

"This is gonna sound weird since we just met, but I missed you. Your being okay and getting back home safely haunted me."

I can hear him take a deep breath before he answers, "It is way crazy, but I missed you too. It was your face I saw in my dreams. And when the shit hit the fan, it was you I fought for."

"Marsh." That's all I could say in response. *He fought for me? Damn.*

"Baby, I need to see you," he says in a deep almost grainy voice.

I need to see him too and this time I want more than a kiss on my hand. "I'm texting you my address, meet me there. I'll leave a key under the blue flowerpot on the porch. I get out of work at five and I'll come right home. "

"What about your dog? Is he a big, mean attack dog?"

Laughing, I answer, "Nope. He's just a big ferocious licker. Be prepared for a major doggie make-out session when you open the door."

He snorts. "I can handle that. I'll be there when you get home."

"Good. I'll leave a clean towel and things for you in the bathroom."

He growls. I mean, a real sexy man-growl. "Sweet thing, are you thinking what I'm thinking?"

"Damn straight."

"Lucky me."

"Yep, lucky you. See you tomorrow, Marsh."

"Night, Sweet thing."

I'm so excited, I text Molly the good news.

*Me: He'll be back tomorrow. He's coming to my house. (thumping heart)*

*Molly: Yeah! (big thumbs-up)*

*Me: See you in morning (wave emoji)*

\* \* \*

## December 18th

My alarm goes off at five a.m., and unlike my regular routine of hitting the snooze button, I jump right out of bed. With a mental list of things to do before work, I know I'll need the extra time. I start by stripping the bed and remaking it with the good linens.

Then I straighten up the living room. I giggle as I work, which is so not like me; I normally hate housework.

In the bathroom, I shower, shave everything below my neck, shampoo and use a dollop of my extra-expensive hair conditioner. Once my hair is dried, I scour the shower, clean the toilet, which is my least favorite task, and lay out fresh towels. Visions of Marsh standing naked in just a towel make my face flush.

Lordy Lordy, tonight can't come quick enough.

Next, I move to the kitchen where I lay out cheese, crackers and the makings for a meatloaf sandwich on one of my nice serving trays and wrap it in plastic.

Grabbing the post-it notes from the junk drawer, I write out two of them.

For the front door: *Hi. Make yourself at home. Can you let Champ out in the backyard for me? I left you a snack in the fridge. Can't wait to see you.*

For the fridge: *Hope you like meatloaf. Enjoy.*

I've decided to wear my baby-blue push-up bra with the matching thong under my work uniform. I love the lace inserts and besides, they match my eyes. But at the last minute I slip on a pair of white panties instead and put the blue ones in my purse, mumbling, "I'll freshen up at work and put these on just before coming home. Don't want to be smelly."

As I'm drinking coffee, I lay down the rules to Champ. "Now listen, I have a very important friend stopping by. Please be nice to him."

Champ wags his tail and answers with a woof.

"Good boy."

Work drags, even with two important meetings and lunch with Molly and Tim. I count the minutes till five p.m.

\* \* \*

## MARSH

I'm sore and bone-tired. It took three planes and a six-hour layover in Atlanta waiting for my last contract flight, but I made it. Stepping outside the terminal, the salty breezes coming off the Pacific greet me like a welcome home gift. God, I love the ocean. When I'm here I swim in it every day, even in the winter.

I chuckle to myself. "Not today, though."

I grab a taxi and ask the cabbie to take me to the base on Coronado; I need to pick up my Jeep. On the way over, I remove the sling from around my right arm. Yes, it's against doctor's orders, but if I arrive on base with it on, they won't let me drive—they'll insist I find a driver. Not gonna happen, not today.

As I sign off base for a month of R and R, pangs of guilt rush over me. Not telling my team members I'm home bothers me, but I don't want the normal party hardy thing. All I want is to see Casey. Hell, I haven't even notified my parents or grandmother I'm home either. I'll contact all of them tomorrow. Today is all about me and my girl.

My girl? Shit, I haven't even kissed her yet and she's already my girl? This feels so strange.

I study my bruised face in the Jeep's rearview mirror. Casey's gonna freak when she sees me. I'm not pretty—two black eyes, a bandage on my right cheek and my nose is taped. I look like I was in a prizefight. Hell, I was. Things got up close and personal; thank God I'm good with a knife. I got to walk away alive, unlike the Taliban bastard who decided to test my skills. He's in heaven right now looking for his seven virgin wives.

My mind switches to Casey. This is the most insane thing I've ever done. Why this woman? Why now? I've never felt like this before. Sure, I've lusted after women, fucked them, even liked some of them, but this is different.

Locating her house is easy—it's right off the main drag, in one of San Diego's planned cookie cutter communities. All the houses have red tiled roofs and cream paint jobs. What sets hers apart from the others is the large variety of potted plants on her small front porch. Pots of every color and shape add a distinct, personal touch.

A big yellow dog head appears in her front window. That must be Champ. Damn, he's huge! He has the jowls and ears of a bloodhound, but he's way bigger, maybe part Great Dane.

I wave at him. "Nice doggie."

I get a few whines and a bark in return. He looks happy to have company; he's probably lonely here alone all day.

Just my luck, there are three blue pots on the porch and I don't find a key under any of them. Shit! She did say blue, didn't she? Champ is whining and scratching at the front door, so I need to hurry up before the neighbors call the cops or something. Where's the damn key? Then I spot a green—okay, maybe it's bluish green—pot that has disturbed dirt rings on the floor all around it.

Ta-da! I find the key and then spot a note taped to the front door.

As soon as I step inside, Champ knocks me against the wall. Placing his front paws on my shoulders, he delivers dozens of sloppy kisses and within seconds my face is covered in dog drool. I know she warned me, but still, Champ really does want to make-out.

Pushing him to the floor, I take back some control. "I like you too, boy. You're a good boy. Now please stay down." Champ does as he's told and I give him another, "Good boy."

Dropping my bag on the floor, and per the note, let Champ out the sliding doors into the back yard. "Okay, boy, you be good out there."

Her house is cute but not what I expected. There are no flowery prints, pink pillows or lace doilies. No shabby chic or French provincial either, her house is decorated in what I'd call early hippie, with colors exploding all over. I like it. It looks lived in and comfortable. Besides, what's not to love about a sixty-inch TV hung over the fireplace?

She left me a snack in the fridge. What a girl! Meatloaf! I could get used to this. With a sandwich in my hand, I walk down the hall to explore the rooms while I eat.

There are two bedrooms and a bath on one side of the house. One is set up as an office and the other can only be described as doggie heaven. A huge pet bed is tucked in one corner, dog-themed wallpaper covers one wall and the floor is strewn with dog toys. Champ is one spoiled guy.

At the other end of the house is her master with its attached bathroom. Her bedroom feels comfortable, no theme decorating here, just mismatched pieces that all seem to blend together. Right smack in the middle of the room is a king-sized bed with both a wrought iron headboard and matching footboard. A lush velvet patchwork quilt covers it.

My cock stirs as ideas run through my head. Hmmm, what fun we can have, playing with scarves, ropes, and other accouterments.

Retrieving my bag from the front hall, I go into her bathroom and strip off my smelly clothes. Next, I peel the medical tape off my cracked ribs and remove the bandages off my shoulder and face so I can take a nice hot shower. The water feels so damn wonderful and the pulsating showerhead helps to loosen my sore muscles. Once clean, I slip into a pair of clean sweats, re-tape my ribs and nose, apply new bandages to my shoulder and cheek, and pop an extra pain pill.

What time is it anyway? 4:15 p.m. She should be home in an hour. Perfect.

* * *

## CASEY

The first thing I see when I turn onto my street is a Jeep with a surfboard strapped on its roof parked in front of my house. My hands tremble as I mumble to myself, "He's here."

As soon as I pull in my driveway, my front door opens and Marsh steps out. Barefoot, he's dressed in a tight black T-shirt, gray sweatpants and the biggest damn smile. He rushes to open my car door. "Casey, I made it."

Concern replaces joy when I get a good look at him. "Marsh, oh my God, your face."

"Oh, it's nothing, you should see the other guy," he says, pooh-poohing the whole thing.

Jumping out of the car, I run my hand lightly down his cheek. "Are you really okay?"

"Yeah, but…" he says with a smirk.

"But what?"

"I sure could use some sugar." He laughs as he pushes me up against the car, trapping me with an arm on each side of my body. Nuzzling my neck, he whispers, "I'm gonna kiss you now, is that okay?"

"Yes, please."

With his lips against my neck, he chuckles, "Please?"

"Yes, please, kiss me. Please kiss me right now," I tell him as I put my arms around his neck.

His mouth moves across my cheek and he places one small light peck on my lips. "Like that?"

With his lips against mine, I whisper, "No, damn it. I want the real thing, please."

This time he doesn't just kiss my lips—he devours my whole mouth. Forcing his tongue inside, he takes me, exploring every inch. My hands move down his back, feeling his muscles ripple under his shirt. As he presses his hot body into mine, I feel like I could spontaneously combust. I've been waiting for this moment every day he was away, and to be honest, I've waited my whole life; I've never felt this before.

"I think we should take this inside, don't you?" he growls as he takes a step backward.

"Yeah," is all I can manage to get out of my mouth.

He pulls me into the house, slamming the door shut and pushing me up against the wall. Like a mad man, he lifts my blouse and places his face between my breasts. "I know I should take this slow, maybe wine and dine you, but that not gonna happen. Do you understand?"

"Yeah." I get it. He needs to feel alive after what he's gone through.

"You on birth control?" he asks while licking up my neck.

"Yeah. You clean?"

"Ran tests in the hospital just this week," he responds as he runs his hand down my side. "You?"

"Oh yeah," Turning, I walk down the hall toward my bedroom, removing my blouse as I go. "Coming?"

"Don't have to ask me twice," he jokes as he joins me.

By the time I'm standing next to the bed, I'm dressed only in my bra and panties, the sexy ones I wore just for him.

His eyes bug out as he looks me over. "Oh, Sweet thing, you are so fucking sexy."

Good, that's exactly the reaction I want. As he takes his clothes off, the beauty of his body is overshadowed by the rest of his bruises, medical tape and bandages. I instantly cool down.

I take two steps over to him, placing my hand on the tape, which is obviously holding together cracked ribs. "Marsh, are you really okay to do this? I don't want to hurt you."

"Baby, you'll hurt me if you don't." He reaches behind me and with one hand unhooks my bra.

"But, but your ribs," I stutter as he rubs his fingers over my nipples.

He moans, "Baby, your breasts are gorgeous," as he bends and kisses each one.

"Your ribs, Marsh."

"They're fine, Sweet thing. Yeah, some of them are cracked, but it doesn't matter," he growls as he shimmies my panties down my hips. "I've dreamt about you every night I was out there and I won't let anything, even some bumps and bruises, keep me away from you."

Then in one quick move he has me flat on my back at the edge of the bed with my legs apart. The smoldering looks he gives me as he steps between my legs takes my breath away. Kneeling down, he puts his face between my legs. "Now, I'm gonna get me some sugar."

He licks me from the top to the bottom and then back up again. With his mouth against me, he whispers, "You taste just like I knew you would—sweet, wet, perfect." His tongue nuzzles its way inside me.

My legs shake in response as I feel his tongue twist and turn.

"I love your big, full pussy lips," he says as he starts to nibble and suck on them.

I want to jump right out of my skin, it feels so good. I can't help but moan.

Looking up at me, he asks, "Like that, baby?"

"Oh yes, love it," I answer as every nerve below my waist feels close to short-circuiting.

"Good, cause I'm gonna eat you up." He attacks my clit with his tongue, licking, sucking and putting pressure on it as he slides two fingers inside me. He growls as he works and rubs his head back and forth. The stubble on his face acting like bristles against my ultra-sensitive inner thighs, adds yet another amazing sensation.

Then, when his fingers rub that special spot deep inside at the same time he sucks hard on my clit, I explode...shattering and screaming his name. "Marsh, oh my God, Marsh!"

Even as I ride through my orgasm, I feel his mouth licking me clean. Then, kissing my inner thighs, he whispers, "You came like a firecracker."

Still out of breath, I pant, "That was the best orgasm I've ever had. "

He chuckles, "You ain't seen anything yet."

At that, he moves and climbs up my body placing kisses all along the way. Stopping and paying special attention to my breasts and nipples, he licks, sucks and bites at them.

"Marsh, please, I need you inside me right now," I tell him as I rake my nails down his back.

He doesn't answer in words; he just moves until his penis is right at my entrance. Looking in my eyes, he whispers, "Feel me," as he slides in, and doesn't stop until his balls slap against my ass.

He holds himself deep inside me as we stare into each other's eyes. This connection between us is so much more than just physical. He knows it and so do I.

"I'm gonna fuck you now, baby. Ready?"

I kiss his neck, right under his ear. "Do it."

He starts to move. Drawing his penis all the way out and then slamming it back in.

It hurts so good. I grunt, "Do it again."

He draws all the way out and slams me again. "Casey, baby, you're so fucking tight, so damn good."

"You're so deep. Feels good."

"Hold on, Sweet thing," he starts the piston action of driving into me over and over, hard and deep.

\* \* \*

## MARSH

Her pussy feels so fucking good: tight, hot, and wet. She fits me like a glove. When I pull all the way out and push back in, her walls feel like they're milking me… fuck, it feels fantastic. I know I sound like a caveman, grunting at each thrust, but I can't help it—they just pop out of my mouth.

I've never wanted to claim a woman before, but Casey, yes, I'm claiming her. Thrusting deep and hard, I stop and grab her chin. "Casey, I want you all to myself, no one else, just me."

"I want that too," she whimpers as I give her pussy an extra push.

"Settled, then, you're mine," I say as I lean in and tongue-fuck her mouth just like I'm fucking her pussy.

Pulling out, I stand at the side of the bed and move her so her pussy is right at the edge of the mattress. Not being a missionary position kinda guy, but still wanting to see her face and her eyes, I keep her on her back. Grabbing her legs, I lift them to my shoulders as I drive my cock inside her again.

She squeals as I bottom out. "Marsh, oh my God!"

"Take it, baby, take it."

Then I start to move over and over as we both enter the ecstasy zone. She screeches my name as she explodes, sending a gush of pussy juice all over my balls. Her squirting orgasm sends me right over the top, and on the next drive inward, I shoot my load and scream like I've never done before.

I drop her legs and collapse on top of her, both of us out of breath. "Oh baby, that was something else," I whisper in her ear.

"Marsh, I've never cum like that before, ever."

Lifting up, I look her in the eyes and tell her, "Me either. It was so much more than it's ever been."

She blushes and whispers, "Did you really mean what you said?"

Leaning up on my elbows, I see a shy, pensive look in her beautiful eyes. There's fear too, that what I said a moment ago was just sex talk. "Come here." Moving to the middle of the bed, I pull her under my arm and up against my body.

Kissing her forehead, I start, "Casey, I'm a guy. I'm not real good with words, but I'll try to explain."

She pulls my hand up to her mouth and places a kiss on it. "Take your time."

"Life has made me a hard man. I've seen and done terrible things, things no man should have to do, but I took an oath and I did them. Don't get me wrong, I love being a Frogman, love my team and love the Navy, but the life has had a negative effect on me. The real reason I went to my grandmother's the last time I was home was to try and restore some of my humanity. I needed to climb out of my dirty black hole. When I saw you in the supermarket helping button that old lady's blouse, it was like a bright light opened up in the darkness, surrounding me, and you were standing in the middle of it. I just knew you were my gift, a precious gift from God or the universe or whatever, but a gift nonetheless."

She starts to sniffle and tears roll down her cheeks. "And you said you weren't good with words. Liar."

I chuckle and kiss her head again. "So do you feel the same thing I do?"

"From the minute you kissed my palm in the parking lot, I knew." She runs her hands lightly through my chest hair as she talks. "I know it's probably way too early to tell you this…" She hesitates, and then she surprises me with a very special gift. She places a kiss on my chest, right over my heart, and whispers, "I love you."

Relieved, I kiss her forehead again and look her in the eyes when I answer. "I know. I love you too."

All of a sudden we hear a loud thud followed by a woof. Champ is standing with his paws against the window and looks very unhappy that he's not inside. We both crack up laughing at the big doofus.

Casey jumps up, reaches for my T-shirt and pulls it over her head. "Poor Champ, he's been outside this whole time."

I laugh, "He's fine, Sweet thing."

"But it's after six and I always feed him at exactly six."

"Spoiled damn dog."

\* \* \*

## CASEY

Later that night, after rounds two and three, I lay snuggled in Marsh's arms when the thought hits me. I fell in love in December.

Smiling, I fall asleep thinking about Christmas trees, lights, presents, parties and love.

# About the Author

Kathy O'Rourke writes woman's romance with both a suspenseful and naughty twist. Always a closeted writer, she took an early retirement to try her hand at being an author. Currently writing book five in her much loved series, The Men of Nirvana Flats, she is an active member of the RWA and her local Los Angeles chapter LARA .

# No Room at the Inn

## By Beverly Diehl

There was no room at the Inn.

Nor anywhere else he checked: at the Chattering Creek Cottages, the Lonely Pine Lodge, or Bobbie's Bodacious Bed and Breakfast.

Benjamin Starr, owner of Starr's Grain, Feed & Gas, shrugged and gazed sympathetically at his sole customer, a slender, dark-haired man pacing nervously on the other side of the counter.

The store, decked out with ancient and bedraggled Hanukkah decorations and an extremely short and bushy Christmas tree bearing multicolored lights, would normally be packed with locals and tourists. Ben had stocked up on last-minute gift items and built up the fire in the Franklin stove. But the comfortable chairs circled around it were empty. With a massive storm front closing in, and it being Christmas Eve, everyone in Lakeside Heights was home with their family.

Family. That word still stung. He wondered what Jess was doing tonight.

"Thank you for checking for us, Mr. Starr. It's not so far to Alta Vista." The accent betrayed that English was not the man's first language, but his diction was crisp. He looked outside toward the small gray car parked by the gas pumps, the thickly falling snow already building up on its roof and bumpers. "Allah will help us."

"I hope Allah provided you with snow chains, because you'll never make it up the 155 without them, and I sold my last set this morning."

"Then we will turn back to Bakersfield."

Ben checked his tablet, then flipped it around to show the man. "Sorry, man. The Canyon's closed because of a rockslide, and so is Walker Pass."

Dignity fought with rising panic on the man's face.

"You said 'we'?" Ben peered outside, but couldn't discern forms through the car's tinted windows. "Who else is in the car? Wife, dog, kids?"

A shadow crossed the man's face. "My wife, Mariam, only."

"Why don't you bring her in, and we'll figure something out? I'm not going to turn you away, now."

"Thank you. My name is Yusef."

Ben watched with amusement as the diminutive man helped a tall, wide woman out of the car, like a tugboat guiding an ocean liner.

His smile melted away as, once by the fire, the layers of coat and scarves and sweaters were peeled off, all but a hijab kept carefully in place, revealing a lovely, slender, and very, very pregnant young woman.

Pain periodically flickered across her face in a way that made Ben feel uneasy.

Shit. Jess might not want to talk to him, but he had to call his estranged wife.

\* \* \*

"Jess? It's Ben. I need your help."

She'd been thinking about him all day. Last Christmas, she couldn't stand to look at him, or let him look at her. Jacinta felt like her guilt and failure couldn't have shone out any brighter if they had been added to the big yellow neon star which hung over his family business. It had been such a relief when Ben moved out.

Lakeside Heights was a small town, and with the store only half a block from the house, it was difficult to avoid him. But despite frequent glimpses of Ben's big green truck, and listening avidly to every story about him she overheard in the local restaurants, she'd managed to evade direct contact. Until now.

"Merry Christmas, Ben."

"Oh. Right. Merry Christmas. I'm sorry to bother you, but I have a situation…"

As he explained, anger rose up in her. "WTF, Ben? What kind of idiot takes his pregnant wife out in weather like this?"

"A desperate one. He has a job offer up at Alta Vista with a cousin, he isn't familiar with our weather, thought they could make it."

"Idiot."

"So, will you bring down some dinner and blankets?"

"To the store? No. No, I will not."

"Damn, I didn't think you'd be so cold."

"You're almost as dense as he is. You've got to bring them here; they can't stay in the store. On the floor, on thin blankets? Especially if you're right and the woman is in labor. Did you think it might be cute to stash her newborn baby in a feed trough? What were you *thinking*?"

"Are you sure you can deal with...?"

"I'll have to, won't I? I'm the only medical professional this side of the lake right now."

\* \* \*

Jacinta—Jess—looked stunning. Ben had missed the silky black waterfall of hair cascading over her shoulders and down her back, the faint blush that rose on her cheeks when she looked at him, the vivacious snap in her dark eyes.

Also, the sparky way she reacted to everything. He'd stopped to make introductions, but Jess wasn't having any of it.

"Ben, did you freeze what little brains you had? You and him—" She pointed at Yusef. "Bring in their luggage, if they have any. We can trade names later," she called over her shoulder as she hustled the pregnant woman into the big recliner by the fireplace.

Ben made the father-to-be stop with him on the porch, to brush off the snow that had collected on the few bags the couple possessed. It was really coming down now, big fat clumps of white. They'd be housebound for days.

Inside, Ben introduced Yusef and Mariam, and the couple shared a little of their story, as Jess passed around hot herbal tea in holiday mugs.

Mariam once taught economics at Damascus University, and Yusef had been top chef at a local restaurant. They waited twenty-eight months for their application to be processed and accepted. Now he had been offered a steady job as a dishwasher at his cousin's restaurant, while Mariam would care for their new baby, and his cousin's children. Perhaps help with the bookkeeping.

Jess had propped up the pregnant woman's feet, and had her wrapped in the granny square afghan his mother had made them.

His mind flashed back to memories of Jess wrapped up in that blanket, her face glowing with happy excitement as the baby kicked. She'd been gorgeous, heavy with their child.

She was even more beautiful now, if a bit brittle. He couldn't help following her with his eyes, as she bustled about, directing Yusef to carry the bags into the master bathroom. She emerged from her bedroom with some of her belongings and her fluffy, ruby-colored robe. Just the sight of it sparked an immediate response in his body. He felt ashamed for desiring her, after everything, but if these guests weren't present, he'd be doing his best to kiss her frown away. He wanted to spread that dark shining hair on the thick rug in front of the fire, to relearn every inch of her smooth olive skin with his fingertips, following the trail with his mouth.

A whimper interrupted his lascivious thoughts. The Syrian woman, Mariam, kept shifting in the recliner, clearly uncomfortable.

It only took Jess one look. "How long have you been having contractions?"

* * *

It didn't matter that the door was closed. Jess could see every stick of furniture, from the rocking chair padded with cheerful blue-print cushions to Ben's battered childhood dresser they'd refreshed and repainted. The murals on the walls, the stuffed bears.

An accidental shrine.

How odd to think there would soon be another baby in the house. And this baby and his mother's needs had to come first.

Jess took a deep breath. Opened the door. Stepped in. Began gathering a stack of soft blankets. The tiny cloth diapers and pins. She placed everything she thought they might need in the small plastic bathtub, avoiding the sight of the empty crib.

Jess didn't realize Mariam had followed her into the too-silent room until the woman spoke.

"It doesn't keep them safe, you know."

"What?" Jess turned to look at the lovely young woman, beads of perspiration beading on her upper lip.

Mariam continued. "The car seats. The bank account. The clothes, made by machine or with love." She waved her hand at the room. "I had a nursery like this in Damascus." She smiled at the beat-up dresser, humor in her voice. "Maybe nicer furniture."

Jess didn't know why, but that struck her as hilariously funny. The laughter bubbled up in her throat, coming out as a bitter, strangled sob.

She needed to confess to someone who might understand. "Sudden Infant Death Syndrome. It happened when we were in the next room." *Because we both thought it was so damned important to make love again, even if the baby monitor batteries had stopped working.* "My baby died and I wasn't even here with him. He was all alone."

Mariam nodded, looking at her with compassion in her own tear-filled eyes. "Pneumonia, in the camps. I held my child in my arms when he drew his last breath, and still I could do nothing. Sometimes that is the truth of it, that we can do nothing. It is a sad, terrible thing, when children die before their parents."

Mariam opened her arms, and the women embraced, tears blending on their cheeks. "I am so afraid," she whispered. "I am afraid this baby will die, too."

"No, he won't," Jess vowed. "I am an awesome nurse and your baby will be just fine."

* * *

Ben had fallen in love with Jess from the moment, new in town, she'd danced into the family store wearing ear buds, looking for a bottled water and her secret weakness, Flaming Hot Cheetos. He'd felt like the luckiest man in the world on their wedding day, and his love had only deepened when she gave birth to baby Micah.

But he'd never seen her in action before.

She braided her hair back out of her face with nimble fingers, then quickly delegated. "Yusef. Bring all the phones in here, plug them into their chargers, and call 911. You're going to use one of the phones to time the contractions, and the others to talk to emergency services. You'll relay to them what's going on here. You can handle it, right? Because Mariam and the baby need you."

The man nodded, looking pale, but resolute.

"Ben. You're going to be my helper."

"Should I start boiling water?"

"What, you think this is a John Wayne movie? No. Go get the shower curtain out of the guest bathroom—and there's a blue tarp in the garage. I need you to lay out the tarp by the left side of the bed and put the shower curtain under the sheets, between the mattress and the mattress pad. Mariam and I are going to do some walking."

Such a difference. Her voice was sharp and no-nonsense when talking to him and the worried husband, but calm, confident and gentle as she encouraged the laboring woman.

It seemed like the women trudged through every room in the house for hours, but eventually they returned to the master bedroom, and Jess had the mother-to-be lie on her left side.

"Mariam, you are doing so very well. It won't be long now until you get to hold your beautiful new baby."

"I—don't—think—I can do this."

"Of course you can. Yusef, tell her."

The man murmured encouragement in a language that sounded like the water rippling over the rocks at Chattering Creek.

Ben asked if they wanted him to leave the room, not wanting to intrude on the Muslim woman's assumed modesty. But when Jess said she really could use his help, the couple exchanged a look. Mariam replied that she would welcome his help, *anyone's* help. So he was fetching and carrying glasses of water. He'd also boiled some water after all, into which he dipped the kitchen shears and some soft strips of cloth for the umbilical cord.

"Ben?"

The look of trust Jess gave him almost melted him into the floor.

"It's almost time. Can you help me get Sef—you don't mind if I call you Sef, do you? Saves time." The man shook his head. "Good. I want to get Sef behind Mariam in 'Papa Bear' position."

Soon the father-to-be was positioned behind his wife so that his chest was against her back, his hands on her swollen abdomen in such a way that he could feel the contractions, and Mariam could grip his forearms.

"This is not how they did it in our hospital," he said. "I like this better."

"Ben, get the phone, put it on the nightstand there so Sef can keep talking to 911. Make sure it's on speaker mode."

She redirected her attention to the perspiring, groaning woman. "Okay, Mama. I'm going to go wash my hands one more time, then we're going to have us a baby."

Jess kept up the encouragement, and not too long later, a tiny, red-faced baby slithered into her waiting hands and began wailing.

"Congratulations, Mom and Dad." Jess held out her hand, and Ben placed a warm, wet washcloth in it, which she used to wipe the baby's face. Then she pressed the infant to Mariam's breast. "Skin to skin, Mama. Let her latch on while we take care of the afterbirth."

"Her? A daughter? We have a little girl?" Yusef had happy tears rolling down on his face, kissing his wife and putting his arms around hers to help cradle the baby.

Ben found that tears were rolling down his own face. All babies were miracles, even those that weren't your own.

He very carefully did not look at whatever it was Jess was doing with the cotton strips and the shears, though he cringed when he heard them snick closed. Instead he riveted his gaze on the baby, now content at her mother's breast.

So tiny, so perfect. So like, and unlike, Micah.

"Yo, Starr-gazer? A little help here?" Jess handed him a small white garbage bag. "Put this in the freezer."

"Do I want to know—"

"No, you don't. But they'll want to check it once she's at the hospital."

When they had changed the bedding and settled the new family comfortably into the bed, Ben and Jess sank into the couch by the fire. His arm went around her, automatically, and she nestled in, letting out a big sigh.

"Jeez, I was petrified. I really wasn't sure I could do it," she said. "But I think she's okay. Both she's."

"Are you kidding me? You were terrific, and you didn't let on for a minute you were nervous."

"I couldn't—Mariam was frightened enough for all of us." She reached out to hold his free hand. "You were pretty amazing too. That was lovely, the way you showed Sef how to give the baby her first bath."

Without thinking, Ben blurted out, "Well, I've had experience."

Her body stiffened. "You think I need a reminder?"

Shit. This was why he'd had to move out, the way they kept reopening each other's wounds. "I'm sorry. I'm so sorry, Jacinta. I know you haven't forgotten for a minute, any more than I have."

The newborn in the next room let out a shrill wail, but was quickly comforted.

"Do you know? Do you really?" She pulled away, pressing her palms into her breasts. "Do you know that whenever I hear a baby cry, like Mariam's, that my breasts still want to let down, even if there's no milk inside them anymore? Do you know how empty and barren I feel?"

Jess started to sob. "I betrayed him. Our baby died because I wanted to feel like a woman, instead of just a mother. What was wrong with being just a mother?"

He gathered her in his arms, feeling stricken and helpless. All he could do was lie down with her on the couch, stroke her hair, and murmur to her things he'd said a thousand times before, "Jess, Jacinta, *pobrecita*, it wasn't your fault. These things happen."

"Yeah, you say that. Everyone says that. And sometimes I even believe it to be true. But my arms are still empty."

\* \* \*

J ess woke on Christmas morning, painfully aware of a crick in her neck, and that swollen-eyed, damp dishrag feeling earned from sobbing half the night away.

And yet…she didn't feel as broken as she usually did.

She eased herself out of Ben's arms. He continued blissfully snoring on the couch. Mouth open, a little drool running into his beard.

How had she managed to get through the past year without this incredibly sexy man?

Not very well, to be honest.

She went to check on the new mom and baby. Mariam's smile was so radiant, Jess almost saw a halo around her head. The baby girl, a solid six pounds as far as Jess could judge, seemed to be thriving and healthy. Bright-eyed, alert, good color, had passed her meconium during the night.

Sef had a request. "If you will permit it, we would like to name our daughter Rasha Jacinta. And call her Jessie."

Tears burned Jess's eyes. "I would be honored."

Mariam spoke. "I am not sure our daughter and I would be alive without your assistance. It is the least we can do. Our family will always be grateful to you."

"You and Sef did the hard part."

"It was not so hard." Mariam's eyes twinkled. "Well, sometimes it was."

"Mariam!" Sef turned the color of a poinsettia.

The women's eyes met, and a message was exchanged, of sisterhood, of amused entertainment at the fleeting prissiness of men.

Of shared motherhood.

Jess called in to the hospital with a progress report. While they were working on it, it would still be another day or two before the Three Drunk Uncles could clear the roads enough so the hospital could send an ambulance for the mother and child.

After getting permission from the new parents, Ben had uploaded some pictures of baby Jessie to his company social media page.

"So, you didn't get to put the baby in the feed trough, but I can't help but notice on this view, your big neon star is directly over her," Jess said.

"I swear, I didn't do that on purpose, that's always been the cover picture for my page." Ben looked embarrassed for a moment, then chuckled. "It *is* kind of ridiculous, isn't it?"

It was so good to see Ben laughing again. Had she seen him laugh at all since they lost Micah? Jess could feel the ice around her own heart cracking, and she let herself laugh with him.

Ben checked out his tablet again. "Hey, the Three Drunk Uncles posted that they want to stop in after they get the roads cleared, visit the baby. Maybe tomorrow?"

"Fine with me, but we need to make sure Mariam and Sef are okay with it."

"Will you ask them? Couldn't hurt them to have the town adopt the baby, so to speak."

Jess's heart contracted for a moment, remembering how lovingly the town had supported them when Micah was born.

And when he died.

She kissed Ben on the forehead, and went to check on mother and child.

* * *

Yusef was helping Ben move firewood from the outside shed to the bin near the back door, which had been almost fully consumed during the previous day.

"So, these men that are coming to see us, are they going to be drunk? I do not wish to give offense, but Mariam and I would prefer not to have strangers who have been drinking alcohol near our baby." He hastened to add, "Though I am sure they are very nice."

"Oh, no, they're not drunks. In fact, they're not even uncles, though we all call them that." It occurred to Ben how confusing it must be to be in a foreign country, or even a different town, with local nuances and history like this always ready to trip one up. Things that he took for granted.

"Uncle Jasper inherited the family tow truck service, and originally it was called Your Favorite Drunk Uncle's Towing Service. But he lost a leg to a roadside bomb in Afghanistan, so he brought in two of his Army buddies to help with some of the things that were harder for him to do. They renamed the company the Three Drunk Uncles, and expanded its scope. They do snowplowing in the winter, rockslide and fallen tree removal and tow services year-round.

"Jasper is the dispatcher and manager. Uncle Mel is a prankster, and he's the one who decided to install gag air horns in all their vehicles."

"Forgive me, what is a gag air horn?" Yusef carefully stacked the split wood in the rack.

"These make weird noises, like a cow mooing, or play 'The Star-Spangled Banner' or something." Ben chuckled. "And he always honks them when he's driving through town. There's on ongoing war on social media between those who think it's charming and eccentric, and those who are really ticked off and want him to stop. But there's nobody better at hauling a vehicle out of a ditch, or fixing a flat, than Uncle Mel."

"And the third uncle?"

"Uncle Baldy? Quite a character. He's African-American, which is as rare in these parts as…" Ben realized belatedly how tactless the remark was.

Sef raised an eyebrow. "Syrian refugees?"

"I'm sorry, man. We might not see a lot of your people around here, but it doesn't mean we don't care and want to help you."

"We know. And we appreciate your kindness, more than I can ever say."

Ben took a seat in one of the deck chairs, gestured for his guest to take the other. "So, Uncle Baldy. The story I heard, they butchered his hair when he was in the service, and he hasn't had it cut since. He wears dreadlocks and tie-dye and is a genius with the snowplow."

Jess joined them outside, bearing steaming mugs of hot tea she handed to them. "Sally and Tony from Shepherd Falls Excursions have offered to run up here on their snowmobiles bringing any supplies we need. I think they just want to take a peek at baby Jessie, but we could use a few things, so I'm making a list. Diapers, wipes, bread, milk, tea… Anything you're craving, Ben?"

"Only you, my sweet." Ben tried to give her a kiss, but she danced out of his reach.

"Not now, Mr. Starr. We have company."

He was both disappointed and elated. Jess said *"we have company."* And she *had* spent the night in his arms, even if that was more passing out from exhaustion than a deliberate choice. "Alrighty then. Ask them to bring chocolate chip cookies. And fruitcake. Sef, have you ever had American fruitcake?"

"I have not yet had the pleasure."

Jess gave him the side eye. "I'm not sure Ben is doing you any favors, or that it'll be a pleasure, but fine. Why should you be spared? Sef, is there anything *you* would like? I know this is not the holiday for your faith, but I can't remember if Ramadan happens around this time of year, or not."

"This year, it does not. I would ask for hummus, but we have discovered that American hummus is not…what we are accustomed to. Perhaps some dates? Mariam loves dates. And pistachios."

"I bet they can find those, and those would be good for her, too. 'Kay, gentlemen, I'm going back inside. Let me know when the Uncles get here, or when the guys from Shepherd Falls arrive."

Before Ben could react, Jess had swooped to give his forehead a fleeting kiss.

He was disappointed it wasn't his lips, but yet…it also felt like progress. And had her hand lingered on the nape of his neck?

\* \* \*

Jacinta was relieved when the visitors departed. The Shepherd Falls peeps had brought in the supplies, worshipped properly, and departed quietly. The Three Drunk Uncles had all left offerings for mother and child.

From Uncle Mel, an Amex Gold gift card.

From Uncle Jasper, a Pier One Imports gift card.

From Uncle Baldy, a gift card from Target.

"What?" he'd asked when the other Americans looked at him oddly. "Everybody shops at Target."

Uncle Jasper shook his head. "We were rocking a gold, frankincense and myrrh theme here, Baldy. Fail, my brother."

"I can leave some weed, if Sef and Mariam—"

"Thank you, but no thank you," Mariam said softly but firmly.

After the Uncles left, Jacinta settled Sef, Mariam, and their beautiful, miraculous baby, with her liquid brown eyes and pink rosebud mouth, into bed for the night. Rather than let the family run up the cost of an ambulance, Ben had agreed to drive to the hospital with the family in the morning, so Mariam could receive a checkup.

For now, Ben was all Jess's. And she wanted him. *Needed* him.

Seated once more on the couch in front of a blazing fire, she met Ben's eyes with her own, drowning in them, as he met her lips and kissed her.

Only he was kissing her tentatively, as if she were made of spun glass and might shatter.

Jess couldn't stand it. It had been too many months since she'd tasted the unique flavor that was Ben. Hunger overwhelmed her, like a long-awaited holiday meal. She needed to bury her face in his neck and breathe in his scent, nip at his earlobes and wind her fingers through his hair, pulling his mouth against hers fiercely, urgently.

"Are you…growling?" he asked with a chuckle.

"Shut up and kiss me!" She reveled in the feel of his strong, firm, yet soft lips. God, she need this, needed him, like the drought-starved land had needed the snowfall. Jess felt the dry, parched places in her heart, her soul, opening up, welcoming the life-giving essence.

She caught his bottom lip with her teeth, nipped it, glorying in his shiver of pleasure. Ben's hands traced a feathery pattern on her shoulder blades, down her back: light, lacy, delicious.

For the briefest second, the ghost of their last lovemaking passed through Jess's mind—only then, she'd been holding back, and Ben had been the eager one. No, it *wasn't* anyone's fault. Time to live in the present, in a world filled with snow and new beginnings and babies.

Falling back onto the couch, she grabbed his ass and pulled him against her, so she could feel that glorious, hard erection against her sweet spot.

Ben pulled his mouth away to whisper, "Jess, I want you but…I don't have any condoms."

"Me neither. Have you been with anyone else, since…?"

"No." He looked shocked, but he was a gorgeous man, she had to assume he'd had opportunities.

"Me neither." Jess looked him in the eye. "I want this. I want you. I want whatever the universe chooses to send us." She couldn't bring the word *baby* past her lips, but it was what she meant, and she could see in Ben's eyes, he was open to it, too.

Ben met her hunger with an urgency that matched, overpowered hers. Pressed her deep into the couch, grinding hard into her, kissing her. His mouth left hers, tracing a heated path down her jawline, to the sensitive spot on her neck, just below her ear, where he latched on, suckling, in rhythm to his hips grinding his cock against her, there, there, there! Jess felt herself coming hard, nails digging through Ben's plaid flannel shirt and under-T into his shoulders.

He lay still on top of her, letting her drift down slowly, then drew a finger across her cheek. "Wanna get naked and do it right?"

"I thought you'd never ask."

They raced into the bedroom, hands entwined.

Her fingers couldn't work fast enough to unbutton Ben's shirt, pull off his T-shirt, trace his sexy jungle mat of chest hair. She had to pause to let Ben pull her shirt over her head, smiling with satisfaction at his indrawn breath at her breasts, firm and inviting in a lacy red holiday bra.

And, as he was soon to discover, matching panties.

Jess had to admit to herself that even with everything else that had been going on, more than a small piece of her heart had been hoping to rekindle the relationship with her husband.

Hence the sexy red underwear.

"Do you have any idea how beautiful you are?" he whispered, his hands blazing a heated trail down her body that his mouth soon followed.

"I *feel* beautiful. When you're loving me like this. Even though I have stretch ma—"

"Battle wounds," he interrupted, kissing the silver-streaked skin with reverence and passion. "And I honor you for them."

"And my thighs have gotten so—"

"Tasty." He knelt before them, caressing them with his mouth as she wound her fingers in his hair.

He pulled her panties down, barely waiting till Jess stepped one foot out of them, and buried his face between her legs, working her pussy furiously until she came again, clinging desperately to his hair for balance.

Tears were slipping down her face as he gently guided her to lie on the bed, and lay beside her, on his side.

"I love you, Ben. I've missed you so much. I'm so sorry. I...I'm so sorry."

"I love you too, Jacinta *Preciosa*. I never stopped. I'm sorry that it has taken us so long to come back together. We *are* back together now, aren't we?" He began kissing her tears away.

"Yes. We are. I don't know how to explain it, but something in me...I still hurt, I will always miss our Micah, but I feel peaceful about it now. Maybe, like Mariam said, it is awful, it is the worst thing that can ever happen to parents, but...maybe it really wasn't my fault."

"*Your* fault? It was my fault, I never blamed *you*."

Jess laughed against Ben's chest, then looked at him, more tears swelling in her eyes. "I never blamed you, either. Can we start over, without the guilt and shame?"

"I think that would be an excellent idea."

"Do you know what else would be an excellent idea?"

"What?" Ben's smile was playful, happy.

She tweaked his beard. "Let's lose this bra. And your boxers. I need to feel you inside me. And no more barriers of any kind between us. New beginnings."

"You're right. A most excellent idea." Ben's hands moved to unsnap the front clasp, then gently kissed and suckled each puckered nipple in turn. "To new beginnings."

When they had removed the last of their clothing, Ben locked his gaze with hers. So beautiful, so intimate, so intense. Was he penetrating her, or was she enveloping him? Or both? Either way, Jess felt not only her body but her heart opening, in a whole new way.

Truly a holiday miracle.

* * *

*T*wo *Christmases later...*

Jacinta Starr felt her husband's arm circle her waist, his big, capable hand sleepily seeking her breast, palming the nipple. He sighed happily and snuggled closer.

She loved being spooned like this. Ben's beard tickled the back of her neck and shoulders, and her nose was filled with the sweet aroma he carried home from the store: dried hay and fresh grains, wood smoke, and a special clean male scent that was all his own.

Reassuring sounds filtered into the bedroom. The calls of ducks and geese flying toward the lake. The "Jingle Bells" car horn of the Three Drunk Uncles passing by on the main street. The soft snoring of the baby, broadcast over two separate monitors from the adjacent bedroom. Jess felt loved and treasured. Safe. Home.

And that delightfully firm cock poking her backside didn't give her a bad feeling, either.

Did they have time for a morning romp before Yusef, Mariam, Jessie and their six-month-old arrived to share the holiday meal? She stole a glance at the alarm clock.

*Yes. Yes we do.* She positioned herself to envelop Ben's erection in her waiting warmth, sinking back upon him as he groaned with pleasure.

"Merry Christmas, Baby."

# ABOUT THE AUTHOR

Beverly Diehl writes romance, women's fiction, and gives a popular online class called *The Business of Writing*. Her memoir *Sex, Drugs, Rock 'n Roll and a Tiara: How I Celebrated Life While Kicking Cancer's Ass* will be released... in 2017. She lives in Los Angeles with two cats, Motivation and Creativity.

Website: www.beverlydiehl.com

# Hopeful at the Holidays

## BY CAMI BRITE

S HY IN STUDIO CITY. You: flexing and posing
for the photographer. Me: the photographer,
blown away by all those yummy muscles but too shy
to say anything. I wish I'd asked you out. You have my
card, please call me any time.

*Ryan Gosling poses, exposing his six-pack (eight-
pack?), his unbuttoned tailored white shirt blowing in the
wind from the large fan in the studio, the hot lights burning
down and bringing a sheen of sweat to his torso like he's
been oiled up. His deep blue eyes bore into me, owning me.*

*"Girl, you've got this," he says just to me.*

*I confidently step forward, my eye to the lens, loving
him with the camera, immortalizing this perfect moment
for all eternity.*

*I hand the camera to my assistant and go to him,
smoothing down a wrinkle on his gray tweed trousers,*

*briefly running my fingers through his hair. For the images, always for the images.*

*We will tell our children and grandchildren about this moment when they come home for Christmas every year, and the photo will hang over the fireplace in our beach-front home, a constant reminder of our deep and abiding love...*

A rush of excitement zipped up my spine, making me tingle. I could almost feel Ryan's silky-soft hair on my fingertips. And then WYSIWYG the monster kitten jumped onto my lap and began kneading my leg. Not quite the Gos, but she would have to do for now. I gently moved her to a nearby chair and grabbed my trusty lint roller. My outfit was not cat-friendly, but I loved that it fit easily without pinching at the waist like it would have a year ago.

It was Thursday, my favorite day of the week. Sure, most people would probably choose Friday, but on each Thursday for the past year, my inbox had been full of hope and magic courtesy of Missed Connections, a weekly email of curated local personal ads.

*Curated* being the key word. Whoever edited this email was a true believer. My previous experience with personals had been a free local newspaper. The ads had seemed sad and desperate, or worse, on the seamy side where the authors were looking for a quick hookup. They were a lot like online dating profiles, which often spurred me to wonder about the requirements for antidepressants.

But now I was hopelessly addicted to the romance, the mystery, the hope of the beautifully crafted messages in these emails. It fit right in with the Christmas holidays, the most magical time of year for sappy romantics like me who thought Valentine's Day was just a bit over the top.

The weekly email was my new drug, and I wanted more, more, more. It counteracted the drudgery of my office job, drafting letters and memos, researching facts and figures, and creating endless presentation decks for my boss. It also kept me from dwelling on the most embarrassing moment of my life, at last year's holiday office party.

Oh, that party. My cheeks flamed even now. I wished I could erase the memory of it. It hung over my head like a cloud of shame for months. I still had trouble meeting his eyes sometimes. And tonight was this year's party. My stomach fluttered with anxiety.

But I was twenty-five now, not the naive twenty-four-year-old I was last year. This year would be different. I was determined to limit my liquor intake and stay far, far away from Rob Andrews with his artfully cut dark hair and smooth, perfect voice.

I turned back to my tablet and poured milk over my cinnamon almond granola, savoring the chances for true connection. My mind filled in the details, building complete stories of hope and love, or sometimes just lust. I soaked in true love near misses, and it stoked the fire of my belief in love at first sight. Or second or third.

I glanced at my watch and groaned. Time for work. I'd have to finish reading it later, no more time for true love this morning.

Suddenly the personals became even more personal. I wished someone would write a missed connection to me. I allowed myself to wallow for thirty seconds, then cut it off. Today, I would choose to be positive. Just because it hadn't happened to me yet didn't mean it wouldn't. I just needed to keep the faith.

\* \* \*

GENEROUS AT GARY'S MARKET. You offered spare change to a stranger at the express register. I was one lane over, trapped behind a father and his two kids with an overflowing cart. Our eyes met, the world stopped for a second. Can I buy you a coffee?

*I stand in the express lane with my organic fruit and herbal tea and my recyclable grocery bag. I see the woman in front of me struggling to find change in her purse to finish her purchase. I open my change purse and offer her what I have. It's obvious she's having a tough day. Her children are sullen and vocal about it. I'm happy to help make her day a little easier. She thanks me and turns to the cashier with the right amount.*

*I glance over to the next register and a beautiful guy watches me with soft green eyes and long lashes a girl would kill for. I get lost in those eyes for a moment and then the woman in front of me leaves and it's time to pay for my fruit and tea. I take one last lingering look at the mystery man in Aisle 2 as I take my recyclable grocery bag from the clerk and leave.*

*I see him again at the store one week later, and this time he switches lanes to talk to me. We laugh over the ridiculous tabloid articles at the register, and he offers to pay for my coconut water and fair trade organic chocolate.*

*He carries my bag to the car and begs me to go to dinner with him at Michael Voltaggio's newest restaurant, the one with a six-month waiting list. I say yes, and six months later, while we're at an exclusive spa resort in Santa Barbara for the weekend, he hands me a powder blue box and asks me to marry him.*

I sat in my postage stamp-sized office at Dunham Tech, basking in the afterglow of my latest daydream. Maybe I should plan a weekend in Santa Barbara. Get away for a bit. And maybe I should carry more spare change. And wear makeup.

When I'd gotten to work, I met my best friend Brenda in the small office kitchen for our morning coffee break. The room was dominated by a fancy machine that brewed specialty coffees. It was very technical, but the two of us had spent a lot of time experimenting to figure it out.

We didn't even have to evacuate the building the second time.

I was currently working my way through the dark roasts. Today was Sumatran Dark Roast, no sugar or milk, just as the good Lord intended. Brenda was a slave to

Donut Shop Blend with Milky Froth and Dark Chocolate. I tried not to judge. She had the same thing every morning, and woe to the poor sap who orders our coffee if the supplies ran low.

We took our mugs to one of the uncomfortably high tables in the break room. I was positive they designed the room that way on purpose, to get people back to work quickly. It didn't work with Brenda and me; we just gritted through it.

"So," she said in a low voice, "did you hear about the big meeting they're having next week before the holiday break? If you didn't, you will soon. Susan's running it."

I groaned. Susan was my boss, and although I enjoyed my job at DT, I did not enjoy the way she delegated everything to me. "How deep is the dive this time? They're changing over the electronic files right now and I can't access any data before last year."

Brenda gave me a knowing look. "Silly Amber. You might not be able to, but Rob can."

"Oh, don't even start this with me. I've been trying so hard to forget the Glare Of Shame, and today of all days you bring him up?"

"The GOS wasn't that big of a deal. I know it's a big deal in your head, but you need to get over it already. We were a little drunk, that's all."

I thunked my head on the table. "Why am I even obsessing over this a year later? It's probably against the employee code of conduct anyway. No fraternizing. I should be grateful for dodging a bullet, right?"

"Actually, you guys are in separate departments, so it's no big deal." She sipped her Franken-coffee and gave a satisfied sigh. "Anyway, you should get your game face on, because you know Princess S is going to assign this to you as soon as she gets in. And maybe it'll turn out you don't need his help anyway."

I was doomed.

\* \* \*

**D**ELICIOUS AT THE DMV. You: rocking blue scrubs, smiling at me when everyone else was sour. Me: tattoo, jeans, digging your gorgeous hazel eyes. You were gone when I got back from my driver's test. I need to see that smile again. Describe my tattoo and I'll know you feel the same way. I want to spend time with you.

*I am a busy, busy doctor and my license is expiring tomorrow. I rush to the DMV between rounds, not changing into my street clothes because I have an appendectomy later. It's a lovely day, the birds are singing, and everything is in harmony. When I get to the DMV, I am helped right away by a charming older woman who recognizes me from the hospital. I smile as I look around, and then I see him.*

*He's standing in a circle of light, like heaven sent down a special ray just for him. A swirling tribal tattoo curves around and down his arm, stark black against his honey-colored skin. He's beautiful and I smile wider as our eyes meet.*

*My attention is called away by the desk clerk, and I take one last look at him before I go to have my picture taken. Every time I look at my license, I will think of him because our encounter is written all over my face in that photo.*

*A few weeks later, I'm covering a shift in the ER and the tattooed god comes in with a laceration on his hand. I stitch him up and we chat about motorcycles and appointments at the DMV, and he tells me he just moved here from New York and this is the first time he's had a driver's license. He's funny and sweet, and he's a stockbroker, but he really wants to be a motorcycle mechanic.*

*We settle down in a charming Craftsman near the hospital, and he starts building custom motorcycles in the garage. He's so good at it that soon every young Hollywood celebrity is haunting our home, begging him to build theirs next. They of course invite us to visit them on set and go to their big movie premieres at Hollywood & Highland...*

"Amber, please come to my office." Susan's voice blared from the speakerphone on my desk. The time had come, there was no way around it. The delegation deluge was about to begin. Might as well embrace it. I grabbed a notebook and pen, twirling in my chair and pushing off to vault out the door of my office.

As I walked down the hall to Susan's office, I saw Rob's tall frame leaning casually against the wall by her door. Pasting on my work smile, I briefly met his eyes and stepped to the spacious cubicle nearby.

Susan's speakerphone echoed from the huge corner office, booming with the distinctive voice of her boss, our founding CEO, Matt Dunham. I sent a questioning look to Brenda, who sat primly at her desk acting like it was completely normal that Rob was also here.

"Traitor," I muttered at her, still maintaining my office smile. "A little warning would have been nice." I surreptitiously pushed a hand through my hair, smoothing down the stray hairs that always cropped up during the work day. I vehemently wished that I had thought to touch up my makeup in the bathroom after this morning's coffee break.

Her mouth twitched. "Sorry, there was no warning. She had me call him while she called you."

Then I felt the warm sensation of someone nearby and smelled a clean, familiar scent. I turned my head and sure enough, Rob had moved to stand next to me, with his perfect teeth and pillowy Brad Pitt lips.

"Hey, Amber."

His voice did funny, melty things to my innards. Even after the Glare Of Shame, I was powerless against him. He smiled a crooked smile at me as if there was absolutely nothing wrong, and we were the very best of friends. Maybe Rob wasn't so perfect after all.

I decided to rip the Band-Aid off. "Hey, Rob. So is your girlfriend coming to the party tonight?"

He glanced sideways at me and cleared his throat. "Um, no. She's not—"

I was saved from making further conversation when the call ended in Susan's office.

"Come on in, you guys, there's so much to get done by Monday!" she called cheerily. And why shouldn't she be cheery? Soon she would have pushed all her work onto my not-so-tiny shoulders.

\* \* \*

SEXY AT SOUTH BEACH. You dropped your towel walking from the beach to your car. I picked it up and rushed to catch you. I just wanted to talk to you and look into your beautiful brown eyes. I'll be on the pier next Tuesday at sunset with a bottle of champagne, waiting for you.

*I'm in a terrible hurry to get back to my glamorous life as a cover girl for a national skincare line. So much of a hurry that I drop my towel on the way to my convertible, but I can't go back for it. I have important things to do. Urgent things. I will buy a new towel.*

*Before I start my car, a man rushes up with my towel. He is tall, his cheeks angular, his eyes piercing. This man is used to power, but it's clear in this moment that he has been felled by my beauty. He doesn't speak, he just carefully folds the towel and hands it to me. I place it on the seat next to me, smile at him in thanks, and drive away.*

*I see the personal ad a few days later. My assistant shows it to me and I know instantly that it's him. I've thought of him so much the past few days, and I want to know more. And now I know he feels the same.*

*I drive to the beach right before sunset, my hair in a soft white scarf, Michael Kors sunglasses on my head, wearing a sexy but demure sundress with matching strappy sandals. I find rock star parking and the day is beautiful as I walk toward the pier, the sun shining like diamonds on the water.*

*And there he is, waiting with a chilled bottle and a wicker picnic basket. He wears distressed jeans and a translucent linen shirt, a tasteful Rolex on his wrist, a bouquet of red roses in his hand. He stands as I approach, a hand reaching out for me, a knowing smile on his lips. True love strikes again.*

After the meeting, which went exactly as Brenda had foreseen, my schedule was full and it was all Susan's fault. It was time to put on my big girl panties where Rob was concerned. His help was going to be vital in getting the information for this presentation before next week.

He followed me back to my office and I quickly trashed the tiny voodoo doll I'd made of him from rubber bands.

Hey, I'm not perfect.

We sat at my desk like two regular adult people who work together and have no strange tension, and discussed the battle plan.

I busied myself with my computer, the dual monitors working effectively as a screen to hide my expression. I cleared my throat. "I appreciate your help with this. As Susan told you, they're migrating our electronic files through the middle of next month, so I only have access as far back as last June. That's not even close to what we need. Can you send me data going back five years on just the two main accounts? Do you have that?"

He leaned back in his chair, looking completely at ease. Of course, he wasn't the one who had been shamed. "We have a lot of information, but it's too much to send, and I need more specifics on what you need. There's a lot to sift through. It would be easiest if we go over it together. Can you come to my office tomorrow? I'll bookmark the relevant records today so they're ready to review."

I grimaced behind my monstrous monitor. Suck it up, weasel. "I'm going to have to put everything else on hold until I get a sense of how long this presentation will take to create. So yes, tomorrow is fine. What time?"

He pushed back his chair and stood. "I left my phone in my office, but I can give you a call when I get back to my desk, or just send you an invite—"

"Sending is fine," I quickly interjected. "No need to call, my calendar is up to date, I'm good." Crap, get ahold of yourself!

He paused at the doorway. "Listen...I'm happy to help you out. I know we had some...is this going to be okay? Us working together? Because you seem a little... not okay."

I turned up the wattage on my work smile and lifted my eyebrows, willing my face to remain a nice, calm pale. "It's fine. Just a lot to process, so many things to get in place by Monday. Everything is A-okay. Can't wait, looking forward to it."

Kill me now.

* * *

**H**OPEFUL AT THE HOLIDAYS. We had a moment a year ago at the holiday party, but it was bad timing. I see your beautiful face every day. I can't stop wondering what might have been. Can we have a do-over? I'll be waiting in the exact same place I was last year.

*I'm at the Dunham Tech annual holiday party, my first ever holiday office party. It's held in the huge atrium of our building with its vaulted glass ceiling and stained bamboo flooring. Intimate sectional seating is scattered throughout the atrium. A table is piled high with shiny silver boxes, the DT logo visible from the side. Festive lights have been hung all around, and a live band plays all sorts of holiday-themed music near a small dance floor.*

*The drinks are flowing, including an especially delicious holiday punch that tastes so good I forget it's got alcohol. I don't worry, though, because there is a car service to make sure everyone gets home safely after the party.*

*Having skipped lunch in preparation for the party, Brenda and I grab passed appetizers of chicken and portobello mushroom skewers, tempura veggies with a spicy ranch dip, and fried calamari with citrus marinara. The dessert bar features a chocolate fountain with marshmallows, graham crackers, and fresh fruit ready to be dipped.*

*I'm feeling loose and happy, my gestures and my smile a little wider than normal. As I look around, people are talking and laughing and having a good time. This is a great party, my very first office party, and I don't know how it can get better. And then I see him.*

*Rob Andrews has been my secret crush ever since I laid eyes on him after I was hired last February. He's so handsome that it took me a month to screw up the courage to even say hi to him in the hallway. Now I can use full sentences around him and my face doesn't get that warm when he's nearby.*

*Rob is friendly to everyone in the office, but I just know we have a special bond. Just last week, he helped me fix a particularly difficult calculation in one of the many spreadsheets I have to maintain for my group. He basically saved my job.*

*At the party, his tie is slightly askew and his eyes crinkle warmly when he sees me. I hand Brenda my drink and whisper loudly that I'll be right back. She laughs and tells me to take my time.*

*I hurry over to him, smiling my huge smile and somehow braver than I've ever been. I realize this is the time, I have to make a move. He opens his arms to give me a hug. I go in, pressing myself to him, and soon I'm nuzzling his neck, breathing in his clean warm scent, feeling his strong hands on my shoulders and I know this is it, this is the moment when everything is changing. Rob Andrews likes me, he really likes me!*

*I move my mouth to his ear and whisper bravely, "You want to go find an empty office?"*

*And then those strong hands pull my shoulders away and set me to one side. Clearing his throat, he slings an arm around a tiny bleach blonde yoga goddess who glares at me like I just ran naked down Hollywood Boulevard, saggy parts and all. I recognize her immediately, anyone would. It figures that my one office crush is dating the daughter of the biggest star in Hollywood, her name and face appearing almost weekly in gossip magazines.*

I stared at the page, blinking. This didn't make any sense. I'd reached the very last entry in today's Missed Connections email, and unless I was taking crazy pills... no. I couldn't even consider it. This was some ploy to either cheer me up because now I wasn't the only holiday fool, or maybe a coworker was playing some sort of horrible trick on me. Screw that. It couldn't be about me, no matter how much I wished otherwise.

Brenda knocked her special knock and waltzed through my door looking fantastic in a red dress with a slit that bordered on NSFW. She gave an approving whistle at my outfit and we had a few minutes of mutual admiration. I had changed into a dark green lace dress that showed off the body I'd been working on every day since the GOS incident. I still towered over my female coworkers, but my BMI was healthy and I looked damn good in that dress. And this year I was not a naive little girl anymore.

I hooked my arm through Brenda's and put on my game face. We arrived at the party two long elevator rides later, just long enough for me to tell her about the new personal ad.

"Well, you have to go for it!" she burst out, shoving me a little. "After a whole year of obsessing, are you telling me that you aren't interested anymore?"

"Come on, B, it's not him. I saw him today. I see him almost every day. He's had every opportunity this whole year to just talk to me. Why on earth would he go through all the trouble of placing an ad? He doesn't even know I read it! It makes absolutely no sense."

"It does to me. I have a good feeling about this. You need to be open to the possibilities."

"Right. And get stomped on two years in a row. I don't think so." I folded my arms and glared at her. "Forget I mentioned it. Let's just have a good time. I'm starving."

Because of course we had skipped lunch again. Rule number one: no alcohol until after food. We made our way to an expansive buffet table full of divine-smelling chafing dishes. I grabbed a plate and chose one of everything, and soon we were sitting near the dance floor where we could watch everyone and chat while we ate. The band was playing a funky rendition of "Rudolph the Red-Nosed Reindeer." People milled about, laughing and eating and drinking. No dancing.

"Does anyone even use the dance floor?" I sipped my lemon seltzer, all wits accounted for.

"Oh sure. Last year I danced three times with Matt Dunham. He's the nicest guy, I don't know why people are so scared of him." Brenda dug into her food.

And then I saw him. Rob was in the very same place he'd stood last year, and he was looking at me expectantly. Like I was supposed to do something. Like maybe that personal ad was really from him...

I nudged Brenda and nodded toward him. "Thoughts?"

She glanced over at him and looked back at me, no surprise on her face. "I told you already. And you got mad. So I'm not saying a word. Except if you don't go over there and at least say hi, you're the biggest chicken I know." And with that, my best friend got up and wandered over to chat with someone from finance.

I thought about today's new personal ad, and my face began to flush. What if it was him? What if it wasn't him? What was the right thing to do?

As if in a dream, I found myself getting up and walking toward Rob Andrews. His smile grew with each step, and I began to allow a tiny seed of hope to flourish in my heart.

When I reached him, he opened his arms to me just as he had last year. New, cautious, sober Amber moved in for a short hug with absolutely no nuzzling. He smelled even better than he had last year and his strong hands were moving from my shoulders to my back, pulling me in tight. A real hug, a hug with potential.

He rested his forehead on mine, and our eyes met as he asked, "Is this okay?"

I nodded. And then he was kissing me. I don't really remember how it happened. One minute I was nodding calmly, and the next my body was tingling in all sorts of interesting places. His soft lips touched mine and I was a goner.

We broke apart and his arm slung around my shoulders. He leaned down and said, "Sorry about last year. I hope this means you're giving me another chance?"

My mind was whirling, going back to last year and thinking about the personal ad. "What about your girlfriend? Miss National Enquirer?"

"We're more like family friends. After I knew you were interested in me, I broke up with her. As soon as I saw you, I just knew."

I smiled, thinking. "But wait. And then a whole year goes by?" I pulled back to look at him.

He looked at the ground. "I had some things to work through. I didn't want you to be a rebound."

Oh man, he was almost too perfect. "How did you even know I'd see that ad?"

He grinned. "Well, you would barely talk to me. I didn't know how to get around all the awkwardness between us, so I got Brenda to help me strategize. She told me if I was really serious, I needed to write you a Missed Connection."

My heart burst wide open with happiness and hope.

This time his mouth moved to my ear and he whispered, "I've waited a year to say this: let's go find that empty office."

* * *

HAPPY AT LAST. I see you every day. When you smile at me, I know anything is possible. Especially do-overs at holiday office parties.

# About the Author

Cami Brite  grew up with a camera in one hand and a book in the other. When not traveling or creating book covers at  Brite Designs, she works full time.  She loves her family & friends: Doris, Reynold, Cindy, Scott, Kyler, Chandra, Cristina, Heidi, Hilary, Holly, Maggie, Maria, Nichole, Yvonne & more!

Website: www.camibrite.com

# A Lares Christmas

## BY CLAIRE DAVON

C atching his foot on the edge of the separator that divided the hallway from her apartment would have been comical if Roald hadn't lost his balance and tumbled inside. His large form slammed into the floor with a loud thwack that Tullia was sure every neighbor could hear.

She tried not to show her dismay as Roald scrambled to his feet, dusting off his coat with quick motions. The flowers he'd brought had also gone sprawling, and the lilies scattered around her in a tangle of stems and bruised petals. He bent to retrieve them, bumping his knee against the floor as he did so.

At this rate, she was never going to get a boyfriend. The Lares power that protected Tullia would make sure of it. Only those with good intentions would ever breach the protection. Roald hadn't failed, but he hadn't passed either. So far he seemed to be in a gray area, proven neither good nor evil. It seemed her power was waiting to judge.

"I…your stoop…I didn't see it," he stammered. His waves of sandy brown hair were also disordered from the fall. Seeming to realize that, Roald pushed his hand through his locks, further mussing them. Roald's face colored red in embarrassment. The small divider was nothing more than a thin strip of wood designed to stop the carpet from becoming unraveled and not to trip up visitors. Yet trip Roald was what it had done in another example of her power at work.

If he had similar talents to hers he would understand, but Tullia's would-be suitor was human. He had no reference point for beings such as the Lares. It was a shame. She liked this man.

"It sneaks up on you," she agreed, bending to retrieve the blooms.

He had gone to great pains to prepare for this date, judging by the newness of his jeans and the crisp fold lines of his shirt, as well as his brushed and styled hair. Tullia cast inside for any sign that her power was going to continue to torment him. While she felt nothing at the moment, she couldn't be sure it wouldn't flare up and send him down a flight of stairs, or crash him into a building. For his own safety, she should make some excuse, turn him away and never see him again.

"Let me put these in some water and get my bag."

"You look nice," he said as she retrieved her purse from the coffee table. "I'm glad you agreed to dinner."

Three dates was longer than any other guy had managed. Some never even got to her door. Most didn't make it all the way through the first date.

She slid into her coat before he could offer to help, but left it unbuttoned. The vain side of her wanted him to check out her curves in her best jeans and form-fitting Christmas-red top. She was gratified when his gaze lingered on her breasts as she moved. She was also pleased that they didn't linger too long. Her power wasn't above throwing someone to the ground.

No rocks fell from the sky as they exited her apartment. No ice patch appeared under Roald's feet. Tullia held her breath when he started his car, but the engine caught right away. Small flakes of snow fell in the cold evening, just enough to melt on the skin and cover the ground in a thin layer of white.

"I've got reservations at Olympia Restaurant. The food is supposed to be great. Tullia, I'm so glad you said yes."

Her power would have told her if his earnestness was pretense. Tullia smiled at him as they drove, the streetlamps casting yellow shadows across the car as they moved. It was quiet in this suburban neighborhood. Cumberland County College was on hiatus for Christmas and many of the residents emptied out for winter break. Her parents lived close enough that Tullia could have been a commuter student, but she wanted to live on her own. Her grandmother's small inheritance had let her have a little financial freedom, enough to have her own place while finishing school and her first year after that.

She became aware of another car revving its engine as it sped toward them. It was going too fast, but that was nothing unusual. Students with a few dollars and no common sense often bought muscle cars and showed them off, as if more horsepower made them men.

Roald glanced in the rearview mirror as the car came up behind them. The light changed to yellow. He stopped and the driver of the other car had to slam on his brakes to avoid colliding with Roald's car. The other car's horn sounded in a continuous blare. Tullia looked behind her and saw the young male driver mouthing curses at them. The driver didn't let up on the horn until the light turned green, tailgating Roald as they continued down the street. With a roar, the other car owner cut into the other lane and screeched to a halt about two hundred yards away, his brake lights red in the darkness.

Roald slowed down and looked at Tullia, then reached over and checked that her seat belt was secured. He signaled to go around the other car, but the driver swerved to cut Roald off, blocking the opposite lane. Fortunately, there was nobody coming in the opposite direction.

Power flared within Tullia. Her tingling fists balled at her side as the energy flowed out of them.

The other car dipped as both tires on the left side blew out, the explosion of air loud on the quiet street. She saw the driver lean sideways at the decrease in altitude and then move to turn his car. Rubber peeled off in strips and the bald rims made a screeching noise across the pavement when he lurched forward. The hideous sound of tortured metal assaulted her ears. Several lights came on in the houses around them.

"We should stop," Roald said, but there was a decided lack of interest in his voice. "See if he's okay."

"We should keep going," she replied, her hands relaxing. "He was being a macho fool. Look, he's fine." She pointed to where the driver had gotten out of the car and stood staring in disbelief at his ruined wheels. He studied Roald and Tullia with a puzzled look on his face. Some part of him understood he'd acted against her and had now paid the price.

Somewhere inside they always knew.

\* \* \*

"You're a Taurus?" She groaned, slapping a hand to her forehead. "That's no good. I'm a Sagittarius. We're not supposed to get along."

Roald flashed an abashed grin, a glint of mischief in his brown eyes before he smoothed his face out. She felt as if she were floating and grounded at the same time.

"I'm three years older than you as well. Is that good or bad?"

She stifled another groan. "Bad. Per Chinese astrology, it's the signs that are four years apart that are compatible."

"I bet we're incompatible in numerology. I Ching, too," he said, and lifted one eyebrow. "That's it. It's over before it began."

Roald gave her a mock crestfallen expression that was so ludicrous she laughed out loud. The tingling feeling intensified, as if her blood were fizzing in her veins. She wanted to reach over and rub her palm over his to feel the kinetic energy there. His fingers were long and tapered to blunt, clean nails. Everything about him showed he'd made an effort for her.

She was a Lar. Crooks could not con them. Accidents could not occur to them. The wrong man could not get close. The yearning in her heart balked at the idea that he wasn't for her.

Roald met her eyes in a sideways glance. Longing thrummed in her belly. She was almost twenty-two, with a woman's desires and needs. This man, whose parents were from Germany, who was working on his MBA with an eye toward the financial world in New York, was the one she wanted. He had been different from the start, opening doors for her, walking on the outside of the side-walk when they strolled, bringing her flowers. He always showed her little courtesies that let her know he was a man who took others into consideration. The fact that he hadn't gotten out of his car and shouted at that silly driver was another mark of his good character. That he was easy on the eyes didn't hurt.

Roald inched his hand across the table, but before he could touch her, a water glass tipped off and shattered on the tile floor. Roald froze midway, a comical look of disappointment on his face. A waiter hustled over to help with the glass, giving them a strained look.

Roald raised his hands and the moment was lost.

"We weren't anywhere near that glass," he said. "How did it happen?"

She was never going to have a boyfriend.

\* \* \*

They walked under the full moon, their hands brushing. It happened so many times she knew it couldn't be an accident.

Finally she couldn't stand it and linked her pinky with his. To her satisfaction he slid his palm over hers, capturing her fingers.

He was German, another point against him. The Germans and her ancestors, the ancient Romans, had often been at war, and her clan had a traditional mistrust of Germans. Yet there he was, a proud German whose family hailed from Dusseldorf. His accent was more British than German, showing his Oxford education. His German heritage was one more thing that said he was all wrong for her. Her mother told old stories of ancient Germanic chieftains betraying Roman soldiers into ambush. Of Vandals and Silingi and Visigoths that swept into Rome and aided in that empire's final destruction.

He felt solid, like a well-built house foundation. She contented herself with the feel of his fingers against hers, and the energy of his palm touching her skin. Liquid desire stirred within her, making her limbs feel heavy and her sex ache. Her nipples pebbled inside her bra. She wanted to strip off all her clothes and fling herself into his arms.

The drive back to her apartment was in a silence charged with many words that could not be spoken. Her power would not allow him to come inside. It would lob him off the bed, or open up a small rift in her floor to plunge him through.

It was the holiday season. This year she wanted a different present, one only Roald could give her. It was the gift of the intimate knowledge of a woman and a man. She needed to lay with him and make snow angels and kiss him when their noses and ears were red.

It would be wonderful to celebrate Christmas with its tree and lights and tinsel and presents. She was familiar with Christmas, of course, even if her family did not celebrate the holiday. She'd seen movies and been to friends' houses around the holiday. Usually she let people believe they also celebrated in the traditional manner. It was easier than trying to explain.

He walked her to her door and paused. Then he kissed her, his lips firm. She sighed, and he seemed about to deepen the kiss when his lips slid and pressed against her cheek instead. He pulled back and a gust of wind caught him, pushing him back from her as they stood in the covered hallway.

"Um," he said. She wouldn't blame him if he dumped her. Usually she didn't care. This time she did. Her heart had become engaged. If she was reading the signals right, she had reason to hope his had as well.

"Um," she returned, bracing herself for rejection.

"Want to get together tomorrow? Doesn't your holiday start soon, you know, what's it called? Saturnalia?

I read something about feasting. It's too cold for outside, but we could set up a picnic indoors. I know just the spot. It could be my early Saturnalia present to you."

Tullia blinked and then smiled. The warm feeling in her stomach radiated out. Every part of her was sensitized, as if she would melt where he touched her.

"In early times there was a sacrifice before the public meal, but I think we can forego that," she teased. Roald smiled and put his hands on her shoulders. Tullia waited for a localized quake or some sort of natural phenomenon to separate them, but nothing happened. Her power appeared satisfied for the night.

"I wouldn't be much good with that," he said with a shudder. "I can pick up chicken. Would that count?"

"Yeah, no sacrifice needed," she said. *Except your heart, since you already have mine.*

She was almost twenty-two and had never been in love, until now. Roald had gotten under her skin and made her crave the things a woman desired.

"See you tomorrow," she said, and opened the door to her apartment. The last thing she saw was Roald watching her go.

* * *

Roald hadn't been the first boy to make her feel, just the strongest. There had been a guy in high school who had hung around her for a brief time. He was the local football star, a senior, and a shoe-in to be homecoming king. Tullia's heart was untouched, but she'd wanted to like him. He was handsome in a boyish way, although she doubted he'd hold his looks. She had discovered he was using her while he and his girlfriend were on the outs. Once Tullia realized what he was after, she ignored him until he came toward her locker, his expression spiteful.

The cuts in his scalp and forehead when the lockers broke free and hit him required stitches. He left her alone after that.

There had been a boss, a man at the coffee shop where she worked part time. One evening when it was just the two of them he tried to grope her breasts in the back room. It had taken three people to extract him from the machines and shelving that collapsed when Tullia leapt back. He slunk around and gave her baleful looks from that point forward. People couldn't feel her Lares power, but they sensed something different about her. Her talent always protected her. Even when she didn't want it to.

Tullia punched her pillow and sighed. She wished that Roald was there with her, filling the ache within her. She would find a way to have him. She would ask her mother during their Saturnalia celebration how to lift this so he could touch her. Then she would know if he wanted her the way she wanted him.

Tullia drifted off to sleep, the memory of their kiss at her door lingering.

* * *

*I*t was night, but she could see. Around her was a glade, with a pond in the center where lily pads floated and frogs croaked. Birds chirped from far away as if they did not want to intrude on this moment.

Roald was with her, his naked form gleaming in the cool light of the moon. He was glorious, all masculine planes and angles, his taut body hard with muscle that wasn't obvious in clothes. She was also nude, and the way he looked at her gave her the courage to extend her hand.

Within this glade, she didn't need the protection of being a Lar. In this enchanted space, only those who were welcome entered it. Those like Roald.

His body hair was sparse, dusting across his chest and down the middle of his torso, creating an interesting line of hair until it gathered at his groin where his phallus was erect. It would have scared her, if it were anyone but Roald.

The touch of another person's body was unfamiliar. The thought of a man inside her both excited and unnerved her. It would happen tonight, with Roald.

Roald held out his hand to her and she went to him. Together they sank down to the bed of moss and leaves that sprang up. There were no words in the glade. When she looked into his eyes, she saw he trembled for the same reason she quaked. Desire and the newness of intimacy warred within her. Then he kissed her and the anxiety began to dissipate. This was right. He pushed her down to the moss, his penis pressing against her hip as his kisses grew bolder. He plundered her mouth, each stroke of his tongue intimate.

His gaze swept down, lingering on her curves. The wordless admiration in his eyes humbled her. He cupped her breasts as he trailed kisses along the column of her neck and across her collarbone. He stroked her pebbled nipples, eliciting moans as he licked first one and then the other.

He drew her nipple in harder, clasping his mouth around it and lashing it with his tongue until need shot straight from her nipple to her core. Tullia cried out, except there was no sound. Then he did the same for the other breast until she was clutching at his hair in silent protest for the playing. She wanted to be one with him. He seemed in no hurry, though. He pressed kisses against her ribcage, her belly, and the splay of her hips. Tullia was sobbing with desire now, his masculine touch sending arcs of sensation through her as he feathered his hand through her soft lower curls. Moisture bloomed there when he slid his hand over her and played at her opening. He touched the small bud on top of her sex and she groaned, thrashing under his touch.

Her clutching hands and writhing body begged him to take her. She widened her legs, letting him have access to all of her. Roald looked into her eyes as if to ask "are you sure?" There was only one answer to that: yes, yes, yes!

He took his shaft in hand, and it was as big and proud as she could have hoped. Uncut and a good size, its veined hardness promised pleasure. He stroked his penis and she watched in fascination as it lengthened further. She gripped at his chest, his legs, and the tip where a drop of liquid emerged.

*She tilted her hips up to give him access. She thought the way would be hard—she was a virgin, after all—but he eased in and then sank into her as if she were made for him. Roald thrust and then went still, his body shaking. Urging her legs up, he began a rhythm that was too slow for her impatient body. She thrashed against him, clutching at his shoulders, and then his mouth rounded and he too was going wild. She felt the warmth of him inside her as he reached his pinnacle. She tightened around him, holding him as reason deserted her and she became a being of sensation and need. With a wordless cry of ecstasy, Tullia erupted in orgasm, the delight pounding through her.*

*The passion retreated, leaving them tangled together in a heap. Their bodies were slick with sweat and moisture from the glade, their mutual fulfillment ringing the clearing with their silent cries.*

\* \* \*

The Saturnalia festivities bursting forth around them, Tullia glanced at her mother. Traditionally Saturnalia was the time of free speech, when people could take "December liberties" and say what was on their mind. Tullia had never invoked it before. She had never needed to.

Her family had kept some traditions, but not others. In ancient times during Saturnalia the fashionable wore the synthesis, colorful clothing saved for this occasion, and pilleus, conical hats that went with the robes. Her family eschewed the hats but donned the multicolored loose garments. Tullia's was a patchwork of red, blue, green and purple that somehow worked together as a whole.

December 19th was the day of gift-giving. Combined with the tradition of honesty, Tullia knew there would never be a better time to ask.

"I would like a present, Mother," Tullia said, shifting and looking down. She could not meet her mother's eyes, knowing what Junia would see there. She could not think of her mother feeling this kind of emotion and yet she must have. A Lares could only accept the worthy, and Junia was still married to Tullia's father.

To her surprise, her mother did not say anything. Looking up, Tullia saw a look of interest mixed with satisfaction on her face.

"It is the Sigillaria," her mother said, "but we have not exchanged our gifts. Would you trade one of yours for another? I am afraid none of mine are valuable."

"I…" Tullia shuffled her feet, words failing her. When she looked up she saw concern and compassion, which gave her the courage to continue. "The gift I ask for is of great value. I want to be with a man, Mother." She paused, unsure if the truth would make it worse or better. "I have met someone, you see, and it has been working— he does not get swallowed by the ground when he tries to approach me—but intimacies trigger my protection. We cannot…" She stopped, her face flaming scarlet, but then began again. "…do more than kiss."

Her mother was quiet for a long time. "You think your power would have him? Are his intentions pure?"

Tullia nodded in an uncertain gesture. "They seem good, but how can I be sure? I know he desires me, I have seen it in his face and...his body."

"Tell me about him."

"He is German," she said, and her mother rolled her eyes. "Handsome, brown-haired, a few years older than me. He has a plan and is working hard to establish himself. He is a good man, Mother, in every way."

"Brown-haired!" her mother cried and threw up her hands, but the glint in her eyes told Tullia she was kidding. "I wanted you to have a blond husband so you could have fair-haired babies. It's time we had some in the family."

"I know, Mother, but he is not blond. Or Roman. Or the right sign. He seems to be wrong for me in every possible way, but he feels right."

Her mother's gaze grew more intent. "Has he come to you in the glade?"

Tullia blinked. The glade was her secret and she clung to the memory with pleasure. Even now her body throbbed with remembered ecstasy.

"Oh, don't look so surprised, Tullia," her mother said, and thwacked Tullia's hand with the wooden spoon. "I was not always this age. I once faced the same choice you did. When your father met me there, that was when my mother knew it was time. So it is with you. Very well."

She studied her daughter. "The power knew your father was right for me, and as much as he drives me crazy, he is the only man I want. That is how the Lares work. We do not allow people in casually. I'm afraid modern ways are not for you." She paused, a look of sadness in her eyes. "It is possible I added my power to yours to ensure you did not wind up with the wrong man. I am glad it has happened to you, but be warned—if he is not worth it, he will have me to contend with."

Her mother was silent for a moment. She breathed in a large gulp of air and closed her eyes. Lifting her hands, she moved them in an arc before clasping them over her head, her fingers pointing to the sky. Her mouth formed words and she opened her eyes. Tullia felt a weight lift away as if a shroud had been blown off her.

Her body came alive with the thought of making love to Roald. The Lares could never be casual about sex, but they took great pleasure in it. So it would be with her.

"Why don't you call this young man and see if he can attend the feast?" her mother said, turning back to her giant stewpot. "If he is worthy of you, then he should meet the family."

"Oh, it's late notice," Tullia demurred.

Tullia heard raised voices in the other room and then someone—she thought it was her uncle—broke into verse. Tullia groaned. This uncle had a penchant for bad poetry, and it was never more prevalent than during Saturnalia. Dice clacked, and although she couldn't hear them land, the shouts of dismay or triumph made it easy to determine the winners. Spirits flowed and the holiday gave them an excuse for letting down their guard.

"There once was a woman from Naples…" Limericks were apparently her uncle's rhyme of choice this season. It would be a long night. He would pass out at some point. Fortunately, his synthesis was long, unlike a toga, and wouldn't show too much skin. All around them raised voices and good cheer reigned.

"Call him." Her mother's large bulk shifted and she looked into Tullia's eyes. It wasn't quite a compulsion, but the words of a woman used to being obeyed.

To her surprise, Roald was delighted and drove over right away. Tullia closed her eyes on a stab of worry when he met her mother and father. Her human father shook Roald's hand and asked Roald about sports. Her aunts and uncles exchanged looks and let her parents take the lead.

As the only daughter and the youngest of the tribe, Tullia was the last to get settled. She didn't mind the scrutiny, as long as the person being scrutinized was Roald. Her skin tingled where he touched her. Here, on this night of Sigillaria, there was laughter and joy. Roald fit right in.

* * *

After dinner they left her car at her place and took a drive up the hill to a famous make out spot. Tullia waited for her power to protest, but it did not. Her body flowed toward his in remembered passion as if the night in the glade had been their first time.

When he took her hand and led her to a tree, she knew the difference between dream and reality. His warm body pressed against hers, filling her curves with his muscles and strength. Roald seemed surprised at first when he kissed her and nothing happened. She sighed and turned her head up to his. His tongue touched the top of her lip and she let him in, exploring, tasting. His arms tightened around her, pressing her back against the tree until she felt the bark on her exposed neck and his hard body in front. She returned the kiss, meeting him with a boldness she hadn't thought she possessed. His body was familiar in that way dreams were, but this was no dream.

"I thought maybe a pinecone would fall and knock me out," he said.

His tone was light, but with an undercurrent that told her he understood something strange had been happening. That he took it with such good grace spoke well of him.

"It won't," she promised.

"Tullia, I…" He faltered, smoothing his hand over her face. "Thank you for inviting me tonight. It meant a lot to me. I…we've only known each other a short time, but I feel differently around you. You're someone I could… love."

He shuffled his feet, looking anywhere but at her. His hand against her face trembled. Never before had a man quaked before her.

"I am glad, Roald. I can see myself with you, too." So could her power although it would continue to protect her. It had its limits. No amount of Lares strength could prevent speech from wounding her. He would never be able to cause her physical harm, but words could do the same amount of damage. She would have to take a leap of faith that he wouldn't hurt her. Tullia didn't think it was too big of a stretch.

His hand went around her neck and Tullia took a breath, waiting for a branch to come and yank it away. Nothing came, and tension she hadn't known she'd been holding flowed out of her.

"I'd like you to kiss me again," she said. His unsteady heartbeat seemed like an off time metronome. The throb of need made her ache to be filled.

"I want to do more," he admitted. "I had the strangest dream last night. We were near this pond in a glade and…" He broke off, shaking his head.

She stared at him, open-mouthed. Was she still a virgin if she'd made love with him in a shared reverie? It was too soon to tell him about the Lares, but that day would come.

"Tullia, since your family celebrates Saturnalia and not Christmas, do you want to spend the holiday with us? It's not fancy—nothing like your feasts—but we have a tree and presents. I'm driving home on the twenty-fourth and staying over at the house. I'd put you up in a hotel; they're a bit old-fashioned that way, but my mom would love to meet the girl I've been talking about."

She would have to watch to make sure her ability didn't interpret pranks as threats. If any of his people didn't like her, it was better that they know now she couldn't be trifled with. She was a Lar. She was the woman who would soon be Roald's lover.

"I'd like that," she said. "Provided you kiss me again."

A gust of wind blew around them, settling in the tree. The branches shook, and for a moment Tullia was afraid it was going to dump the snow onto Roald. Then the wind sighed and moved on, leaving them unscathed.

He was the wrong sign and nationality, the wrong everything and he was all she wanted.

Roald kissed her with a fervent desire that took her breath. He slid his hands over her butt and pulled her to him. The evidence of his passion was clear. Her power didn't stir. This Lar had found her mate.

She sighed into his mouth, rubbing her body over his, and was delighted when he gasped and let out a strangled moan. It matched the excitement sparkling through her heated blood. If they'd been inside she would have moved his head down to her breasts, asking him to taste her aching nipples. There would be time.

"God, you don't know what you do to me."

"Oh, but I do know," she whispered, feathering her hand through his hair.

"I'm so lucky," he murmured, pressing kisses over her cold reddened cheeks and nose until kissing her lips again.

It wasn't a word most associated with a Lares, but she let it pass.

"Kiss me again, Roald. Kiss me and kiss me. I need you so."

The Christmas season beckoned like a new beginning. Everything was going to change now. Roald wasn't frightened away and he'd shown through deeds and words that he was the one for her.

She turned her face up to his and gloried in a different kind of power, that of a woman desired by her chosen man. Soon she would know the secrets of a man's body and share hers with him. It would be a magnificent Christmas.

# Bed of Sweet Surrender

## By Kadee McDonald

"Cassandra Anne Jennings, why are you hiding here in your father's library? We must leave for Mr. Ashton's dinner party in an hour and you are not yet dressed. What in the world is wrong with you, girl?"

Seated in the large wing chair in front of the fire, Cassie watched her mother advance into the room. A tall, imposing figure clad in the finest gray silk, Henrietta Jennings possessed as strong a mind as any of Wellington's generals. She would never understand the fear that pierced her eldest daughter's heart at the thought of seeing John Ashton again.

"Mama, I do not think I can marry him." Cassie sat forward, twisting her handkerchief in agitation. "He is so practised in the world and I know very little of it."

"Not marry him?" Mrs. Jennings looked at her in apparent amazement. "Mr. Ashton is a gentleman and

189

he has properly asked your father for your hand. He possesses his home here in London, in addition to what is, by all accounts, a fine estate in Sussex. I also daresay his countenance is fine enough to please a girl with as much to offer as you and one who is younger than you, as well."

"He is beyond handsome, 'tis true. And well to do. But I have spent so little time with him. How am I to know if I can ever truly love him?"

Despite the warmth of the fire that warded off the December chill, Cassie's hands trembled now almost as much as when Mr. Ashton had taken them securely in his the first time they'd danced. Even through the barrier of the gloves she'd worn that evening, his steady, confident grip on her fingers created a sensation such as Cassie had never experienced before. It started in her palms and shot up, making her head spin, then plunged down to the pit of her stomach, causing an unfamiliar spasm. She didn't know how the feelings could both thrill and terrify her in equal measure. She longed to experience them again—almost as much as she feared them.

"Cassandra, you must put aside these odd notions." Her mother settled in the chair opposite hers. "You have been reading the novels of Miss Burney again, I fear. I did not love your father when we married, but I soon grew quite fond of him, and I remain so to this day, despite the fact that he is a timid sort. It shall be the same with you. Mr. Ashton seems to be an amiable young man, even though he has a bit of a…reputation, shall we say? If you try very hard, you shall make him a suitable wife. You should be on your knees in gratitude to the Almighty that such a man has decided to marry at all, let alone ignored the Great Beauties of the past season and chosen you instead."

Cassie took no exception to her mother's opinion, for she spoke the truth. Now at the age of three and twenty, and blessed with more than a fair amount of common sense, Cassie had only a year or two at most before she would be so firmly rooted on the shelf that she might as well be seated in a pot of dirt, sprouting leaves and attracting honeybees.

"Why did he choose me, Mama, instead of one of the younger girls?"

"We may never know the answer to that question, child. Men are often not such logical creatures as women and they marry for reasons quite different than we do. You are a gentleman's daughter and passably pretty. Your marriage portion is also sizeable, so perhaps that combination is just what Mr. Ashton is looking for in a wife. Now you must hurry upstairs and find Molly at once or we shall be late. Whatever his reasons are in asking for your hand, I doubt he will appreciate a fiancée who keeps him waiting for his dinner."

Cassie sighed and, with reluctance, rose from her chair and did as her mother bade her. As she climbed the staircase and turned toward her bedchamber, images of John Ashton flooded her mind.

She'd seen him the first time at a card party just after Easter, now eight months past. His immaculate manner of dress, his curling dark hair styled in the latest fashion, and his confident air had intrigued Cassie, so later she asked the family governess, Miss Parton, if she knew of him.

"Yes, dear, I do, and I suggest you avoid him." Here the woman paused to ensure she had her former pupil's rapt attention. "He is rich, to be sure, but he is rumoured to be a flirt and a notorious rake. Those failings will steer him to a dramatic downfall, I fear."

That had not happened. Cassie met him at numerous occasions later in the season and he continued to be more handsome and stylish than any man of eight and twenty with such a reputation had any right to be.

Every touch, dance, and whispered word they'd shared had drawn her in. She began to look for him at each new entertainment, longing to see his smile, hear his compliments, and spend a few more moments in his company. She thought of him during the day and dreamed of him at night.

When the season ended, she'd heard he returned to his country home. Why had he not remained there in Sussex and invited friends to make up a house party for the holidays instead of coming back to London in December for the Christmas season?

And why in the world would a gentleman such as he wish to marry someone as ordinary as she knew herself to be? As Cassie entered her bedchamber and submitted to the hurried attentions of her maid in dressing for dinner, the answer to that question came to her.

Mr. Ashton must want an heir and needed a respectable wife—preferably one with a large dowry—to provide him with a son. No other explanation made any sense.

Cassie yearned for a husband and children and a comfortable home to manage. She also longed to be out from under her mother's strict rules and often withering gaze. With wide hips and full breasts, she should be able to birth easily and feed her own, just as Mama had with Cassie and her younger sister Elizabeth, who, at the age of fourteen, would remain at home tonight with Miss Parton.

But rearing children with such a man as Mr. Ashton as their father? He'd provide financially for them, to be sure, but wasn't a man's devotion to his wife and family just as important? Cassie had heard little to recommend her newly acquired fiancé in that regard.

Still, off to dinner she must go. Now that Mr. Ashton had secured her hand, perhaps tonight she could discover not only his motives but also his plans for their future.

If she could manage to stand long enough on her wobbly knees the moment he came near her.

Cassie had lied when she'd asked how she would know if she could love John Ashton, and she would carry that secret with her to dinner tonight. Despite her concerns about the kind of husband he would make, her real fear occupied her mind.

She had already fallen in love with the gentleman who intended soon to wed her and bed her. But was he in love with her?

* * *

"John, please come away from that window. Staring out into the night will not cause the Jennings family to arrive one moment sooner."

From where he stood watching the carriage traffic below in Harley Street, John Ashton glanced back at his sister, Margaret, who sat near the hearth, busy with her embroidery.

"They're late." He took an impatient turn about the room, stopping at the mantle clock. "The invitation was for seven o'clock and it is now ten past."

Margaret's husband, Duncan, looked up from his newspaper. "Your bride-to-be and her parents must not wish to appear too eager."

John frowned. "When I say dinner in my home is at seven, then we should be sitting down to table at seven."

Duncan chuckled. "You do understand, Ashton, that when you marry this young lady, she will have the running of this house as well as the country estate, or at least the indoors of it. It is what women do."

"What women do?" John arched an eyebrow. "When they become wives, don't women do what their husbands tell them to do?"

"My dear brother..." Margaret began, then shook her head. "Ah, well, I suppose it doesn't signify. Miss

Jennings, whom you profess to be your ideal of loveliness, good sense and decorum will no doubt set you straight on matters even more quickly than she will salvage your reputation."

"What is wrong with my reputation?"

Margaret merely smiled and went back to her sewing while her husband returned to his issue of *The Morning Chronicle*. Voices from the entry hall seconds later indicated their guests were arrived at last, forestalling any further discussion of the matter.

Unable to wait a moment longer, John strode across the room and met Cassandra and her parents as his butler escorted them to the drawing room door. The mother was tall and imperious, the father a good two inches shorter as he trailed behind his wife.

Cassandra entered last, her small gloved hands clasped tightly together, looking as if she'd rather be anywhere else in the world except here, in her future home. Her tentative step and frightened look reminded him of a tiny kitten he'd rescued when he was a boy. The memory caused an unexpected wave of protectiveness to sweep over him.

Margaret and Duncan rose to greet them, Margaret acting as hostess. "Ah, Mr. and Mrs. Jennings, and you must be the charming Miss Jennings. Allow me to introduce myself and my husband, since my brother does not seem disposed at the moment to do the honours. I am Margaret Galesworthy, John's sister, and this is my husband, Duncan." The requisite number of bows and curtsies followed before Margaret motioned them closer. "Pray, do sit down."

At his sister's implied reproof, John recovered his manners. "Yes, forgive me, and do take a seat. I was growing concerned that you wouldn't be coming tonight after all."

"Not coming?" Mrs. Jennings frowned. "La, nothing could keep us away. Isn't that right, Mr. Jennings?"

Cassandra's father jumped a bit in his chair, as if startled to be asked to join in the conversation so early. "Oh, of course. But you know the ladies, Mr. Ashton. Sometimes they require more effort to make ready than at others. I'm sure our Cassie wanted to look her best tonight."

John turned toward Cassandra and nodded. "She has succeeded admirably." He hoped to draw a reaction from her and was gratified when she blushed before lowering her gaze, which up until that moment had been fixed on him. Her pretty eyes had seemed curious as she'd watched him, and her hair, the colour of fresh honey, gleamed in the glow from the evening fire.

Her soft skin and generous mouth had prompted him to ask their host for an introduction when he'd first seen her in April. A few moments of conversation showed her to be an intelligent young woman. Those traits combined to lure him to her side on each occasion he saw her afterward. He also appreciated the curves evident in her fashionable low-cut evening gowns. She possessed the innocence and respectability John needed in a wife contained within the body of a woman he wanted as a lover.

When they'd danced, he'd felt her tremble at his touch. Was it fear that caused the reaction? Or desire? Once they were wed, he would find out. If she was afraid, he would reassure until her apprehensions were gone. If it was desire, he knew how to fan the embers into flames that would keep both of them warm for the decades they would be together.

Most gentlemen of their day saw no purpose in sleeping every night in the same bed with their wives. John was not most gentlemen. His parents had spent every night together unless his father traveled on business. Even as a boy, John saw the felicity they found in such an arrangement. Now that he was engaged, he'd relegated the dalliances he'd enjoyed over the years to the past, and intended to devote himself to his wife and be just as happy.

The butler announced dinner a few minutes later. John took the foot of the table with Cassie on his right and Margaret, as his hostess, at the head. Mrs. Jennings was next to her daughter with Mr. Jennings and Duncan on the opposite side.

"May I enquire as to your plans for the rest of the Yule season, Mr. Jennings?" John asked as the footmen served the final course of fruit, nuts and cake some time later. "I hope you stay in town." He meant to spend time with Cassie and get to know her better now that he'd returned from Sussex with the plan to marry her and had been accepted.

Cassie's mother spoke before her husband could begin. "Indeed, Mr. Ashton. We shall remain here until

Twelfth Night at the very least and quite possibly several weeks beyond, depending on the condition of the roads."

"I'm glad to hear it."

"We hope that you wish for the wedding to take place early in the new year, but if you prefer a later date, then of course we'd be happy to delay our return to Somerset."

"Marrying by Twelfth Night would suit me well, if the bride agrees." John looked to Cassie for her answer and had to be satisfied with a slight incline of her head as concurrence. She'd said no more than a quiet "yes," "no" or "thank you" since their arrival or during the meal. "I hope, Miss Jennings, you find ways to amuse yourself while forced to stay inside in the cold weather that has seized London this year?"

He made the question sound casual, but it was not. He wanted a helpmate, as the Good Book said, a wife who kept herself always occupied and interesting, not one who would expect him to entertain her.

Except in the bedroom, of course. There he would be willing to devote hours to her and her pleasure.

"Amuse myself, Mr. Ashton? There is no need. With my sewing, my music and my father's excellent library, I stay quite busy. In fact, I often find there is not enough time in the day."

"Really, child," Mrs. Jennings said, arching an eyebrow in admonishment. "I'm sure Mr. Ashton does not wish to hear of the hours you waste with all those dusty old books. Furthermore—"

"I beg to interrupt," John spoke over her, causing the woman to sit back in her chair and close her mouth in surprise. "I did ask your daughter how she spends her days, after all, and I'm delighted to hear she has an appetite for learning that matches my own. Also—" He turned back to Cassie with a slow smile. "—anyone can tell at a glance that Miss Jennings is far from being a child."

There it was at last, that becoming blush to her cheeks and the sparkle in her eyes he'd waited to see all evening. Once they were married, he would do everything within his power to ensure she wore such a look every day.

* * *

Cassie coughed, choking back a laugh at the way Mr. Ashton reprimanded her mother. No one, not even her dear Papa, had ever done so, which would explain her mother currently wearing the look of a fish that had suddenly found itself on the sharp end of a hook.

Mr. Ashton's butler returned at that moment, leaned toward him and used a hand to shield his words as he whispered something which made the gentleman frown. With her chair close to his, Cassie overheard the servant say "tradesman" and "waiting in the library, sir." The butler stepped away and his master nodded, as if he'd debated and then made up his mind to proceed.

"My apologies." He rose and dropped his napkin to the chair. "A most urgent matter has come up that I must attend to at once. Margaret, I'll ask that you see to our guests. I'll join you all again for coffee as soon as possible."

Without waiting for his sister's answer, he gave a curt bow and quitted the dining room.

Cassie watched him go and turned back, puzzled. Her mother looked annoyed and her father bewildered as he announced, "I must say, that was most odd."

Mrs. Galesworthy shook her head. "My brother is not one to hold too tightly to convention, Mr. Jennings, but I'm sure the situation is vital or he would not have left us. Now, unless you and Duncan wish to stay over port, I suggest we await John in the drawing room."

"Of course, of course." Her father nodded. "As you say."

They rose at once and moved from the room, giving the servants access to clear the table. The house seemed to run with great efficiency and Cassie longed to meet the housekeeper. In fact, her mind whirled with a thousand questions about this home she would soon take charge of. She also wanted to speak with Mr. Ashton alone. Of course, it was not done, but for the first time in her life, she felt it was necessary to step outside the bounds of propriety.

"Mrs. Galesworthy…?" Cassie came up to her, seizing the instant when the others had walked on and were out of earshot. "May I excuse myself for a few moments?"

"Of course, dear." Their hostess called for an upstairs housemaid, who appeared at once. Cassie followed the young woman farther down the hall to a smaller room, where the maid showed her the chamber pot, then filled a washbasin halfway with warm water. After she was finished, Cassie straightened her skirt and rinsed her hands.

"D'ye need me to show ye the way back to the drawin' room, miss?" The maid stood ready with a small clean towel. Did the servants know she was to be their new mistress and, from what had been discussed at dinner, in only two weeks' time?

"No, I'm certain I can find it, thank you."

She left quickly, determined in spite of the guilt of the ruse she'd put forth, to find Mr. Ashton and speak to him. As much as the idea of marriage to him thrilled her, their engagement was none of her own doing. She had every right to discover his true feelings and prepare herself for what her life was soon to be.

The butler had said the library, so she crept downstairs in search of it. The house, though comfortable and tastefully decorated, was not large and she discovered the room in a minute. Fortunately, no servants were about in the front hall as she approached the door, finding it ajar.

Mr. Ashton's voice came from within. "The date is set. Delivery has to be prior to Twelfth Night."

The tradesman must still be with him and Cassie could only guess at the behavior of her future husband. The host of a dinner party leaving to tend to business was strange enough, but surely a meeting with a carpenter or a brick mason could have waited until morning.

"Completing the work is not the problem, sir. It's your…requirement for this particular piece that concerns me. I beg you to look at these pattern books I've brought once again and choose a style that is more…appropriate, if you will."

Pattern books? Cassie frowned. So the tradesman was an upholsterer?

"I perused your books and decided on the design for the new bed over a week ago. You said you'd begin at once, ordering the hangings and so forth. Is it only the slight modification I require you to make that seems to be an issue?"

"Yes, sir, that is the case, although I would hardly agree with the term 'slight.' I admit I've only seen such a thing once before, when I apprenticed, and it was intended for a woman of, shall I say…questionable virtue?"

Cassie clapped her hand over her mouth to cover a gasp of surprise that would surely give away her presence just outside the library door. She stepped back, grateful for the wood paneled wall there to support her.

"The woman who will sleep in this particular bed, Mr. Henderson, is none of your concern." Mr. Ashton's tone was firm. "Your commission is simply to build it."

There was only one possible explanation for his words and shock coursed through Cassie as she grasped his meaning. The reality hit her with the same force as the strong wind gusting outside in the freezing December night. Her fiancé was at that moment ordering a bed and arranging for its delivery, but it was not meant for her.

They weren't even married yet and he was already setting up a residence for a mistress.

\* \* \*

Cassie fled upstairs, her hands clenched in anger. She must leave this house at once, before she fell into a sobbing fit.

She found Mr. and Mrs. Galesworthy and her parents seated comfortably near the drawing room fire. They turned as one when Cassie practically tumbled through the door and stopped just short of falling onto the Aubusson carpet at their feet.

"My dear!" Mrs. Galesworthy jumped to her feet, looking alarmed. "Whatever is the matter? You seem… ill."

Not prone to histrionics, Cassie seized on the lady's opinion and saw the opportunity to use it to escape. "I am afraid…" she began, then drew in a deep, shuddering breath. "That I am indeed suddenly quite unwell. I am most grateful you have made us feel welcome here tonight, but—" She turned to her father, for her mother would make any excuse to force her to stay. "Please, Papa, take me home at once?"

To his credit, her father agreed and Cassie hated being the cause of the worried look he now wore. Her mother tried to delay, saying they must remain until Mr. Ashton rejoined them, at least to say a proper farewell, but her father overruled her. He made their apologies and they were downstairs and out the door as soon as their cloaks could be fetched and their carriage brought round.

As the horses set off, Cassie turned away and sank back against the plush seat of the coach, unable to bear the sight of Mr. Ashton's puzzled face as he stood at the front window of the library, witnessing their hasty departure.

\* \* \*

"She was ill, you say?" John gripped the mantle, his gaze fixed on the dying fire. "Please assure me, Margaret, that it didn't seem to be a serious malady."

"I wouldn't be too concerned. It was likely only the lateness of the hour, and Miss Jennings did seem a bit overtired to me."

"Overwhelmed might be more like it," Duncan spoke in a matter-of-fact tone. "What with that shrewish mother ordering her about and an unexpected engagement foisted upon her, it's a wonder to me the poor girl could swallow a bite of dinner or form a coherent sentence."

"I don't understand. Isn't this how such things are normally arranged?"

"It's the nineteenth century, Ashton. A gentleman courts the lady first these days, not her father."

"Have I gone about it the wrong way then, and ruined it?" The thought of losing Cassandra made John's insides tremble as violently as when he was a schoolboy and required to recite the soliloquy from *Hamlet*. "What if she calls off the engagement—?"

"Go see her tomorrow and speak to her alone," Margaret urged. "You must realize what she faces. She will acquire a husband she barely knows, a new home to be mistress of, and a change in everything she is accustomed to and comfortable with."

*Of course. How could I have been so dense?* He would call on his bride-to-be on the morrow, and see her every day after that if need be, to put her at ease and secure her good opinion.

\* \* \*

Cassie watched from her upstairs bedroom window the following morning as Mr. Ashton left after paying a short call. She'd wondered if he would, but told herself she didn't care if he did. Mama had summoned her, of course, but Cassie sent word back with the footman that the headache persisted and she could not come.

Elizabeth sighed as she craned her neck for a better view of her sister's intended. The girl grew as fast as summer grass and was now only a head shorter than Cassie. "Oh, he's beautiful. Every lady will be jealous and want a husband as handsome as yours, Cass."

"Eliza, please. 'Tis not proper to say such things." From what Cassie had overheard last night, it seemed she really would have to share Mr. Ashton with at least one other women. The idea of it cut through her like a sharp knife. "Why aren't you busy with Miss Parton and your studies?"

"She always needs to rest after my French lesson. I believe my atrocious grammar actually makes her ill."

The bedroom door swung open and their mother stood there, her look stern and unforgiving. "Elizabeth, return to the schoolroom at once."

"Yes, Mama." Eliza possessed more spirit than Cassie, but the girl knew when not to argue. She cast a sympathetic glance Cassie's way as she left.

"You could not be bothered to make your fiancé feel welcome in our home." Her mother closed the door behind her. "Tomorrow at church, you will behave as you should, Cassandra. I've also invited Mr. Ashton and the Galesworthy family to join us Tuesday night for Christmas Eve dinner and carol singing. You must impress them with how well you play the pianoforte."

"Mama, you don't understand. Last night, I heard him say—"

"Men say a great many things, daughter, and you would be wise to disregard most of them. Remember that it's not what they say that matters, it is what they do."

* * *

Services on Sunday morning at St. George's in Hanover Square strained Cassie's nerves even further. Mr. Ashton occupied the pew directly behind them and she could feel him watching her. After the sermon concluded, he walked out with them, past the tall Corinthian columns and down the steps, commenting on the fineness of the day.

"I am most grateful to see you looking well, Miss Jennings," he said with a warm smile. "I was quite concerned for you." He trailed his gloved fingertips across her arm briefly but in a most intimate way before continuing, seeming not to notice her sharp intake of breath as that strange feeling rushed through her again. "I pray you'll be as pleased as I am that I've spoken with the bishop and procured the special license. At times I still cannot believe you shall meet me there at the altar a week from Saturday."

He turned then to motion to his driver and, as his carriage rolled away moments later, a strange mix of joy and sadness washed over her.

Mr. Ashton was undoubtedly practised in love-making, and there would likely soon be children to adore and care for. But would any of that help her forget that when he left her, he would go to his mistress's arms, in a bed he'd had crafted especially for the illicit hours they would spend together?

Fitting for a new gown for the wedding day at the dressmaker's took hours on Monday. Cassie and her mother returned to find that Mr. Ashton had called again, leaving behind only his card.

Final preparations for Christmas Eve began in earnest at dawn the following morning, with evergreen boughs and sprigs of holly brought into the house and arranged in the front hall and up the staircase for deco-ration. Mama closeted herself with Cook to plan for the increase in the number of guests. The size of the plum pudding was a great concern. Since it was a family evening, with the children invited, it would be informal, with meat, savories, vegetables and pies on the dining room sideboard and the drawing room readied for games and music.

Cassie dressed for the evening with a heavy heart. She would speak plainly with Mr. Ashton tonight and tell him what she'd overheard. She would not embarrass him in front of their families, but she needed a plan to lure him away and be alone with him.

Mr. and Mrs. Galesworthy arrived first, bringing their twelve-year-old twins, Henry and Edward. Henry had his father's paler coloring and ready smile, while Edward looked to be a younger version of Mr. Ashton, with more handsome features and dark hair. They made proper bows to the Jenningses, regarded Cassie with great curiosity, and seemed particularly entranced to meet "Miss Elizabeth." Cassie tried not to laugh when Eliza sighed in resignation as the boys followed her to the dining room like eager puppies.

Mr. Ashton came in fifteen minutes later with the explanation that his favorite horse had come up lame and he'd had to order his carriage fetched instead.

"Oh, tosh, you're not late at all," Mrs. Jennings assured him as the butler took his hat, coat and gloves. The sight of him in his well-cut evening clothes and neatly tied cravat made it hard for Cassie to breathe. She'd never wanted anything, much less anyone, so much in her entire life. She was grateful, for once, when her mother continued to speak. "Do come and fill a plate, Mr. Ashton. I hope I've had some of your favourites prepared. Why, it was quite a chore to—"

"Uncle John!" Edward raced across the front hall to greet him and stumbled to a stop. "Mrs. Jennings, may we begin the games now? I wish to show Miss Elizabeth how I can snatch the raisins out of the flames in Snapdragon more quickly than my brother can."

"Heavens, we shall have none of that, young man!" Mrs. Jennings shuddered. "Believe me, I'm not in the habit of helping any guests in my home set themselves on fire."

Mr. Ashton pulled his nephew close. Cassie saw how he rested his strong hands on the boy's shoulders with evident affection. "We'll be content with carol singing or charades or whatever is planned for the evening, won't we, Edward?" He glanced at Cassie with a hint of a smile. "'Tis Christmas, after all, a time to be happy and thankful. For myself, tonight, I am both."

Before carols commenced, punch with brandy was fetched for the adults, along with tea for Eliza, and milk for the Galesworthy twins. "Deck the Halls" led to "Here We Come a-Wassailing." After several cups of the punch, even Cassie's father joined in on "Adestes Fideles" and "I Saw Three Ships Come Sailing In". Cassie declared herself quite done in at that point and asked Eliza to take over on the pianoforte. The younger sister was not as talented or well practised, but she played the simpler songs well enough to not be an embarrassment.

Cassie took a cup of the fortified wine and left the drawing room as the strains of "The First Noel" began. *Good, five verses. Plenty of time for Mr. Ashton to come in search of me, if he intends to do so.*

A footman in the front hall stepped forward, but she waved him off and proceeded to the now empty dining room, where she helped herself to a small plate of gingerbread. Her mother declared it too indulgent to be a common treat, but Cassie loved the flavour, and looked forward to enjoying it during the Yule season.

She'd be Mrs. Ashton next year, celebrating the holiday with his family's traditions, whatever they might be. The uncertainty of that future threatened to overwhelm her yet again, but she pushed her fears away. If Mr. Ashton followed her to the dining room, they would have more important matters to discuss that night than gingerbread.

\* \* \*

By the middle of the carol, when "the Wise Men came from country far," John wondered where Cassandra had disappeared to. Standing at the rear of the group assembled around the pianoforte, he slipped away and went to look for her. His plan to see his fiancée and convince her of his affections had so far been less than successful.

He paused at the open door to the dining room and found her there, seated alone, with no servant in sight. For once, she looked relaxed, her eyes closed as she put the last bite of a piece of gingerbread in her mouth, then licked the crumbs from her fingertips and sighed in pleasure, obviously savouring the taste. Her hair shone in the candlelight, making her an entrancing sight to behold.

He started to speak, then realized he first had to breathe again. "Miss Jennings." He found his voice at last, even if it came out barely a whisper.

Her eyes flew open and she gasped, bolting upright in her chair. "Mr. Ashton, I'm sorry, I—"

"Don't." He held up his hand to stall her as he advanced into the room. "You have no reason to apologize. Once we're married, if you wish to eat gingerbread every day of the year, you may do so."

She stood then with a sway and grabbed the table for support. "I fear the wine has gone straight to my head, sir."

He covered the distance between them in seconds and pulled her against him, afraid she might fall if he did not. She turned her face up to his, looking startled.

Whether it was the two cups of the fortified punch he'd had or simply the opportunity, he would never know, but he would kiss her now or die in the attempt. He touched his mouth to hers gently and felt her go pliant in his embrace. He traced her delicate skin with just the tip of his tongue, finding her lips warm and tinged with spice.

She didn't resist, so he went deeper, exploring, teasing, hoping for and finally hearing a soft moan from her in response. She slid her hands up his chest and around his neck, pulling him closer.

A moment later, with his last ounce of self-control, he broke away. They were, after all, in her parents' home and might be discovered at any moment. "We cannot," he managed to say at last, hating the look of hurt and confusion on her face and loathing himself even more for putting it there. "I will not have it said we began with a scandal. Our lifetime together deserves a better start than that."

* * *

At midnight, after their guests had departed, Christmas Eve turned to Christmas Day, and Cassie sat before the fireplace in her bedchamber, bewildered. She knew not what to think of Mr. Ashton's behavior or, for that matter, her own.

He'd looked for her, as she'd hoped he would, but instead of confronting him about the bed he'd ordered for a mistress, she'd fallen into his arms without a thought. Shivers of delight had raced down her spine as he held her and his kiss had made her forget the world and everyone else in it.

After they'd pulled apart, he'd made sure she was seated and steady again, then had called for the footman and ordered him to bring her a large cup of strong coffee. He'd left her with a promise that they'd meet again soon.

Not marrying him was not an option, as her feelings were too strong. She could imagine no future without John Ashton as her husband. But could she hope to harden her heart sufficiently to survive years of his leaving her to be with another?

She slept little and rose at dawn to breakfast and dress for church, intending to focus on the sermon instead of Mr. Ashton. Her preparation, however, proved unnecessary, for he did not attend.

"Called away?" Mrs. Jennings repeated Mrs. Galesworthy's explanation for her brother's absence. "What in the world could be so urgent in Sussex to cause him to need to travel on this holiest of days?"

Mrs. Galesworthy spoke of a fire in the kitchen of the family estate. "The agent wrote that damage to the property was not extensive, but our family cook was injured. My brother felt it necessary to ensure she received the proper care and also arrange for the repairs himself." She laid a gloved hand on Cassie's arm with a kind look. "Don't worry, my dear. John will return in plenty of time for the wedding."

That he did, and at eleven o'clock in the morning on the fourth of January, he stood tall and handsome next to Cassie at the altar of St. George's, repeating his marriage vows in a reverent tone she would never have believed him capable of. Becoming his wife would be the most natural, thrilling and perfect event of her life.

If not for the mistress…

\* \* \*

The wedding feast seemed interminable to John and it was with a great sense of relief that he saw his own family and the Jenningses finally take their leave just before dark. He heard Mrs. Jennings whisper to her daughter, "Do your best," although he had no idea to what she referred. Mr. Jennings kissed Cassie on the cheek and turned toward the door, wiping his eyes.

"I shall await you, Mr. Ashton." Cassie moved away at once. "I'm sure my maid has my trunks unpacked by now."

He wanted to say something, but he let her go. Their first real conversation as husband and wife should be private, and not conducted in the entry hall with Christmas greenery still draped all around, and servants within earshot. He retreated to the library and poured a brandy, surprised that his hand trembled as he raised the glass.

What was wrong with him? He knew the ways of love, indeed had bedded a dozen women in his time. *Ah, but,* his conscience reminded him, *you've never gone to bed with your wife.*

After a quarter hour, during which he paced and debated how best to approach the lovely, innocent young woman he'd married, he followed her upstairs.

\* \* \*

Molly helped Cassie change into a nightgown with delicate Brussels lace sleeves, then unpinned her hair and brushed it till it flowed around her shoulder in soft waves. Cassie dismissed the maid until morning and stepped through the door leading from her private dressing and sitting rooms to the bedchamber she would share with her husband.

Winter darkness had settled. Candles flickered from the fireplace mantel, throwing fingers of light throughout the large room. Thick draperies covered the two tall windows, keeping out the chill of early January frost. A massive four-poster bed sat between the windows, dressed with fine linens and hung with blue silk damask curtains pulled back and tied in place.

Cassie moved toward the fire, hugging herself and shivering despite its warmth. The door on the opposite side of the room opened a moment later and Mr. Ashton came in on bare feet. His coat, vest and cravat were gone, and his shirt open. He paused a second, making her feel self-conscious as he took in the sight of her. He stepped forward and brushed her hair back, then leaned down and pressed his lips to the delicate skin of her neck.

She gasped at his touch. Then, without thinking, she tilted her head away to grant him easier access. He trailed kisses down her throat, untied the silk strings of her nightgown, and continued to explore. She clutched his shoulders, experiencing again those same strange jolts she now recognized as her desire for him.

"Mr. Ashton, you…quite overwhelm me."

He raised his head then, the flames from the hearth reflected in his dark eyes. "Cassandra, 'Mr. Ashton' will do in the drawing room, I suppose, but here, when we are alone, I am John."

"Of course. John."

"Do you like the bed I had made for us? I chose the fabric because it matches your beautiful eyes."

She frowned, perplexed, and glanced at the four-poster. "This is the bed you left us at dinner to speak to that tradesman, Mr. Henderson, about?"

"Yes." Now it was his turn to look confused. "How did you know his name?"

*In for a penny, in for a pound,* as Miss Parton often quoted. "I wanted to speak with you that evening, so I came downstairs. I overheard you in discussion with him in the library. He said the bed you'd ordered must be intended for a woman of…questionable virtue. I'm afraid I assumed the worst."

"The worst?"

"Yes. I believed that, even as you planned our wedding, you were also setting up an establishment for…a mistress."

His eyebrows rose in surprise, then he startled her with a bark of laughter. "My dear, keeping a smart and beautiful wife happy is occupation enough for any one man to handle, if done properly. I can assure you, I have no lightskirt now and no intention of ever acquiring one."

She blushed at his compliments to her and at his frank speech. "Then why not tell us that you were commissioning such a fine new piece?"

He took her hand and led her to the side of the bed. "Cassandra—"

"If I am to call you John, then I must be Cassie."

"Very well, Cassie it is." He dropped a kiss on the tip of her nose. "I said nothing before and now I must insist that no one else ever discovers the secret of this particular bed because it is meant for us alone. Let me show you."

He moved one layer of the hangings out of the way, exposing two hidden cords. He tugged gently on one, causing the fabric under the canopy to gather and gradually be drawn toward the foot of the bed. Underneath, safely secured by strips of wood nailed to the canopy frame, was a mirror.

Cassie gazed at it in astonishment, then realized with a rush the intention of it. "No, I would never tell anyone about this."

"Cassie, come here." John whispered as he gathered her into his arms. "I've admired you since the first night we met and, over the last few weeks, I've come to love you, as well. I want to make love to you night after night, until the coming of children prevents it. If the mirror makes you uncomfortable, we can cover it, but I hope someday you'll want to explore with me all the joy that our hours together can bring."

She looked into his eyes and found honesty, acceptance and trust there. "I have one question, John. In your country house—"

"Our house," he corrected her. "You shall see it very soon."

"Yes, our house. Is there such a bed there, as well?" Encouraged by the assurance of his love for her, she pressed closer to him, feeling his body grow hard against hers.

"An old one," he finally managed to say, though not without some difficulty, it seemed. "It belonged to my parents. It wasn't until after they both passed a few years ago that I discovered their secret."

"And will that be our bed?"

"No. I thought we would decide on new furniture together. It can all be as ordinary as a warm summer's day if that's what you wish."

Cassie glanced up. "No, I believe I'd like another new one just like this. Do you think Mr. Henderson could be prevailed upon to craft it and bring it to us in Sussex?"

Her new husband laughed in surprise, a sound that brought delight to her heart. "I was not aware I'd married such a bold woman, Mrs. Ashton."

"Well, you have, sir. Your love has given me courage. I suggest you get used to the idea."

"Indeed, I shall. With great pleasure."

Christmas was truly a season for miracles, granting her this amazing man to share her life with. She kissed him until they were both quite breathless, then pulled him down on the bed with her. She gazed up at the reflection of the two of them as he gently slipped the nightgown off her shoulders and brushed his lips over the swell of her breasts.

Nothing in her life had ever felt so wonderful and so right, and Cassie surrendered with a happy sigh. "I love you, John Ashton."

# About the Author

Kadee McDonald writes traditional Regency romance and was a Top Pick at the AReCafe. Her titles are available at most online retailers. She's a native Texan, supports pet rescue and animal rights, and is currently on the staff of two black cats. Kadee enjoys connecting with readers at  www.KadeeMcDonald.com

# Ghosted: Christmas Present

## By Roxann Breazile

"**O**h, my gawd. You are stupid, stupid, stupid."

I know. It wasn't the most positive self-talk. *But really!* As I rhythmically thumped my head on the steering wheel of my hopelessly stuck car, the contents of my purse emptied on the passenger seat, I knew myself to be my own worst enemy. Here I sat, trapped in the sludgy mud a hundred yards from the quaint farmhouse belonging to my ex-boyfriend's family, with my cell phone charging in my kitchen, ten miles away, instead of sitting in my pocket or in my purse. I was miles from anywhere on a cold, snowy Christmas Eve. And it was about to get worse.

The nearest neighbor lived almost a mile away, so my only option was to walk up to his family's front door and ask them to let me use their phone to call a tow truck. *Yay! Outstanding.*

I could only pray that Patrick was somewhere else. His mother already thought I was an ignorant hick, and his father kept his opinions to himself. He might have even liked me a little a one time, but I felt pretty sure that train had left the station.

I scooped everything back into my purse, pulled on my hat, scarf and mittens, and got out of the car. Squishy, cold, wet mud instantly froze my feet, even through my heavy-duty boots. But I persevered, and after fourteen exquisitely careful steps was rewarded with the feel of asphalt under my feet. I could have felt my relief at remaining upright down to my toes, if they weren't frozen numb, so I had to content myself with trying to stamp feeling back into them, while stamping off as much of the mud as possible.

In the surprisingly bright light of the full moon, I could see the path of tire tracks leading up the driveway to the farmhouse. Patrick's mom called it the Pond House. I thanked God that the pond was quite a way from the road, because with my luck I would have ended up there instead of the shallow muddy ditch.

Hitching my purse higher on my shoulder, I marched with determination to the cheerfully decorated home. Last year, I had been Patrick's guest and loved the extravagant lights, toys and gadgets. Their house was strewn with every kitschy Christmas-themed object known to mankind. Pot holders, tea towels, singing Santa dolls, pine tree candles, and at least four different kinds of Nativity scenes, including a chocolate one. Which was bizarre, because who eats the holy family? But apparently, there is a Nativity candy mold, so you can make your own. I ate the angel and the Star of Bethlehem, but no way was I going to pop the Baby Jesus in my mouth.

The snow in the tracks wasn't the kind of crispy snow that people think of with a white Christmas. It was gray and soft as biscuit dough to walk on. I followed the tracks to where they veered off towards the barn. Fortunately, the path through the front yard to the porch had been shoveled and the light-colored ribbon of concrete reflected the moonlight and pointed like a runway to the house. The entire front of the farmhouse was ablaze with Christmas lights. Every window was bordered in those big-bulbed lights in alternating red and green. White icicle lights hung from the eaves, a huge lit wreath adorned the door, and through the big picture window, I could see the Christmas tree with twice as many lights as any tree I had ever had, and I really like lights. Last year, this had been a fantasy come to life. But that was before everything turned to crap...before I screwed everything up.

With all the enthusiasm of a dog headed to the vet's clinic, I made my way to the house. My foot lifted to take the first step up to the porch, but for the life of me, I couldn't force myself to put it down. This was a mistake. A big, fat, giant mistake. What if Patrick was there? What could I possibly say? *Oh, hey, Patrick. Long time, no see. I was just in the neighborhood, ten miles from anywhere, gazing lovingly at your parent's Christmas decorations, like some kind of crazy stalker chick. I'm sure you can get a restraining order come Monday.*

But what the heck else could I do? I already knew the nearest house was a mile away. It had sure seemed like a good idea when I started out. Just going to drive around looking at people's Christmas lights. I shook my head, closing my eyes to try and shut the truth out of my own head. I knew when I pulled away from the curb at home that I was going to end up here, looking at *these* Christmas lights, dreaming about what could have been, if I hadn't been a complete, frickin' idiot. Time to suck it up and show myself as the fool I had been all along.

Emboldened with *that* encouraging pep talk, I climbed the steps. Faced with the mondo-sized wreath that covered most of the door, I tried to remember if the doorbell worked. I couldn't remember that specific detail, but I did recall that Patrick's mom was an anal retentive control freak. Lauren Murphy would never allow anything to remain broken on her house. I pushed the doorbell and waited. Each second ticked off like a century, and I could feel the flush rising up my neck, despite the cold. Yeah, that's why they call folks like me rednecks. *Great.*

I heard the deadbolt click open, followed by a spill of light, golden and warm. Patrick stood in the open doorway. Of course.

I could have sworn he swayed a bit when he recognized me. But that was ridiculous.

"Callie?" His voice was as dark and silky as really awesome, expensive chocolate.

I closed my eyes for a moment. God, I forgot how his voice felt. Reopening my eyes, I looked at a spot just above his left shoulder. "Hey." I jerked my head toward the road. "My car's stuck and I accidentally left my phone at home. Can I use your phone?"

He immediately reached for his jeans pocket. "Yeah, sure. C'mon in. It's cold."

I scooted in past him, just enough to let him shut the door, but ready to bolt at any moment. He unlocked the phone and handed it to me. It was warm from his body. Trying not to let the thought of what body parts that phone had just been near distract me, I used my teeth to remove my mitten, so I could open the Google app.

*Yeah, smooth.* At the ex's house with a bright pink mitten hanging from my mouth. I shoved the mitten into my pocket, and spoke in a search for towing companies in Columbus, Ohio. Picking the first one, I put the phone to my ear and waited for the line to connect. I stared at Patrick's shoes, black and gray Nikes, and did my best to ignore his cologne. All I wanted to do was wrap my five foot two frame around his long, lean body and squeeze him like a starving python.

The voice in my ear said the name of the towing company twice before it sunk in that it was my time to talk.

I only had to cough once, before my heart, inconveniently lodged in my throat, allowed me to speak. "I need a tow out just off Route 16."

"Are you in a safe place, miss?" the towing guy asked.

I don't think he intended it as an existential question. Safe...safe from what? Patrick? Myself?

I made the mistake of glancing up at that moment and became ensnared by Patrick's sage green eyes. God, I loved his eyes.

Returning my gaze to the floor, I said, "Yes, I'm in a safe place. I'm in a house nearby. My car is just stuck. It doesn't need towed anywhere, except out of a muddy ditch."

"Unfortunately, it's going to take us a couple hours to get out to you. It's been crazy tonight."

"It'll take that long for someone to get out here?" *Terrific.*

"I apologize for the wait. Would you like to contact another company, or schedule the tow with us now?"

"I'll schedule it now." I gave the man the address and Patrick's phone number.

I handed Patrick back his phone, realizing with a start that I hadn't laid eyes on him since August. Three months. But, of course, I knew exactly how long it had been; I'd thought of him constantly every day of those three months.

"Well, hey! Merry almost Christmas. This is awkward as shit." I try not to swear as a rule, but, well, there was no other word that seemed to fit the occasion.

Patrick chuckled, his laugh low and smoky, almost as sexy as his speaking voice. "Yeah, it is. From your side of the conversation, it sounded like it's going to be a while before the tow truck can get out here. Can I take your coat?"

I hesitated too long. Another question not intended to require a great deal of thought, but it brought me up short just the same.

"You *are* in a safe place, Callie."

*Damn.* That made me want to cry.

"Yeah. You can take my coat." I shoved my other mitten in a pocket, snatched off my hat and pocketed it, feeling the electrified strands of my bone-straight hair lift from my head. After putting my purse on the floor, I unzipped my coat and shrugged out of it. It was then that I realized we matched. Jeans and olive-colored sweaters.

"We match. You're going to have to change." I fell into the trap of our long-standing inside joke.

He laughed again, taking my coat and tossing it over one shoulder before reaching to gently unwrap the scarf from my neck and smooth down a few of the fly-away strands of my hair. I was grateful that he immediately turned to the nearby coat rack, because the tears were threatening again.

"Can I get you anything to drink? Green tea, Diet Coke?"

"Some tea would be nice."

"It'll just take a minute. Why don't you relax in the living room?" He lifted his chin toward the living room entry about four feet away and headed in the opposite direction through the dining room to the kitchen.

I stood immobile, stuck in my memories just as hopelessly as my car was stuck in the mud. The tires of my mind spun uselessly.

It had been three months since I cut him completely out of my life. No texts, no voicemail. I deleted my Twitter account and deserted Facebook like it carried a disease. Not for anything he did, but because I needed to carry out the most jacked-up preemptive attack in history. I hurt him before he could destroy me, and there I stood in his home, while he fixed me a cup of tea.

Lacking anything else to do, I picked up my purse, walked into the living room, and was struck dumbfounded by what I saw.

If I thought last year's decorations were over the top, the Murphy Yuletide offerings this year were insane. Dominating the display were the train sets. Plural. The tracks for the largest train set rested on shelves that encircled the room about eighteen inches from the ceiling. A more intricate set perched on a large circular table and wound through and around a miniature Christmas village that glowed with the light from tiny street lamps and itty-bitty interior house lights. The third set encircled the Christmas tree in a wide orbit that allowed for a dozen or more animated Santas, reindeer and elves to sit between the tracks and the tree.

The tree was simple in comparison to the rest of the room with its profuse multicolored twinkle lights and white hand-crocheted snowflake ornaments. I knew they were handmade, because I had made them.

Drawn to them, I walked mesmerized and leaned over the train set to touch one. A feeling rattled around inside my hollowed-out heart, knocking me off balance. Why had he kept them?

"What do you think?" Patrick's question made me jump.

With as much nonchalance as I could manage, I walked over to the sofa and tossed my purse into one corner of it. "I think this is what happens when an electrical engineer and his mother have too much time on their hands." I smiled, hoping he didn't think I was being bitchy.

He responded with a grin and a nod, before following me to give me a mug of jasmine green tea. I inhaled the fragrant steam.

"It smells good. Thanks."

"You're welcome. And I have to take all the credit for the decorations this year. My parents have been in Barbados for the past two and a half weeks."

"Really? I'm surprised. Your mother always seemed like a total workaholic."

"She is, but my dad can be persuasive when he puts his mind to it."

"Huh." I didn't know what else to say that wouldn't be...too much. I had no desire to talk about his mother. I don't know why I even brought her up, except for the obvious reason. The Voldemort reason...the Reason that Cannot Be Named.

We stood in awkward silence. Maybe I could just run away, or spontaneously combust. Anything, other than stand there.

"So, what brings you out this way?" Patrick asked, gently, with no discernible anger or resentment.

"I was just conducting my yearly Christmas light pilgrimage." That at least was partly true. I left out the part that I only really had one destination, this house.

"How did I do? Did I rate a GTF?"

It was my turn to laugh, surprised he remembered my Christmas light judging awards. "Oh yeah, you definitely have 'Gone Too Far'."

"Did you decorate this year?"

"I give myself an 'E for Effort', but nothing like this." I waved my hand around the room.

"I was hoping you'd come by. Last Christmas was good."

"Yeah." Last Christmas had been a slice of heaven.

We both became fascinated with reexamining his Christmas decorations. I walked back over to the tree and lightly ran my finger over one of the crocheted snowflakes. The shimmery white yarn reflected the colorful lights. I could see that they had held up well to sitting in storage from last year.

"I made a killing on Etsy selling these this year."

"Did you? That's cool."

"I branched out and made some with a gold metallic yarn and some in a silvery blue color. The blue was my favorite, but it didn't sell as well as the white or the gold. I sold over a thousand pieces."

"Wow, that's a lot of crocheting."

The poor guy, his eyes were probably glazing over, but I couldn't meet them anyway, so he would just have to suffer. "It's not too tough. I've done so many that I can practically do them in my sleep. I crochet a couple during my lunch and breaks, and then a few more after work."

Okay, now I was boring myself.

I finally turned back to look at him. And, *damn*, he still looked like an Irish Adam Levine. Lean, almost skinny, but a total hardbody and sexy as hell with his wavy reddish brown hair cut short and his permanent five o'clock shadow. "How are things at solid state and photonics land?"

"I got my Masters, so now I'm working on my Ph.D."

"Congratulations. I take it you're still loving life at the labs."

"Yeah, But it's completely different now that I'm doing my own research, on my own designs. I thought I was working independently before, but this is a whole new level."

I thought about how much I used to know about his work. He's eighteen kinds of intelligent, but I used to feel pretty good that I could follow a lot of what he said. Contrary to his mother's opinion of me, I'm not stupid—I'm just not well educated. But after three months I didn't think I could process the details of his new work.

"I'm sure you'll kick butt." I tried to smile at him, but couldn't quite manage it. I know I sounded like a total jerk, because that was obviously an "I'm done with this topic" thing to say. But I didn't want to feel dumb if he tried to pick up where we left off.

I reached for my phone to check the time and remembered with a grimace that it was busy charging at home, ten miles away.

Patrick pulled out his phone. "It's 8:39."

"Thanks. The tow truck guy said it could be a couple hours. Is that okay with you? Uh, for me to hang out that long?"

"Yeah, sure," he agreed readily. "I've been wanting to talk to you, well, since…" He trailed off after banging straight into the Reason that Cannot Be Named.

"Let's not go there, Patrick." I hoped he could recognize the sound of all my walls grinding into defensive positions.

"We need to go there." It was obvious he missed the warning tone in my voice. "I tried to be there for you, to explain what my mom meant, to apologize, but you ghosted me." I could see the sincerity in his face. I knew that he wanted to give me the benefit of the doubt and let me explain why I had up and left him without a trace.

It would have been kinder of him to stab an ice pick into my chest, because I didn't deserve his understanding. I was the villain in this movie, and I never wanted him to figure that out.

This was why I should have stayed in the damn car.

The only sound that could make its way past my lips was a strangled gasp, the inarticulate admission of my bottomless pain. I set the mug down on the end table, hard. Harder than I meant to. I grabbed my purse and retreated backwards, so I could move around the coffee table, get to the front door.

Somehow I did manage to reach the door first. Snatching my coat and scarf from the coat tree, I reached up to flip the deadbolt. I only pulled the door open a couple inches before his hand appeared over my head to slam the door shut.

Suddenly furious, I spun around and pushed him hard in the center of his chest with both hands.

"Goddammit, Patrick!" My curse fell into a weird silence between us. I don't think I had ever laid a hand on anyone like that before, not even when I was a kid. I'm not sure who was more surprised.

Patrick lifted his hands in a gesture of surrender. "You can't go," he said, contradicting his body language.

"I surely can." My voice came out a mix of gravel and broken glass.

"Seriously. It's cold. Even with your coat, I can't allow you to sit freezing in your car half the night."

"Fuck you! It's not about what you allow."

I stalked up to him and pushed him again. "I'm in charge of my life. You don't get a say. And we don't need to talk and you don't need to explain shit to me."

He opened his mouth to speak.

"You are going to shut up, now. And I'm going to get my things and get out of here. This was a giant fucking mistake."

"Callie, I'm sorry you lost the baby," he blurted out. *Oh, shit.*

That quick, I got sucked into an all-too-familiar vortex of grief and guilt. So much so, I felt like I was having a goddamned out of body experience. I could see my body deflate like a balloon toy with a slow leak. I wasn't going to collapse all at once, but inevitably, I was going to lose whatever allowed me to keep standing. I clutched my coat to my middle as I bent forward with the pain.

I just wanted to disappear, collapse in on myself like a dying star surrenders to gravity and becomes a black hole.

But instead of folding, I got mad. Really mad. Fury stiffened my spine. I snapped up straight like one of those creepy undead horror flick zombies that move too quickly and all weird.

"Well, I feel so much better that you're sorry I lost the baby. It wasn't *the* baby. It was *my* baby...*our* baby. And I'm way more than sorry about losing *my* baby."

There was some satisfaction in watching him lose color, get tight around the lips, like he does when he's emotional. There's no defense like a good offense, and he had gotten way too close to the Reason that Cannot Be Named. I needed him off balance, because I was a mile off my center and lashing out wildly.

I could hear my yoga instructor's voice in my head telling me to connect with my spirit. To dwell on my innate goodness. *Christ.* Her mouth would be hanging open if she had seen me in the last three minutes.

Calmer now, I looked up at him. "There's a reason why I didn't take your calls, or listen to your voicemails, or read your texts. You and your family are toxic to me."

He visibly reacted to that, his eyebrows creased into a frowning vee shape.

"Maybe it was me," I went on, trying to soften the whole toxic comment, which was totally unfair. I was the toxic one. "Or maybe it would be the same for anyone who tried to enter your sacred circle."

He cocked his head, looking at me like I was a baffling experiment result. It was too clinical for my comfort.

"I'm going to go now. I shouldn't have come here."

"Callie, it's still freezing out there. Stay. We'll talk about the weather, or watch a movie, or something. Nothing heavy. I promise."

He looked defeated. It wasn't a good fit for him. Even though he's four years younger than me, I had gotten used to his strength in the face of adversity, his relentless optimism.

This is what my crappy decisions had brought us to. I'm sure I looked pretty defeated at that moment, too.

"Let's watch TV or a movie together like we used to."

I wanted to stay, to be like we were one more time. Last Christmas glowed brightly in my memory. For an incredibly lovely moment in time, I stood as part of a family, like I was worthy of that privilege. I longed to recapture that feeling.

Earlier in the day I'd almost called him, but decided it felt too weird to reach out to him on Christmas Eve. Kind of like only going to church at Easter and Christmas, it didn't seem like the right thing to do.

I called Tracy instead, who told me once again, loudly and clearly, as only a best friend can, that she thought I was nuts. She was so good to me after I lost the baby, supporting me even when she told me that I should be letting Patrick be there for me.

"Please?" His quiet question wrapped itself around me. He was a good man, too good for me, but I wasn't strong enough to walk away from him at that moment.

I nodded.

I followed him into the family room at the back of the house. It was colder back here courtesy of a large picture window that looked out onto the snow-covered backyard. The full moon's light reflected off the snow, making the landscape appear almost surreal in its wintry perfection. I gazed outside for long moments, avoiding even thinking about the door to my left that led to the kitchen. The Voldemort reason began in that seemingly innocent room.

I jerked my attention back to Patrick.

He was crouched in front of a low shelving unit beneath the big-screen TV, looking at rows of DVDs. "Of course, we've got all the Harry Potter movies." He had grown up with the movies, but I love them just as much, maybe more so, because it was something we shared. "If you want a traditional Christmas movie, there's *Bad Santa.*"

I smiled at his joke, or at least I moved my lips into something that looked like a smile. "How about some music?"

"Christmas music?"

"Sure."

He picked up a remote and pointed it at the stereo. A symphonic version of "Hark! the Herald Angels Sing" filled the air.

I sat down at the beige L-shaped sectional, feeling awkward with my booted feet firmly planted on the floor. I always put my feet up.

"Feel free to take your boots off." He smiled suddenly. "I've got something for you."

I watched as he left the room and came back, holding a small red and green gift bag. I'm sure my face was the textbook example of total dismay.

"Relax." He chuckled as he knelt down in front of me. "It's a pair of fuzzy socks, Cal. I saw them in the store last week and they reminded me of you."

Without asking, he gripped my right boot and pulled it off of me, and did the same with the left. Like a parent with a reluctant toddler, he stripped off my plain black knee-highs and put on the bright pink fuzzy socks.

I don't know why I just sat there and let him do this, but it comforted me in some strange way. So few people have ever taken care of me...did things that I'm perfectly capable of doing myself. I can't say I encourage that much. Years in the foster care system taught me to be self-sufficient.

"Let's try the beverage thing again." He smiled, straightening. "I'm getting some coffee. Still green tea for you?"

I nodded, not trusting my voice. How long could I indulge in this fantasy? I always thought it was weird how everyone faked happiness on Christmas. Even in totally messed up situations, I found that people went out of their way to maintain the fiction of a merry Christmas. I curled my fuzzy sock-clad feet underneath me and covered my legs with a velour throw. Patrick had left the door to the kitchen open and I caught glimpses of him as he prepared his coffee and my tea.

My mind reached back to late August, the day we told his parents I was pregnant. We had only found out a few days before that our birth control strategy of mini-pill and admittedly intermittent condom use had failed.

The farmhouse felt completely different in the summertime, like it was in an alternate universe at Christmastime. The big trees completely shaded the back of the house, so I remembered feeling a little chilly in my tank top and shorts. Patrick was out at the barbeque with his dad, and I was in the kitchen, cutting vegetables next to where his mother stood putting together the ingredients for a macaroni salad.

"So, big news you gave us today." Her perfectly modulated lawyer voice sent a shiver of unease up my spine.

I glanced sideways warily; her tone was too neutral for me to gauge what she thought of the fact that I was pregnant.

She didn't elaborate. That silence of hers made me nervous. It always seemed like she was waiting for me to trip up. For once I didn't say anything, and just kept focused on slicing the red bell pepper in front of me.

"Patrick seems to be taking it well." She folded mayonnaise into the salad, mixing it in with a sure steady hand.

"Patrick is so excited." I hesitated, knowing I didn't feel the same way he did. "I'm just scared." I couldn't believe I confessed that to the woman who already thought I wasn't good enough for her son.

I looked at her and her eyes were intent on me, and they were so much like Patrick's. I tried to explain why I was fearful. "My mom lost custody of me when I was six, and she was dead of an overdose by the time I was nine. I don't know anything about how to be a mother. I don't know if I'm ready for this."

"Have you talked about this with Patrick?"

"He knows about my mom."

"No, I mean, does he know that you don't want this pregnancy?"

I scrunched up my face in confusion, not liking the way her question sounded. "It's not that I don't want the baby, exactly. I wouldn't want to get an abortion or anything. It's just scary. It's like getting lost in the woods... you're probably going to be okay, but it's hard, like, when you're out there, I mean." *Damn.* I wished I could be at least a little more articulate. I sounded like an idiot.

"So, you won't terminate your pregnancy without talking with Patrick, will you?"

Shocked, all I could do was stammer, "I, uh, I'm not getting a, an abortion." I turned away from her, giving her as much of my back as I could while standing next to her. It was like she was wanting me to have an abortion, or maybe she wanted me to not have an abortion. I couldn't tell. I shouldn't have said anything to her.

*Stupid, stupid girl.* You would have thought I had learned through five foster homes that no one wants to hear the dark thoughts, the deep fears.

The next time I spoke to her two weeks later, I was lying in a hospital bed, recovering from the d&c that had taken the last remnants of my baby from my body. Patrick had been with me, but he left to get something to eat.

She patted my arm awkwardly. "Sometimes these things are meant to be, especially considering your ambivalence toward the pregnancy."

I went hot and cold at the same time, like being plunged into a vat of ice so cold, it burned. Somehow, she knew. She knew that when the doctor said that there was nothing they could do, that I had miscarried, I felt a sharp breath of relief. The tiny life inside of me had been extinguished and I was relieved. My fear had allowed me to celebrate, however briefly, the death of an innocent baby. And worse than that, my fear had anticipated this very situation. In the darkest part of my heart lurked the knowledge that my fear had wanted this to happen.

That was when I drew deep inside myself and walled out everyone else, because I deserved to be locked away in this hell of my own making.

I didn't ghost him right away. At first, I just tried to hide everything I was feeling, to keep the man I damn near worshipped from learning the truth that would make him hate me. But it got harder and harder to be with him with this ugliness eating me up inside. I had to get away from him, so he wouldn't ever know. And I wouldn't ever have to see him despise me.

Even after Tracy finally talked me into seeing a counselor in November, I couldn't find my way out of this giant black pit. The counselor said grief and depression was normal, but I didn't feel normal. I felt like I would always have this huge weight crushing me. I went to work, crotched snowflakes, watched TV and went to dinner once with Tracy, but I disconnected somehow. I did everything I was supposed to do, but it was like I was a robot. A busted robot, I guess.

"Callie, baby." Patrick's voice dragged me back to present. "You've got to talk to me." He bent over me, his thumbs sweeping the tears from my face. I hadn't realize I had been crying.

"You'll hate me." My voice sounded small, distant in my ears. I pulled away from his gentle touch.

"Whatever it is has already taken you away from me. And you've allowed it to take me away from you. How much worse can it be?"

I shut my eyes, because I couldn't bear to see the contempt that would soon replace the concern on his face.

His hands wrapped loosely around my hands. He situated himself on the coffee table directly in front of me, and waited without a word.

"When I miscarried…" I tried to actually say the next words, but they refused to be said.

I tried again. "When I miscarried, I had been so scared about having a baby, that for just a little bit, I was relieved that it had happened. And…and I think maybe I was afraid enough that I caused it to happen."

There it was, naked and ugly. The Reason that Cannot Be Named. The shame that caused me to ghost the man I loved.

I nodded with my eyes still tightly closed, my head bent forward, as if giving permission for him to drop the axe on me.

Impossibly, his hands pulled me forward into his embrace, his hand cupping the back of my head and holding it against his shoulder. "Callie, you didn't cause the miscarriage. Are you hearing me? I don't blame you, no one blames you, because you didn't do anything wrong."

"I blame me," I wailed, loud, because the pain tore at me with vicious claws.

Suddenly I was no longer seated in front of him. He scooped me up in his arms, sank back down onto the sectional and gathered me tight against his body. I wrapped my arms around his neck and held on.

I don't cry pretty. I only cry when my heart is being ripped out of me, and there's no room for prettiness then. "I'm sorry," I said again and again. I was sorry for the miscarriage, and for crying, and for running away from him, and for locking him out of my life. I was sorry for so many things.

He just rocked me and held me until my tears slowed. I scrubbed at my face with the sleeve of my sweater. My kingdom for a box of Kleenex.

"Better?" he asked, tilting my face up to check.

I nodded, not trusting my voice.

His beautiful green eyes locked on to mine. "I meant what I said. It wasn't your fault. It was just a really sad event that wasn't anyone's fault. Do you believe that?" His mouth kicked up on one side in a half smile. "Do you at least believe that I believe it wasn't your fault?"

"Yeah," I mumbled.

Leaning in, he kissed my forehead. "Where do you want to go from here?"

"I don't know," I lied. Of course I knew what I wanted. I wanted him, and us, and a life together. "What do you want?"

"I want you to marry me."

"What?" I blinked stupidly at him.

"You heard me." His voice dropped into that dark chocolate range, vibrating through to my core.

"Your mother hates me."

He grimaced at that. "My mother doesn't hate you. She's...different, complicated. " He worked hard to find the right words. "She sucks at emotional things. She shuts everything down and whatever she says comes out like she's totally cold-hearted. In some ways you two are kind of alike."

I looked at him. My expression must have conveyed my thoughts on that last statement, because he laughed sheepishly.

"On second thought, you two are nothing alike, except in one way. You would do anything for the people you love. Even ghost them, if you thought you didn't deserve to be with them. "

*Oh, damn.* I started crying again. What a difficult, loving truth.

"The house, the decorations, they're for you. The fact that my parents—my mother—is a thousand miles away, that's for you. I knew I had one more shot. And that Christmas was my best chance of getting through."

"Really?" The sheer sweetness of his words seeped in, potent and healing.

"I knew that you had to be in a dark place to ghost me. I didn't want to keep hounding you, and drive you farther away."

"I wanted to call you. Tracy tried to get me to call you today."

"Ehh," he said, a pained expression on his face. "I know. I've been talking with Tracy, making sure you were okay."

"Oh, my God." I know my mouth was gaping.

"I finally got up the nerve and texted you a couple hours ago, asking you to come over."

"I must have already left."

He nodded. "Even though I texted you, I was still shocked when I opened the door and there you were. "

*There I was.* Wonder and disbelief warred within me. "How can you possibly want to marry me? I've messed everything up."

"There's a big difference between a bad person and a hurting person." He arranged me up against the corner of the sectional, so I could see him easily, but still had my legs draped over his lap and our fingers were laced together. "I love you," he said simply. No pretense, only honesty.

He wouldn't let me hide my face from him. His eyes searched mine and the smile on his face told me that whatever he saw there was what he was looking for.

I swiped at fresh tears with shaky fingers. *Would I never stop crying?* "I'm sorry."

"You don't have to apologize."

"Yeah, this is what every guy wants, an uber-emotional chick."

"I don't know about every guy, but you're what *I* want. I like it when you don't hide your feelings. That was the worst, when you went all cool and withdrawn after you got out of the hospital. I should have known. I should never have left your side until you talked to me."

"I'm sorry. The guilt was killing me." I smoothed my hand over the stubble on his jaw, loving the rough texture against my palm. "I love you so much."

Fiercely, he caught my face in his two hands and brought his mouth down on mine. It wasn't a gentle kiss, although I knew he was capable of great tenderness. It was a possessive kiss, designed to reclaim me, to reclaim *us*.

I swung my legs off of his lap and surged up on my knees. Basically tackling him, I pressed him down into the couch cushions and climbed on top of him. His fingers threaded through my hair, holding my head steady as he took my lips with hungry kisses. His need went straight to my head like a shot of Patrón, leaving me reeling and breathless.

"Oh God, Patrick. I missed you so much," I whispered against his lips.

My hips pressed against his erection and I shuddered with the stab of lust that shook through me.

"Callie, we better slow this down." His breathlessness pleased and emboldened me.

"Or what?" I locked onto his green eyes. My own eyes widened when his pupils dilated even more in reaction to my challenge.

"Or I'm going to take you upstairs and make love to you until we can't move."

"I'm good with that." Oh yeah, I was *way* good with that.

He tilted his head and narrowed his eyes, assessing just how ready I was to jump back into bed with him.

"Patrick, I love you and I want this."

To make my point more clear, I pushed myself up to sit straddling his hips, and took off my sweater. I slid my hands under his sweater and over the warm, taut skin of his chest. His breath hitched when I took my hands off of him and reached back to unhook my bra. Ever so slowly, I slipped the straps down my arms and let the bra fall to the floor.

"Jesus, Callie." His hands cupped my breasts and his thumbs rubbed over my nipples, sending a shockwave of sensation through me. "We aren't going to make it to the bedroom," he growled, flipping me over on the wide sectional and started making good on his word to love me until we couldn't move.

Eventually, we did make it up to his bedroom, and though Christmas Day dawned gray and cold, I was deliciously warm, lying on my side with Patrick's body spooned perfectly behind me. I wore my new fuzzy socks and one of Patrick's long-sleeved T-shirts, which hung to mid-thigh on me. He wore nothing at all.

Under the heavy quilt, I wriggled around until I faced him and smoothed my hand over his hard, muscled chest. He was all angles and planes, with no softness in his physical body, which made the tenderness of his soul that much more precious to me. Without opening his eyes, he captured my hand and brought it to his lips.

"Merry Christmas, Patrick."

I felt his smile against my fingers. He opened his eyes; the sage green captured me.

"I was having the best dream," he murmured drowsily. "And then I woke up and it's even better than the dream."

God, that was so sweet. Every word he said acted like a balm on my heart, healing all the cracked and brittle pieces.

He rubbed his calf over mine. "Did we get everything taken care of last night?"

I grinned at him. "Heck yeah, baby." I leaned in and licked at his ear.

Actually, last night we were very mature and responsible, and in between going at it like rabbits, we cancelled the tow, discussed my new and improved birth control pill regimen, and talked about how I was never going to ghost him again.

Chuckling, with that laugh that should be registered as a lethal weapon, he threw his leg over me, trapping me against him. "What do you think next Christmas will be like?"

I took a little too long to answer, and he grew more serious, knowing my tendency to overthink everything. I reached up and drew his head down to kiss him softly on the lips, on one sharply defined cheekbone, and on his brow.

"As long as it's with you, it'll be perfect."

# About the Author

I grew up in Ohio, dreaming of California, reading voraciously—especially Harlequin Presents—and writing fiction since the second grade. Although I write Regency-era historical romance, this foray into short-story contemporary romance truly delighted me.

For excerpts from my *Love and Deception* series, please see my website, RoxannBreazile.com.

# The Santa Shack Up

## By Susannah Erwin

M y mom ambushes me the night of Thanksgiving.
She picks her time well—I'm in my bed, lulled
into a false sense of security by an overdose of trypto-
phan. Just as I wonder if I should sneak downstairs to the
kitchen and take the last piece of pecan pie, she appears
in the doorway. To be fair, I knew it was coming. But
things are so topsy-turvy this year, I'd hoped she forgot.

I should've known better. Her expression is ready for
battle. And in her hands she holds…

"No." I shake my head and scramble backwards on
the bed, the better to avoid the certain disaster staring
me in the face. "Just…no."

Mom continues to thrust the red-and-white striped
tights and short green tunic at me. "Lizzie, we all need to
do our part."

"Fine. I'll help Pete with the tree baler." I am not wearing that costume. It was bad enough I wore it during my high school winter breaks. But I graduated last summer. I'm too old to be an elf. Officially.

Mom gives me her patented Mom stare. "You're allergic to sap. I'm not going through that again." She puts the pile of colorful felt and Lycra on the bed and sits down next to me. "Honey, I know these last few months haven't been what you wanted. Dad and I appreciate all you've sacrificed. It hasn't gone unnoticed."

My face feels hot enough to roast chestnuts. "It's okay. I just want Dad to be healthy again." I glance around my bedroom to avoid Mom's sympathetic gaze. It hasn't changed much since my sister Angie moved out when I was twelve. A queen-sized four-poster bed replaced the two narrow twins, and romance and fantasy novels occupy the space on the bookshelves where Angie's prized porcelain pig collection once resided. But other than that, same yellow buttercups on the wallpaper. Same scratched oak furniture, heavy and stout, a hand-me-down from my grandparents, whose house this had originally been. Same travel posters of Spain and Dubai and Tokyo, mocking me with their cheerful exhortations to fly and see the world.

I love my family. I do. But I want more. I had plans. Then the stroke felled my dad and put him in a rehabilitation center the week before I supposed to leave for college.

"You kids have been so great. Joe stepping up to run the financial side of the business, Angie working on the marketing after she's finished teaching for the day, Pete and Paco taking care of the trees. But I couldn't have survived without you, Lizzie Belle. If you hadn't offered to stay home and help out full time..." Mom's jaw makes a chewing motion, and I feel tears forming in the corners of my eyes.

This will never do. We Sandovals like to keep our emotions tightly bottled inside, the better to preserve them. "So to thank me, you're making me wear an elf costume," I point out. Not only do I hope it will make her smile, but it's true.

A smile does indeed form. "No one can run Santa's Workshop like you do. You manage to keep both the children and the parents happy while they wait for their turn with the big guy. " The Mom-briskness tone is back in her voice. Emotional crisis averted. We're both relieved.

"I'd be happy to run Santa's Workshop. In flattering street clothes."

"People come here to make holiday memories and relive their family traditions."

Yeah. I know. *Sandoval Family Holiday Farm, Putting the Holly in Your Day Since 1953.* It's engraved on the gate over the driveway that leads to the cut-your-own-tree area.

"And holiday memories mean holiday elves. Not a teenager in jeans and a parka." She gets up, her body language indicating the conversation is over and the matter is settled. "Make sure you find the boots. Children notice if your toes don't curl up," she says from the doorway.

"I'm only a teenager for another year!" I call after her, but all I hear are the echoes of her steps as she descends the stairs.

Great. Just…peachy keen awesome great. I sigh and throw myself backwards on the bed. There's only one good thing about manning the Santa Shack, as we kids like to call it. After high school graduation, Sean Boswick went to Florida to play college football and his team is slated for a New Year's Day bowl game. If, heaven forbid, another Incident of Hot Shame happens this season, he won't be around to see it.

The next morning I'm up by five A.M. To most people, the day after Thanksgiving is Black Friday. But to us, that Friday is red and green, silver and gold, and blue and white.

We need a good Christmas this year, more than ever. I couldn't sleep after Mom's ambush, so I left my bedroom and went downstairs to get a glass of water. When I passed the dining room on my way to the kitchen, I heard my mom curse.

She never curses.

I stayed in the shadows and watched her face crumble and her shoulders fall. Joe was with her, shuffling through a pile of paper on the dining room table. His lips sat in a straight line and his eyebrows made a "v" in the middle of this forehead as he entered numbers into a calculator. When my calm, placid brother slammed his fist down, scattering the bills, I fled back upstairs.

So this morning I put on my costume and I make sure to give Mom and the rest of my family a huge smile whenever they see me in it. They don't need the aggravation of my aggravation. The smile falls as soon as they walk away.

The costume is even more unflattering on me than before. The waistband of the candy cane striped tights digs into my hips, leaving an angry ridge. The hem of the kelly green tunic hits at the widest section of my thighs, never a flattering length. The rubber elf ears smell like wet clothes left in the washing machine too long, and a procession of tiny red bumps are forming where the fake ear rubs against my real ear. And the boots pinch. But Mom's right—the feet are one of the first places children look when they meet me.

"Looks like shooting season is almost ready to begin." Lena smiles at me as she finishes securing her camera to the tripod. One of the few bright spots to Santa Shack duty is I get to work with my brother Paco's fiancée, who I adore. She's the cool older sister I didn't get in Angie, who thinks Hershey's qualifies as single origin chocolate because it's made in Pennsylvania.

"Yep. Just about." I run my gaze over the Santa Workshop area. The line ropes are in place. The old fashioned cash register is set up and ready to accept money, although I'll probably use the credit card reader attached to my e-tablet to take orders. The Shack itself has never looked better. Paco and Pete did an outstanding job with the pine swags, dripping from the eaves. Fresh wreaths of dark green holly, cheerful with bright red berries, decorate the door and windows. Twinkling multicolored lights reflect off shiny ornaments packed tightly among the greenery. "Everything's all set. Except for the most important thing of all. Where's Santa?"

Lena shrugs. "I'm sure Mr. Boswick will be here any minute."

Sean's grandfather is our Santa Claus, has been for as long as I've been alive. Which, as a small kid running around the farm with Sean during the holidays, was pretty cool. When we were older—and especially after Sean became Mr. Awesome Spectacular Football Hero and I was, well, that weird girl who would rather read or watch a *Doctor Who* marathon than go to a pep rally—it wasn't so cool. Sean stopped visiting his grandfather sometime during freshman year, until he showed suddenly last season with a bunch of his friends.

My cheeks flame at the memory, and Lena gives me a pat on the arm. She's the only member of my family who knows about the Incident of Hot Shame, and I made her swear to never mention it to them. Not even Paco. "Don't worry. New holiday, new you. You look—" She runs her gaze up and down my costume. "—very…festive."

"Gee, thanks." I surreptitiously adjust the waistband of my tights under my tunic.

"But don't do that," she continues, shaking her head. "Just…no."

Adjusting my costume is part of what led to the Incident of Hot Shame. I drop my hands. "Grand opening is in half an hour. He's really running late."

Just then, my gaze catches a flash of red and white through the pine trees and I breathe a sigh of relief. "There he is," I start to say. But the words die on my tongue as a tall man steps into the clearing.

It's not Mr. Boswick.

It's Sean.

I'm rooted to the ground. I couldn't move my arms or legs if I try. My eyes are scratchy-dry and I realize it's because I can't even blink.

What the *BLEEP* is Sean Boswick doing on my family's farm, wearing a red velour suit trimmed with fur? He's supposed to be practicing for the bowl game. Did his coach give him permission to come home for Thanksgiving weekend?

Sean carries something white and fluffy, and it takes me a second to recognize it's a Santa wig and beard.

"Hi!" Lena steps forward, her hand outstretched. "We've met, but in case you don't remember, I'm Lena. I'm the photographer."

Sean shifts the beard to shake her hand. "Sean," he says. He still hasn't looked at me. "Granddad has gout and can't walk. I said I'd fill in."

"How awful," Lena says. "Tell him we hope he gets well soon. We like working with him."

"He'll be back. This is temporary." Sean keeps his gaze focused on Lena.

Not that I blame him. She's gorgeous. But his deliberate avoidance of me is starting to rankle. The anger unthaws my limbs and I cross my arms over my chest as much as the tunic will allow. I can feel it pulling across my back. "Santa needs to have his wig on, his stomach stuffed and his butt in the chair. Now. Children will arrive any minute."

Finally he turns his head and looks in my direction. His gaze stuns me, almost more than when he first showed up. As long as I've known him—so, pretty much my entire life—Sean has been confident. Bold. Secure in himself. I floundered rather badly when I ran smack into puberty, but Sean? Never.

When his eyes meet mine, he's seems...defeated. Ashamed, even. The ground beneath my feet feels like it's shifting, as if I'm trying to stand on one of those giant inflatable balls they have at gyms. Sean and I aren't friends. Not even on Facebook, much less Snapchat. But knowing Sean was out there, sailing smoothly through life, was kind of my rock. The one thing in my life that makes sense and would always make sense.

If Sean Boswick feels lost, what chance do any of us have at finding firm ground?

He abruptly pulls his gaze away from mine. I can almost hear the *pop* as our gazes disconnect. "I know the drill." He tugs the wig down over his ears and pulls up the beard. "See?"

"Hat," I snap, trying to cover my disorientation. "And belly."

Sean crosses his arms and grabs the hem of the loose red jacket, pulling it up to reveal rock hard abs that would make a Greek statue feel inadequate. I force my hands to stay relaxed and by my side, because I'm dying to know if his muscles are as smooth and firm as they look. Just out of curiosity, of course. "Ready."

"For what?" I blurt out, just as my sister Angie runs up with a pillow in her hand. I take a closer look and recognize the faded blue starflowers on the case. "Hey, that's mine! What are you doing with it?"

Angie is puffing hard, but then, she's six months pregnant. "Mr. Boswick tried to reach you, Sean, but you didn't answer your phone so he called the main number," she says in between wheezes. "Said he forgot to give you the belly." She holds out my pillow. "Here. This should do for today."

"But that's my—" I start to protest. Angie cuts me off with an eye roll so hard, I'm surprised her baby doesn't get seasick by proximity. She holds the pillow against those sculpted abs, and for the first time I'm truly jealous of my sister.

Sean lets the jacket fall and together they figure out the best way to use the belt to keep the pillow in place. It's not perfect, but when he's sitting on the Santa throne it will work well enough. And just in time—I hear the jingle bells announcing the opening of Sandoval Holiday Farm for the Christmas season.

Sean makes a great Santa. He puts on a low, growly voice that, if he weren't wearing a gray beard and my down pillow, would be really sexy. His "Ho-Ho-Ho" is deep and cheerful, and he really listens to what each kid has to say. There are fewer screaming babies than usual, and I wonder if it's because Sean handles them like he handled the football in high school: with utter confidence. Before long, we're working like a well-oiled machine, trading riddles and jokes—G-rated Christmas ones, of course—as we play our roles of Santa and Chief Elf.

But when the day is over, the easy camaraderie that had developed between us disappears. We're back to being Sean and Lizzie. And Sean and Lizzie don't speak. He hands back the pillow without saying a word, nods at Lena, and walks back into the pine trees the way he came.

"That was nice of him, to fill in for his grandfather," Lena says, packing up her camera gear. "Especially after what happened to him at college."

I almost don't hear her because I'm focused on the pillow in my hands. It still holds a tiny trace of warmth from his body. "Wait. What happened?"

"You didn't hear? He was suspended from the football team last week. He'll miss the bowl game." Lena finishes putting her gear away and looks up at me. "Want any help? Have you restocked the candy canes yet?"

"Suspended?" My jaw nearly hits the ground. "For what?"

Lena shrugs. "Something about breaking the team's rules? It made ESPN." She stands up and swings her camera bag over her shoulder. "If you don't need me, I'm going to head home."

"Sure. Yeah. Of course." I finish my duties, sweeping up candy wrappers and straightening out the line stanchions. As I turn off the lights, I grab the pillow. Yes, I have other ones on my bed. And yes, Sean wore it under a heavy velour jacket on what turned out to be a rather hot day for the end of November, so, y'know, ew. But it's a reminder that, if only for a few hours and if only when we were playacting at being mythical holiday figures, Sean and I could laugh and joke with each other like we did when we were small.

I'll wash the pillowcase, however. I'm not desperate enough to hold a sweaty pillow to my face and pretend it's him. I'm almost nineteen, not thirteen. Or so I tell myself.

The next morning, my green glitter manicure is nearly gone by the time I make it to the Shack. My breathing stutters as I wonder if Sean would continue being Mr. No Words, or if we might be able to finally break through the awkwardness of the last few years. But when I arrive, the man in the red velour suit isn't Sean. Mr. Boswick gives me a cheery hello and then I learn far more than I ever need to know about gout. He doesn't mention Sean, and I don't ask. Google isn't much more help. Lena was right: Sean earned his suspension for breaking team rules and that's all the internet has to say.

The days go by quickly, as they always do during the run up to Christmas. I take parents' money, I announce kids' names, I hand out candy canes. I don't see Sean again. Before I know it, we're heading into Countdown Week, or the seven days before December 25. This is our last chance to bring in the income we need to survive until Easter and our annual Easter Egg Hunt and Bunny Hop Ball (we tried to create a Valentine's event, but the farm in mid-winter turned out to be too cold for hot romance).

Joe calls a family meeting the night before Countdown Week begins. Two deep creases have been added to my oldest brother's forehead since he started keeping the farm's books on top of his law practice. We gather around the dining room table: me, Mom, Joe, Pete, Paco and Lena, Angie and her husband Sven.

Joe doesn't waste time jumping with both feet into the bad news. "We've all worked hard, but it's been an unseasonably warm holiday season," he starts. "Visitor numbers are down, which means our receipts are down. And with Dad's care facility bills taking most of the family savings…" His voice trails off.

"Just spit it out," Paco says. "What's the bottom line?"

Joe looks at Mom, who looks down at the table. He sighs. "If we don't take in double our sales projections during Countdown Week, we need to think seriously about selling the farm."

We swivel our heads to take in Pete's reaction. Of all of us, Pete is the most connected to the land. In fact, he's far more comfortable around the trees than he is around people. He nods his understanding, but his gaze is bleak.

Angie pats Pete's hand, and then turns back to Joe. "And if we increase sales? We can keep the farm?"

Joe shrugs. "It will be tight, but if we have a good Easter, maybe add some more activities, we should be okay. "

Mom looks up. "Your father will be able to come home around March. We might need a part-time nurse, but the bills should decrease."

Pete speaks for the first time. "All that matters is Dad gets well. We'll make it work. No matter what."

The room is quiet as the implications of losing the farm start to sink in.

"I have an idea," Angie says slowly. "What if we added a new feature to the Christmas options, went after a new demographic?"

Joe raises an eyebrow. "A new demographic?"

Angie nods. "Single women. Maybe single men, too."

I do not like where I think this is going. "No," I say firmly.

"I haven't even said my idea, Lizzie."

"No," I repeat.

Angie huffs and turns to Joe. "The other day, Sean Boswick filled in for his grandfather as Santa. I'm telling you, that kid has a body of death. What if we offered—" She makes quote marks in the air. "—'Santa After Dark?' Lena can be a sexy elf for those who want a photo with a female."

"Hey!" Paco and I protest at the same time.

"That's exploitive," I add. "Plus we're Sandoval *Family* Holiday Farm. It's off-brand." Let's see how Angie likes it when I throw her marketing buzzwords back at her.

"It's not a bad idea." We all turn to look at Lena. She shrugs. "I saw Sean's abs, too. Angie has a point." Paco opens his mouth, but Lena cuts him off with a reassuring squeeze of her hand. "If a sexy costume can help save the farm, I'll wear one. This is my family, too."

I can't decide if I am angriest with Angie for suggesting Santa's Workshop as an exercise in sexist objectification, or for suggesting Lena as the sexy elf but not me. "So who takes the photos if Lena is dressed up?" I ask.

Ha. Let Angie figure that one out.

"Sven can take the photos since it's after work hours," Angie says. Sven nods. "And we'll offer selfies. Twenty dollars a photo op, and some of the money can go to charity. We'll make it a fundraiser for the National Stroke Association."

I sink into my chair, my objections deflated. I can't argue with the charity angle. And I know it will bring our friends and neighbors out, too. So many asked us what they could do to help, but we didn't want to take their charity for ourselves. But for the National Stroke Association? Sure. "So who is going to ask Sean?"

This time the family swivels as one to look at me.

No. Hell no. No. No. No.

An hour later, I'm cutting through the pine trees. There's a party at Phil Cheng's house tonight, a gathering of kids from my high school graduating class who are home from college for the holidays. I'm pretty sure I only scored an invite because the Chengs own the property next door and they're using some of our land as overflow parking. I wasn't going to attend, but Angie is convinced Sean will be there, making it the perfect opportunity to hit him up with her idea.

"He'll have some booze in him, he'll be relaxed—go for it," she urged as she pulled an outfit out of my closet and thrust it at me. It's the only time I've heard Angie endorse underage drinking. I was about to call her on it when she shoved me out the door.

I catch sight of the Chengs' house through the trees. Light pours from the windows and I hear pounding dance music and laughter. If I didn't fit in during high school, what chance do I have now? Everyone has moved on to his or her next stage of life while I'm stuck in the same old place. Not to mention the Incident of Hot Shame, which lingers like the memory of a bad smell .

I turn around and walk away from bright glow of the party. But I can't go back to the house. The family is still there, running sales numbers and making contingency plans. The breeze picks up and I shiver. Stupid unseasonable weather. I went out without a coat, but with the sun long gone I need one now.

There's only place left to go: the Shack. At least it has four walls and a roof to keep out the worst of the cold.

I can hang out there for a few hours—or until my phone battery runs out and I can't read on it anymore—and then sneak home. When Angie asks, I'll tell her I didn't see Sean at the party. Hey, it won't be a lie. Technically. I turn around and trudge toward the area of the farm that holds Santa's Workshop.

Through the tall pine trees I see the Shack's squat bulk, dark—wait. It's not so dark. There's a light, a dim one, visible through the windows.

I know I turned off the electricity before I left. If I hadn't, the entire Shack would be lit up, from the multi-colored strings on the roof to the tiny white twinkle lights in the garland lining the door. My heart speeds up until I can practically see it jumping through my cardigan. I'm about to run to the house to get one of my brothers, not caring it will expose my party pooper status, when the light reveals a very familiar profile.

Sean Boswick is in the Shack.

I rub my eyes and blink hard. Then I focus again on the window. Yep, he's still there. The square outline of his jaw is unmistakable, lit by the phone screen in his hands.

Why is he here? Did he bring—my heart pings, hard, a sharp stabbing pain—a girlfriend to the Shack?

Then a wave of anger makes me forget the cold. Seriously? He brought a girlfriend to a place where babies sit on Santa's knee?

I march to the front entrance. Slapping one hand over my eyes so I won't see the defilement of the Shack,

I use the other hand to wrench open the door. "Have you no shame?" I cry.

I hear a grunt of surprise, followed by the sound of something clattering to the ground. "What the hell, Lizzie!" Sean growls.

No one else speaks, so I figure it's safe to take my hand off my eyes. Sean is standing up, his fists clenched as if ready to defend himself. His phone is on the ground, the screen playing some sort of video. Headphones cover his ears, the unplugged cord dangling down his chest. As I watch, his fingers slowly uncurl.

He's alone in the Shack.

"Good reflexes," I say.

Sean gives me a look of utter disgust before he bends down to pick up the phone. "Good job knocking," he says, examining the device for any damage.

Now that I know the Shack isn't being used as a love palace, my heart rate slows down. Still, I can't let his remark go unchallenged. "This is my family's property. I don't need to knock. You're the one trespassing." I know the words are a mistake even before they leave my mouth.

"Yeah. I know. I'm leaving." Still looking at his phone, he moves toward the door.

I shut it behind me and stand in front of the doorknob so he would have to physically move me to get out. "Wait. You can stay. You just startled me, that's all. Please don't leave on my account." I look around the Shack. The moonlight streams in through the two small windows and I see Sean brought a blanket, a greasy sack from the local burger joint and a thermos with him. "Looks like you were planning to be here a while," I say.

He shrugs. "Just a few hours." Then he looks at me, and his blue eyes are deep pools in the moonlight. "So why are you here? You haven't—" He stops speaking abruptly and begins fiddling with his phone again.

"I haven't what?"

He shrugs again. "Been to the Shack at night before."

"You've come here every night? You mean—wait. You don't sleep here, do you?' The thought at once saddens me and sends a thrill down my spine. Sean Boswick, sleeping less than a hundred yards from my bedroom.

He shakes his head. "No. I just needed to get out of my house."

I exhale. "Boy, do I understand that."

And for the first time in a long time, Sean catches my gaze and smiles at me. A real smile. The kind of smile we used to exchange on an hourly basis when we were kids, but became few and far between once puberty kicked in.

"So why are you here?" he asks.

I sigh. "Trying to simultaneously avoid and attend Phil Cheng's party."

His brow creases, but he nods. "I think I'm doing the same thing. You want people to think you're out having fun with your friends. But it's the last thing you want to do."

"Sort of," I say. "They're not my friends. But my family likes to think they are. Hence, the Shack." I sweep my arm to indicate, and suddenly I am very aware of three things:

One: With the door shut, the Shack is not a big space.

Two: I'm standing closer to Sean than I have in a very long time.

Three: Sean is even more devastating gorgeous up close than he is from my usual worship-from-afar vantage point.

My knees start to buckle, just a little, and I manage to scoot past Sean and sit on Santa's throne. "Do you mind if I take your chair?"

He smirks. I'd forgotten about the dimple that flashes in his left cheek. Now it will haunt my daydreams. "It's Granddad's chair. But I did have fun."

A vision of Angie, hands balled on her hips, pops into my head. "Ask him!" vision-Angie hisses.

I ignore her. Instead, I nod at his phone. "What were you watching?"

He shrugs and puts the phone in his pocket, taking a seat below me on the plywood steps that lead up to Santa's Throne. "Just some game film."

We sit together silently. I can hear him breathe, soft exhalations in the dark. I'm used to Shack's usual scent of pine needles and cranberry air freshener, but there's something different in the air, a tangy mix of leather and citrus. My cardigan begins to constrict my limbs, the wool too heavy to bear, and I shrug it off before I suffocate. I clear my throat. "So what—"

"Why did you—" he says at the same time.

I laugh. It sounds nervous even to me.

He flashes a close-lipped smile and says, "Ladies first."

"No, you go ahead."

He shifts on the steps, the better to look at up me. It's oddly disconcerting. I've never been the one able to look down before. "Why didn't you want to go to the party?"

A harsh chuckle bursts from my lips. "What would I want to go? That's my definition of the Seventh Circle of Hell. The real question is, why aren't you there?"

He looks away. "Like you, I'm not in the mood."

I scoff. "Yeah, right. You're the returning football hero. It would be oh so difficult for you to walk into that room."

His shoulders come up, almost as if my words physically delivered a blow, but he doesn't respond.

Me and my big mouth. "Sorry." I leave the chair and sit down next to him on the steps. They're just big enough to fit the two of us side by side. "I heard you were suspended from your team. That must be rough."

He nods, his gaze still fixed on the opposite wall. "I've had better weeks." Then he turns to face me. We're so close, I can see day-old whiskers shading his jaw. "Did you ever think things would be different after high school?"

He holds my gaze with his. And I know we aren't talking about the Cheng party anymore. "Yes," I say softly. "I thought I would go to college and high school Lizzie would cease to exist. I counted on it."

His shoulder brushes mine. His body heat scorches through the thin blouse I'm wearing. "How's your dad? Sorry I didn't ask sooner."

"Getting better." My nose starts to tingle, as it usually does when I think about Dad, and I clear my throat. "But hey, you did go away. You got out of here."

He grunts. "You take yourself with you wherever you go."

"Oh, c'mon." I dare to nudge him with my shoulder. "Most people would think taking Sean Boswick with them would be a good thing, Mr. Homecoming King and Most Likely to Succeed and All State First Team."

"Even you?" His gaze bores into mine.

I glance away and giggle. I'm not proud of it. "Of course."

"After what happened last Christmas?"

I feel a blush spreading over every inch of my body, and it has nothing to do with Sean's proximity. "Gee, thanks for bringing that up. And I thought we were talking like two adult humans." I stand up and shrug my cardigan back on. "Make sure the door is closed when you leave. We don't need more vermin breaking in to the Shack."

Sean springs to his feet and grabs my hand before I can take two steps. His grip is warm and firm as his fingers curl around mine. "I'm sorry."

I know this time he's not talking about my dad. But I can't look at him. "Yeah, well, none of us are perfect. Not even you." I try to pull my hand free. I need to get out of the Shack. I refuse to break down in front of him.

My dirty secret? I've been in love with Sean since he offered to share his ice pop with me in kindergarten. And all the way through elementary school, I saw no reason why my "Mrs. Sean Boswick" doodles wouldn't become a reality.

Then the hormones kicked in. Mine made me even more aware of Sean. The way his blue eyes crinkle in the corners when he's amused but doesn't want to show it. The way he catches his lower lip with his top teeth when he's concentrating. The way he focuses his full attention on you when you're speaking, as if you are the only person in the world in that moment.

The way he fills out those skintight football pants.

When high school started, I tried to get over Sean. By that time, he was firmly in the school's upper echelon and I was at the bottom. The kicker—and I don't mean on the football team—is Sean is smart. So every time I thought, *This is it, he is an erased smudge on the journal of my life*, Sean would say something brilliant in class and I'd tumble down the well of longing once again.

Damn him for coming here and reminding me of what I want but cannot have. I tug my hand again, and this time he lets it go.

"See you around," I say over my shoulder.

I won't, though. Not if I can help it. And there is no way I'm going to ask him to play Sexy Santa now. Let Angie do it if she is so keen on the idea.

"Lizzie," he says, and there is something in his voice that makes me turn around. "Do you know why Coach suspended me?"

I give him a half-shrug. "Google says you broke team rules."

"I punched a teammate. Made his nose bleed."

"What?"

"He was going to assault a girl." His eyes glitter in the dim light.

"That's horrible!" I gasp. "Why did you get the suspension?"

He ignores my question. "She was another freshman. I didn't really know her, but she used to hang around the older guys. And then..." His gaze drops to the floor.

"What happened?" I ask tightly.

"We were at a team party. I didn't know she was there until people started talking. She'd had too much to drink and passed out. And when she did, her skirt—" He makes a lifting motion with his hands. "—was at her waist. She had underwear on," he hastens to add.

An unpleasant chill runs down my spine. "And?"

"Some guys took their phones out to take pictures."

My mouth tastes of iron and salt. Perspiration dots my palms and I rub them on my jeans. "No one helped her?" I asked.

He shakes his head. "Jesse—that's the guy I punched—kept others away. He thought it would be funny to take off her panties. And do who knows what else. I couldn't let him." He takes a deep breath.

I walk back and sit down next to him again. "I'm glad you punched him," I say. The words are inadequate for the emotions I dare not examine swirling around me.

His lip curls. "He deserved it. Then a bigger fight broke out. By the time security came, someone had taken her to the hospital and it was my and my friends' words against him and his friends. Jesse's a potential NFL draft pick. So." He shrugs. "I got the suspension."

"That sucks." I mean it. Sincerely. "You're a hero."

Another shake of his head. "Nah. It was too little, too late." He reaches his right hand out and takes mine again. "I'm sorry, Lizzie."

The warmth starts where our fingers join and it spreads, tendrils unfurling through my veins. "You already said that," I blurt out. Moments like this don't happen to me. I don't get an apology from the football hero. "They were your friends, but you weren't a part of what happened to me last year. And it didn't go anywhere near what Jesse tried to do."

"What they did to you was mean. And cruel." His thumb rubs over my knuckles. The tendrils grow blossoms, bright joyful bursts of electricity making my pulse quicken. "I could have tried to stop them from putting it on the internet."

I can scarcely breath. Part of me wonders when I'll wake up and realize it's a hallucination brought on by sleeping with the pillow he wore during his day as Santa. "They uploaded it immediately. Nothing you could have done once it got out. But it was just a photo. Nothing critical shows."

"But—"

"Yes, I was embarrassed." And that's the understatement of the century. "But it could have been worse." Also true.

"They were at the farm because I brought them here. I should have known they were planning a prank." His thigh presses against mine, a solid, comforting presence.

I don't want to cry. But if he keeps talking, I'll have no choice. "Thanks," I say, just managing to keep my voice from cracking. "Apology accepted."

"I never thought through how the prank must have affected you until my fight with Jesse. I guess I thought you were invincible. You always seemed so strong."

A strangled laugh escapes. "Me? Strong?"

"Well, you ignored me for four years." He grins. "That took strength, right?" He waggles his eyebrows for extra effect.

"Egotist!" I knock his shoulder with mine. "And *you* ignored me. I thought we were friends."

"No, *I* thought we were friends. And then you froze me out."

"No, you—" I stop. Does it really matter? The only things that concern me right now are the tight grip of his fingers, the warm press of his arm and leg against mine. Let me have this moment, to keep stored up after Sean goes back to Florida. "Thank goodness high school is over, right?"

Sean turns his head and suddenly his face is right next to me. His breath stirs the locks curling around my ear. My pulse accelerates like a racecar about to take the pole position. A pleasurable-painful tension pools in my stomach, tugs deep between my legs.

"Yes," he says, his voice a low rumble. "Because otherwise I wouldn't have the courage to do this."

And he lowers his head to mine.

You know how when you're a kid, you imagine what certain things will be like when you finally get to experience them? And then you do, and you're horribly disappointed? Take coffee. When I was a child, I thought coffee would taste like really, really strong chocolate. I was wrong.

I spent years imagining what kissing Sean Boswick would be like. And the reality—the reality blows away my imagination. It's anti-coffee.

Sean's lips are hot and firm. They fit against mine as if they were created just for each other. When his tongue sweeps the seam of my pursed kiss I eagerly open them for him. He tastes of candy canes and cocoa (now I know what is in that thermos). Then he shifts on the steps, angling his torso so he can draw me closer, and I stop making mental notes. All I can do is feel: the lick of his tongue against mine, the combustible fire of his mouth, the sizzling pops traveling up and down my nervous system.

Sean's right hand tangles in my hair, while mine clutch his broad shoulders, loving the play of muscles under his shirt. He disengages just enough to lean his forehead against mine. "So, this is okay with you?" His breathing is harsh.

I'm also out of breath, but I manage a short laugh. "What do you think?" My fingers find the buttons to his shirt and I undo enough of them to allow me to finally explore that sculpted chest. Again, my imagination was woefully inadequate. My senses gorge on his smooth, warm skin paired with just the right amount of crisp hair. "I've wanted to do this since seventh grade."

"I'm a late bloomer," he says. "I've wanted to do this since ninth. But you stopped talking to me." His hands cup my face, and he brushes his right thumb across my lips. It causes a shiver that runs from the crown of my head to the tips of my toes.

I open my mouth to retort, and then think of better uses for it. It doesn't matter who ignored whom first. What matters is we're communicating now, and with more than words.

I kiss him, my tongue dueling with his. With our mouths still exploring each other, he pulls me up to stand with him just long enough to climb the two steps to Santa's Throne. Then he tugs me down on his lap.

The bottle storing my emotions overfills and breaks into a thousand pieces. I want him. I do. And he wants me. The proof is hard against my thigh. He groans, and the sound goes straight to my core. I need to be closer to him. I—

His phone buzzes. We ignore it at first, but the caller is insistent. Holding me on his left leg with his left arm, he digs into his pants pocket with his other hand and draws out the offending instrument.

"Everything okay?" I ask, enjoying the opportunity to put my arms around his neck and curl into his side.

He grins and shows me the screen. "Should I say yes? Apparently she got tired of waiting for you."

I grab the phone and read the texts. If she weren't pregnant and I wasn't looking forward to being an aunt, I would so kill my sister.

I hand the phone back to him. "I kind of like the thought of having your abs all to myself," I say, and lean down to explore the skin between his ear and neck with my lips.

He shudders and settles me more firmly on his lap. "I like the thought of helping your family so you can go to college."

Right. College. The sweet hot haze enveloping me begins to dissipate. This is a Santa Shack shack-up. A few hours of magic, but ultimately only as real as the guy in the red suit himself.

I get off Sean's lap. Without his body acting as the world's sexist furnace, the Shack is cold. I pick his blanket off the floor and wrap it around me.

Sean's forehead creases. "Lizzie? What's wrong?"

"You said the 'c' word. College." I chew on my lower lip. "I just realized this is a temporary thing. Not that I thought this was anything but, y'know, what it is," I rush to add. "Don't worry, I'm not a clinger. It's just…I guess I didn't think about it until now."

"Why?"

"Why didn't I think about it? I was a bit preoccupied with kissing you."

He huffs, but there's a smile on his face. "I mean, why is this only temporary? Granted, we haven't had our first date—"

"You want to go on a date?"

"—so this could fall apart, sure. But why assume the worst?"

I stare at him. He returns the stare, his gaze frank and open. Doesn't he get it? I'm Lizzie Sandoval. Good things don't happen to me. Incidents of Hot Shame happen to me. Part of me is waiting for this to be revealed as another prank and the video of my make-out session with Sean to be uploaded to YouTube for the world to laugh at the deluded girl who thought she had a chance with the sports star.

Sean unfolds himself from Santa's throne and walks to my side. He takes the blanket off my shoulders, drapes it across his, and then pulls me close so we are both enveloped under the red and black wool.

"It's Christmas," he says. "Believe in miracles. I think we're both due one."

I put my head on Sean's chest and listen to the thump of his heart, steady and constant. Maybe he's right. Maybe I should start realizing good things *do* happen to me. Like my family, who loves me. Like my dad getting better. Like going to college. Maybe a year or two late, but I can still follow my dreams.

Like Sean.

"I can't go to school in Florida," I say, my words somewhat muffled by his shirt. "I like winter."

"Good," he says, the words a comforting reverberation under my ear. "Because I'm transferring. That's what I was watching. Game films from teams that might take me. Maybe we can look at schools together."

Then he kisses me again. And my last conscious thought, before the heat takes over and the blanket falls off our shoulders, is that miracles do happen. I believe.

## About the Author

Susannah Erwin is a former Hollywood studio executive who appreciates intelligent heroines, independent heroes and happy ever afters that leave the reader sighing. She lives in Los Angeles with her husband and one very curious cat.

You can find her at www.susannaherwin.com.

# My Oktoberfest Escapade

## By Jewel Quinlan

## Chapter One

"Oh my God, he's going to be hurting tomorrow." Dana stared wide-eyed at one of the Italians at our table and tucked a cluster of her glossy dark curls behind one ear.

The guy was chugging his third mug of beer in the last ten minutes and, instead of stopping him, his friends chanted and goaded him on. Another of their crew had already passed out. That guy was propped upright against the back of the bench. But his head lolled to the side, and drool dripped from his parted lips.

I shook my head at the spectacle. "They're absolutely crazy."

Dana and I had scraped together money we'd earned at our part-time jobs over the course of our sophomore and now junior years in college, and we'd been looking forward to this trip for a while. It was the first time either of us had been to Europe. And Oktoberfest turned out to be even better than we'd imagined. This was our second day at the festival, and today we were drinking beer in the Augustiner tent.

Upon arrival, we'd discovered that inside the beer tents you had to be sitting at one of the long picnic-style tables in order to be served. Unlike in the US, the tables were not exclusively yours. If there were open seats, they were filled with people whether you knew them or not. Yesterday we'd sat with a variety of people over the course of the day. And, like the people around us, we'd stood on the bench at our table singing along to the songs the brass band played. The men in today's band were dressed, as usual, in *lederhosen* and their female singer wore a *dirndl*, the traditional clothing of Bavaria from a time long past. They played on a raised platform in the center, the rich sounds and tempo of the tuba, trumpet, accordion, guitar, and flute combining to create a lively rustic atmosphere.

Aside from Germans, there had been Scandinavians, Brits, Spaniards, Irish, Scots, and more. Most of whom had either been fluent or spoke a better-than-basic level of English, in addition to their native tongue. I felt kind of dumb now for only knowing one language. Why hadn't I continued with French after high school? Regardless, it was tons of fun talking to them, hearing their accents, and having my eyes opened to their perspectives on the world. Being here brought to mind the German exchange student I'd had a crush on in high school, and I wondered what he was up to now.

The Italians we sat with now didn't speak a single word of English. But, true to the stereotypes about their nationality, they were good with hand gestures.

"Do you think that guy's going to be okay?" I glanced again at the one who had passed out. He twitched unnaturally as if in response to a dream.

Dana's soulful dark brown eyes filled with concern. "I wonder if he needs to go to the hospital."

I agreed with her, then felt bad for not being the one to summon help for him. But if his friends weren't concerned, why should I be? Didn't they carry more responsibility for his welfare than I did? *I don't even know how to call an ambulance in this country*, I reminded myself, and that made me feel better.

As if in response to our stares, the guy stirred. He heavily blinked his eyes open and lifted his head. Then he straightened and wiped his mouth with the back of his hand. When his friends noticed his movement, a couple of them slapped him on the back, and he rose to his feet in response. He swayed where he stood, gazing blearily around, then reached for the half-empty mug of beer in front of him and took a swig.

Dana and I looked at each other in shock and started laughing.

"Oh my god!" I said. "That's hardcore."

Twenty minutes later their group left and Dana and I were alone at the table. Their rapid departure probably had more than a little to do with the fact that some of them were looking distinctly green. Our solitude lasted about two seconds before the waitress showed up with a group of men following her. She wore a dirndl, as all the waitresses did, and carried ten *Ma*, the one-liter heavy-duty glass mugs, clutched in her fists. I was impressed every time I saw one pass by with such a load. The heavy glasses and the beer in them had to weigh a ton. How in the world did they do it?

The new group of guys squeezed in around us and we became a full table again. The newcomers were also dressed in the traditional Bavarian outfits; short or long lederhosen embroidered with gold thread, hunter green jackets, and matching hats. I had to admit that the leather pants and shorts looked good on men. The leather molded itself well to the thick muscles of their thighs and buttocks. Somehow this type of garment on guys just looked downright…manly, way better than denim.

They nodded at us politely in greeting, and we nodded back.

The one next to me reached his hand out to introduce himself. He was tall and had sky-blue eyes. Blond hair peeked out from beneath his hat.

"English?" I asked, as I grasped his hand. His strong fingers enveloped mine, and my skin tingled from the contact. There was something familiar about him. Had I seen him yesterday?

"Yes, I speak English," he said. "Where are you from?" The words, though accented, flowed from him with ease.

"Florida." *Man, he's hot.* He had full, succulent lips that screamed sensual pleasure.

He turned to point at each of his friends and name them. "That's Markus, Tim, and Benedikt—"

A thunderbolt of memory and astonishment streaked across my brain. "Lars? Is that you?"

## CHAPTER TWO

He stopped short and looked at me with surprise. "How do you know my name?"

I pressed a hand to my chest. "It's me, Arianna, from Stratford High School."

He brightened, and I could see in his eyes that he remembered. I was swept immediately into a giant hug, and my feet left the bench.

"Arianna!" Our bodies pressed together, and his breath came warm in my ear. "I can't believe it's really you." He kissed me on the cheek before setting me back on my feet, and the warmth of a blush crept over my face. God, he smelled good. He wore one of those mellow musky colognes that made you feel as though the earth itself were wrapping around you.

Lars grinned at me then turned and spoke to his friends in rapid German. I guessed he was explaining how we knew each other.

"You know that guy?" Dana asked me.

"Yeah. He was an exchange student at my high school." *The same one I was just thinking about two seconds ago.*

"Wow. Was he as hot then as he is now?"

"No. Yes. I mean, he was hot as a teenager, but he's even hotter now." In high school he had been lean and gangly. But now, four years later, that framework was filled in with layers of muscle. His chest and shoulders were broader and his arms thicker than my faint memories. The youthful roundness that had softened the planes of his face was gone, which was why I hadn't recognized him right away. His jaw had more definition, as did his cheeks. Hints of light-brown stubble shadowed his features, further demonstrating that he wasn't a boy anymore.

"Did you guys date back then?" Dana asked me.

I shook my head. "He was friends with my brother. But sometimes we all hung out together." My brother was a year older than me, and I remembered feeling shy every time he brought the sexy foreigner around. There had been a couple of times Lars had come over when my brother was late getting home from his part-time job. So we'd hung out and chatted, just the two of us. For me, those had been sweet electricity-filled moments where I'd had his full attention. He had seemed to enjoy our time together as well. But nothing had ever happened, even though there'd been moments where I thought it would, electricity-filled ones where I'd blushed all the way to the roots of my hair.

Lars had been at our high school for only six months, but I still remembered the day he came to our house to say goodbye. The longing looks he and I had exchanged were etched in my memory. He'd kissed me on the cheek when he said goodbye. And for months, every time I thought of it, the skin there heated with memory. It was silly, but in that half second of contact, the simmering attraction had spiked into full bloom when his lips touched my face. In that instant my entire body had become acutely aware of him. Not the teenage crush type feelings, but something rawer from deep in my core. I thought I had seen the same sort of jolt in his eyes, but there'd been no chance to talk about it. And the next day, he was gone.

Lars and his friends lifted their beers from the table and raised them in a toast. He glanced over at Dana and me and invited us to do the same. We happily joined in, and I even said, "*Prost!*" as the guys did. It was the German word for cheers.

I went to take a sip from my mug, but Lars stopped me with a hand on my arm. "You have to touch it to the table first or it's bad luck." I hadn't noticed that custom yesterday, but we hadn't sat with any Germans then.

"Oh, okay." I did as all the boys were doing and touched the bottom of my glass to the table. Dan joined in, too.

"And when you drink you have to make eye contact," Lars said. Using two fingers he pointed at his own eyes then mine.

"Got it." As I drank, I maintained eye contact with Lars. The blue I remembered from high school had taken on more depth. There were facets to it now, like a diamond, and I had a hard time looking away. I could have stared at him for hours on end. He was just that damn good-looking.

The tent was loud from the music of the band, the voices of people singing along, and the random chatter of multiple languages. It was so loud Lars had to stand close in order to converse with me, which I didn't mind at all. He was on the ground and I stood on the bench but, even with that, I wasn't much above his eye level, which meant he had to be over six feet tall.

"So how did you end up here?" he asked.

I glanced to the side to make sure Dana was doing okay. She was already flirting with Lars's friends, who were all pretty attractive as well, though not as cute as Lars.

"We're on vacation. We went to Italy for a couple of days before coming here. We're headed to France next. After that we go home." We hadn't been able to afford more than this one precious week. Now that I was here, I couldn't bear the thought of having to leave. I think I fell in love with Europe the second I glimpsed it from the plane.

"When do you leave Munich?" he asked me.

"Tomorrow. Our train leaves in the morning at nine." I took another long swallow from my mug and the chilly liquid helped to sooth the fire of attraction smoldering in my belly. Standing so close to him allowed me the pleasure of leisurely examining every feature of his face, from his full lips to his chiseled cheeks and onward to the darker curls of blond hair skimming his neck, which I was dying to stroke with my fingers.

I'd stared at his profile so many times on Facebook. I assumed that my brother was connected to Lars on there, but I wasn't sure. Years ago, my brother had refused to friend me because he didn't want me "spying" on him. He'd even gone as far as blocking me. If he kept in touch with Lars other than that, I had no idea. Probably not. Guys made that whole "out of sight, out of mind" thing true. I had come close several times to just pressing the stupid Friend button. I had known Lars, why not just do it myself? But I was too painfully shy back then to risk the pain of rejection, as minor as it was. And, after talking it over with my friends, we unanimously decided it would have been a lame move. If Lars had wanted to keep in contact with me, we reasoned, he would have friended me himself or taken down my email address so we could write to each other. But neither of those things had happened. So I'd let it go and tried to forget him.

I should have been over him after all this time. But no, I wasn't. The attraction came rushing back full force. Even now, I was debating over faking a fall just so I could grasp those strong shoulders of his, but I didn't. I also knew I had an idiotic smile plastered on my face. But who cared? There wasn't much I could do to stop it. Everyone here was drunk and acting stupid, no reason for me to be any different. Besides, just like before, I would never see him again after today.

"What have you seen of the city?" Lars asked.

"Not much," I admitted. "We arrived late the day before yesterday and had dinner at Hofbräuhaus. We slept in and then came to Oktoberfest around eleven and ended up spending the whole day here. It was so much fun we decided to come back instead of seeing the sights."

"Were you in this tent yesterday?"

I shook my head, frowning as I tried to remember which one we'd been in. "Can't remember the name. Something with an S."

"Schottenhamel?"

"Yes! That's the one."

"Did you get a chance to go on some of the rides? Or try the food from the vendors outside? It's very different from the US."

I remembered tantalizing aromas in the air on our way in and out of Theresienwiese, the festival grounds where Oktoberfest was held. But yesterday Dana and I had been on a mission to get into one of the crowded tents because it had been chilly and drizzling. We'd passed some outdoor beer gardens on the way there and neither of us had felt like standing outside in the fall weather away from the excitement. "No, we haven't had time to do that."

"Oh, well you have to—" He was suddenly distracted by the band's shift to another tune. As one, he and his friends cheered then sang along to the German tune. After sharing a grin with his friends, Lars turned back to me, wrapped an arm around my waist, and, still singing, pulled me close. He had a nice deep singing voice that welled from his gut. It was like chocolate to my ears—if they could eat, that is. I laid my arm around his shoulders and together we swayed back and forth to the tempo of the music. That's when I realized his friends and many of the people in the crowd were doing the same, arms interlocked or wrapped around each other.

He glanced at me. "This is called *schunkeln*," he said.

"You mean the swaying back and forth together?" I asked.

He grinned. "Yes. Exactly."

It was funny how much I enjoyed something so simple. It was just plain fun to be here. Everyone was participating with the antics of the band and the atmosphere was warm and joyful. Being tucked into Lars's side perfected the moment. Even when the music changed and everyone else stopped schunkeln-ing we remained clasped together. I was totally fine with that. Even through his green wool coat, I detected firm muscles and didn't really feel like pulling away. Lars snuck his long warm fingers under my coat and rested them on my side just above my waist, the pressure and heat of them almost burning a hole through my T-shirt. I couldn't have been happier. If ever there was a moment I wanted to freeze in time, this was it.

"How is your brother?"

Talk about a buzz kill. "Good. He's graduating from college this year with a degree in business. He's not going to believe it when I tell him I ran into you."

Lars's fingers stroked my side in a minute gesture that made me want arch against him. "Make sure to tell him I said hello."

"I will." Was it the beer, or was Lars acting interested in me? Wouldn't an uninterested guy have let go of me by now?

"And you? Are you at university, too?"

I nodded. "I'm in California, at UCLA, studying marketing."

His eyes lit up. "How do you like it there?"

God those lips. He was so close I would just have to tilt my head and lean in… "At first it was hard to be so far away from home, but now I really love it. The weather is great and so is the school." *Focus, Arianna, he's just an old friend.*

"Do you have a boyfriend?" His eyes were locked on my face. The intensity of his gaze showing that this wasn't a casual question.

I shook my head and felt a zing of pleasure shoot through my heart. I'd had a few boyfriends over the years, but nothing serious had evolved. And, right at this moment, I couldn't be happier to be available.

I turned the question back on him. "Do you have a girlfriend?"

"No."

"Why not?" I found it hard to believe.

"I met someone special a long time ago and no one I've met since compares to her."

From the way he was looking into my eyes it was clear whom he referred to, but I was stunned. *Does he mean me?* No, it was impossible. My heart soared with joy anyway. Our gazes locked on each other and worlds of meaning passed between us. It was as if we were standing frozen in time, in our own dimension, as the festivities went on around us.

Dana broke the trance. "Hey, Arianna, do you want another beer?"

I tore my eyes away from Lars to see that the waitress stood by our table taking orders. I looked down at the glass clutched in my hand. Somehow it was empty again. Was that the third one I'd had? Each of the German Ma was roughly equivalent to three regular beers. How much time had gone by, and how was I still standing upright? And why the hell would Lars be interested in me now, after seeing me for five minutes, when he'd done nothing back then?

He unwrapped his arm from around my waist and took my hand. "Come on, let me show you more of the festival. We can go out for a little while and come back."

It was the gentle look in his eyes and his eager tone, rather than my curiosity about the other attractions, that made me nod my head.

## CHAPTER THREE

I glanced at Dana. "Lars and I are going to walk around outside for a little bit. You want to come with us?" I invited her even though I didn't want to. It wouldn't be right to abandon my friend.

A knowing look swept over her expression. "No, I'll stay here. I just ordered another beer. You guys go ahead."

"She'll be fine here with my friends," Lars said. He lifted me from the bench and set me on the ground. His breath against my ear and his deep rumble stirred a primal instinct within me and my gut quivered with pleasure. "I'll make sure my friends look after her. Hold on."

"Okay."

It took a few minutes to make our way out. We stepped outside to see a horde of people crowded around the door waiting to gain entry.

I tugged on Lars's hand. "Wait a minute. How are we going to get back in?" Dana would kill me if I didn't come back for her.

"Don't worry. One of my friends is working the door at the other entrance."

I relaxed and allowed him to pull me along beside him. Oktoberfest was unlike any other festival I'd ever been to. Every couple of steps a different language or accent could be heard. It was amazing how, within a few feet, I heard people speaking Italian, German and French. Amid that there was also English, but it was laced with accents, like British, Indian or Irish. It was as though Oktoberfest was the place where all the countries had been squashed together into one cosmic meeting point.

Aside from beer tents, there were booths along the side of the thoroughfare selling crafts. Then we turned down a section with carnival rides.

Lars must have seen me staring because he stopped in front of a ride that reminded me of one I'd ridden back home when I was a kid. People sat in pairs strapped into seats enclosed in wire cages. Not only did the cages themselves spin around, but they were attached to a belt on the oblong oval frame. As the long oval rotated like the blade of a giant fan, the belt ran the spinning cages around its perimeter creating three sources of spinning motion all at the same time.

"You want to try it?" Lars asked.

"No way." I took a step back. "I rode that thing once back home and that was enough to last my entire lifetime."

He laughed. "When we were younger, a couple of my friends made the mistake of getting on after drinking. One of them made it off of the ride before he was sick. The other wasn't so lucky."

"Ew! Gross!" Another good reason not to get on something like that. With all that whirling and spinning, there must have been a vomit shower.

Lars resumed walking again, holding on tight to me so we didn't get separated in the crowd. He paused in front of a snack vendor and the sweet, rich smell of something yummy wafted to my nose. I wasn't able to identify the lumpy golden brown treats behind the glass partition though, and of course I couldn't read the signs.

"Are you hungry?"

"Yes." My stomach squealed in agreement, reminding me that it had been hours since I'd eaten the scrumptious roast chicken and potatoes in the tent. The food here was surprisingly good. Dana had ordered some kind of bratwursts or other that had come with sauerkraut and they had been totally tasty as well. The hearty Bavarian fare definitely suited me.

After a brief exchange in German with the vendor, Lars handed me a small warm paper cone. He opened the top, pulled a misshapen brown ball from it and lifted it to my mouth. I parted my lips and he popped it in, the tips of his fingers lingered on my mouth making me blush. Whatever it was, it was sweet and crunchy. "Mm." I reached into the bag for more. "What are they?"

"*Gebrannte Mandeln*...roasted...candy nuts." His sandy blond eyebrows scrunched together in thought for a second. Then he snapped his fingers and said, "No. Almonds. They're coated in sugar and spices and some other things. Do you like them?" He snagged a few from the paper cone and popped them into his mouth.

"Love them."

He glanced at the next booth over. "How about currywurst? Have you tried that?"

I shook my head and glanced skeptically over at the booth. "What is it?" I was suspicious when it came to food I couldn't immediately categorize. Simple food with recognizable ingredients was more my thing. Something sweet, like the coated almonds, was easy to take a chance on. But I was wary when it came to other stuff.

"You'll like it. Here, come."

He pulled me into the short line, and a few minutes later we were standing off to the side with a small steaming paper plate. The currywurst looked like a chopped up hot dog with barbecue sauce ladled over it and some kind of mustard-colored powder sprinkled on it. *Ew.* I took a cautious sniff. The odor was pleasant enough. Like before, Lars speared a piece with the plastic fork and lifted it to my mouth to feed me.

His blue eyes were plastered on my face and I felt self-conscious about chickening out, so I closed my eyes and opened my mouth. *If this tastes nasty I can always spit it out—there's a garbage can nearby.* But the spicy flavor of the curry sauce combined with the rich, meaty taste of the sausage combined to make an entirely new flavor, not the gross hot dog and barbecue sauce combo I thought it would be. I opened my eyes.

Lars was grinning at me. I smiled back, still chewing, and nodded my approval. "That is really good."

"I told you."

We ate as we continued our stroll through the fairgrounds, and had fun pointing out people who'd drank too much and were now stumbling home. A group of men sang as they walked, towing their worse-for-wear friend along. Others, both men and women, had glazed eyes. I wondered if they would remember what they'd been doing when they woke up in the morning. But none of it seemed out of place—it was one big happy atmosphere of celebration.

Lars stopped us again, this time at a hat vendor. There were all kinds of hats. Some were traditional Bavarian ones like Lars's. They came in green, gray, and brown with all different kinds of trim and decorations on them. Other, less expensive hats were on the comical side and shaped like kegs or mugs. One had beer holders with straws so the wearer could drink as they walked.

"You can't leave without a souvenir," Lars said.

I looked up from the stand of felt A-shaped hats I was examining.

He shoved some money and a receipt into his pocket and then presented a hat to me that looked like a full beer mug, complete with froth, and placed it on my head. I held still as he tugged the brim into position and arranged my hair, pulling the light-brown locks forward over my shoulders. He trailed his fingertips down the length of the last cluster of strands, making the base of my scalp tingle. We stood so close I could detect the mild scent of beer on his breath.

The boots I wore had a decent heel on them, but I still had to tilt my head back to meet his gaze. "How does it look?"

"Perfect."

Our eyes locked, and it was as if time sucked us backward to that day so long ago when we'd said goodbye. It overpowered the world around us, forcing it into the background. All that existed was the two of us. As the longing in his gaze registered, my breath caught. *Does he feel the same way I do?* I got my answer when his lips pressed down on mine, and he wrapped his arms around me, pulling me tight.

## Chapter Four

I had the strange, fleeting thought that I was in heaven. He moved his lips slowly on mine, as though savoring every second. The sensual contact, especially when our tongues met and mated, awakened a place deep within me that stretched with pleasure. The onslaught of sensations made me curl my fingers into the fabric of his jacket, and a deep moan of pleasure rose in my throat. It was low and guttural, a sound I never knew I could make…

He eased his head back. "I've wanted to do that for a long time."

"I wanted you to do that, too." Then I blinked as his words registered. "Wait a minute. You have?"

He grinned and touched the strands of hair near my cheek. "Yes, it's was just…"

"What?"

He sighed and glanced away from me for a second before answering. "Your brother. He made me promise I wouldn't try anything with you."

"He did what?"

"He made me promise—"

"Nevermind. I heard you. And you listened to him?" I pulled away from him, anger driving away all other feelings.

He looked surprised. "Well, yes, he was my friend."

"So? What kind of friend does that? Why would you even listen to him?" I paced away from the booth. My voice had risen and people were glancing at us. I had been denied love because of some stupid fricking guy code? How moronic!

And then my feet slipped out from under me, and I sprawled onto the ground.

*Smooth, Arianna. Really smooth.* The embarrassment of it reduced my anger to irritation.

Lars kneeled beside me. "Are you okay?"

"Yeah, I don't know how the heck I did that..." I glanced down at my boots. Three fourths of the sole of the right one had become detached. The thick two-inch heel now dangled uselessly from the flap of leather. "Shit! I loved these boots."

"Did you twist your ankle?"

I frowned. "I don't think so. Nothing is hurting, anyway." Crap. Now I was going to have to go back to the hotel and change shoes.

"We'd better make sure." He began to remove my boot.

"Hold on," I said. "I'm sure it's fine. Let me see if I can walk on it."

"Okay." He set his hands on my waist and then stopped, sat back on his heels, and gazed at me.

"What?"

"I just want you to understand, Arianna, that I was young and in a foreign country. I was trying to fit in."

I huffed out a breath, understanding but not caring.

"I know now that I shouldn't have listened to your brother. I've never been able to forget you." He said the words softly, and they were like a caress that crossed the space between us.

A ridiculous smile spread across my face, and a full-body flush swept over me making the cool September air feel like a summer breeze. "I've never been able to forget you either."

He smiled and leaned in to kiss me briefly, then rose and pulled me up next to him. "Besides, I've never seen anyone succeed in looking mad wearing a hat like that."

I smacked him on the shoulder in reply and we both laughed. Just like that, the tension dissolved. "That's nothing. I'm still going to kill my brother when I get home," I said.

Lars chuckled.

I set my foot down and tried to stand on it, but it was extremely awkward. "The problem now is, how do I get to the hotel to change my shoes without having to walk barefoot?"

"Where is your hotel?"

I glanced at the surroundings. Fortunately, we'd somehow made our way to the entrance Dana and I had come through earlier. "It's just out and around the corner."

"I'll carry you," he said. "Better not to walk on it until we know more, especially with the way your shoe is. It might make it worse." He turned to present his back to me, and motioned with one of his hands for me to hop on.

"Okay. Thanks." I climbed on. His form was thick and strong and, with the way he strode easily forward, I doubted he felt my weight. It was silly, but clutching on to the back of someone so powerful made me feel girly and dainty. Plus, it was wonderful to clutch my arms around his broad chest and rest my cheek against the side of his neck where I could inhale his scent. His forearms were wrapped beneath my knees, and the movement of his hips between my thighs as he walked had my mind circling in a new, more intimate, direction.

"Are you still in school?" I asked, trying to focus.

"No, I'm finishing training to be a mechanic at Lufthansa."

"An airplane mechanic?"

"Yes."

"That's cool," I said. "So you'll be working here at the airport in Munich?"

He glanced back at me. "I could. It's a large company, though. I've actually been looking at positions in Los Angeles." He squeezed my calf.

I couldn't stop my mind from processing the millions of possibilities for us if he moved to LA. Then I scolded myself for getting so irrationally excited over something that wasn't even a thing. A short while later, we entered the hotel room Dana and I shared. Clothes were scattered on most of the available surfaces, which was embarrassing, but thankfully, there was no underwear lying around.

Lars lowered himself at the edge of my bed until my butt touched the mattress. I let go and slipped out of my jacket while he turned and unzipped my boot. He glanced at my damaged boot before setting it on the ground beside him. "That's easy to fix."

"It is?"

"Any shoe repair shop should be able to do it." He pulled my rainbow striped sock off and inspected my ankle. "It doesn't look swollen. Does anything hurt?" He pressed his fingers into different spots and rotated my foot, looking up at me inquiringly.

I shook my head at each movement. "How do you know so much about ankles?"

"I've played football—I mean soccer—since I could walk. Ankle injuries are pretty common."

It was surreal to be here with him now, alone in a hotel room. He stripped off my other boot then pulled his hat from his head, set it on the edge of the bed, and shrugged out of his coat. Beneath he wore a white shirt and the traditional suspenders that held up his lederhosen. Across his chest, an embellished crosspiece held the suspenders parallel to each other.

He sat next to me and took my hand. "I can't believe we ran into each other at *Wiesn*. It's really lucky...I'm really lucky." The look in his eyes made me feel like a treasure. His blond hair glinted in the light, mussed from being under a hat, but still sexy.

"Wiesn?"

"It's what we call Oktoberfest here." He touched his fingers to the brim of my hat. I'd totally forgotten I still had it on. "It looks good on you."

I laughed. "Yeah? Having a giant beer on my head looks good?" I tugged it off self-consciously.

"You make it look good." He cupped my cheek in his hand, and time stood still again.

I didn't wait for him to lean in. I did it myself, and we picked up where we'd left off at the fairgrounds. Together we reclined onto the bed, our hands roving across each other's bodies. The slow, intense way his mouth moved over mine had me smoldering within minutes. I snuggled closer and closer to him until, finally, I pushed him onto his back and lay on top of him. My body exploded with lust when I felt the hard ridge of erection pressing into my hips. I writhed against him instinctively and it felt wonderful.

"Wait," he gasped. He pushed gently on my shoulders. "Wait."

"Why?" This was what I wanted. There were no doubts in my mind. Being with him now was a dream come true.

"Because..." His eyes shifted to the side and he sighed. He ran a hand through his hair with frustration.

That's when it registered. "Oh my god! Seriously? Because of my brother again?" I pulled back, but he wouldn't let me go.

"Arianna. Stay. It's just…you're special. I want to do the right thing."

I glared at him. "Yeah. You both decided what was right for me then. And, guess what? You were wrong!" Rejection and disappointment speared through me along with the anger.

Lars caught my face between his hands. "Don't you see? I don't want to be wrong. I don't want to hurt you."

I was immediately lost in his gaze. I could see that he really cared about me. The knowledge warmed my heart. "Then let me decide what's right for me this time." I pulled one of his hands to my lips and kissed his palm, trying not to plead. "Even if we never see each other again, I'm absolutely sure that we shouldn't let the magic get away again."

His brows drew together in concern. "Are you sure?"

"Yes. I'm sure."

"Good. Because, Arianna, there's nothing I've ever wanted more."

A brilliant smile lit my face. "Me, too." I trailed kisses down his cheek to the thick cords of his neck and, before I could stop myself, I nipped his skin with my teeth. His answering moan made me feel mad with power. His fingers slid beneath the waist of my jeans, and he stroked the bare flesh of my ass cheek and fingered my thong.

"You are even more beautiful than I remember, Arianna."

He rolled us over so I was on my back and pushed his hips between my thighs. God, yes. There was no doubt in my mind at all. I wanted him. Even in high school I'd wanted him, but was too young and shy to know what to do about it. I swept back the soft golden strands of hair that fell across his forehead.

"This is too good to be true," I whispered. And, as his lips caught mine again and his fingers kneaded the flesh of my waist, I knew this was something I couldn't pass up. Some mysterious arcane knowledge told me so. Tonight was about soaking up every last bit of electricity amplifying between us.

He pressed himself against the most intimate part of me and I encouraged him, tugging at the soft leather of the lederhosen covering his hips.

Suddenly, I was impatient for us to be skin-to-skin. I wanted to feel the heat of his body on mine. I frantically undid the buttons of his shirt then tried the fastenings of his pants and suspenders, but couldn't make sense of them. I was momentarily interrupted by him stripping my shirt off in one smooth move. He unhooked the blue lace-and-satin bra I wore and then his mouth was on my breast, sucking in that oh-so-good way while his teeth teased my hardened nipple.

"Oh!" I tugged at the front of his pants, not able to see what I was doing with his head bowed over my chest. "Lars, I want you." The words came out low and urgent.

He pinned my hands above my head, then lowered himself to cover my body once again. "Are you sure?" Though his face was filled with passion, concern held him still as he regarded me.

I was flattered by his concerned. But everything was so right between us, the only regret I would have was if we *didn't* have sex right now. I was old enough to be comfortable with my sexuality, with having sex purely for pleasure. The antiquated rules of conduct society tried to place on women had no hold on me. There would be no guilt later. I wanted this, I wanted *him* and the pleasure we would create together.

"Absolutely."

He took a second to absorb my answer, obviously weighing the pros and cons in his mind. Then he gave me a quick peck on the lips and pulled away to undo his pants.

While he stripped out of his garments, and I the remainder of mine, our eyes stayed locked on each other, passion building as more skin was exposed.

He kneeled on the edge of the bed and ripped open a small square packet. God, he was beautiful. His wide shoulders tapered to a waist thick with muscle, and there between his legs throbbed an erection so large and enticing I reached out to stroke it, marveling at the soft skin. He paused to enjoy the feel of my hands. And the sight of him kneeling on the bed, his blue eyes piercing into me, called to mind images of sword-wielding warriors for some reason, which was completely sexy.

He rolled the condom over his length, but rather than wait for him to settle on top of me, I took over, pushing him down onto his back and straddling him. He clutched the hair at the nape of my neck as he kissed me.

And I took his full, thick, wonderful length into me all the way to the hilt in one smooth, slow motion. I was so wet and turned on that there was zero resistance, and we came together as though designed to be one.

We groaned into each other's mouths at the feel of it. My hips rocked of their own accord in a motion that was primal and instinctual. Lust practically seeped from my pores. I gave the reins of my control over to my subconscious and allowed it to drive us both toward climax. It was a delicious winding road, and as the molten surge of pleasure built to a crest in my belly, Lars seemed to sense it somehow because he switched our positions in an instant and drove into me with deep, steady strokes that made me cry out. I'd never been so in sync with anyone before. I knew this was special.

"So beautiful...you're so beautiful. Oh, god, Arianna!"

We climaxed at the same moment, our hands in frenzied motion on each other's bodies, eyes locked on each other's faces as ecstasy flared from the power of our unity.

## CHAPTER FIVE

We lay in each other's arms breathing heavily until *dinging* of both our phones penetrated the quiet cocoon of our bliss.

"We'd better go back," I said. "They must be wondering what happened to us." I wished with all my soul that I had the ability to freeze time. But I settled for trying to burn into memory all that had just happened between us and the tender way he looked at me now.

"Okay." He trailed a finger down my cheek and skimmed it over the rise of my breasts. "I'll send them a message and let them know we're on our way."

We rose, used the bathroom in turns, and dressed, neither of us in a hurry, then walked back hand-in-hand to our friends. We were quiet on the way back, but I think both of us were comfortable allowing each other the space to savor what we'd experienced.

Back in the tent, the chaos and excitement of people celebrating hit like a crashing wave of reality, bringing me down to earth. When we reached the table, I could tell Dana was ready to leave. She wobbled on her feet and yawned. "I'm tired. Did you have fun?" Her voice was slurred and she blinked at me, trying to focus on my face.

I nodded, certain she would grill me later for more details when she was sober. "We can go back to the room now if you want." It wasn't what I wanted to do, but it was what my friend needed.

"Yeah, I think that's a good idea."

"You're leaving already?" Lars said. "But it's still early."

I cast a rueful glance toward Dana, who was hugging one of Lars's friends goodbye. "She's had enough to drink, and we have an early train to catch."

He pulled me into his arms for a hug and one last long, deep kiss. I felt the pressure of his fingers on my back as he clutched me to him. And then I felt the odd sensation of him pushing something into the back pocket of my jeans with his fingers. But I didn't get a chance to ask him what it was. And, from the expression on his face, I figured that I should check it out later.

I made it just to the outside of the fairgrounds without looking. Dana chattered to me drunkenly, and most of her attention was centered on walking straight, so I figured it was as good a time as any to see what he'd slid into my pocket.

It turned out to be a note, written on a piece of hotel stationary. He must have jotted it down while I was in the bathroom.

*Arianna,*

*Now I am determined to get the job in Los Angeles. Until I do, let's stay in touch. I'm not letting you go again.*

*Yours, Lars.*

At the bottom, all of his contact details were written out—phone number, email, and Skype. A huge smile broke across my face and the high I had felt earlier in his arms returned to fill me with a warm glow. I had no doubt now that fate had brought us together tonight. And I was certain we would have the chance to grow even more what had been planted so long ago.

# About the Author

Lover of ice cream, beer, and red wine, Jewel Quinlan tries to stay fit when she's not typing madly on her computer concocting another tale. She is an avid traveler and, in her spare time, she likes to do yoga, hike, learn German, and play with her spoiled Chihuahua, Penny.

Website: jewelquinlan.com

# *Home for Christmas, Act 2*

## By Teri McGill

## Chapter One

### Holly

"Why would I need a Dustbuster? I have a brand new, top-of-the-line Electrolux Ultra!" I scoffed, taking another sip of my mojito.

"You've been living like a damn nun for years, so I'm betting there's a shitload of cobwebs up there!" Gina's boisterous squeals had me scanning the bar for unwelcome attention. "It's got that long, narrow attachment—"

"Ssh!" I cautioned, embarrassed she was aware of my nonexistent sexual encounters, although I had never divulged that information. Gina knew *everything*. She was a bloodhound, capable of sniffing sexual afterglow a mile away. *Note to self: fabricate some imaginary hookups to throw her off.*

"You're pushing thirty, Holly. You gotta get out there before you—"

"What? Turn into an ancient, wrinkled-up prune?" Sometimes Gina overstepped her best friend status and it pissed me off. I didn't need another painful reminder of my age nor the fact that I was alone. *Jamison was my soul mate, the absolute love of my life. We spent the week before he was deployed in bed, making love like there was no tomorrow. Ironic choice of words. We didn't know we had made Jamie.*

"No, before you expire!" Gina placated earnestly. "Wait, I didn't mean it *that* way. Don't you want a father for Jamie? Maybe a sibling?"

"Jamie has a daddy. He's just...gone." A heavy sigh whooshed from my lungs. I bit my lip to quell the tears clogging my throat.

Gina empathized, the corners of her mouth drooping. "Sweetie, I love you like a sister. Jamison has been gone over four years. You deserve to find love again. So, with that in mind, I am officially inviting you to the holiday party. Mr. Goldstein insisted on it!"

My face scrunched. "Why?" *Crap. Not again.*

"There are two new partners at the firm who are single, and Mr. G hinted that extra women would be welcomed. He also knows your *situation*. I have a sneaky suspicion his wife will be playing matchmaker again."

"No. Freakin'. Way! Do you recall that *loser* she set me up with last year? Ugh! Repulsive is an understatement." I shivered at the memory.

Gina scowled. "Are you shittin' me? He was smokin' hot. You're too picky," she huffed.

I snorted, rolling my eyes. "I stand corrected. He *was* smokin'—a stinky *cigar*—and he had his hand on my ass before we were formally introduced."

Gina had the good sense to act contrite. "I wasn't aware of that. This year will be better, I promise. It can't get worse, right? So you'll come? It's at the Universal Hilton."

Gina's eyebrows arched upward. She knew that hotel was my favorite; my wedding had been there, in the magnificent rose garden.

Seeing my reaction, Gina wrapped me in her warmest hug. She assured, "Mrs. G has a guy in mind for *me*, so you are off the hook." I heaved another sigh as my shoulders sagged. I was putty in Gina's hands and she knew it. "It'll be fun, my jolly Holly girl! Think about it. You never know what could happen."

I gulped down the rest of my drink and ordered another. *Maybe Gina's right.*

# Chapter Two

## Jake

Aaron Goldstein, my new boss and former brother-in-law, greeted me with open arms. We hadn't seen each other in several weeks.

"Jake, single life continues to agree with you! You look terrific, like you've lost a hundred pounds. *Beth*, to be exact. My sister has always been the spoiled, self-centered brat of the family, but how she treated you? Appalling. Naomi still refuses to speak to her. 'That bitch is *dead* to me!' were her exact words, and I agree." Aaron stopped for a second to inhale some much-needed oxygen. "All settled in your office? I gave you the northwest corner—best view of the Santa Monica Mountains."

"Yes, thank you, it's perfect. Your paralegal, Gina, gave me the grand tour. That girl is a hoot. Already invited me to the Holiday Gala, as she called it." Gina was sweet, but loud and too flirty. Not my type.

"Gina knows every employee, which is why she's in charge of the guest list. You're coming, right? If you don't, Naomi swore she would bludgeon me to death with the sterling silver menorah. Please, Jake, have mercy."

"Wouldn't miss it. I'm looking forward to meeting my new co-workers."

*Especially the intriguingly beautiful Holly. I have not been able to get her out of my mind. The total opposite of Beth is exactly what I need. New friends, different surroundings, and a new life with endless possibilities would be a pleasant change too.*

## CHAPTER THREE

### HOLLY

It was impossible to ignore Gina's disdainful scowl. I tossed my hair defiantly, channeling my inner rebellious teenager. "This is the third outfit I've tried on. What's so terrible about it?" I blew out an exasperated sigh.

Picking nonexistent lint off my charcoal-gray pencil skirt, Gina grumbled, "It's perfect for a librarian convention, *chica*, but not for my Holiday Gala! Remember that fabulous emerald-green satin ensemble you wore to our college reunion? You were a knockout in that! It's the perfect Christmas color and matches your eyes, not to mention your name."

"You don't think it's too over-the-top? My boobs were popping out all night, for fuck's sake."

Gina pouted. "And since when is that a *bad* thing? You were sexy as sin. Every eye was on you. And besides, those were your breast-feeding boobs, so they're a tad smaller now." She wore a triumphant grin. "Let's try that beauty on. You'd better still have those silver fuck-me stilettos." Gina's giggle was infectious and, as usual, I had no other option but to join in. Striding into my walk-in closet, I quickly found the items in question.

"I got you a little pre-holiday giftie!" Gina teased in her signature singsong lilt, as I emerged from the closet's depths. "That's more like it. You look dazzling! Now, spritz a bit of this on your secret girly-parts," Gina ordered as she pressed something into my palm. I peered closely at the tiny purse-sized perfume bottle, deftly opening its cap.

"*Decadence?*" I whispered skeptically. "Hmmm..." I took a tentative sniff and was immediately transported to a fragrant garden. "Oh my. That is heaven." I examined the luxurious gift, remarking, "Who's this Marc Jacobs fellow? A friend of yours?"

Gina's mouth fell open in appalled indignation. Teasing her was too easy.

* * *

Holiday decorations abounded and Christmas music blared as we strode through the lobby and into the banquet room. Gina grinned, confidently linking our arms together.

"You two look like a million-dollar Bloomies holiday ad!" Naomi Goldstein gushed as we approached the table. "Aaron, please introduce these gorgeous girls to your new partners."

"It's a pleasure to meet you, Holly." A deep, sexy voice on my left instantly garnered my attention as steel-gray eyes met mine. He took my hand in his and a tingle of electricity passed through us. "I'm Jake McKenna, an old friend of Aaron and Naomi."

For a brief moment I forgot how to breathe. The man was *that* handsome. Strong jaw, prominent cheekbones, and full lips that were begging to be… *Wait. What? I needed a sip of water. No. This calls for wine and lots of it. Where's the bar?*

I inhaled deeply, licked my lower lip and smiled. "Jake. It's so nice to meet you. How do you know the Goldsteins?"

Jake shifted in his chair, then downed a shot of amber liquid. Aaron had been subtly eavesdropping and interjected, "Jake used to be married to my sister Beth."

Naomi nodded vigorously, chiming in with her own declaration. "We got custody of Jake in the divorce settlement. He will always be part of *our* family."

Gina shot me a knowing glance, eyebrows raised.

\* \* \*

"What's with the *look*?" I hissed at Gina as we checked our makeup in the ladies' room mirror. Her eyes sparkled mischievously, as if withholding secrets.

"I suspect that something—or should I say some*one*—has caught your eye."

"What are you talking about?" I deflected.

Gina's retort was quick. "Whenever you blush, your freckles become obvious. I could see your attraction to

Jake a mile away, and I'm pretty sure the feeling was mutual."

Her words caused my stomach to clench, but I needed answers. "Do you know anything about his divorce?"

Shaking her head, Gina sighed. "Only a bit of office gossip that Beth cheated on him. I met her once. She's a bitch with a capital C, if you know what I mean."

My heart sank. "The last thing I need is to get involved with a divorced man who has a nasty ex." Gina took my hands in hers, shooting me a glare with her trademark pleading puppy-dog eyes.

"But he seems soooo nice, not to mention drop-dead gorgeous!"

*I certainly couldn't argue with that.*

# Chapter Four

## Jake

I first saw Holly a few months ago while out to dinner with Aaron and Naomi, who caught me staring at the beautiful blonde. Aaron mentioned that Gina, Holly's dinner companion and best friend, worked for him and he would be happy to "hook me up" with an introduction. I'd declined out of sheer nervousness—*or was it downright terror?*—at the thought of jumping into the dating pool after the Beth nightmare.

I had fantasized about Holly for a while, so I thought I'd be prepared for how I would feel when we finally met. I was wrong. Her shy smile, the softness of her hand, and her radiant green eyes far surpassed anything I could have conjured up in my dreams.

I was captivated by her voice and her whispered first word: "Jake". Most people say hello upon meeting, but she spoke my name, like a prayer. On her lips it sounded magical, full of promises and possibilities. For the first time since Beth left me, I felt ready, willing to take a risk and venture out of my comfort zone.

The group made pleasant small talk over dinner, but I was itching to get some alone time with Holly. The band began to play and I heard the familiar melody of "White Christmas". I took a deep, fortifying breath and turned to face her as I gently covered her hand with mine.

"May I have this dance, Holly? I love this song."

Apprehension flooded her beautiful face, but she nodded and my racing heartbeat calmed.

As I held her close, a subtle, floral fragrance wafted upward and I inhaled deeply. Beth always doused herself with heavy, musky perfume. I hated it. Holly's delicate scent was pure woman. Intoxicating. I was hyper-aware of her body against mine, my hand on her lower back—firm, not overly familiar. I wanted to know everything about her, but would not cross-examine her as if she was one of my witnesses. Naomi had shared a few facts. Holly was a widowed stay-at-home mother who helped run a family business.

Suddenly those breathtaking eyes were upturned, studying me. "I think I know why you like this song." Her rosy lips curved upward.

"Is that so?" I challenged, in what I hoped was my sexiest tone. *Fuck me. That was lame.*

"I overheard that you used to live in Manhattan, so I suspect *dreaming* about a white Christmas is far more pleasant when surrounded by sunshine." Her long lashes fluttered coyly. "Am I right, Jake?"

Her soft giggle was infectious and we shared a heartfelt laugh as I nodded. I felt her relax in my arms. My cock had the opposite reaction, standing at attention.

"I grew up in the Village, went to NYU School of Law, and then moved to L.A. I love it here and do not miss the winters one bit. You?"

"Born and raised Valley Girl, and my birthday is December 25th. At least my parents didn't name me Mistletoe." Her emerald-green eyes had me hypnotized.

The music morphed into another slow tune and Holly abruptly stiffened, her fingers gripping mine. Her eyes shone bright with sudden tears. *What the…?*

"*I'll be home for Christmas,*" the bandleader's voice crooned. "*You can count on me.*"

Her hand fell from my neck and I missed its warmth immediately as she took a small step back. "Jake, I should go. I'm so sorry." I could hear the panic in her breathy whisper.

My hand had not moved from the small of her back. *I can't let her leave. Not like this.*

"Holly, stay. Please? This will be my first Christmas alone." I sighed, then added, "Since my divorce. Will you at least finish this dance? If Naomi sees you abandon me, I will never hear the end of it."

Biting her lower lip apprehensively, Holly gazed up at me and nodded, returning her soft hand to my nape. We spent the next hour deep in conversation, while moving slowly on the dance floor. No topic seemed off-limits: books, movies, religion, even politics came under discussion. She eventually revealed the loss of her husband, reining in her emotions as best she could. My heart ached for her; my misfortunes paled in comparison. Oblivious to the rhythm of the music, all I could hear was her sweet voice and the beating of her heart against my chest.

## Chapter Five

### Holly

The gala was winding down; I was shocked to see it was past midnight. Gina nodded approvingly, her inner musings on full display. She was overjoyed I hadn't run for the hills when the sudden rush of sadness overtook me. Her eyes were on us while we danced, her relief apparent as Jake and I immersed ourselves in conversation. My heart broke as he recounted how his wife had an affair and then left him for her lover. I suspected there was more he wasn't telling me. I included only the pertinent facts when sharing the loss of Jamison. It was comforting to be with someone who understood my pain. It also was nice to have a gorgeous man hold me so snugly in his strong arms.

Jake invited a few of us, including the Goldsteins, Gina, and Marco, the other new partner, up to his suite for a nightcap. Naomi cornered me in the elevator, whispering, "You two look great together. Jake McKenna is one of the best men I know." She shot me a sly wink. "You're in good hands, dear." Her words caused my stomach to flip-flop.

A pleasant hour of mingling passed, and I realized Jake and I were alone in the suite once Gina and Marco departed.

"Can I get you anything, Holly?" Jake had been a perfect gentleman all evening and now that we were alone, my heart fluttered inside my ribcage. I was terrified. Feelings rushed through me that I hadn't experienced in years, emotions I willingly suppressed now threatened to resurface.

"Just a water. No more wine tonight, thank you." After grabbing two bottles from the fridge, Jake sat next to me on the couch. Close, but not too close.

"Holly, I have a confession to make." Turning to face me, Jake took my hand in his. "Several months ago, the Goldsteins took me out to dinner. We ate at the new Palm in Beverly Hills."

*Hmmm, I recall seeing an extremely good-looking... Jake?*

"You were with Gina, and I spotted you from across the room. Naomi—damn that eagle-eyed woman, she misses nothing—mentioned how distracted I was and Aaron offered to arrange an introduction. I was caught off-guard and didn't feel ready, so I declined. I regretted that decision and have wanted to meet you ever since."

"Truth be told, I noticed you too. I think you may have passed our table, and our eyes met for a brief moment." I felt my cheeks redden as I stammered, willing my racing heartbeat to decelerate. I hadn't flirted in years and felt ineptly out-of-practice. *Breathe.*

Another hour or two sped by as our comfort level with each other deepened. Jake had casually draped his arm around my shoulders and I found myself snuggling with a hand pressed to his muscular chest. We covered so many topics from how we'd met our spouses and online dating horror stories, to our distaste for reality TV shows. A mutual preference for a meaningful relationship instead of casual sex gave me hope. He also volunteered that regular STI tests, as well as sharing the results, were important and I agreed, gnawing on my lip nervously, relieved to get *that* awkward issue out of the way.

His beautiful eyes lowered, lingering on my mouth. I had only kissed one man in the last decade, and had never wanted to kiss another until this moment. Guilt tugged at my heart, or was it a feeling of infidelity? My conscience was conflicted, but the need that bloomed elsewhere in my body could not be denied.

"Holly, I need to kiss you more than I need air at this moment, but if you're not ready, I'll wait."

A war waged in my head: guilt versus desire. His sweet words put me at ease, but something told me it was too soon. *We just met a few hours ago.*

My chin fell to my chest and I heaved a sigh, stumbling over my words. "Jake, I..."

His hand cupped my cheek, raising my gaze to his as his thumb brushed a lone tear that had escaped my eye.

"No worries." After pressing a few tender kisses on my forehead, he pulled back and studied my face. His serious expression filled me with trepidation until he spoke.

"Holly, I don't want to look back on this moment after more lonely years have passed me by and feel any regrets. There is something extraordinary happening between us and I'd love to see where it leads. What do you think, my beautiful green-eyed girl?"

*What should I do, Jamison? I know you don't want a life of loneliness for Jamie and me.*

# CHAPTER SIX

## JAKE

I decided our first official date should be back at The Palm. I hadn't been here since that fateful night when she captured my attention from across the busy restaurant.

Holly opened up during dinner. Her husband was killed in Afghanistan; a hero who sacrificed his life to save others. He never met his daughter.

"Jamison kept a journal while he was deployed. It's been under my pillow since it was returned to me. I'm not ready to read it yet."

I caressed her hand but refrained from asking any questions; grief was still raw in her voice.

I shared how my marriage gradually deteriorated and eventually fell apart when I opted to pursue sports law instead of criminal defense, which I loathed. Beth aspired to be the wife of a prominent ADA and didn't hide her disapproval of my decision. I mentioned her affair but omitted the unpleasant details.

Over coffee, I pressed Holly for more information about herself. She had a bashful side, which I found endearing. "Tell me about your family, Valley Girl!"

Her giggle warmed my heart. "I live in Encino with my daughter. We have a duplex and my mother-in-law lives upstairs. Jamie has her grandma nearby and I have the world's best built-in baby-sitter! My parents and older brother live in the Napa Valley where they own and operate a vineyard. I run their website and online store."

"I have never been to Napa," I volunteered.

"It's incredibly beautiful. We'll have to take a trip up there one day."

Continued chatting revealed we shared many interests, which bolstered my courage, along with her mention of a Napa trip together.

"Holly, I know the perfect place for our next date. Tomorrow, around noon. Interested?"

\* \* \*

## HOLLY

I hadn't been to the Huntington Library and Botanical Gardens in years, forgetting how much I enjoyed the grounds. Strolling for hours, hand-in-hand, we often found ourselves alone on the tranquil paths. We dined at the Chinese Tea House, which overlooked a serene lake.

Despite the peaceful surroundings, Jake was not himself. Something was troubling him and I was determined to ferret it out. I suggested we relocate to a lounge chair near the water's edge where we could snuggle. He kissed the top of my head as I relaxed against his firm chest.

"Holly…" Jake began, placing a gentle kiss on my nose. "I've spared you the nastier details regarding my divorce, but there are things you should know." He brushed his fingertips down my cheek; tingling sparks followed.

"When I was sixteen, a routine checkup showed a large, non-malignant tumor in my pituitary gland. I had surgery, it was removed successfully, but the doctor warned that infertility was likely. I never hid it from Beth and she seemed okay with it—until her biological clock sounded the alarm. We tried unsuccessfully for a while, then a year ago she announced she was pregnant. Something seemed off. We rarely had sex and she was never home, so I became suspicious. After confronting her, she admitted she was sleeping with an ex-boyfriend. Long story short—they're married with a five-month-old son. I got a paternity test, just to be sure he wasn't mine. Further tests showed that I was, indeed, sterile." Jake looked so despondent, my heart broke for him.

"I'm sorry you had to go through that." I grasped his hand, entwining our fingers.

"The toughest thing to deal with is I *love* children, but everything happens for a reason. I do volunteer work with a local group called Boys to Men and I don't mean the singing group. They match at-risk young males with mentors who act as role models." Jake's expression did a one-eighty as he lit up with excitement and pride.

"I've been Donovan's mentor for two years. He's ten, in fifth grade, and a really great kid, despite the shitty hand life has dealt him. I'm not gonna lie, it was a struggle at first. There's never been a dad in the picture, just a string of his junkie mom's abusive boyfriends. He kept a lot of pent-up anger inside, but things improved when I took him to Staples Center last year to see Kobe Bryant's final game. That was an emotionally bonding experience for us both. He lives in a group home, but I've been considering the possibility of..."

"Adoption?" I couldn't help myself—the thought excited me. Jamie brought such joy to my life and I wished that for Jake, too.

"I'm working on it. I haven't mentioned anything, don't want to get his hopes up."

"I'd love to meet him. Let's set up a play date!"

"I know the perfect place. Wanna hear my plan?" Jake caressed my cheek, his warm hand stirred something deep in my belly.

Licking my lower lip in anticipation, I whispered, "Later. Right now I need you to kiss me." His lips brushed the corners of my mouth, softly at first. His warm tongue teased the seam of my lips. I wanted more, opening and inviting him in. The kiss intensified, startling me until I succumbed to the tidal wave of desire surging through my body. Jake's fingers tangled in my hair as he broke the kiss, gasping for air. His warm breath fanned my ear, teeth grazing my neck before softly biting my earlobe. I moaned as a rush of wetness flooded between my thighs.

Jake chuckled as he reached to subtly adjust his jeans. "We need to continue this back at my place."

## CHAPTER SEVEN

### JAKE

I barely remembered the drive home; the sweetness of her lips had me craving more. After encouraging Holly to get comfortable on the couch, I opened a bottle of wine and lit the fireplace. The night was chilly, even for Southern California. I snuck a glance at her, the flames reflecting in her sparkling eyes. Her beauty took my breath away as warmth flooded my chest, accompanied by a twinge of anxiety. Holly was nervously raking her full lower lip with her teeth. *So fuckin' sexy and she doesn't even know it.* God made this woman to my exact specifications: hourglass figure, heart-shaped ass, and lush lips that I envisioned screaming my name.

"Hey, Jake? A *Country Christmas* is on tonight."

I grabbed the TV remote, grateful for any distraction. I needed to rein in my libido.

"Found it. Looks like we didn't miss much." The music became ambient background noise as we snuggled on the couch, exploring each other's lips.

After opening another bottle of wine, we settled back, focusing on the screen, as a group of military personnel took the stage. A somber voice announced, "This one's for all the men and women who keep us safe."

As the solo guitar's opening chords filled the room, my heart plummeted. I knew this song and the lyrics were gut-wrenching—"You Should Be Here" by Cole Swindell.

"We can watch something else, Holly."

I reached for the remote, but her soft hand rested atop mine as she whispered, "It's okay."

I flipped my hand over; we were palm-to-palm, fingers laced together. Her head rested on my shoulder as she hummed the poignant tune's melody. I heard a quiet sniffle, but simply pressed kisses to her temple until her breathing calmed. The music awards continued; I was content to hold her, reluctant to break the comfortable silence.

A while later, a muted snore emanated from her throat. I grinned at the sleeping angel in my arms. *I could get used to this.* Grabbing my universal remote, I turned the TV off and dimmed the lights. Holly rested against me, her back pressed to my chest—the classic spoon position. My favorite, although Beth hated it. I never understood why.

I eventually fell asleep, but became aware of Holly stirring in my arms. I heard a soft sigh followed by a moan but said nothing, unsure if she was awake or asleep.

*Holy Hell!* Her hand stealthily crept under her shirt, skimming her breasts as she moaned softly, lips parted. The same hand started the journey downward, fingers deftly sliding over her stomach, under the waistband of her leggings, then down lower as she arched her back. Her hand moved in a sensual circle, and I groaned as my cock swelled, straining painfully against my jeans. *I need to touch her.*

Before I could stop myself, my hand joined hers, moving in sync with a singular purpose. Her eyes suddenly fluttered open, connecting with my own. Desire burned in her green irises.

I licked the shell of her ear, then whispered softly, "Holly, you've started something and I'd like to help you finish. Will you let me?"

Casting a glance downward, her eyes widened. A crimson blush started at her neck, moving quickly to cover her cheeks. Meeting my gaze again, she nodded.

"Yes, Jake. Please."

Two fingers found her warm, wet channel and gently thrust inside. Her hips gyrated against my hand, begging for release, as my fingers slid in and out, curling while caressing that elusive spot. In seconds she moaned, in the throes of orgasm, her body shuddering against mine, her walls relentlessly squeezing what I wished was my aching cock.

After her body stilled, I removed my hand, bringing it to my lips, her scent overwhelming my senses. *I can't wait to taste her.*

Holly lay in my arms for a while, as her breathing became steady. A dreamy smile graced her lips as my fingertips caressed her cheek. I thought perhaps she had fallen asleep, until her breathy whisper caught me off guard.

"That was amazing, Jake. I should be embarrassed that you caught me... you know, pleasuring myself."

Holly tried to hide her face between my neck and shoulder, but I wouldn't allow it, as I reached to sweep a stray tendril that had fallen in her face.

I tried to conceal my smile but failed miserably. "Don't be, sweetheart. I've never seen anything more beautiful."

## Chapter Eight

### Holly

O h. My. God. Every time my eyes closed, the image from the previous night reappeared. Me. In Jake's arms. Masturbating. My face flushed hot with equal parts arousal and shame. He reassured me a million times, claiming it was "smokin' hot," but I was still a bit mortified. Bringing myself to orgasm was my nightly ritual and I often woke up with my hand *down there*. I recalled the exquisite sensation of his fingers inside me, filling me. *Imagine the orgasm his cock could...*

*Bzzz!* The doorbell sounded and Jamie bounded into the living room.

"Momma, they *here!*" She seized my hand and pulled me to open the door, revealing Jake and Donovan sporting giant grins. The boy held a long, thin package wrapped in purple paper, and a DVD. Jake made the appropriate introductions after depositing a chaste kiss on my cheek, causing a rush of heat to my core. *Focus.*

"Momma! Donovan is *dark* just like Gramma Polly!"

*Shit!* Did my blabber-mouth daughter really just say that? "Jamie's grandmother is part African-American. It's so nice to meet you, Donovan!"

"Nice to meet you too, ma'am." Jake motioned toward the gift. "This is for you, Jamie," Donovan whispered shyly. "Open it later when we watch the movie, okay?"

"Okay, thank you. Wanna see my room?" Grabbing Donovan's hand, she pulled him down the hallway, squealing, "You're gonna *love* my dollhouse!"

\* \* \*

## JAKE

I couldn't help but notice D's fascination with Jamie as we walked through the Wizarding World of Harry Potter, the new attraction at Universal Studios. He had never met a mixed child before, especially one with such fair skin and pale blonde hair. Golden locks, just like her gorgeous mother's, but curly. I worried at first. The "dark" comment could have been offensive, but my boy had a sweet, accepting nature and was immediately smitten with the little girl.

Donovan had read the Harry Potter books and patiently answered the child's numerous questions. At one point, Jamie—who'd been sitting on Holly's lap during a live interactive show—squeezed in to sit beside Donovan. A rush of warmth infused my chest as

I watched them interact. The identical emotions played on Holly's face: joy and contentment. I longed to give her all that and more.

We had just exited the child-friendly mini-roller coaster, and Jamie was breathless with excitement. "We was up *soooo* high, Daddy could see us from Heaven! Right, Momma?"

Holly's lovely face paled. "Of course he can, baby. Daddy sees everything, and he was proud of how brave you were!"

Donovan leaned against me and I wrapped a comforting arm around his shoulder. I'd shared Holly's loss with him, knowing he could identify with Jamie somewhat, having never known his own father. Donovan's forlorn, dark eyes gazed at the little girl and a myriad of compassionate emotions colored his face.

"Hey, D, where should we take our girls for lunch?" I knew that would lighten his mood. The boy could eat!

# Chapter Nine

## Jake

The kids giggled in the back seat, and relief flooded me as we drove back to Holly's. It had been the perfect day. I chuckled, recalling the many curious looks we attracted: two whiter-than-white adults with two obviously non-white children.

"Jamie's grandma has planned something fun for us. I hope you both like homemade Christmas—"

"Cookies! Gramma Polly's bakin' cookies, and we gonna help!" Jamie bellowed, bouncing as much as her seatbelt would allow.

"I'll help with the eating," Donovan chimed in, high-fiving Jamie.

Holly's mother-in-law was an attractive woman in her mid-fifties; warmth and kindness exuded from every pore, especially when her eyes landed on Donovan.

"Come here, darlin'. You remind me of Jamie's dad when he was your age. Such a handsome boy you are! You can call me Gramma if you like. Jamie has another grandma, so I know she won't mind sharing me." She winked, then hugged him to her ample bosom, planting several kisses atop his head. D was often shy around strangers, but his expansive grin spoke volumes.

"Okay, y'all, time to start mixing the dough." Polly's grandmotherly voice suddenly became that of a drill sergeant. "Jamie, your job is to stir, and Donovan, you're responsible for choosing the cookie-cutter shapes, okay?"

\* \* \*

Polly had retired to her apartment, and the children were contentedly stretched out on the floor watching the movie, enjoying chocolate milk and cookies. Jamie lay clutching her gift, an official Harry Potter magic wand.

Holly and I relaxed on the couch, agreeing that the day had been a resounding success. As I cuddled her in my arms, I noticed her hand caress a chain she wore around her neck. I'd witnessed this action previously, but couldn't see what hung there until her fingers extricated the chain and rectangular metal shapes became visible. Dog tags.

Grasping them firmly in her hand, she took a deep breath. "Jamison was my entire world, my reason for living. I fell into a deep depression until Jamie arrived. When I held her in my arms, her daddy was right there with us. She saved me, and continues to make my life worth living every day."

My heart warmed at the scene around me. Holly nestled into my chest as my fingers ran through her silky hair. Donovan on his stomach, still watching Harry

Potter, head propped on his hands with Jamie curled up asleep, using his shoulder as a pillow. I caught him more than once glancing affectionately at the sweet child.

When the time came to say our goodbyes, Jamie would not let go of Donovan's hand as her hazel eyes overflowed with tears. "Momma, can D sleep over? Please?"

Donovan looked up at me, panic-struck. *Get used to it, kid. A beautiful girl's tears will be your undoing someday.*

I squatted in front of Jamie, cradling her face in my hands. "Sweetheart, D had a big project he needs to finish for school, but we'll see you soon, okay? I promise." I pressed a quick kiss to her forehead.

"Okay," Jamie lamented, wiping her cheek with the back of her hand.

Holly added, "Thanks, Donovan, for keeping an eye on Jamie today. Please come visit anytime. Oh, and Gramma Polly packed some cookies for you."

Hugs ensued all around, and the two of us headed home. Donovan was quieter than usual, contemplating the day's events.

"What was the most fun part of today?" It was easier to start the conversation myself.

He sighed. "Everything. I have no grandparents, and I never baked cookies, or played with a little girl before. It was…" His faltering words trailed off.

"Overwhelming, right?"

"Yeah, but good. My weekends with you are so fun, but then I gotta go back…"

"I know, buddy. I'd like you to spend more time with me. I'm working on it with Child Services. It'll take some time, but remember, I'm a lawyer. It's what we do."

Later that evening, I was tucking D in for the night, when he shocked me with an out-of-the-blue revelation.

"Jamie asked me about my dad. I said I didn't have one. She thought maybe mine died, too. I said no, he just went away. Then she asked if I missed him. I wanted to scream that I hated him, but didn't want to scare her, so I explained I didn't know him. Jamie's only four, but really smart. You know what she said? She whispered in my ear, like it was our special secret, 'Don't be sad. Momma says sometimes daddies *have* to go away but they never, *ever* stop loving you!'"

## CHAPTER TEN

### HOLLY

After listening to Jake boast about his cooking skills, I agreed to dinner at his house. The first thing I saw was a huge Christmas tree in his living room.

"What a gorgeous tree! Is that a basketball on top? No angel?" I teased.

"D and I decorated it together. I wanted it to be special for him. He's never had a real tree before."

I realized, in that moment, this thoughtful, generous, breathtaking man was one in a million. He'd awakened an unexpected longing that had been dormant for far too long. It both excited and terrified, flooding me with waves of conflicting emotions.

Somewhere in the madness I found Jamison's soothing voice. *It's time, baby. Don't use me as an excuse to avoid happiness.*

"Holly? You okay? You zoned out for a second. Get comfortable on the couch and I'll bring you dessert." Jake eventually emerged from the kitchen carrying a huge tray, which he placed on the coffee table: choco-late mousse, fresh whipped cream, assorted berries, and one spoon. He approached me, wearing a Cheshire Cat smirk. A long, black silk scarf dangled from his hand. *What the hell?*

"Holly, do you trust me?" He brushed the soft material against my cheek. His eyes were compelling—sky-blue flecks swimming in smoky gray, a storm cloud of emotions.

"Yes, Jake, I do." I anxiously pulled my lower lip into my mouth, but he gently dislodged it with his thumb as his palm cradled my cheek tenderly. His warm breath fanned my face with the sweet scent of red wine.

"Good. I'm planning to feed you dessert, but I'd like every bite to surprise your taste buds, so I'm going to cover your eyes. Is that okay?"

A *blindfold.* I simply nodded, not trusting my own voice to form coherent words. Images were ambushing my brain—naked limbs, tangled up in sweaty, bare skin, Jake pounding into me. My core quivered as a lone bead of sweat trickled down between my breasts. I held my breath as my eyes fluttered closed.

I expected the scarf, but his soft lips came first. He languidly kissed my face everywhere—nose, eyelids, forehead, cheeks. I parted my lips as if to say, *Please. Kiss me. Now.*

He slipped the material over my eyes and knotted it at the back of my head. Complete silence followed, except for one word. "Open."

Jake placed a bit of mousse on my tongue, followed by a plump strawberry. The delicate flavors exploded as

I licked a drop of juice from the corner of my mouth. A soft finger spread whipped cream on my lower lip. Wet kisses were next, as his tongue explored my mouth, greedily sharing the sweet flavors.

A lightheadedness overwhelmed my already laden senses as I swayed and fell into Jake's muscular arms. He carried me to another room, gently placing me on a bed, my head resting on what felt like satin pillows.

Four years of pent-up lust threatened to erupt, and the blindfold heightened every sensation. My chest heaved in a vain attempt to catch my breath.

Jake's warm lips descended on mine and our tongues gently explored each other's mouths. After what seemed like hours of erotic making out, his ministrations began the exquisite journey down my neck and lower. He sought my permission before removing each article of clothing. His mouth and tongue trailed over every bared body part, licking and sucking each nipple until both ached with pleasure. Sliding my panties off, he rained kisses on my lower abdomen, inner thighs, calves, and toes. I lay before him, naked. Exposed.

There was a prolonged moment of absolute silence. *Zip. Click. Thud.* Jeans unzipped, belt off, shoes tossed somewhere.

"Holly?" His gravelly voice startled me out of my naked-Jake fantasy.

"Hmmm?" I murmured dreamily. My ability to form a coherent sentence vanished with the whipped cream.

"Should I remove the blindfold?"

Licking my lips, I tentatively mouthed *No*, shaking my head. I wasn't quite ready for intimate eye contact yet. I only wanted to feel.

After spreading my legs, Jake knelt in between as his fingertips traced a slow, seductive path along my inner thighs, moving upward. His lips and tongue followed, so warm and wet. My core throbbed with an indescribable need, skin sizzling as if electrified. *Oh, my God. I am going to combust. If these sheets are flammable, I am toast. Literally.*

His rough, demanding tongue had me writhing in seconds, forcing me to reach behind my head for something to grasp. *Headboard. Perfect.* Spreading my sensitive folds with his thumbs, Jake licked everywhere, except where I craved him the most. Deliberately skirting around my clit drove me wild, heightening my arousal until I was pushing against the headboard, grinding my aching pussy against his face.

"Jake. *Please!*" I implored, fingers yanking his hair. His mouth vibrated against my mound. *Is he laughing or humming? Damn, it feels amazing. Oh God.*

Several flicks of his talented tongue on my clit and the familiar tingling pressure intensified. I tried to prolong the sensations, but shockwaves of ecstasy engulfed me and I was transported out of my body, over the cliff, then…

"Jaaake!" My hips bucked uncontrollably, but Jake held on, laving and sucking my clit like a starved man. *Eleven on the one-to-ten orgasm scale. Wow!*

Jake inched slowly up my body, covering it with his own. Soft lips found mine and his kiss overflowed with urgency.

"Holly, I miss your beautiful eyes. May I—?" I shook my head.

"Not yet." I could barely hear my own voice as my legs wrapped around Jake's broad back. "I want you inside me first. Please?"

Reaching down between us, I gripped his rock-hard cock, palming the underside while stroking the head with my thumb. I was still drenched and pulsing from the powerful orgasm; I wanted...*needed* him to fill me, but he hesitated, poised at my entrance. My hands snaked around, cupping his ass cheeks firmly.

In one, swift movement, Jake thrust into me fully. Exquisite pleasure mixed with a bit of pain overwhelmed me as my inner walls stretched to accommodate his girth. His hips began to circle slowly, altering the angle of penetration, caressing my G-spot so precisely I nearly lost consciousness.

"Holly, I can't hold back any longer," he pleaded. "I *need* to see you."

I nodded, as he slipped the blindfold off, careful not to pull my hair. Our eyes locked and a myriad of emotions were exchanged. I knew in that moment Jake would never hurt me. I trusted him completely.

Locking my ankles behind his back, his hips sped up, plunging in and out of me, faster, harder, until my pussy clenched around him as he groaned out his release, collapsing on my chest. I came seconds later, waves of heat liquefying my core. I lay panting in a pool of sweat. Our sweat.

"You okay?" Genuine concern laced his tone as his kindhearted eyes searched mine. Although I suspected tears might make an appearance later when I was alone, there were no immediate feelings of guilt.

"Yeah, I'm good. You're my first since…" My voice trailed off as he captured my lips in a tender kiss.

"I thought so. I wanted our first time to be perfect for you."

As we snuggled, I felt secure in his arms, enjoying the soft kisses he lavished on my face. "Holly, can you stay? I hate the idea of waking up without you."

Jamie was sleeping at her grandmother's, so I could. I worried about it being too soon, but agreed, sending Polly a quick text.

Jake made love to me again, slowly, almost reverently, and any uncertainty I had been experiencing melted away. We climaxed together, fingers entwined, eyes connecting, every deep-seated emotion plainly written on his face.

I awoke to Jake's distressed muttering in my ear a few hours later. He lay behind me, arms still encircling my waist.

"I love you. Please don't leave me." I froze. *He's dreaming.*

"I'm here, Jake. Everything's okay. Go back to sleep," I soothed. He did. I didn't.

There were two possibilities: Jake still loved Beth. Or...?

I pushed the thought away.

## CHAPTER ELEVEN

### JAKE

Naomi relished the moment: brunch at Canter's Deli and giving advice to the lovelorn. *Me*. After sharing the G-rated version of last night's activities, she pondered while chewing a toasted bagel.

"Jake, honey, it's clear to me. Holly knocks you off your feet. Beth never had that effect on you. Go for it!" Aaron nodded in agreement.

"But this morning something was *off*, like she had second thoughts. I'm falling in love with her but—"

"Jake!" Naomi suddenly shrieked, her panicked expression startling us. "Were you sleep-talking? Beth told us you often mumbled in your sleep when things were bothering you."

"What the hell are you—?" My thoughts scattered as an icy chill crept up my spine. Jumbled words and images echoed in my brain.

*Fuck me. I need to fix this. Now.*

I excused myself and headed back to the office, dialing her number as I walked. *Shit! Voice mail.*

"Holly. Please listen, sweetheart. What you heard me babbling in my sleep…did you think that was meant for Beth? She moved to Chicago, I haven't thought of her in months. I was dreaming of you. I love *you*, Holly. Please call me ASAP! I have client meetings all day, but I need to know you got this message."

* * *

## HOLLY

Gina was speechless, a rare occurrence. Catching her breath, she squeaked, "He said *what?*"

"You heard me! So, who was he dream-talking to? Me or his ex?" I couldn't bear to utter her name.

"Hon, it *has* to be you. Don't worry about going too fast. Love doesn't follow rules. All the hot romance novels prove that. Be grateful he's not some crazy-ass tiger-shifter!"

I rolled my eyes, giggling as we embraced. Gina could always lighten my mood.

As I left Starbuck's, I noticed a voice message. My heart just about burst through my ribcage when I heard Jake's sweet, sexy, and very frantic message. During the drive home, I wondered what Jamison would think about all this. The answer came like a bolt of lightning. I couldn't wait to get home and dashed straight to my bedroom.

Willing my tears not to fall, I opened the beat-up journal. A few worn photos of me and Polly fell out, along with a folded note.

*My dearest Holly... If I don't make it back to you, please know how sorry I am. I never meant to leave you alone with our baby girl. Promise me you'll fall in love again. Find a good man, a good father for our daughter. I will watch over you both, living in that corner of your heart that will always belong to me."*

I clutched my pillow as a waterfall of tears streaked down my cheeks. Jamison's comforting presence enfolded me, lifting a weight off my heart.

## CHAPTER TWELVE

### HOLLY

"**M**omma, hurry. We gonna be late!" Jamie hollered as I grabbed my car keys.

Plans had been made for later that evening to visit Santa Claus at a huge Christmas bash hosted by the Los Angeles Big Brothers/Big Sisters organization in conjunction with Boys to Men. Jake texted he had a work emergency, but he'd just dropped D off at the party and promised to join us soon.

I spotted Donovan, looking adorable in his red and green elf costume with matching jingle-bell-adorned pointy hat. He waved for us to get in line.

Santa reached down to assist Jamie onto his lap, as he ho-ho-hoed boisterously.

"What can I bring you for Christmas, Jamie?" Santa's gruff voice was vaguely familiar, as were his penetrating steel-gray eyes.

*No. Freakin'. Way.*

Jamie's answer was immediate. "A baby brother!"

Santa chuckled. "Babies are a lot of work. How about a big brother? He could teach you how to skate, ride a bike, and—"

"That sounds fun, Santa. Yes, I want a big brother!" Donovan's grin was a mile wide.

"And what does your momma want for Christmas?" Santa continued, his twinkling eyes shifting to me. *My heart pounded, ready to detonate in my chest.*

"Someone to love her a lot, just like Daddy did." My daughter's soft voice caused Santa to lean in close.

"Well, Jamie, I think Santa can do that for your beautiful mom."

Santa's bristly beard tickled my lips, and as my eyes filled with tears, I heard a song blare from the loud speakers: "I Saw Mommy Kissing Santa Claus."

## Epilogue

### Holly

I t had been an exhausting but exhilarating evening, filled with laughs and an abundance of tears. Disbelief, doubt, and uncertainty engulfed Donovan, until Jake assured him that his adoption had been approved and it was just a matter of time until the paperwork was signed. When Jamie finally seemed to comprehend what was happening, she clapped her chubby hands, then turned to me, squealing, "Momma! Can D sleep over? We gotta pwactice to be brother and sister!" My attempt to fend off the happy tears was an epic fail.

I was still in a state of shocked euphoria as the four of us arrived at home to find Polly putting last-minute decorations on our huge live tree. Festive holiday music emanated from the TV and the mouth-watering aroma of freshly baked cookies hung in the air. A high-pitched squeal burst from Jamie as she spied her grandmother and Jake, who had carried her from the car, could barely deposit her on the ground quickly enough.

"Gramma Polly, we gonna be family! D's my brother now, Gramma!" My sweet girl dragged Donovan with her, while bouncing excitedly, all the while clutching the boy's hand in a near-death grip. Polly wrapped him in a comforting hug, pressing a kiss to the top of his head. Stealing a glance at Jake, I could see the Christmas tree lights' reflection in his shimmering eyes.

"Baby, why don't you show Donovan and Jake all the gifts Santa left under the tree, but no opening until Christmas Eve like you promised, right?"

"Okay, Momma," she agreed, tugging Donovan behind her while I made a beeline to a shell-shocked Polly. Her countenance was a myriad of bewilderment, shock, wonder, and what I prayed was happiness. I was comforted by the knowledge that she always encouraged me to date in the hopes of finding love again.

Before I could open my mouth, Polly grasped my hands in her own. Her brown eyes became huge in excitement as she stage-whispered, "Jake proposed? You two are getting married? Oh my Lord! I'm thrilled for you, darlin'!"

Barely suppressing my grin, I shared, "Well, his proposal was anything but traditional. He said he loved me madly, then asked if I would be Donovan's mother, and I said yes! We'll wait until the adoption is finalized." Polly's arms engulfed me in warmth, as her tears flowed.

"I prayed for this day. I know Jamison would approve." She kissed me on both cheeks, then we turned our attention to the heart-warming scene unfolding on the living room couch. Donovan sat reading "'Twas the Night Before Christmas" to Jamie, who was in Jake's lap, her small back snuggled against his chest, with her feet on D's thighs. Polly gently shoved me toward them, murmuring, "Go join your new family, sweetie."

*Jamison, I found someone. He loves me and Jamie too. Plus, your mom approves! That's gotta be a good sign, right? We miss you terribly, but we'll be okay.*

I quietly watched them for a few moments before sitting down. Jake snaked his arm around my shoulder and our gazes locked. Donovan beamed through tearful eyes, as he closed the storybook and began to speak softly.

"Thank you for my new family. I...I'm happy to finally have a *real* home." Jamie pressed her curly head against her new brother's chest, causing warmth to rush through me, as I beheld the miracle of unconditional love. Polly's booming voice rang out, putting a sudden halt to my reverie.

"Who wants cookies?" Both children bolted towards the kitchen, leaving me to fall into Jake's open arms as a song began on the television. The all-too familiar melody, "I'll Be Home for Christmas", filled the room as I raised the volume...much to Jake's surprise.

I assured him, "It's always been my favorite holiday song. So, are you ready for kindergarten, Jamie's first boyfriend and the eventual walk down the aisle at her wedding?" Jake nodded as his soft lips met mine.

He challenged, "Can you handle basketball games, soccer practice and teaching them both about safe sex?" I attempted to stifle a gasp.

"Deal! As long as we're always home for Christmas. Just like this. Together."

# ABOUT THE AUTHOR

Teri moved from NYC to Los Angeles in 1994. She retired after 30 years of teaching mathematics to deaf high-school students, and now enjoys life as a proof-reader/beta reader and romance author. Teri loves watching sports (NHL, NFL, NBA), creating mosaics, playing golf, and daily workouts at LA Fitness.

Website: www.TeriMcGillAuthor.com

# Sorcha in Snowflakes

## By Kate Bigel

## Chapter One

This year, Sorcha wasn't going home for the holidays. It was the night before Christmas Eve and she was going to meet her best friend for a drink and a girlfriend chat. She had lost track of time while drawing and headed out later then she intended. She had decided to walk instead of spending money on a taxi but it started raining, a cold mist so typical of San Francisco in December. The dark sidewalks were slick with water so she ran with care trying to avoid the puddles. Her long red hair was turning into a mass of crazy, frizzy curls making her look like a windblown Celtic witch but it didn't matter, it was just Vicky, her best friend.

Stepping inside the bar, she looked up to see the ceiling glowing with strands of little white lights that almost looked snowflakes. The lights made the space look magical and festive. There were little flags with an offset red cross hung in looping lines across all the walls. She was pretty sure it was the Danish flag.

She spotted Vicky at a small table talking to two men in business suits and Vicky waved her over to the table. So much for the girls' night out. Vicky was a petite blonde who talked fast and laughed loudly – she was in real estate sales. Sorcha guessed she was in the process of trying to sell the men some property.

Vicky waved her over to the table, "Sorcha, come meet Bob and John — I just met them while waiting for you." She threw her arms around Sorcha and whispered, "Happy Holidays. Sorry, I couldn't resist talking to them while waiting for you."

Sorcha gave her a warm hug. "It's my fault. I lost track of time drawing. It was dumb, I kept thinking I knew the person I was drawing and if I kept drawing, I would remember who it was. It was tall man standing in a forest but I never figured out who it was. Lame excuse, I know but you have to forgive me," she explained.

"Sorcha, you're an artist and I love you so don't worry. The drawing sounds cool but just don't tell your mother because she'll tell you it's a *vision*." Vicky said half-seriously.

"Da-shealladh – the two sights. *Art is the way to see the future and Irish artists are doubly blessed*," Sorcha said in an exaggerated Irish accent and then grimaced. "I couldn't get the face, just the gesture of how he stood so it will be tough to know if I meet him," she laughed.

Vicky smiled. "Show it to me later. Now, say hi to Bob and John. They're waiting for a friend too. We have late friends in common." She put her hand on Bob's arm and said, "Sorcha is a talented artist. Do you need an amazing painting for your apartment? A Sorcha Rosenbloom is a must-have."

"Hello. Nice to meet you." Sorcha waved. A *must-have?* Maybe Vicky was laying it on a little thick but she had great track record. Sorcha's paintings hung in various newly purchased condos of young professionals.

Bob scratched his chin. "I gotta confess - most modern art confuses me. I'm just not really into it. Sorry." He turned away to order a drink.

Her mouth hung open in shock. How could a human not like art? What was wrong with him? Art was the heartbeat of the human race, it was everything. She filled her cheeks with air and crossed her eyes at him. Vicky saw it and tried hard not to laugh.

"Are you feeling okay?" said a deep voice.

Sorcha flinched in surprise and looked up to see a tall, broad shouldered man in a business suit. He looked at her with beautiful golden-brown eyes that had crinkles in the corners. His dark blond hair was messy as if he had just run his fingers through it, his face was all chiseled lines with a strong nose but he had a kind smile.

She gave him an apologetic, embarrassed grin. Probably thought she was crazy making silly faces and, of course, she had to be caught being a goof by a man so handsome he made little butterflies dance in her stomach.

\* \* \*

Alexander walked through the bar looking for his friends. He froze in disbelief as the face of the woman with long red hair became visible. He walked up to her in stunned disbelief and caught her making a face at Bob. He asked her if she was ok which was stupid of him.

She looked up and blushed. Inhaling sharply, he froze unsure of what to say. How could his beautiful Sorcha from his painting be here? How could she be real?

Bob shouted, "Alexander — you made it! Ladies, my friend and last year's MacArthur Genius Grant recipient and SF's entrepreneur of the year, Alexander Macklin. Alexander, this is Vicky and her friend, Sorcha."

Vicky shot him a sharp look and salesman smile. Sorcha just stared at him with beautiful blue eyes and her mouth slightly parted. She had dimples and little freckles. He hadn't realized this. He winked at her and she snapped her mouth shut and swung her long red hair forward to cover part of her face. He would bet her cheeks were pink.

Alexander shook Vicky's hand, murmuring his hellos and then turned to shake Sorcha's. Her hand was small and cool. "Sorcha. A good Irish name," he said.

Her eyes lit up. "My first name is a peace offering to the Irish side of the family. *Erin Go Bragh*, keep that Celtic pride alive. My last name is Rosenbloom," she said, and rolled her eyes. "Confuses everyone."

He gave her a wry smile. "Alexander Larsson Macklin. My Irish father's peace offering to my mother's Danish family was that I was born and raised in Denmark. He was a wee man and they're all Vikings."

"A wee man?" Sorcha grinned. "Maybe in a land of giants. But families are crazy, aren't they?"

"Absolutely but my family thinks that they're very normal." He shook his head in mock sadness. "They're crazy eccentrics. Inventors, writers, and musicians. All that Irish temperament in big Viking bodies – my home was rambunctious."

She laughed. "It sounds wonderful."

"Hey, you wanna order some food? It's a Danish bar and they've great Scandinavian food. Look, see how they have little Danish flags everywhere." Vicky pointed to the little flags that were hung in decorative groups and in long strands.

Alexander scratched his jaw and thought he needed to defend his country. "Danish people are just crazy about their flag, we use it in all our celebrations," he explained. "Birthdays, National holidays and Christmas. See, everything is red and white. It's funny, huh? What if you decorated at Christmas with the US flag? A Christmas tree in red, white and blue?"

Everyone laughed at the idea. John started telling Bob and Vicky a funny story about Christmas decorations. Sorcha was sitting on a barstool listening to everyone so Alexander took the opportunity to slide his barstool closer to her. He wanted to tell her that he owned her painting.

* * *

Sorcha was only half-listening to the funny stories as Alexander turned to face her. She had trouble not staring at him, he took her breath away. That strong Scandinavian face and the cute accent. She liked how he talked about his family, with love and warmth in his voice.

He tapped the bar table with his long, elegant fingers and tilted his head. "I wanted to tell you that I've one of your paintings – a portrait of you in a window and in the background there is a forest and snow falling. It's called *Sorcha in Snowflakes*. But, you know that." He rubbed the back of his neck while he looked at her intently.

Oh, that's why he had been staring at her. "Yes, of course, my self-portrait. You own it?" she asked feeling pleased he owned her painting. Realizing that he looked at her face everyday, she suddenly felt self-conscious. She tucked her hair over her ear and sat up straighter.

"Yes, one of my employees bought a condo and a painting last winter," Alexander told her softly. "He told me a pretty blonde real estate agent convinced him to buy a painting by the little known artist."

"I never met the man but it was my first major sale. I was sad that I didn't know where it was," she told him with great seriousness. Her paintings were like children and she liked to keep track of them.

Dragging his stool, he moved right next to her. He sat so close, she could feel the heat from his body and his long legs were almost touching her knees. Her mouth went dry thinking about his long legs, his body. She cleared her throat.

He furrowed his brow in though. "The moment I saw it, I had to own it. I bought it from him that day. Thank you for painting it. I love it. It's my favorite painting." He took in a breath as if he was going to say something else but then simply shook his head.

"Oh, thanks. It makes me happy that you enjoy it. I'd like to know where my paintings live. I might have to come see it," she said looking into his golden eyes. She speculated on how to make that color with paint.

He breathed deep and gave her a hopeful look. "Anytime." He said it firmly.

They just stared at each other for a while and then looked down at their menus. She couldn't stop smiling while she pretended to read the menu. Everything felt bright and loud around them, the bar buzzing with chatter and laughter. She bit her lip thinking how to ask him out on a date.

Suddenly, he slapped the menu down. "You know, you can come to see your painting right now. I live a two-minute walk from here," he said. "Come look at my Sorcha Rosenbloom collection. Only one painting so far." He smiled and waggled his eyebrows.

"Haha. But, really? I could see it right now?" she said in a surprised voice.

"Two minutes and then we could come back here."

"Okay, let's go."

"Really? Alright," he said. His eyes sparkled when he smiled.

"Yes. Unless you were just joking then forget it. But I do kinda want to see it and, well, you *are* a patron of mine. You might want to buy more Rosenbloom paintings to add to your collection." She blushed again and tried to hide it by covering her mouth with her hand. Damn that fair Irish complexion.

His eyes crinkled up and then a small smile appeared. "It's around the corner. Your friend can come with us. I'd like you to see it." He reached out and shook her hand, he held it like they were making a deal.

"Ok. Let's go."

Vicky turned from her conversation and looked at them. "What's up?"

Sorcha straightened her shoulders and gave a brisk nod. "Alexander owns one of my paintings. The self-portrait."

Vicky narrowed her eyes in thought. "But wait, Tim Moulton bought it."

"But Tim works for me and I bought it from him." Alexander said drily.

"I got him to buy the self-portrait from a picture on her website when I sold him his condo," Vicky said proudly.

"That was a great sale. Um, Alexander lives two minutes away and I was going to look at the painting then come right back. Will you come with me?" she asked Vicky.

Vicky smirked, "No. You go. I'll wait here for you. Bob and I are going to eat dinner together. Run along! Text me when you're done and we can get dessert together."

Sorcha grinned. "I'll text you." It was girlfriend code for making sure all was kosher.

Vicky hugged her and whispered, "I command you to have fun."

Sorcha laughed and kissed her friend on both cheeks. "Merry Christmas, Vicky."

"Happy Holidays, Sorcha."

Bob looked up from his iPhone. "What? Alexander, we need to talk," he said.

Alexander shrugged. "Call me, let's grab lunch together." Bob looked pleased and waved goodbye.

He held her hand again as they walked through the bar as if he needed to guide her but it really wasn't crowded at all. She pretended she needed the guidance. He held her hand so lightly so she could have pulled her hand away easily if she wanted. She didn't.

Alexander stopped to introduce her to Gusion, the owner of the bar which was named after him. Gusion was a huge, handsome man with red hair and a movie star smile. Alexander and Gusion had a brief conversation in Danish and then shook hands.

Gusion said "Gladelig Jul! That's our Merry Christmas or 'Joyful Christmas' in Danish. Come back again, Sorcha."

She nodded happily "I will. I like this place. Merry Christmas and Happy Holidays to you."

They walked out and Alexander looked at her with a crooked smile.

"I don't usually don't invite people to my place. Really, I just come down here to eat and then I go back to work but you're my favorite artist." He shook his head and looked slightly embarrassed.

"This is your informed opinion after having seen one painting of mine." she said with an eyebrow raised.

"One amazing painting that I own. Let's go look at it to help you remember," he stated.

## CHAPTER TWO

W hen they emerged from the bar, the light rain was still coming down and a chill wind was coming off the bay, sharp and cold. Alexander kept her tucked next to him while he guided her quickly down the street. She was slim with a small waist that accented by long skirt and close-fitting jacket. He liked the little dimples that appeared when she looked at him. He was enchanted with her. She was so much prettier in real life.

"I'm glad I came tonight," he said, "I haven't been social lately. I tend to space out on people when I am focused on work. A lot of people want my attention." He frowned thinking about it. "I can be rude." He surprised himself with his bluntness. Perhaps talking to her painting for months and confessing things had made him grow accustomed to being honest with her.

"Huh…you should see me in a creative groove. I just grunt at people, live in my pajama pants and don't answer the phone," she confessed and looked up at him. Her blue eyes sparkled like the raindrops in her hair. Up close, he could count the tiny freckles across her face.

"A fierce vision of an artist at work." He pulled her close to him and then dropped his hands. He leaned forward and asked in a husky whisper, "Can I kiss you?"

She widened her eyes and nodded. "Yes, please."

Alexander leaned down to kiss her softly and gently. A hello kiss. A get-to-know-you kiss. Her lips were cool. He leaned forward to protect from the wind and kissed her again to warm her up, to feel her breath, to receive her hello. He wrapped his arms and hugged her lightly, she fit nicely in his arms with the top of her curly hair tickling the bottom of his nose. The real woman was sweet and lovely, he liked how she slid glances at him, all flustered with her mouth slightly open.

"Hello, lovely Sorcha," he murmured, "Let's get you inside." He tucked her hand in the crook of his arm and heard a stomach gurgle. It wasn't his. He arched his eyebrow at her.

She blinked at him and said, "Excuse me. I was busy drawing and missed lunch. I'm really hungry. We are coming back to eat, right? If not, I might have to gnaw on your fancy Italian loafers."

Grinning, he tapped his temple. "Way ahead of you. We stopped to chat with Gusion so I could order some food from the restaurant to be delivered. I'll feed you while we look at your painting. And my shoes are Danish. Italian."

"You are super smart, ordering food on the sly. I heard you were a genius," she teased.

"Yes, I order food brilliantly and buy amazing paintings." He bowed slightly.

They were almost at the corner of block and he took the left, opening the door on the side of the building. She lifted an eyebrow. "Umm... this is the same building as Gusion's Bar."

"Yes, this is the official entrance to the upstairs apartments. Gusion only rents to friends. Come, he is having four different entrées delivered so you could pick what you want. We go back downstairs for dessert."

She widened her eyes. "Forget my painting. You said four entrées? I got a little dizzy with joy when you said that. You've heard of the proverbial starving artist – that's me."

"I'll give my Danish shoe to gnaw on while we wait," he laughed.

"How about a bread roll instead?" she retorted.

\* \* \*

Sorcha was amazed how naturally their conversation flowed. It was like talking with an old friend. It was sweet of him to ask if he could kiss her. Such old-fashioned manners. She had been about to lean forward and take a kiss anyway. She wasn't old-fashioned.

Men she usually dated liked the idea of being with an artist but they never were genuinely interested in art. Alexander was different, he bought a painting because he saw it and loved it. He was smart, interesting and yes – handsome-hot. He made her heart beat fast when he smiled at her with those golden eyes. She wanted to see her painting but also, she wanted to get to know him. She wanted to laugh more with him.

There were prints and drawings on the walls of his living room and a shelves filled with books. On the side of the room was a large comfortable leather couch with a rough wooden coffee table piled high with books and magazines.

Sorcha adhered to the advice of the film director, John Waters. He said, "If you go home with somebody, and they don't have books, don't fuck 'em!" Well, maybe she was old-fashioned because she wasn't going spend the night but she wanted to see him again.

She slipped her coat off and looked up to her painting *Sorcha in Snowflakes* alone on the back wall of the living room. A dominant position. It was the largest self-portrait she had ever done and one of her bigger canvases — four by five feet. In the painting, she was turned partly away from the viewer in a forest with the snow falling lightly all around her. It was maybe nighttime or a dream – it was painted from an idea of how being in the forest felt. The light fell across her features softly. Her body was hidden in darkness. Her face was like a source of illumination in the scene.

She narrowed her eyes and tilted her head to look at the painting. She realized the painting had dedicated track lighting above it. She flushed with pleasure at the care he took with the piece.

"It looks good," she sighed approvingly.

"Wait, let me adjust the lights," he said and turned the lights up just a little.

"Perfect, Alexander. The lighting is just perfect."

* * *

Alexander was glad she approved. He had bought the painting after his fiancé dumped him. It was a totem for healing his heart. A picture of another woman to remove the memory of a terrible relationship. She had been kind of girl he thought he should marry but she fell in love with another man. Boom, in a blink, it was over. He wasn't heart broken which told him something but he had descended into a slight depression over the idea of relationships.

When he first saw the painting, something in him responded and he bought it immediately from his hapless employee. He loved the name of the painting, *Sorcha in Snowflakes*. In the painting, the woman's eyes were closed and her mouth open like she was singing. She had been caught in a song while the snow fell. The colors were soft and dark except for her skin, which glowed in a golden light. There was landscape behind her — strange trees and spaces fading into forests. It was a mysterious painting. It calmed him when he was stressed out. It made him believe in women again.

"Wait, let me adjust the lights. It looks best when it's not so bright," he said.

She stood there, mirroring the woman in the painting. "You picked a nice frame."

"What's the story behind *Sorcha in the Snowflakes*? I have a story in my head that I've made up staring at it but I want to hear what you were thinking when you made it." he asked.

She pushed her long hair away from her face. "I can talk about the light or the painting technique, but talking about the idea is very personal which is obviously normal with a self-portrait. This painting is about dreaming and my nostalgia for home, missing the warmth and comfort of the known and familiar. I tried to infuse it with optimism. That's why I am singing in the painting. Singing is kinda optimistic," she said with her eyes half closed like she was remembering how it felt to paint it.

Her words echoed in the big room. Everything was still and quiet. He could feel his heart pounding in his chest.

"How did you start this painting? Did you do sketches or studies? Did it come the idea come quickly or did you revise it?" he asked in rushed voice.

She laughed softly. "Lotta questions. Well, I was working on some studies of forest landscapes. That forest in the painting is not a forest that's anywhere specific. I dreamt it and in the morning, I drew the first sketch for the painting. The figure is a counterpoint to the darkness of the forest, that's how it felt in the dream. I work from my imagination but from dreams – well, that was a first."

"That's amazing. It does feel like a dream painting."

"Yeah, I think the weird light in the painting helps. Ya' know cause light in dreams is always weird."

He cocked his head thinking about what he wanted to say. "The colors, the light of the forest in the painting reminds me of northern Denmark. It reminds me of h-home," he stammered and cleared his throat.

She gave him a quick, shy glance. "That's cool. Maybe it's like a universal forest that everyone recognizes as their own home in a primal way. Like a collective unconscious forest."

"I wish I could say something more profound about the painting. Saying it reminds me of home and I love it makes it sound trivial," he muttered.

"Saying you love it is pretty much the best thing to say to an artist," she assured him.

\* \* \*

She could feel her heart beating a little faster as she stared at him. He stood in the light of her painting. His long lean body was like an artist's dream. It reminded her of something.

He stepped toward her, looking all thoughtful and sexy. "I think I'm going to kiss you again," he informed her.

"Really?" She smiled. She meant *yes, please.* She reached out to him and he took her hands.

She pulled him close and kissed him firmly. She didn't know if she could tell him the right words but she could kiss him like she was telling him her thoughts. Be with me, her kisses said. Her breath was shallow and fast and she pulled away to look at him. He simply smiled and dropped little kisses on her head and jaw. She opened her lips and he slanted his mouth over hers and kissed her deeply. The warm male scent of him enveloped her and she absorbed his warmth, his smell in some primal part of her brain.

She pressed herself against him, feeling his strong, lean muscles hidden under his business wear. She laid her hand against his cheek and he pushed her hair back with his index finger. A warm contentment bloomed, flowing up from her belly to her head like a shot of whiskey.

Then, the doorbell rang and he whispered, "That's your food. We could ignore it and keep kissing."

"Oh!" she swallowed hard. She was hungry but she also needed a moment to collect herself from the intensity of that kiss. "Don't let them leave with the food. Please," she said and waved him towards the door.

Laughing, he opened the door and took the food from the delivery guy. He gave him a hefty tip and told him to thank Gusion. He placed the containers on the breakfast counter and took out some plates. "Come on, my hungry artist. I don't want you fainting and chewing on my shoes."

They sat and traded the dinner containers back and forth, putting a little bit of each on their plates.

"So, can you tell me about what you do in software while we eat?" she asked.

He poured her some red wine in her glass before he answered. "I wrote some algorithms and software which are really good at analyzing data and that software became the foundation of my company. I released the basic algorithms for free and public use. It's used in a lot of things most famously in medical research to assess and locate data problems. I love my work and building my own company. But it's amazing to help save lives with my work, I mean I have actually shook the hands of people who are alive because of my algorithms." He shook his head in amazement. "That's humbling and awesome because I didn't set out to do that."

"I guess that's why they gave you the Genius grant," she said.

"Well, you know it's mostly lots of hard work and a tiny spark of a good idea. It seems to me that you and I have a lot in common in what we do. We both need great ideas and a strong work ethic. Look at you, you've done amazingly well. You're in a show at the Center for Contemporary Arts. You're a rising star."

"How'd you know that?" She hadn't told him that. She had recently received some great reviews for the paintings in that show.

"Googled you on my phone. Have you Googled me? Don't. You'll find a lot of very boring articles on my software and the math behind it." He made snoring sounds. "Not like the amazing young painter who…" he glanced at his phone, "and I quote 'transforms the ordinary into a magical realism'.

She shook her finger at his phone. "No fair to Google me while we are talking. It was a nice review even if it was just a local paper because everything ends up online.

I'm just trying to figure out how to support myself more consistently."

"Can you teach?" he asked.

"I do. I teach part-time at the local community college. I'm getting more teaching gigs and maybe a fulltime position next year at the State College." She furrowed her brow. "I like teaching – it's very gratifying to help other young artists." He leaned toward her while she talked, like every word she said was fascinating. It made her feel special to be listened to so intently.

"The students will be lucky to get you." He poured each of them a little more wine. "*Skoal.* A toast to you and your beautiful paintings, Sorcha!"

She laughed and did a little Miss America wave. "Thank you, thank-you, everyone! Peace on earth."

He cupped his hands around his mouth "And the crowd roars…rawraw-aahhh."

They smiled big, wide smiles at each other. It was fun being a goof with him.

Her phone buzzed with a text. "I gotta go. That's Vicky, we're going to have dessert and exchange presents at my place."

"What are you doing tomorrow for Christmas Eve?" he said in a rushed voice.

"Nothing," she said smiling broadly. "I'm not going home this year. Planes tickets were crazy expensive. Vicky is leaving town so I just planned to stay home, binge watch shows and paint."

"Please come to the party at Gusion's bar with me. My family is in Denmark so I'm alone. Gusion throws a big party for employees and I'm invited since I live here. It'll be lots of fun. It's a mad shindig. Lots of crazy Danes. Free taxis for everyone to and from the party – Gusion insists or you can't drink."

"It sounds like fun. My parents usually have a mad Hanukkah-Christmas-Winter Solstice shindig. Lots of crazy people come to our house and I'm going to miss that."

"So, say yes. Say you're coming. Danish Christmas is delicious." He gave her a grin. "Lot of meat, cookies, cake and booze. Since I'm part Irish, we'll have some singing."

"Of course but I must warn you, I only know one song and it's *Galway Girl*," she said laughing. "I learned to sing it with my Dad who learned it to sing to my mother because her hair is black and her eyes are blue."

"And I never seen anything like a Galway girl," he said the words of the song softly.

She nodded. "I'll go to the party with you, Alexander Macklin." She kissed him on his cheek and wrapped her arms around him. He hugged her back. Just for second, they stood, quiet and wrapped up in each other. It was a wonderful hug.

He gave her one soft kiss on her mouth and she closed her eyes with a sigh. He was more then just handsome. He whispered in her ear, "Don't tell anyone about all the hugging or I will lose my street cred."

She giggled and put her finger to her lips. "Here's my number. Text me and tell me when to come over to the mad Danish Christmas shindig."

He tucked the number in his pocket and helped her on with her coat. She smiled and brushed her long hair back over her shoulders with her hands. "Thanks again. I'm glad you bought my painting."

"See you tomorrow!" he called out as she left his apartment.

## Chapter Three

Sorcha was ready to go to the Christmas Eve party. She had on a low-cut crushed velvet top in bright blue with slim black pants. Her hair was back in a ponytail with a sparkly sequin ribbon and dangling earrings with long rhinestone strands of little snowflakes.

She was looking forward to a fun holiday party. And Alexander? He was like an intense painting that she wanted to look at for a long time. Alexander was more than handsome—he was a lovely person, maybe a little lonely from being so far from family, she understood that, but she enjoyed his intelligence, passion and enthusiasm. Oh but his kisses made her dizzy with joy.

As she grabbed her coat, she looked at the drawing of the strange man that made her late to meet Vicky. The way he stood with his head tilted looking out the window, he looked just like Alexander. That's why he looked familiar yesterday. Perhaps her mother did know something. Yesterday, the man in the drawing looked lonely but today he looked strong, looking ahead to something. She would draw a better picture of him soon.

She grabbed the little gift bag with his holiday present and put it in her coat pocket. She had spent all morning on it, making it just for him.

Alexander sent an taxi to pick her up. He stood waiting in front of the bar in a blue button down shirt without a coat, shivering slightly but he gave her a huge smile when she stepped out of the car. He opened his arms and said "Merry Christmas! Happy Hanukkah! A Joyful Winter Solstice to you!"

"Wow, that's the best, most inclusive holiday greeting I've heard all day. Happy, Happy to you too!"

"Come in, quickly. I'm freezing out here. The Danes have been drinking Akvavit already. It's strong Danish liquor – be careful. But there is lots of food."

He opened the door to the bar and music and laughter spilled out. A huge man with brown skin and large dark eyes stood just inside the door. "Welcome, I'm Marcus. All the girls must kiss me to get inside."

Sorcha looked at Alexander, who laughed and shook his head in the negative, mouthing *no*. She smiled.

Another man shoved Marcus aside "Don't worry about this asshole. I'll protect you. I'm Barth, the smarter and handsomer brother. Ignore this sad fellow. Happy Holidays!"

"Happy Holidays to the both of you!" Sorcha responded. She knew it was going to be a fun evening.

Alexander put his arm around Sorcha's shoulder. "Go away, annoying ones. This is Sorcha Rosenbloom and she's with me."

Gusion came to greet them, all flashing blue eyes and charming smile while he shoved Barth and Marcus out of the way. "Sorcha, we're so glad that you could join us. You look beautiful. That blue color of your shirt makes your eyes sparkle. Ignore these boys—soldiers are a rowdy lot and my staff is not much better, so you must excuse us. Now, let me introduce you to everyone."

Gusion glanced at Alexander, who nodded his approval before she was swept away. Gusion introduced her to lots of different people. Some of the men looked like Viking marauders but shook her hand gently like she was made of glass. The women laughed and welcomed her with kisses on both cheeks.

They all sat at long tables and ate huge amounts of food and people gave multiple toasts. She laughed a lot and drank way too much. Akvavit was yummy on ice. She chatted with some women who worked at the bar who regaled her with funny stories about customers. Some had husbands with them and there were children dashing around giggling with toys that they had been given by Gusion. Little red and white flags of Denmark decorated the table.

She sang her song "Galway Girl" with Alexander singing the chorus with her. Everyone cheered. Gusion sang a Danish song that Alexander vaguely translated but she guessed it was naughty from the raucous laughter from the men and the eye rolling of the women.

At the end of the evening, people hugged and kissed goodbye. It felt so warm and family-cozy. They were good friends to Alexander and they all were excited that he had brought her to the party. Several gave obvious thumbs-ups and side winks. "*Ja*," they said which was Danish for *yes*. Alexander covered his eyes in mock embarrassment but smiled fondly at them and nodded.

Marcus hugged her hard while yelling at Alexander. "She's too sweet and pretty for you. You call me if he treats you bad. I'll rescue you, my lovely princess." He was more then a little drunk.

Sorcha knew she was tipsy because she giggled and kissed Marcus on the cheek, which made him shout with delight. Everyone applauded. She slid Alexander a smiling side-glance.

Alexander rolled his eyes and pulled her from Marcus's arms. He helped her with her coat and led her out of the bar into the cold night. "I'm sorry for all my friends, but particularly Marcus."

She shivered and rubbed her arms. "Everyone was so welcoming. It was lovely with the kids. Loud and crazy. I loved it. I drank way too much of that Akvavit. Dangerous stuff." She shook her head mournfully. "I'm wobbly drunk."

He smiled. "Come up for coffee. And really just coffee, that's not just a line."

She wanted to be honest. "I can't spend the night, Alexander. I'm a lightweight with booze and I drank too much."

"It's because you're so little," he said, "It's fine but yes, I'd like to spend the night with you but I would like to do so when you're not drunk so we'll leave that for another time. Come home with me, just for a little bit, I want to give your Holiday present and I'll make you Danish coffee."

"Okay, I have to give you your present too."

He led her upstairs holding her hand in his big, warm hand.

## CHAPTER FOUR

Sorcha leaned against the wall in the hallway while Alexander opened the door to his apartment. He stood back and gestured her in. "Happy Holidays!"

She stood in the door and looked up laughing because the apartment was full of glowing white Christmas lights. Everywhere. Crazy amounts of lights. They were hung in great loops from the ceiling and around the counters and cabinets and windows. He must have hung twenty boxes of lights in his apartment. There were nine candles, one large and eight small, together on the coffee table.

He ran his hands through his hair, making it stick up in blond tufts. "You like it?"

She nodded enthusiastically. "It's wonderfully ridiculous. Your impromptu menorah arrangement is inspired and the explosion of lights. It reminds me of home."

"It's like snowflakes if you squint your eyes." He pulled her close and whispered. "Try it." They squinted their eyes together then laughed because they made funny faces. He pulled her close and kissed her gently on her lips. "Your Christmas-slash-Hanukkah present is on the coffee table."

She saw a beautiful wrapped present with an extravagant gold ribbon on it. She pulled out her little gift and handed it to him. "Wow. I got you a tiny, little gift. You out-Christmased me. Open mine first."

He opened her gift bag and pulled out the large hand-painted dreidel and a bag of chocolate coins. "You painted this! There are little snowflakes on this dreidel. Look at the details, the miniature landscapes behind the symbols. Oh, it's beautiful," he said delightedly.

She nodded. "You like it? I'll teach you to play. A little gambling for chocolate. My favorite gambling game involves food, of course."

"My second artwork from the famous Sorcha Rosenbloom."

She sat on the couch, picked up the large box for her and shook it. She pretended to guess and furrowed her brow as if thinking very hard. "Sneakers?" she asked as a joke.

He grinned.

She pulled off the ribbon and opened the box. She gasped in surprise when she saw a hand painted box with dragons and flower designs, a leather sketchbook and colored pencils.

"It's a pencil box," he explained. "I found it today at a folk art gallery in the city near my office. I saw it and thought of you."

"It's beautiful. Oh look, it has a little piece of paper inside. It says it was made in Sweden with the name of the artist and biography. Thank you – it's perfect."

"You have to give me the first drawing for my art collection," he said with a little smile.

She bit her lip. "Ok. But not tonight though." She wasn't nervous about him. She couldn't resist him. Those crinkly golden eyes made her dizzy and hot.

"Of course, I'll take you home in a taxi. Our first night will be later, perhaps?" He looked at her with a mix of concern and hope.

"Hmm." She leaned forward. "Yes, I'll have another night. I demand another night." She needed more of his kisses and touches. Sorcha turned her face up and kissed him, softly like a snowflake.

* * *

Alexander's heart pounded in his chest. Here she was like a fairy princess sitting on an ogre's couch. He held her glowing face in his large rough hands. He tugged her down on the couch and trailed his lips down her long neck. He reached back pulled off her ponytail tie and set her curls free.

"You are wonderful, Sorcha. I've stared at your face in my living room for six months but you're more amazing then my imagination. Your lovely face and red hair like an Irish fairy tale princess," he marveled.

She held a finger up. "My hair is from the Jewish side of the family. My Dad's a proud ginger. My mother is a true Celt with black hair. And there's blue eyes on either side of the family. I think my Jewish ancestors roamed Europe falling in love with handsome local lads with red hair and blue eyes and causing all sorts of mischief. Ya'know because it's matrilineal, so it would had to have been the girls."

"You are carrying on a grand tradition, Sorcha," he observed.

"I thought you were verra, verra handsome when I first met you. You made me feel all flushed and hot," she blurted out then knitted her brows as if surprised to say that out loud.

"You're a cute drunk." He went to the kitchen and filled the drip coffee maker and started it brewing. "Coffee will be ready soon."

She waved her hand at him. "You know I drew a picture of you before I met you. My mother would call that da-shealladh—foresight. She says all Irish artists have it." She stared at him with big eyes. "But really, I kinda drew you and then we met. Weird, huh?"

"What's the word?" he asked.

"Dah-haloo is how you say it. It's spelled funny 'cause it's Gaelic."

"Well then, I had a foresight vision of you, too. It's on my wall. It's my Irish showing." He winked at her.

"Wow. That's right. Double crazy." She leaned back in the couch with a sigh.

"Now my little seer, since I plan to spend a lot of time with you." he declared, "Tell me many hours do you spend in your studio? I want to arrange my schedule." His voice was light and full of laughter yet he was serious about the question.

"I have never had a man ask me when I need to work."

"Really, why not?"

"I don't know. They probably didn't think it was important."

"Well then, they hadn't really looked at your paintings," he observed.

"You've only seen one," she pointed out.

"That's all I need and you'll show me more." He said firmly. Who were these jerks she had dated?

"If I am not hung-over…" Sorcha rolled her eyes at him and smiled. "I like to work a solid four hours a day, sometimes all day." Her face was a little pink making her freckles stand out and her hair danced around her head.

"Excellent."

Sorcha gave him a sultry, drunken smile. She pulled herself to her knees on the couch and leaned over him. Her hair fell like curtain around his head and she brushed his lips with hers. Then, a lick and a nibble. He let her taste him and let her run her hands over his shoulders and chest. He cupped her face and kissed her with all his heart and hope.

She pulled away and licked her lips, looking at him with heavy-lidded sleepy eyes. He trailed small kisses on her neck. She tasted like cake and liquor and smelled like flowers.

"Sorcha, you could kiss my good sense away but your kisses still reek of Akvavit. I will kiss you a little more then I take you home." He tucked her close to him on the couch and kissed her while she made happy humming noises.

"My sweet Sorcha," he whispered in her ear. They lay there tangled in each other, just breathing and looking up at the lights. The apartment was quiet except for the muted traffic sounds floating up from the street.

Sorcha turned and nuzzled his neck with her nose. "It's very naughty, making out on the couch. I feel kinda high school."

He groaned and pulled himself close against her. "Bringing up the image of a naughty teenage Sorcha in high school is not helping me. I want to strangle those booze-swilling friends of mine who gave you all that Akvavit to drink. It's stronger then Vodka. We're going to wait, Sorcha but, please no drinking tomorrow or I'll cry in a unmanly way."

She giggled and snuggled her head next to his shoulder. "You're a funny man, Alexander. Okay. Tomorrow only water and coffee – and popcorn at the movies." She yawned.

"The coffee is ready. Let me get it for you."

She grinned but closed her eyes almost sleeping.

He couldn't believe that he could be perfectly happy lying on a couch with a fully clothed woman who was drunk and sleepy. Damn booze. But this wasn't a date, this wasn't a hookup. This was a dream made real. This was different. Her curly hair tickled his cheek so he rubbed his face gently against her neck.

"Scratchy man," she mumbled.

"I'll shave in the morning. I'm getting you the coffee and no more making out." He shook his head. He was an idiot. An idiot falling in love.

She looked up at him with heavy eyes. "I didn't expect you. I didn't expect love and kisses. I didn't think...I want to see you *more*." Her eyes widened as she declared this with a tiny bit of a slur and then she shut her eyes. He heard her breath in and out. He realized she had fallen asleep. He would need to hear that again from her. He smiled.

"You will, you will see me lots but no more drinking," he told the sleeping Sorcha. He didn't expect her either. She was like the sun and he wanted to bask in the warmth of her, he needed her light.

He kissed her forehead and went to pour coffee. He needed to get her home. He requested a taxi on his phone. It was a busy night so it would be twenty minutes.

When he came back into the living room with the steaming mugs of coffee, he looked out the window and laughed. Oh, wow. Who would have thought, snow in San Francisco? A Christmas miracle or perhaps, it was the second Christmas miracle in his life.

He put the coffee down. Shaking her gently awake, he pointed to the window. "Look, Sorcha. It's snowing. Gladelig Jul!"

She blinked her eyes and standing up, she leaned against the window to watch the tiny snowflakes coming down. "Oh," she whispered, "It's beautiful. It's joyful."

He gazed at her standing in the window with the snow falling fast. His beloved painting had come to life. This Sorcha was real. A beautiful, messy woman with long red hair and sparkling eyes. He opened his arms and she walked into them, leaning against him while he tucked her coat around her shoulders, ready to take her home.

# About the Author

Kate Bigel has always loved stories and romance. She studied Literature and Fine Art in College. She has been a visual artist and worked in computer games. Her stories are rooted in the fantastical, paranormal and speculative but with a strong romantic center.   There is kissing and more in her stories.

Website: www.katebigel.com

# The Christmas Encounter

## By Belle Ami

Mandy had never hated Christmas, but now she did. The holiday time was like a big exclamation point, an emphasis on the failure of her life. Only the truly lost were alone at Christmas, and here she was Christmas Eve without family, friends, or someone to love and be loved by.

She stared out at the sea that danced chaotically before her. Each breaking wave flailed drops of spume that lashed out, basting her face in a fine coat of salt. The angry water seemed to scream and howl as if in protest of being returned to the churning sea from which it came.

Hypnotized by the rhythm of the breathing sea, she wondered what it would be like to walk straight into the churning cauldron. She shuddered. *The first icy impact would be terrible, but probably in a few minutes you'd go numb. Kind of like getting a Novocain shot in a dentist's chair. I bet once anesthetized, it'd be easy to surmount the tide and wade into the slumbering arms of nothingness. What a romantic end of life. Didn't I see that in a movie once?* She searched her memory. *Yes, of course, Frederick March and Janet Gaynor,* A Star is Born, *and that* wonderful remake with Barbra Streisand and Kris Kristofferson. *Why don't they make movies like that anymore?*

Movies had been one of the great joys of her life. What had happened to all those hours spent in the darkened chambers of theaters watching other people's lives unfold in reels of silvery light? When was the last time she'd been to a movie theater? She couldn't remember. She'd cast away that attachment, like so many others, that no longer fed her soul. The magic was gone. *Thank God for Netflix. The beauty of anonymously surfing through cyberspace, virtually thumbing through the archives of hundreds of films.*

The thought of sitting in a theater with strangers, listening to the sounds of candy wrappers being greedily fingered and kernels of popcorn ground to pulp between greasy, buttered lips, enraged her senses and felt about as appetizing as the hysterectomy she'd endured last year.

*Whatever you do, don't think about the children you'll never have.*

What had driven her to the shore, especially on a day like today? She didn't know. It was almost as if something or someone other than herself was exerting a power over her. This wasn't the Mandy who meticulously ordered the hours and minutes of her life. She had meetings in the city, an office Christmas party, her time accounted for. Yet here she sat, staring at an endless expanse of ocean, contemplating…what?

She tried to clear her head and think rationally, but all she could think was how tired she was of living. She wanted to care about something, but life and its endless battles had worn her down. The daily routines of existence, just putting one foot in front of the other, could not hide the maelstrom of her life. It was like threading the eye of a needle blindfolded. She stabbed blindly in the dark, hoping for an answer, but with each miss, the opportunity of understanding slipped through her fingers like the grains of sand that she now dug her hands into. Every day it became harder to convince herself that there was anything meaningful to live for.

It was true that her failed marriage—or rather the marriage that had failed her—had proven to be a study in diminishing returns. She and Serge had parted amiably, their marriage easily dissolved. Seven years had yielded little: no children, no pets, and no attachments. It had been easy to divide the accumulation of things, the outward signs of a successful marriage. With a mutual sigh of relief, they had parted ambivalent as to the causes, grateful to be free and unencumbered. He'd found someone else, someone he told her he couldn't live without. With those words he had completely eviscerated her world. Without his saying it, she knew that he'd never felt that way about her, but more importantly, she'd never felt that way about him.

It wasn't until some months later that the reality of an empty bed had made an impact on her. She'd reached for him out of habit in her sleep and had been stunned awake. The physical emptiness of the bed had revealed the emotional vacuity of her world, and with this realization all of her sense of purpose had vanished. She had rushed into therapy hoping for a cure, but all the pundits and their steady stream of well paid for analysis had done little to restore her broken spirit. She might as well be drowning in the arms of the turbulent sea, then continue to pretend that tomorrow held a key to her happiness.

What an overrated word, "happiness", tantalizing with its equal promises of reward and redemption. She recalled her mother's words, prior to the divorce, that had set the end in motion. "Are you happy, honey?" Four little words had revealed the failure of her marriage and with it went the idealistic propensity of youth when one believes all things are possible.

She had built a successful career through hard work and determination, something solid and fulfilling that she could depend on. The truth was that even her work, that last bastion of pride and accomplishment, no longer fulfilled her. She thought about praying, but that would be like believing in the intervention of angels or God himself. It was all pointless, bringing her to this precipice of emptiness that held her immobile, staring out at the gloomy sea.

Lately, self-deprecation had become her armor. It precluded any disapproval from the outside world, but unwittingly encouraged her self-created demons to thrive. She had become reclusive but thought herself in splendid isolation, alienating friends and colleagues. She had told herself that her work demanded no distractions and that eventually she would find the time to mend her frayed relationships. Her self-denial was one more nail in the coffin, and in her heart she knew it.

She shivered as a blast of cold, wet spray pummeled her, raising goose bumps on her arms and legs. Her natural inclination should have been self-preservation, but instead of protecting herself from the bombardment of salt and spray she welcomed the chilly embrace, her physical discomfort proving that she was still alive.

Somewhere down the beach, faint in comparison to the thunderous pounding of the surf, she heard a dog barking. Turning her head, she focused her eyes along the gray path of shoreline to a distant intruder. A dog ran in and out of the effervescent foam of dying waves, barking with bravado at the walls of water that threatened to engulf him. Then, with carefree aplomb, he trotted back to his master, barking his daredevil exploits as he danced with leaps and bounds around him, shaking from head to toe, freeing the beads of salty water that clung to his shiny black coat. Once satisfied with his owner's approval, the dog turned and ran barking towards the surging tide daring it to envelope him again. The diversion arrested her attention, allowing a momentary respite from the unrelenting despair of her thoughts.

It occurred to her that the approaching stranger introduced a new impediment to the drama she contemplated. It was irritatingly apparent that if she tried to swim out through the crashing surf, he might intervene. After all, only a mad person, or someone contemplating suicide, would willingly ignore the dangers of frigid water and undertow.

Staring out over her shoulder, her eyes blurred by the damp tendrils of hair that clung to her face, she watched as the man and his dog continued to approach. With growing apprehension, she wondered, could she, even without the intrusion, find the determination to truly end her life? As she contemplated her unease, the air thickened and darkened with an impending threat of rain as the stranger and his pet approached.

*Damn it*, she thought, *there's no question I'll have to wait until the guy and his dog are gone. I can't just walk fully dressed into the icy waves and not expect that he won't play hero.*

The whole scenario was beginning to feel like a soap opera. She glared out at the grayness of sea and sky where a seagull struggled against the wind, his screeching barely audible above the roar of rushing air and pounding waves. *Maybe he'll pass me by, or better yet, turn around and disappear.*

She stole one more look at the man and dog before turning her attention once more to the black rain-gorged clouds that moved slowly across the sky. Taking a deep breath, she shrank into herself, hoping to project a desire for privacy. She closed her eyes so she wouldn't see them or encourage any curiosity from the man or his dog. She wanted no contact, accidental or otherwise, with the intruders. She wondered if he'd even notice. It didn't seem too unusual for someone to sit on the beach meditating, connecting with the spiritual and the natural world. Frozen, her posture rigid like a statue, she sat barely breathing, her senses tuned to the deafening struggle of wind and surf.

Then the unthinkable occurred. A warm, moist tongue licking the salt from her face, startling her with its persistence. Reacting instinctively, she opened her eyes as her hands rushed to protect her face from the onslaught of animal affection.

A man's voice broke the spell as he ran up grabbing the dog by the collar and gently reprimanded, "Anaia, no. Bad girl. Not everyone wants a dog licking them all over their face." Reluctantly the dog allowed herself to be pulled away as the man quickly clipped a leash to her collar. "I'm sorry. I hope she didn't frighten you. She loves people and you were a temptation she couldn't resist." His pale gray eyes changed color when they met hers, deepening to the color of sky and sea.

"No harm done." She forced herself to return the smile. "I just didn't expect it."

Anaia tugged on the leash, determined to return to Mandy. "She certainly likes you. Anaia, sit!" The dog obediently sat as her eyes shifted back and forth from her master to Mandy. Whining, she pleaded to be set free, her tail fervently fanning the air.

"Yes…well…no problem." Hoping that the fewer words exchanged between them, the more likely he would be to continue on his way, she turned back toward the sea, ignoring them both.

"It looks like a pretty big storm is coming." She could sense his eyes searching her as she stared intently toward the seascape. "Beautiful, isn't it?" he continued, not waiting for her to reply. "I love when there's no one on the beach. It's like opening a window and seeing the world anew. It really puts things in perspective…"

His words hung in the air, an uncompleted thought. She could feel him turn toward the sea, following her gaze.

She hugged her legs as a chill swept through her. Unbidden, he sat beside her. Anaia laid down in the sand, her head resting on his leg, her eyes fixed on Mandy. She and the stranger stared silently out over the whitecaps to the darkening horizon.

"Listen, I know you might think I'm crazy, but I just live about a half mile from here on the beach." He nodded back toward the direction in which he'd come, his eyes never leaving her face. "Would you like a cup of coffee? I could really use one, and you look pretty chilled. Besides, it's Christmas Eve and you'd be doing me a favor. It seems I find myself alone this year, which is pretty depressing."

Mandy turned and met his eyes, "Tell me something—is there a meaning to your dog's name? I've never heard it before. Does Anaia mean something?"

For a moment he seemed taken aback and hesitated. A smile shaped his lips and then faded as his face settled into seriousness matching hers. "It's a biblical name, it means…God has answered."

He watched as she inhaled, her chest rising with her decision. "I think I'd like that cup of coffee." It was daring of her, perhaps desperate of her, but she felt unable to say no. The pleading whine of the dog called to her. It was as if Anaia had seen deep into her soul and knew her intentions.

"I think that's the best news I've had all day." He smiled, his full lips lifting at the corners. "I've had a tough week."

She thought of asking him what had happened, but hesitated, not wanting to be intrusive. "I'm sorry."

"Yeah, it's a bitch. I'm divorced and my ex decided last minute to take my girls away for Christmas. So, here I am, Christmas Eve and alone. What about you? Do you have plans for the holidays?" He rose, extending his hand. She took it, allowing him to help her up.

They walked side-by-side across the dunes with Anaia running, chasing seagulls into flight. Mandy stared ahead, keeping her eyes on Anaia. "No, I lost my mother this year. I'm also divorced, he left me for someone else." She steeled herself against the cold feeling that usually engulfed her when she acknowledged her failed marriage, and the grim fact that she'd never see her mother again.

He grabbed her elbow, gently turning her so she would have to see his face. The color of his eyes changed again with his emotion, filling with compassion. "I'm sorry, that makes my problems pale in comparison. It's funny about life, how it sometimes knocks the wind out of your sails, and then just as suddenly something happens that renews your belief that there's a greater purpose. I think it might be nice to know each other's name. Mine's Jake."

He held her gaze, forcing her to look into the kindest eyes she'd ever seen. It occurred to her, she'd been willing to follow a stranger, a man whose name she didn't even know, wherever he might lead her. It was so unlike her.

"Mandy, I'm Mandy." The unexpected warmth of his hand still holding hers travelled through her body like a shot of whiskey.

He turned, never letting go of her hand, and they continued to walk toward a group of houses that seemed to appear out of nowhere. She should have pulled her hand away, but the strength that emanated from him made her feel safe and cared for. Holding his hand felt natural, friendly, not intimidating. *He's probably a serial killer and I'm making the mistake of my life,* she mused. *On the other hand, he just might be an angel sent from heaven to save me. You're an idiot, Mandy. God has bigger things on his plate than you.*

They arrived at what looked to be an old English cottage. Climbing roses, which in summer would be full and in bloom, were trellised against the house between the diamond-shaped pane windows. The house, painted white, was crowned with a thatched roof that hung low over the white plastered walls. The house was incongruous set among the modern structures that surrounded it, making it seem a figment of one's imagination.

She entered his home thinking she'd entered a fairytale. It was quaint and charming, with distressed wood floors and nooks and crannies where antique cabinets displayed delicate porcelain teacups and plates. The living room held an overstuffed blue chintz sofa with antique side tables, cozily arranged before a large river rock hearth. She couldn't imagine how this masculine man would come to own such a romantic cottage. She looked around curiously until Jake interrupted.

"If you're wondering about the Disneyland digs, chalk it up to my mother. She's a writer of fantasy romance books. When I was young, I used to complain to her that this place was embarrassing. She'd laugh, ignoring my complaints. *C'était comme dans un rêve*, this is my dream come true. I suggest you get used it. She's quite the eccentric. It was like growing up with Auntie Mame. I was always the laughing stock of all my friends and the envy of all the girls," he chuckled. "I guess it was my rebellion to her feminine sensibilities that made me into a super jock, outdoorsy type. I spent most of my youth trying to prove my manhood to myself." He grinned, scratching the dark stubble that shadowed his face. "Finally figured out that I don't have to."

Mandy couldn't help but smile at the thought of the teasing he must have withstood. "All I can say is I'm jealous. Your mother was right; this is a dream come true."

He beamed. "To tell you the truth, for some reason, that's all that matters to me—for you to feel comfortable."

She could feel her cheeks redden as she reluctantly drew her eyes from him. She brushed her damp, dark curls out of her face. "I must look like a drowned rat."

He studied her with an intensity that scared her. "I think you look beautiful."

She nodded. "That's very sweet. You certainly know how to make a girl feel appreciated." *Why the hell am I feeling so shy and timid? Maybe it's because he's so damn nice and so good-looking.*

In fact, the more she looked at him, the better looking he got. When he'd taken off his coat, she'd nearly gasped. His shoulders were wide and his torso tapered into a trim waistline. The gray eyes, which never seemed to leave her face, were so confident and honest that they seemed to see right into her heart. The cold wind had made his cheeks ruddy with color, and blown his dark hair into a crown of waves. When he smiled deep dimples sank into his cheeks. It occurred to her he must have been an adorable child. His was a face that took every opportunity to smile and found humor wherever he looked. Instinctively, she knew that this man did not dwell on the morbid, but reveled in the challenges life provided.

Guilt assailed her. What would a man who radiated such confidence and control over his world think of a woman who'd sat on the beach contemplating suicide? She shuddered to think of how close she'd come to giving up on herself and on life.

"Would you mind if I use your bathroom? I'd like to clean up a bit, and maybe drag a brush through these curls."

"I love your curls; you look like an angel." As if he'd revealed too much, he quickly continued, "The bathroom's down the hall—there should be everything you need. My mother's well equipped for receiving her women friends. If you want to take a hot shower, there are towels in the corner cabinet. In the meantime, I'll get a fire going and brew a pot of coffee. Then I'll take you on a tour of the Rose Queen's cottage." He laughed. 'That's what I call my mom, the Rose Queen."

Disconcerted by his compliment, the best she could muster to say was, "Thanks, Jake." She picked up her purse and started toward the hallway.

"Mandy?" She turned, expecting him to disclose something else about the hidden secrets of the bathroom. "You're safe, now." His voice was deep and reassuring.

She hurried from the room before he could see the tears that welled in her eyes.

The hot shower cleared her head, allowing her to think about Jake. Just as he'd indicated, everything a woman could need was provided in the feminine bathroom. The shower and backsplash tiles were all hand painted with roses. She giggled to herself. *I think there's a definite theme happening here.* Roses figured prominently in Jake's mother's house. His mother must be a real character.

She looked in the mirror for the first time in a long time, trying to see who she really was. Jake, a total stranger, had done that. With only a few words, a handful, he'd managed to make her want to live, to believe there might be possibilities to explore.

*No makeup, ugh. Well, there's not much I can do about it. Maybe he's farsighted and won't be able to find his eyeglasses. Hell, with my luck, he probably has 20/20 vision and could pluck my eyebrows for me without even squinting. I'm so out of my comfort zone. I've never done anything like this before. How far do I go with this, with him?*

She could almost see the haloed angel and the red devil sitting on each of her shoulders. The angel said, "Behave yourself, be careful. You don't want your heart broken," but the devil, that was another matter. That devil grinned at her and smirked. "No guts, no glory. What do you have to lose? Absolutely nothing. You have no life. It's Christmas, treat yourself to a present." She brushed the two opposing advisors off her shoulders. She'd trust her heart, something she'd failed to do since her divorce.

When she walked into the living room, Jake stood before the hearth, his back to her. It was a brooding stance, his legs squarely set apart. He stood still, and she wondered what he was thinking. She cleared her throat, not wanting to startle him. Slowly he turned, his eyes seeking hers. She couldn't fail to miss, the slight intake of breath when he looked at her. Her own heart was beating thunderously in her chest. Did he just get better looking?

"It looks like you took me up on the shower invitation. You look . . . happier."

She blushed. "Yes, I feel much better. As if I washed away more than just the cold and salt."

He nodded. "Let me get you the cup of coffee I promised. You sit. How do you take it?"

"Cream or milk, two sugars, please." She sat on the couch and tucked her legs beneath her. "Jake, you'll never know what a difference you made in my life today. I can't thank you enough."

His head tilted with curiosity. "Save that thought, we need to explore it."

"I don't know if I can."

"Trust me, you will." He walked to the kitchen. She wondered whether she could trust him or anyone. It scared her.

In a minute he was back sitting on the sofa next to her, handing her a steaming cup. The aroma of freshly ground coffee beans scented the air. "You know, I'm thinking we should decorate a tree."

She looked around, perplexed. "I don't see a tree to decorate."

"It's in my bedroom, bare, unadorned, just like you right now."

She huffed. "Is that a disparagement of my fresh, clean, scrubbed look?"

"On the contrary, it's a compliment. You're beautiful. You must know it."

She ignored his comment, refusing to believe it was more than a gratuitous remark. "Why the bedroom?"

"Well, if you're going to be alone for the holidays, there doesn't seem much point in wasting the effort of decorating and scenting the air with fresh pine if you're not going to spend time enjoying it. I figured in the bedroom, at least, it would keep me company while I sleep. These days a few dreams about sugar plum fairies would be welcome. But now, if you decide to stay, we can move the tree in the living room and decorate it."

With his emphasis on the word "stay," her pulse quickened. She looked into her cup, hoping for an answer. Maybe, like tea leaves, the cream in her cup would magically show her a sign of what she should do. Seeing nothing but foam, she made her own decision. "I'm staying, Jake. I don't want to be alone. I want to be here with you."

"You won't be sorry, I promise you." He took her hand, brushing his thumb over her palm.

Anaia rushed into the room, her tail wagging, and jumped on the sofa between them. Mandy nearly spilled her coffee. "Anaia, you're just a big bundle of love, aren't you?"

"Anaia, you're wrecking my moves," he laughed. "You're supposed to help me with the girl, not come between us."

Anaia licked first Jake and then Mandy all over her face, throwing them both into a fit of laughter.

* * *

With a Herculean effort they managed to get the tree into the living room and set it in a corner. Jake carried in a box of ornaments and placed it on the ground at Mandy's feet. "Why don't you get started emptying this box and laying out all the ornaments and then we can decorate together? I'm going to whip us up a little dinner."

"Don't you want me to help you with the cooking?"

"Nah, I'm a pretty good cook. Actually, cooking's a passion, something I got into during law school. I made extra cash by making gourmet meals for students. You might as well know, I'm really into food." He patted his gut. "As you obviously can see."

"If that's what eating does for you, keep eating." She blushed. "I mean, you don't look overweight to me. Shit, I better stop while I'm ahead."

"Hell, don't take back the compliment."

"Besides," she confessed. "Cooking is probably a skill set you'll be happy you have with me around, since I'm a disaster in the kitchen. Maybe you can teach me, and I can be your sous-chef?"

He chuckled. "I think I'll take a rain check on that. No sharp knives for you tonight, missy. I don't want to spend my Christmas Eve at the emergency room."

She bent to the box, opening it. An eruption of laughter stopped him in his tracks.

"What's so funny?" *That laugh is so damn cute, I'm tempted to tickle her just so I can make her laugh all night.* He turned, folding his arms over his chest, his eyebrows raised quizzically.

Mandy held up four ornaments. "They're all roses, every single last one of them. The Christmas tree is going to look like a rose bush. I feel like Alice in Wonderland in the queen's garden. Where's the Christmas?"

He couldn't help but join in her amusement. "I told you the Rose Queen was eccentric, didn't I? I'm lucky she didn't make me sleep in a room wallpapered with roses. Believe me, she tried."

It took Mandy a minute to subdue her laughter. "By the way, you forgot to give me my tour of the Rose Queen's palace."

He grinned. "Oh, I didn't forget. I just wanted to keep a few carrots dangling, something to keep you here."

He watched a smile fill her luscious lips. He wondered how long it'd been since her lips were properly kissed.

"Go on." She waved him away. "I'm getting hungry."

He shot her a parting grin and headed to the kitchen. A half hour later he returned carrying a tray filled with steaming plates. He looked at the tree that she'd nearly finished decorating. "Hey, you were supposed to wait for me to decorate."

"Sorry, but I had to get the roses up. I was afraid the queen would come running in and shout, 'Off with her head!' Speaking of the queen, how come you're not spending Christmas with your mother?"

"She's at Sandringham in Norfolk visiting the Queen."

"Are you serious?"

He shrugged. "The Rose Queen has friends in high places."

"Wow! That's impressive."

"Trust me, the Rose Queen is impressive. My mother's a one of a kind. She'll love you, I can tell."

"Why would she love me?"

"She loves a woman who's not afraid to laugh. Pretentious people get her goat. I can already picture the two of you in a fit of laughter, probably at my expense."

"Isn't the Queen a little pretentious?"

"Not with the Rose Queen. Together they're a couple of cackling old dames. I've seen them in action together, it's scary."

"How the heck did she become friends with the Queen?"

"I know it's hard to believe, but Her Royal Highness is an avid reader of my mother's books. Jeez, I think if it were allowed the Queen would knight her. Instead, she had to settle for being made a Dame."

"Your mother sounds like quite a character."

"You don't know the half of it. Now, I want the truth—has anyone ever told you that you have a killer laugh? It puts Julia Robert's laugh to shame."

"No. I don't think I usually laugh as much as I have today, with you."

His brows wriggled. "I promise you, you're going to do a lot of laughing from now on." When she dropped her eyes, it was obvious to him that every time he got up close and personal, her guard came up. *I don't care how long it takes, Mandy, but you're going to trust me.*

"That smells fantastic. What did you whip up?"

Jake placed the large silver tray on the coffee table. A dishtowel was wrapped over his arm. "Well, signorina, we have an arugula salad with shaved parmesan, and risotto al tartufo."

Her eyebrows lifted; she was obviously impressed. "Risotto with white truffles? On the spur of the moment you're serving truffles?"

"A confession: if I was going to spend Christmas alone, I intended to do it well. Wait until you see the wine. I'll be right back."

He left her with her mouth hanging open. *That look on her face was priceless. You're not getting away from me, Mandy. Now that I've finally found something I want, I'm not letting go.*

Smiling, he returned with two crystal glasses and a bottle under his arm. "Now, m'lady, you're in for a treat." He poured a couple inches of red wine into the wine glasses. "Taste this and tell me life isn't good."

She took a sip, allowing herself to savor the flavor. "It's delicious. What is it?"

Inhaling a deep sniff of the bouquet, he sipped. "One of the best Barolos on the planet." He leaned back, against the sofa. "Man, life is good. To you, Mandy, and our chance meeting. To you too, Anaia, for finding me this woman." Anaia lifted her head from the carpet in front of the hearth and looked at Mandy, her tail wagging in a happy dance.

"Now, my darling girl, let's eat."

\* \* \*

"Come on, you have to finish that risotto or I'm going to have to do it for you," Jake eyed her plate.

Mandy leaned back against the sofa. "It was so good. You weren't kidding about your cooking—you're like a master chef—but I can't eat another bite or I'll burst."

"Then it's mine." Jake heartily ate her last few bites and took a deep drink of wine, smacking his lips. "You and that food have made my day." She could see by his face that he was considering what to do next. "Mandy…"

"Jake—" She smiled. "You first."

The look in his eyes disconcerted her. "You know what I'd like for dessert?"

Timidly, she asked, "What?"

"I'd like a kiss."

She leaned in and gave him a peck on the lips. "How's that?" she teased, giggling.

"Very nice, but not quite what I had in mind. Why don't I lead this time?"

He took her in his strong arms and kissed her so passionately that her legs began to shake. His tongue prodded until she opened, and then all she felt was swept away by the tide of his kiss.

When they finally broke, his lips were on her ear, husky with yearning. "I know this is going fast, baby, but I've wanted to kiss you from the first moment I saw you today. I've been alone since the divorce two years ago. I've dated, but no one, and I mean no one, has affected me the way you have." He kissed her lobe, nibbling, his breath steamy with desire.

Her breath came unevenly, his words and hot breath on her ear reached deep into her soul and kindled her body. Her emotions were like the tumultuous sea outside, tossing her in every direction. She wanted him to make love to her more than she'd ever wanted anything in her life before. But she was afraid. Afraid that somehow it would all be over in an instant, some kind of a dream, and she'd wake up alone without him. Afraid that it was happening so fast and they were beginning this romance at such a great height, there would be nowhere to go but down.

*I may be a lot of things, but I can't be a one-night stand.* A war was raging within her. Her rational mind said no, but her body and heart said yes. Jake's arms around her felt so right, his kiss made her body come alive. She knew she had to make a choice. This man came into her life for a reason.

She pulled from him, needing to see his eyes. He stilled, as if hanging on to her every word. "I don't know where this is going, Jake. But if I don't take a chance and trust my heart, then I'm lost."

The smile that lit his face told her she'd made the right decision. But when his lips once more enfolded hers, it felt life changing. Was it possible that she was falling in love with a stranger?

They kissed until she was wet with desire. He leaned his forehead against hers, his breath uneven. "Mandy, kissing you is like heaven, but I can't take much more. I want all of you. Come with me to my bedroom. I want to make love to you the way you deserve to be loved. I want to hold you all night in my arms, and I want to do it again tomorrow, and the next day, and for as long as you'll let me."

"Are you sure this isn't a dream?"

"It isn't a dream, it's a prayer answered." He stood, and held out his hand to her. His gaze hot and filled with desire.

She took his hand and he pulled her through the house until they came to a set of double doors. He opened them and her eyes widened. The room was fit for a king, decorated like a huntsman's lodge. It shouted M-A-L-E. Everything was oversized and masculine and exquisitely tasteful. Her own humble home paled in comparison.

As she looked around, she wondered about Jake. Who was he? But before she could ask him anything he swooped her up in his arms, his lips once more sealed over hers in a kiss that set her heart pounding against her chest.

He murmured, "I don't know why this is happening, Mandy, but I feel like we were meant to find each other. You feel it, don't you? Our connection?"

She rained kisses over his chin, his lips. "I can't deny it. I don't know whether Anaia is my guardian angel or God intervened before I did something stupid. I only know I don't want to lose this feeling and I don't want to ever feel that lost again."

"I told you I'm never letting you go."

He gently laid her on the bed and began to undress. Her imagination hadn't failed her—he was gorgeous. Sculpted muscles and a broad chest with a Navy SEAL tattoo emblazed on one forearm. *Military,* she realized. A gasp escaped her lips when he removed his pants. He smiled devilishly.

He walked to his dresser and removed a gleaming gold packet. Tearing it open, he slipped a condom onto his hard-on. He tossed the foil in the trash.

"And we're not using these anymore, once you're comfortable. I need to be skin-on-skin with you. I've been celibate for quite some time now, Mandy."

She could see the intensity in his eyes.

"I want to take my time kissing you and exploring that perfect little body of yours. I want to know everything about it, every inch of it. Why don't you get undressed, or do you want me to do it?"

There was a hint of amusement in his eyes. She didn't move at first, she was so taken aback by his words. He stroked himself, and she felt herself break out in a sweat.

"Don't be afraid, baby, I'm not that asshole you were married to."

The mention of her faithless husband was like fuel rushing through her veins. She shimmied out of her pants and underwear, and slipped her sweater and bra over her head. Now naked, her body arrayed before him, she could see his chest swell with his breath, his muscles and cock hardening. He was all man.

Taking a moment, he surveyed her. "You're beautiful, Mandy, sexy as a siren. Just the way I imagined you'd be." He moved to the bed and lay beside her. He ran his thumb over her lips, then he kissed her, his tongue demanding her to respond, and respond she did. Her hands explored his chest and back, his firm buttocks, her body pressing hard against him. She couldn't get enough.

"Oh, Jake," she whispered, "I don't think I can wait for you to discover every inch of me. I need to feel you inside of me. I want you now."

He growled. "Finally, you're acting like the woman you're meant to be. Unafraid to take what she wants. I love that. We have all the time in the world to figure each other out. You're right, I can't wait either."

His fingers traced down her body, settling on her mound. She was wet, her clit plump as a rosebud as he caressed her. His head dropped to her breast, sucking her nipple into his mouth, eliciting a moan of pleasure. Her hips rose against the pressure of his finger and her back arched in response to his teasing tongue. Her body simmered at a slow boil, on fire from the way he was loving her.

Two fingers filled her. "You're so ready, baby, and so am I."

He lifted her leg over one arm, and pressed against her wetness. With a passionate kiss he thrust, slipping between her folds, his hardness filling every inch of her.

"Jake," she gasped. Her eyes locked on his.

He grinned, and pumped her with even strokes. "Fucking beautiful, we're beautiful together. Look," he commanded.

She gazed at the wonder of his cock glistening with her juices as he rhythmically fucked her. "I don't think I've ever really watched myself being made love to."

"Well, now you know what you've been missing." He deepened his thrusts, hitting her on her most sensitive spot.

Her breasts shook from the intensity of his strokes. "Oh, Jake…so…good. Don't stop."

\* \* \*

Jake didn't know what he'd done to deserve Mandy, but he was damn sure he wasn't going to ever let her go. Fucking her was the best thing he'd ever felt. He watched the color fill her face, the soft moans that escaped her lips, and he knew that he wanted to spend the rest of his life holding her in his arms. He planned on doing whatever it took to supplant the sadness that dwelt in her beautiful eyes with a love that she could trust. He'd take care of her body first, and then he'd take care of her heart and her soul. If he had his way, she was never leaving this bed.

*Nah, I have an even better idea. I'll fly her to Paris for New Year's Eve and treat her like the princess she deserves to be. Yeah, that sounds like fun.*

"Oh, baby, this is good, you feel so good." He began to thrust harder, pounding, driving them both to ecstasy. He knew she was close and he sure as hell wasn't going to be able to keep this up much longer. Besides, he knew this was only the first of many orgasms he planned to give her. He'd never be able to keep his hands off her body or resist the way her full lips felt against his, so soft and pliant; it was all he could do not to nibble them raw.

Her cry of his name hurtled him over the top. Her body trembling in bliss, reverberated through him, drenching him in her pleasure. He came with an explosive growl, rocking her body with slow deep thrusts. They lay spent in each other's arms, nestled together in a perfect fit.

As their heartbeats returned to normal Jake murmured in her ear. "God, Mandy, that was amazing. I'd almost forgotten what it feels like to be crazy about someone, to care."

She placed her fingertips on his face and gazed into his eyes. "Jake, I've never felt anything like this before. Even with my husband . . . I . . . it was never like this."

*Good. Whatever's happening here is happening to both of us.* "Mandy, today on the beach—you seemed—I don't know? Lost."

She took a deep breath. Tears filled her eyes. "I have to tell you the truth. Please forgive me?"

"Forgive you for what, baby?" He pulled her closer, protectively.

"I...I think I was going to give up on myself. I was going to walk into the pounding surf and leave the world behind. I just felt so alone."

"Oh, baby, thank God Anaia and I found you. You're never going to feel that alone again. I promise you." His arms drew her closer, his lips kissing away her tears. "Jesus, baby, don't you ever think about doing anything like that again."

"Don't let go of me, Jake." Her pleading eyes made his heart melt. She nestled deeper into his embrace.

"I'm not letting go. You're my Christmas miracle. We'll take it one day at a time. Let what we're feeling grow."

"I want that Jake."

"Yeah, me too." He smiled. "How soon can you move in?"

Her surprise brought a burst of laughter. "I'm just kidding baby. Everything's up to you, we'll move at your pace. But you'll stay the week?"

"The week? I . . . I . . . yes."

"When my girls get home, I want you to meet them. Are you okay with that?"

He watched her face as she thought about what that would mean. "Yes, of course. That's important to both of us. I need to meet them."

"Don't worry, they're going to love you and you're going to love them."

The sincerity of her smile warmed him. "I'm sure anything that's a part of you I'll love."

He beamed. "Anaia lived up to her name didn't she? How that dog knew to bring us together?" He shook his head in amazement.

Anaia who'd been asleep in her dog bed on the floor woke when she heard her name. She jumped on the bed, wedging herself between them. Their laughter erupted as she smothered them in doggy affection.

The day that had started out with two lost, lonely people ended with two people who'd found something to look forward to, something that felt like love. They held each other thinking about what a wonderful Christmas they'd have.

# ABOUT THE AUTHOR

Belle Ami writes romantic/suspense with a teaspoon of sex. Her latest is entitled One More Time is Not Enough. Coming 2016/2017 Saving Layla will be published by Hartwood Publishing. She lives in Southern California with her husband, two children, a horse named Cindy Crawford, and her brilliant Chihuahua, Giorgio Armani.

Website: http://belleami.us

# Glow

## BY PAMELA DuMOND

"**D**on't look now, Jenessa, but the hot guy in the 'Naughty but Nice' T-shirt is totally checking you out," Angie Papadakolis said.

"Stop making things up." I jabbed the button that cranked up the incline on my treadmill. I loved my BFF almost as much as she loved gossip magazines and exfoliating facials that made you look younger for two hours. But I also knew that she loved exaggerating.

"I'm totally serious." Angie tossed her thick ponytail over her shoulder, and dabbed her bone-dry brow with the edge of her T-shirt. "He's hanging out with Mario Tesla, the club's manager. Maybe Mr. Tall Dark and Ripped is the new towel boy. The way he's staring at you I suspect things could get slippery when wet."

I shook my head. "Read my lips. I was married for fifteen years. It killed me. Romance is dead. I'm not stepping back into the dating pool. Ever."

"It's totally happening," Angie said. "I'm a bit psychic, you know. I predict that you will need a towel in your near future."

"I'm fifty-something, a woman of substance, and not a money bunny. Besides, this is Marina del Rey, California," I said. "The mother country of aging swingers and silver-ponytailed aging hipsters with hundred thousand dollar sailboats and memberships at Del Rey Yacht Club. They're more than willing to drop a credit card or four on holiday shopping for a twenty-something starlet-wannabe. They're not interested in dating a woman like me."

"There are still a few good guys out there," Angie said.

"Exactly. And the last thing I'm interested in is dating a ninety-year-old billionaire with a fat pocketbook and nothing else interesting in his pants."

"Age discrimination!" Angie said. "I would totally date a hot ninety-year-old billionaire—"

"—if said billionaire owned a Caribbean island, gave you unlimited access to his platinum American Express card," I said, "and turned a blind eye when you fooled around with the cabana boys."

"How well you know me," she said. "But the guy who's checking you out isn't ninety. He's thirty-five tops, has ripped arms, and a cleft in his chin that's deep enough to hide a nickel. He looks like the kind of guy that could make a girl grow weak in the knees, or cry—in a good way, if you know what I mean. I think that's what he means by 'Naughty but Nice.'"

"Since when do you interpret T-shirts? Besides, I can make you cry in a good way." I jammed my finger on her treadmill's incline button.

"Stop it!" She batted my hand away and punched the decline button. "I don't even know why I try and cheer you up anymore. Would it kill you to try and be just a little more positive? Mario Tesla and the chiseled mystery man are walking in our direction. I've had my eye on Blonde Italian Prince Charming for three months now and I don't think that's coal in his stocking. Be personable. Put your 'Ho-Ho-Ho' face on." Angie yanked her hair out of the ponytail holder and ran her hand through it. "And don't be a bitch."

"Just because I've been a little crabby the past six months does not make me a bitch!"

"Ladies!" The hot guys approached much faster than I expected and paused in front of us. "Exercise doesn't have to be a bitch," Mario said. "How's the workout coming today?"

"Awesome, thanks." Angie smiled, tossed her brunette mane, and shot me a cautionary glare.

"Excellent. Either of you need a towel?" Mario asked.

"Jenessa would love one," Angie said. "She gets sweaty when she does cardio."

"I'm fine," I said. "Besides, isn't handing out towels to club members a little beneath your pay scale?"

"Hah!" Mario said. "Everyone who works for the Solstice Club is here to help you enjoy your journey toward fitness."

"He's not passing out the towels today. I am," the hot guy with the cleft in his chin wearing the "Naughty but Nice" T-shirt said. He took the stack from Mario, grabbed a crisp white one off the top and offered it to me. "Hi. My name's Aiden Black. You are...?"

"Jenessa Rousseau," I said, and took the cloth from him. "Thanks."

His fingers grazed mine for a millisecond longer than most towel transfers required, and I couldn't help but notice his hand: tan and muscular, tendons flexing on the back. My gaze traveled up his forearm to his biceps muscles: firm and defined as they disappeared from sight under the short, fitted sleeve. A quick pang of disappointment pinged in my chest when I realized I wouldn't be able to see their destination into his rock wall of chest muscles that filled out the rest of his goofy T-shirt.

"Is something wrong?" Aiden asked.

"Nope," I said. Oh God, I was staring at him like a six-year-old at a petting zoo seeing an alpaca for the first time. Even worse—he'd caught me. I felt my face flush and I broke out in a sweat. I didn't need a mirror to know this wasn't a delicate glow of a twenty-something girl out at a nightclub caught up in a fit of flirtatious laughter with a cute boy. Nor was it the soft, hopeful blush on a thirty-something year woman's face when she peered up into the face of the man she was about to marry on her wedding day.

"Are you sure?" he asked.

"I'm absolutely fine," I said, as big, peri-menopausal sweat droplets erupted on my forehead like a long dormant volcano had finally blown. Perspiration blos-somed on my chest and trickled down my cleavage like fat, juicy snowflakes smacking and melting down a car windshield during an early winter snow.

Angie looked concerned. "Are you having one of your hot—"

"No!" I said, and patted my face, neck and chest with the towel because apparently just looking at this guy close up was dangerous, or I was too stressed out, a hot hormonal mess, or all of the above. "I'm just working out extra hard today. Look, Alvin—"

"Aiden."

"Aiden. Must run. Got to get back to work. Thanks for the towel." I punched the treadmill's off button, hopped off the machine, and walked as fast as I could toward the locker room.

"See you later, Jenessa," Angie said, then turned and returned to flirting with Mario. "Don't forget the holiday party at Il Cielo tonight!"

"Yes! Can't wait!" I said. Couldn't wait to call in sick and stay home with my new boyfriend, Mr. Netflix.

"Merry Christmas, Jenessa!" Aiden called after me.

"Yes, thank you, same to..." I stopped, swiveled in my tracks, and face him. He was too cute, young, and naive. "How do you know I celebrate Christmas? There are so many holidays this time of year. Hanukkah. Kwanzaa. Rohatsu—"

"Your Baby Jesus in a manger earrings were a tip off," he said.

I frowned. "They're Santa in a sleigh earrings."

"Nice to meet you, too." He winked and walked away.

\* \* \*

I t was New Year's Day and the gym was packed with people of all ages, races, and varying degrees of fitness and health. I stood next to a workout bench and waited my turn to slip in a set of back exercises. I didn't have to make a New Year's resolution to get fit. Exercise was my therapy. Exercise was my sanity. I showed up every day and just got it done, which was pretty much the way I approached the rest of my life.

The fifty-something man with the dyed auburn hair like a sportscaster rose from the work out bench and checked me out. "Happy New Year."

"Happy New Year to you." I took a seat, leaned over and adjusted the pin in the weight stack to a reasonable level.

"You know that if you start coming to the gym regularly," he said, "you'll see that weight drop away in no time."

"Thank you." I grabbed the wide horizontal bar hanging from the weight deck and pulled it toward my chest.

"I'd be happy to give you some tips if you wanted—"

*Eyes forward, Jenessa*, I told myself. *Don't be a bitch. Just pull the weights down, release them slow on the way up, and repeat. That's how everything gets done. Slow. Steady. Repeat.*

"Thank you," I said. "I appreciate the offer, but I'm good."

I put my ear buds in and cranked up the music. I was here to show up for myself. Not to get skinnier, or tighter, or hotter—Lord knows the hormones had that covered. But I was on a quest to take care of Jenessa. Rebuild my existence. My divorce had gone through and I was a free, albeit fractured woman. Now what would I do with the rest of my life?

I'd carved out a new routine: Wake up alone. Eggs on toast in the morning with black coffee. Shower. Floss. Go to work. Cry a little. Read a self-help book on middle-aged women who reinvent themselves after divorce. Sorry, no, I refused to make a stupid vision board. Cry some more. Go work out. Facebook while I eat my dinner salad. Read a book. TV. Bedtime. Rinse and repeat.

"Hey—great to see you! How's the workout going?" a familiar male voice asked.

"Really, I'm fine!" I said, swiveling, and bumped face to waist with a rock solid male torso. Directly above my nose I saw faint outlines of ripped hard, abdominal muscles through the quick dry moisture-wicking fabric that I was now breathing on. I surmised that dangerous territory lay below my nose, and instead of looking down I tilted my head back and glanced up.

*Not* Sportscaster Auburn-Haired Man who was concerned about my weight. Mr. Naughty and Nice— Aiden stood next to me. Okay, the gym was so crowded, technically he was almost on top of me. My face tingled and I prayed to every god known to womankind that I would not break out into another embarrassing sweat.

"I can tell you're fine," he said. "You're in here almost every day."

"Someone has to hold down the fort in the bleak days between June and January 1st," I said. "Who are all these people? Where did they come from? It's crazy busy."

"They are the People of Magical Wishes." He looked down at me and smiled. "I'd rescue you from them, Fair Maiden, but they will most likely vanish from the Kingdom of Weights and Exercise of their own accord by February 1st. Besides, you look just fine. You don't appear to be the kind of woman who needs saving. Happy New Year, Jenessa." He turned and walked away toward the far side of the gym.

"Happy New Year, Aiden," I said. "No towels today?"

"New year, new task at hand," he said, as he made his way to a weight rack and picked up the dumbbells that were scattered across the floor and returned them to order.

\* \* \*

"Any Valentine's Day plans?" Aiden stood behind me, spotting me as I lay on my back on the workout bench struggling with a bench press.

"Gah, no!" I said, grunting, and pushed that bar up as hard as I could. "Suckiest holiday of the year. It's crass. Commercial. Hyped by multi-billion dollar corporations who want you to crave things you don't need, let alone want. Too much pressure to conform to standards which I do not believe in."

"Tell me what you *don't* believe in." He added a five-pound weight to each end of the bar and locked them in.

"I *don't* believe in happily ever afters. I don't believe in fairytales. And I don't believe I can lift this weight." My arms shook as I tried to lift the weighted bar over-head. "I think I've hit my limit."

"I disagree. You've been at the same level for a while," he said. "You need to push your comfort zone."

"Said the man who is not my trainer."

"Said the man who got his degrees in biomechanics and kinesiology, and is well on his way to earning his Masters in exercise physiology."

I took a slug of my water and placed the bottle back on the floor. I'd gotten used to being around Aiden. I didn't break out in huge, embarrassing sweats anymore from just looking at him. He was hot. He was kind. He was smart. He was a dangerous trifecta, and if I had never gotten married and was twenty years younger, I would have gone for him in a heartbeat.

But I was in my fifties, and it felt like time was speeding up and life was passing me by so very quickly: it was too damn late. "Nope," I said. "I'm done for today. Got to get back to work. Someone has to make the donuts."

"Come on. It's Valentine's Day. Don't you want to know what your pal Aiden believes in?"

"Of course." He *had* to have plans for Valentine's. Girls were all over Aiden at the gym like cinnamon on sticky buns. Someone needed to press warning labels on him. *Do not Touch! Verboten! Priceless Jewels Must Not Be Disturbed!*

He leaned down toward me, and, just like that, I was enveloped in the heady scent of musk and one hundred percent man. "I believe in second chances, Jenessa. I believe that one percent of the one percent of people walking this earth luck out, and get something handed to them on a silver platter. The rest of us folks have to work really fucking hard for it. We have to push weights. Sweat. Get dirty. Make ourselves do a little more. Punch out one more set, Jenessa," he said, "and then I'll tell you something funny. Something that will make you laugh."

"Fine." I snuggled back onto the bench, strained, and lifted that bar up and down, rinse and repeat.

"Way to get it done. Did you know that St. Valentine pissed off a Roman caesar so much"—Aiden placed his hands close to mine on the bar and helped me return it to the rack—"that he ordered that asshole's head chopped off?"

"Served him right!" I laughed.

He leaned in and wiped the sweat from my brow with the edge of his T-shirt. "You're glowing again," he said. "You do that on occasion. Hey, want to grab a bite on the way out?"

I restarted my heart and looked at him. "You don't have plans for Valentine's Day?"

"Hell no. Stupidest holiday of the year," he said.

\* \* \*

The weeks flew and the months passed. I ran into Aiden frequently at Solstice gym in Marina del Rey, California. He was a full-time trainer now, making a decent living at it until he graduated with his Masters degree, but he still spotted for me on occasion. We chatted and hung out a bit. Nothing special, nothing fancy, and no, we definitely weren't dating. There was that seventeen-year age difference.

Around Easter I decided to give Mr. Netflix some competition, went to the shelter, and adopted two rough and tumble kittens. But then Memorial Day arrived—my wedding anniversary. I fell into a tiny abyss, had a mini-meltdown, and didn't leave my apartment for the three-day weekend.

It was early Saturday evening on July 4th weekend and I couldn't have been happier to have the gym to myself. Everybody wanted to hit a barbeque, and if they didn't have one, still felt compelled to wear something red, white, and blue. Me, on the other hand? I had a date with gray and black: some barbells, the treadmill, and the stretching mat.

Angie had successfully made her play for blonde Prince Charming a few months back only to discover that Mario had been promoted as the club's Midwestern regional manager and was moving to Chicago at the end of July. I wanted to cheer her up, and promised that I'd brave the holiday traffic in Marina del Rey and find my way to a penthouse party in the City Club Condos before nine p.m. in time for the fireworks' show.

I cleaned up in the Solstice locker room, dressed in a cute skirt, top, and carried a jean jacket for when the ocean air grew chilly. I styled my hair, threw on some makeup, and walked out the gym's door right as the club was closing at eight p.m. I spotted Aidan sitting on the outdoor benches frowning as he texted.

"Happy July 4th, dude." I waved and walked past him.

"Jenessa," he said, and put his phone away. "Do you need to be anywhere in the next half hour?"

\* \* \*

We sat on the rooftop of the same office building complex that housed the gym, a picnic of burgers, fries, and lemonade spread out in front of us on top of paper bags. In the distance tiny fireworks popped and fizzed through twilight skies.

"So, what are you going to do about the girl?" I asked, my heart sinking a little in my chest. Because—of course—Aidan had a girl. He hadn't posted about it on Facebook because he wasn't "that guy". He was old-fashioned in that he kept his private life private and his public life on social media to the bare minimum.

"I don't know. She wants to move here from Portland. We've been doing the long distance thing for a few months." He bit into his hamburger. "I don't know if I'm ready for commitment."

"Did you give her false signals?" I said, and munched on some fries.

"Maybe," he said. "Probably. Not intentionally."

The first big fireworks display of the night shot off with a bang above the Marina.

"Crap, I'm late," I said, wiping my hands on a napkin, and gathered my things.

"I'm sorry. We've been talking for an hour," Aiden said. "You look like you need to be somewhere."

"I do," I said. "But it's a party. They're not going to miss me. They don't even know who I am."

The explosions had started and there would be no stopping them now. The whizzing, cracking and hissing rockets red glared as the bombs burst in the air.

Aiden stood up, held out his hand and helped me to my feet. "Of course they'll miss you, Jenessa. Anyone with half a brain in their head would miss you."

"You're sweet," I said, and lifted my purse over my shoulder.

"I'm honest," he said, not releasing my hand, and suddenly I wondered what we were doing. "Why aren't you and I dating?" he asked, and tugged me toward him.

"Because I don't date." The nickel-size cleft in his chin grew closer.

"But you would make an exception for me," he said.

"I'm seventeen years older than you, Aiden."

"What does it matter?" He gripped my hand tighter. "I don't care."

"You have a girlfriend who wants a commitment."

"Maybe I can't make a commitment because my heart's already with another woman," he said, and pulled me flush against him.

I stared up into his dreamy hazel eyes and wondered for a few seconds what it would be like to be with Aiden. Kiss him. Touch him. Wake up next to him in the morning. Get naked, slippery when wet, and crawl on top of him at night.

"I'm late for the party," I said. "I've gotta go."

He released my hand and I walked away from him, a bit unsteady on my low heels. "You didn't answer my question."

I paused at the stairwell. "Answer your girlfriend's question first."

\* \* \*

I switched memberships from the Solstice gym in the Marina to the branch in Santa Monica. No big deal, really. The facility was actually closer to my day job and had even more workout classes. Aiden texted wondering where I was, if I was okay. I told him I was fine, just needed to change up my routine a bit. I unfollowed him on Facebook, which I imagined was a bit like weaning oneself off of crack.

One night after I hit the gym I decided to go window-shopping at the enormously popular tourist mecca, the Third Street Promenade, and ran into a friend of my ex-husband. Mark was my age, nice, recently divorced and in a similar line of work. We shared a cocktail. He was funny and we chatted for an hour. The next few months we took in some movies, went to a few plays, got in the habit of going to a farmer's market on Sundays.

On the outside it seemed we had a lot in common. Not so much on the inside.

One night after dinner with Mark, I went home, hopped on Facebook and checked Aiden's page. He was in Portland on a job interview. Guess he had answered his girlfriend's question. I broke it off with Mark and returned to my comfortable gym in the Marina the following week. The staff had changed since I'd left. New trainers, new front desk people. No Aiden. Probably for the best.

In the blink of an eye, Christmas holidays were upon us, and I was staring down another New Year's Eve, amazed at how quickly the year flew. Fractured Jenessa had transformed into Jenessa who showed signs of healing. Apparently one could fall down, split open, and bleed for a while. But if a girl was lucky, if she just showed up and got it done, she could build up some scar tissue, restart her heart, and live to fight another day.

Late afternoon on New Year's Eve, Angie and I shared treadmill gossip time while she dished about the guy she was seeing from work. He had a condo on a walk street in Venice, and was having an open house that night. I was welcome to attend.

"I need to go get ready," she said. "Cocktail attire. You should come," she said. "You never know who you're going to meet."

"I kind of hate those things, Angie. All these people I don't know. Another holiday celebration that feels contrived. Like, seriously—why do we have to stay up to midnight and count down, and then yell and scream with random strangers like we're teenagers at a football game?"

She looked past me as she frowned and blinked. "OMG. Don't look now, Jenessa, but you're not going to believe who's checking you out."

"Who is it this time?" I asked. "The dude with the dyed sportscaster-auburn hair? The billionaire with nothing but enormous credit cards in his pocket? Or the hot towel guy who will come in handy when slippery when wet?"

"Who's the hot towel guy?" Aiden asked as he walked up.

"Um," I said.

"Gotta run. Happy New Year, Aiden!" Angie said as she raced away.

"Haven't seen you in a while," I said. He looked good. He looked too good.

"I don't work here anymore. I'm doing my internship at a sports med clinic in Compton."

"What happened to Portland?"

"Portland?"

"I thought you were getting a job in Portland. You know. To be with your girlfriend." I felt beads of sweat pop on my forehead as my entire body heated up like a small combustion chamber.

"I never moved to Portland. The girlfriend and I broke up. We weren't a good fit," he said. "What are you doing tonight, Jenessa?"

"The usual fun stuff," I said. "A little free weights, some stretching on the mat. I might get in some time on the ellip—"

"You're glowing again," he said, leaning in, and drew his fingers across my forehead. "You've got that damn glow, Jenessa. I've got a better idea. Why don't you and I ring in New Year's together?"

"Um," I said. "Okay. But what should we do?"

"I'll think of something," he said, and smiled.

\* \* \*

Valentine's Day. I slept in. Finally got up and made the coffee, poured two mugs and placed them on a tray alongside a small plate of foil-wrapped chocolate kisses.

I carried them back into my bedroom. Aiden was sprawled sleeping on my bed, the duvet twisted around him. I placed the steaming cups on the side table, lifted the cats off the mattress and deposited them on the floor, and climbed back in bed.

I stared at him while he was sleeping. Black hair, nickel-sized cleft in his chin. I traced the biceps muscles that didn't need a silly T-shirt to cover them. I kissed his forehead, and he stirred.

"You spoil me," he said, and glanced at the coffee and the chocolate. "Happy Valentine's Day, Jenessa," he said, pulling me top of him, and kissed me. "What should we do to celebrate?"

"I think we should fool around for a couple of hours," I said.

He smiled, flipped me onto my back, and climbed on top of me. "Or at least until we're both slippery when wet."

# About the Author

USA TODAY Bestselling author Pamela DuMond discovered Erin Brockovich's life story, thought it would make a great movie, and pitched it to 'Hollywood.'

Pam writes Romantic Comedy, Historical Fantasy, Cozy Mysteries, YA, and Self-Help. She likes dogs and cats equally, prefers her coffee strong, her cabernet hearty, her chocolate dark, and her foods non-GMO. She lives for a good giggle in Venice, California with her two cute, opinionated, and spoiled cats. She loves hearing from readers. You can sign up for her newsletter for info on upcoming books, deals, and special events on her website.

Website: www.pameladumond.com

## Conclusion

You have reached the end LARA's "Holiday Ever After" anthology. We hope you enjoyed the stories. If you did, please consider returning to the retailer or visiting Goodreads and leaving a review!

To learn more about Los Angeles Romance Authors and Romance Fiction, and to find out when the next steamy anthology is coming, please visit us at www.lararwa.com and join our reader mailing list.